D0561525

A WAVE OF PASSION

"There are some people who thrive on danger," Eden said. "Most are gamblers and adventurers who don't feel alive unless something's at risk. I'm beginning to suspect you're that kind of man."

"That's possible," Raven agreed with a slow smile. "The placid life we could lead at Briarcliff has never appealed to me."

Briarcliff was associated with too many poignant memories of her late husband for Eden to want to talk about it. "No, a quiet country life definitely does not suit you," she said instead.

"Going to sea as young as I did spoils a man. There's only one thing that compares with the constant challenge of sailing."

"And what is that?" Eden asked.

Raven did not respond with words. Instead he slipped his arms around her waist to draw her near for a kiss he did not end until she had not only relaxed in his embrace, but had begun to cling to him, silently begging for more . . .

PHOEBE CONN

Swept Away

ZEBRA BOOKS
KENSINGTON PUBLISHING CORP.

ZEBRA BOOKS are published by

Kensington Publishing Corp.
475 Park Avenue South
New York, NY 10016

First Printing: March, 1994

Printed in the United States of America

Swept Away is gratefully dedicated to Adele Leone, who is a marvelous agent, and a warm and sympathetic friend.

Prologue

Jamaica, Late Spring, 1863

Consumed with a restless energy, Raven changed his pose frequently as he leaned against the mantel in his uncle's study, for the subject under discussion was not one he cared to pursue. "The very last thing I require is a bride, Alex, and you know that as well as I do," he insisted for what seemed like the hundredth time. His voice was deep, yet soft and amazingly gentle to the ear despite the exasperation of his mood.

While he readily understood the cause of his nephew's pensive frown, Alexander Sutton's own expression was filled with a warm glow of admiration and pride. Raven Blade was always described as tall and dark but Alex knew that was no more than the superficial impression one gathered at first glance. While the words were true, they revealed far too little about the complex young man whose dashing good looks fascinated women, and made men so envious they frequently failed to notice the brilliance of his mind.

Years at sea had enhanced the bronze tones of his skin with a deep tan that never faded. The somber effect of his coal black hair was softened by thick, boyish curls but there was nothing youthful about his eyes. They were so deep a brown they appeared black and his gaze was often guarded, for Raven sought to see what others missed: the secrets that lay hidden beneath the layers of pretense that passed for fine manners in polite society.

An active man, he had an athlete's grace and superbly muscled build. He wore finely tailored garments with the same ease he had once worn rags: with a careless nonchalance that belied their princely cost. He gave his extensive wardrobe no more thought than a horse gives his blanket, but despite the elegance of his apparel he had not once been called a dandy. He was now in his shirtsleeves, but that provided scant comfort in Jamaica's sultry climate.

Alex nodded slightly to acknowledge Raven's view, but he was too intent upon making his point to give in. "Julian thinks I may have a year left, but certainly not two. Before I die, I want to see you have a suitably adoring wife to look after you. I'm doing you a kindness by insisting upon it. You may not realize that now, but you'll thank me for it later. I was married by your age, so my advice is based on my own experience, and it's probably the most valuable I've ever given you."

Raven turned his back on his companion and rested his outstretched arms on the mantel. Taking a deep breath, he valiantly fought against the pain that Alex's casual mention of his impending death had caused him. At thirty-eight, Alex had already outlived his father by five years, and his grandfather by seven. While he was clearly able to accept the heart disease that had plagued the Sutton family for generations, Raven could not.

"There are other doctors. Why must you accept Julian's prognosis as though it were a death sentence?"

Annoyed, Alex shook his head sadly. "I refuse to fool myself, Raven. I would only be wasting whatever precious time I have left if I used it to travel Europe searching for a physician who could extend my life. I prefer to take each day as it comes, and to enjoy it as best I can."

Alex's relationship with Raven often mirrored that of a father and son despite the fact only twelve years separated them. While they were not even distantly related, when Alex had plucked Raven from a Kingston gutter, made him his cabin boy, and then later introduced him as a nephew, the story had never been questioned. After so many years, their closeness was deeper than blood, so the fact their relationship was of their own making did not matter to either of them. Rather than uncle and nephew, on that afternoon they seemed more like brothers arguing over how one would live the rest of his life without the other.

Alex noted the tension that had stretched the fine linen of Raven's shirt taut across his broad shoulders and realized how difficult a time the young man was having. "I swear if you start to weep, I'll get up and beat you with the poker!" he threatened as convincingly as he was able before breaking into deep chuckles. "I know you possess a healthy passion for women, Raven, and if you choose the right one to marry, you'll love her so dearly you'll find it no effort to be faithful to her. Had Eleanora not died so young, I know she would still be making me as happy as she did on our honeymoon."

Raven did not understand how Alex could speak of love and death in the same breath. Nor could he fathom how Alex expected him to throw his heart into courting when the man who was the only family he had ever known might not live to attend the wedding. "What you ask is impossible," he refused again.

"No, it is not," Alex argued. "We'll spend the summer in London, and attend as many parties as we have to in order to find you a wife. I can guarantee it will be an extremely pleasant enterprise rather than the ordeal you imagine."

Seizing upon the most obvious complication, Raven turned back to face Alex. "I'm accepted as your nephew, but surely if I were to propose marriage, the young woman's family would ask which branch of your family I represent. How am I to answer such a question?"

"You will reply, and I hope smugly, that it matters not at all whose son you are, when you are my heir. That you'll someday inherit not only my title but my estates and fortune as well, will make up for the fact we can't name your parents. But I'm willing to wager that your heritage is an insignificant detail that will never be raised."

They had had this same argument so often, Raven knew Alex would never back down from his demand. While he could not bear to think what his life would be like without the best friend he could ever hope to have, Raven did not want Alex to spend what could well be the last summer of his life worrying about him. Not pleased with what he would have to do, he began to pace up and down, his long stride readily conveying his distress.

"All right, I'll go to London, and I'll be as charming as I can possibly be to the young ladies. But if none proves tempting, I don't want you to complain that I haven't given them a fair chance."

Delighted that he had finally wrung that concession from Raven, Alex broke into a wide grin. He was also a fine-looking man, his hair still thick if prematurely gray, and his eyes a warm, clear blue. Rising from his chair, he extended his hand and Raven stopped his restless pacing to take it in a firm grasp.

"You'll not regret the decision to marry, Raven. I can promise you that."

Raven responded to that enthusiastic prediction with no more than a rueful shake of his head, for he had already begun to regret it, and deeply.

One

London, July 1863

At her first opportunity to slip away from the ball, Eden Sinclair sought the inviting solitude of the dimly lit library. She closed the ornately carved door and leaned back against it, but she failed to shut out the lilting waltz melody that floated on the warm night air to the farthest corners of the spacious Carlisle mansion. Rather than soothing her troubled mood, the lyric beauty of the music served only to mock her cruelly.

It was all so unfair, the slender blonde fumed angrily as hot tears of frustration spilled over her thick lashes and slid down her flushed cheeks. Had her parents been blessed with a son rather than a daughter, she would have been in uniform that night, fighting for the Confederacy beside her father, but no, she was the Sinclairs' darling daughter and she had been banished to England to await the outcome of the War. While she knew her parents had meant well, she could not abide being surrounded by luxury when she had heard the good citizens of Vicksburg had been reduced to eating rats.

Alexander Sutton had been dozing in front of the unlit hearth when the sound of the door closing awakened him.

Aggravated at having his dreams disturbed, he leaned forward to peer around the side of the red leather wing chair to see who had dared to disturb him before shouting an emphatic demand to be left in peace. Finding a tearful beauty rather than a lazy servant avoiding his duties, or an amorous couple seeking a trysting place, his frown instantly relaxed into a welcoming grin.

"You're far too beautiful to be so miserably unhappy. Come take my handkerchief and dry your tears. You must hurry back to the party before your absence is noted."

The timber of the friendly man's voice was rich and deep, as soothing as a caress to Eden's ravaged emotions, but she was astonished to find someone else had sought refuge in the library when the Carlisles' ball was one of season's most lavish. "I'm so sorry," she rushed to apologize, the slurred tones of her Southern drawl made husky by tears. "I didn't mean to disturb you." She attempted to brush away her tears with her fingertips and, failing, came forward to accept the monogrammed handkerchief the helpful stranger had offered.

Through a mist of tears she had seen only the silver sheen of his hair and had mistaken him for an elderly gentleman, but when her vision cleared, she realized he was far closer to forty than sixty. While his hair was gray, his brows and lashes were black. His skin was deeply tanned, with laugh lines etched at the corners of his vivid blue eyes. He was a handsome man with a charming smile, and while she knew she must have met him, she was embarrassed she could not recall his name.

Rather than rise as a gentleman should, Alex patted the hassock in front of his chair. "You must sit down a moment and compose yourself," he invited with another enticing smile.

Eden hesitated, for she knew she should not be alone with him, but then, what did it matter? she wondered. She

14

had no interest in the party, and sharing a few moments' conversation with a pleasant gentleman might be the only enjoyment she would have that evening.

Eden artfully arranged the voluminous folds of her white satin gown and its stiff crinoline petticoat so she could sit down with a ladylike grace. She then apologized again, "I truly am sorry, but I've met so many people of late that I'm afraid I've forgotten your name. Should I be addressing you as m'lord? I constantly forget to do that and I don't mean to be rude."

A slow smile played across Alex's lips before he broke into an amused chuckle. Eden looked at him askance, clearly offended by that response, and he reached out to pat her hand lightly. She was wearing gloves, as was he, but that did not minimize the pleasure he received from their brief contact. "Most of the pompous fools here have as many titles as the books on these shelves," he explained with a sweeping gesture toward the crowded stacks at his right. "It's no wonder you can't recall a name or two. I would be pleased if you called me Alex. You're Eden Sinclair, are you not? Lady Lawton's niece?"

Eden looked down at the linen handkerchief he had so thoughtfully provided. If he knew her name, then he knew everything there was to know about her and she saw no reason to be coy. "Yes, I am, and I've had quite enough teasing about being a beautiful rebel for one night. If only England had agreed to be our allies, then surely things would not be going so poorly for the Confederacy."

Alex reached out again, this time to tilt Eden's chin up so her gaze was level with his. She had remarkable eyes for a blonde, for rather than the usual blue or green, hers were a rich golden shade, a sparkling topaz deepened with flecks of brown. Such a remarkable color would have been fascinating in itself, but Eden's eyes were framed with a lush border of long, dark lashes that made her glance utterly devastating. Her hair was the glorious golden blond of ripening wheat, streaked with silvery sun-kissed highlights. Her crown of curls gave her a deceptively childlike innocence at first glance, but her golden gaze held a wisdom far beyond her years. Her preoccupation with America's Civil War showed Alex she possessed a depth of character most young women her age lacked, and he immediately decided he liked her far too much to tease.

"I think your aunt must be looking for you," he cautioned slyly before dropping his hand, but he purposely did not urge her to rejoin the party.

"I doubt it. She is devoted to her daughter, while I am merely a burden to her," Eden responded much too quickly.

"I fail to see why you would be jealous of Stephanie. Her beauty does not begin to compare with yours," Alex assured her with the same easy confidence that marked all his comments.

"I am not jealous!" Eden squared her shoulders proudly, and as she took a deep breath, another inch of the smooth swell of her bosom showed above the deep ruffle that edged her low-cut bodice. Unmindful of that tantalizing sight, she was horribly embarrassed she had thoughtlessly revealed so much to a stranger.

"Forgive me, I misunderstood," Alex replied with a knowing smile. He held Eden's attention with a teasing glance until she began to smile too. His gaze then strayed down the elegant line of her throat to the lush swell of her breasts. Her skin was a lovely shade, a pale creamy gold rather than the lifeless ivory so many women thought men admired. Eden Sinclair struck him as a rare beauty, glowing with the pride and spirit she seemed to find so difficult to contain.

From what he could recall of her mother, she had been

a similar high-strung beauty who had spurned several titled Englishmen to marry a Virginian whose family fortune had been derived from shipping American cotton to English mills. Alex had never met the man, but was nevertheless impressed that he had sired such a lovely daughter.

As Alex studied her, Eden was observing him with equal interest for he was unlike the other Englishmen she had met. He was neither cold and aloof, nor overly friendly. His clear blue gaze held the sparkle of polite interest rather than the amused disdain she had so often observed. Her aunt had insisted she attend a near endless round of balls and parties since she was of an age to take a husband, but Eden was wise enough to know few men would consider her when they were ready to choose a wife. She had once been a pampered Southern belle, an heiress whose only care had been which of her many beaus to favor with a smile, but with the War going so badly for the South, there was too great a possibility her once highly respected family would find themselves impoverished to make her worth courting.

Her aunt had sought, without success, to squelch her rebellious spirit, to discourage all interest in the progress of the War as unladylike, but she had succeeded only in making Eden aware of a stubborn streak of defiance she had not even realized she possessed until she had been sent to England the previous fall.

"I must be more careful of what I say," Eden admitted regretfully. "I'm afraid I frequently fail to display the elegance of manner my aunt and her friends require, much to her regret."

"That isn't true, Miss Sinclair. Your deportment is flawless," Alex contradicted firmly. "I have observed you on several occasions and your aunt has no justification for complaint on any account. It should be obvious to all that you're a young woman of refinement and breeding."

Eden drew back slightly, uncertain whether or not she liked the idea of his watching her so closely as he had just admitted. "Leaving the ball to wander the house was an unforgivable breach of etiquette as I'm sure you must know, as is being here with you, but I could not pretend for another minute to be enjoying the party when those I love best are suffering so terribly."

When Alex nodded sympathetically, Eden was sufficiently encouraged to continue. "Tonight, and everywhere I go, I'm surrounded by pretense. I am eager for any news from home, but all I hear is insincere flattery rather than true conversation. I prefer silence to the outrageous flirting most of the young women receive."

Puzzled, Alex leaned forward slightly, "Most of the women, but not you?"

"No, the men are very cautious where I'm concerned. I have a sizable dowry, but it doesn't compensate for the fact that, if the South loses the War, my family may lose all they own."

Alex could not recall another woman mentioning the size of her dowry to him. It was a shocking remark actually, and yet, it did not seem out of place between them. A most intriguing thought occurred to him, and he could not ignore it. "What if the South were not at war? What if you were here merely to become acquainted with your English relatives, and had your parents' permission to stay for as long as you desired? Would your opinion of the evening be different?"

Eden took a deep breath and held it a moment as she gave his question the careful consideration it deserved. "I'm sorry, but the War has been far too costly for me to pretend for even a minute that it does not exist. I'm afraid that even when it's over I'll have no home to which to return. It's only the young women without such serious concerns that can find a ceaseless stream of empty compliments amusing."

Alex knew he should escort Eden back to the ballroom, or at the very least tell her to go but he was loath to do it. It was so very pleasant sitting there talking in the cozy confines of the library that he had as little interest as she in returning to the crowded party where none of the remarks would be so delightfully spontaneous. He again took her hand and slowly drew it to his lips.

"You're a treasure, Eden, and any man who does not see that doesn't deserve even a moment of your time."

His manner was too sincere for Eden to think he was merely trying to flatter her, but before she could thank him for that compliment, the door opened and a strikingly handsome young man strode into the room. He was tall and dark, with eyes so deep a brown they appeared as black as the unruly ebony curls that dipped low over his forehead. While he was as well dressed as Alex and the other male guests, there was a wildness about him his splendid evening clothes could neither disguise nor contain. The boldness of his entrance shattered the calm mood of the library as surely as the first bolt of lightning announces the coming of a storm. His piercing glance frightened Eden and she was relieved when he dismissed her quickly and spoke to her companion.

"I'm ready to go now if you are," he announced confidently to Alex.

Alex rose, and after helping Eden to her feet, he introduced the young man as his nephew. "You must forgive Raven's rudeness, but he shares your view of tonight's guests. Only in his opinion, it's the women who speak nothing but flattering lies."

Eden's eyes widened at that jest and she suddenly felt very foolish for having confided such private thoughts without any assurance Alex would keep them to himself. Terribly embarrassed to have made so potentially disastrous an error, she returned Raven's brief greeting then excused herself and hurriedly left the library.

Raven turned to watch Eden depart, his stare mocking as it swept over her fair curls, narrow waist, and the long, graceful stride the fullness of her skirts didn't hide. "Have you taken to seducing comely virgins?" he asked as he turned back to face his uncle.

"That I prefer a beautiful woman's company to my own shouldn't surprise you," Alex responded readily, but he was puzzled by the sudden aloofness of Eden's manner when she had been so delightfully open, and he could not dismiss her from his mind. "I know I said I'd like to leave early, but I've decided to stay awhile longer."

"Why? You can sleep at home in your own bed far more comfortably than you can in here."

Alex moved toward the door. He was almost as tall as his nephew, and his build was also lean. In finely tailored evening clothes his every gesture displayed the elegance to which he had been born while as usual Raven's motions showed only the tension of his mood. "I've no intention of sleeping. It's been a long while since I felt like dancing so just go on ahead and send the carriage back for me if you can't wait."

"You want to dance?" Raven gasped incredulously. "But aren't you afraid that—"

Alex raised his hand in a demand for silence. "My heart isn't that weak, Raven. A dance or two won't kill me. Of course, if it does, I'm afraid the Carlisles will be so angry with me for ruining their ball they'll refuse to attend my funeral." Amused by that macabre thought, he began to laugh to himself. "Please convey my apology should it be necessary."

Raven quickly caught up to Alex as he left the library

and walked with him back to the ballroom. "You mustn't make jokes about your death. It isn't in the least bit humorous to me. How can you even imagine that it is?"

"Forgive me. I know that comment was in poor taste, but even if my attempts at humor fail to cheer you, they do serve to keep me in good spirits." Alex smiled far more frequently than his dark-eyed companion, but the subject of his own demise did not depress him. In his opinion he had lived a full life, but as he scanned the guests looking for a certain fetching blonde, he was filled with a poignant longing for time enough to replace the sorrow in her golden eyes with the warm sparkle of happiness.

"Where have you been?" Lady Lawton scolded crossly as Eden returned to her side.

Lowering her voice to a discreet whisper, Eden provided the first excuse that occurred to her. "My hair needed attention, Aunt Lydia. I feared it would come loose and went to arrange it more securely."

Lydia's sharp eyes quickly assessed her niece's golden curls, and finding them neatly arranged, she gave her an approving nod. "Your appearance is perfection, but you mustn't wander about alone. It might cause speculation that you're meeting someone, and your reputation must remain above reproach."

Eden turned away to hide her smile, but she thought her aunt's fear truly ludicrous. The music ended then and her cousin, Stephanie, joined them for a few minutes. Petite and dark like her mother, she never lacked admirers, and when the musicians began the next tune, she was again invited to dance while Eden was left standing by her aunt's side. It was one thing to know why she was seldom asked to dance, but quite another to smile bravely as though she did not care when she had once been the most popular girl in Richmond.

When she saw Alex across the room, Eden quickly directed Lydia's attention to him. "I can't recall the name of that silver-haired gentleman. Do you know him?" She had not realized she still held his handkerchief until she had left the library, and not wanting to return and intrude upon Alex and his nephew, she had quickly slid the damp square of fine linen down her bodice. She could feel it now, touching her left breast in a shameful reminder of how foolish she had been to speak her mind so freely.

Always well mannered, Lydia nodded, but did not reply until none of the dancing couples was near enough to overhear her words. "He is Alexander Sutton, Earl of Clairbourne, my dear. He's a widower who spends most of his time in the West Indies. In fact, I can't recall when he was last in London. It's been several years since I've spoken with him although his late wife was at one time a dear friend."

"Lord Clairbourne," Eden whispered softly so she would not forget the name but her heart fell at the realization Alex was not someone she would be likely to meet again. When he and his nephew began making their way toward them, Eden felt the heat of a bright blush fill her cheeks but it was her aunt Alex invited to dance, not her.

While he had reluctantly agreed to seek a wife, Raven found himself hating every minute of the search. He felt on that night as he had all the others: like a prize stallion on display before an auction, and he was eager to leave. When his uncle invited Lydia Lawton to dance, he had no choice but to escort her niece out onto the floor; however, he made no attempt to make the experience enjoyable for either of them.

Eden searched her mind for something amusing to say, then recalling Raven had apparently found his other part-

22

ners' conversation wanting, she gave up the effort and remained silent. He was so tall the top of her head barely reached his shoulder so she knew it would have been difficult for them to converse even if she had been able to think of something witty to say. She winced as he stepped on her toe, and only nodded in reply to his mumbled apology.

As Alex and her aunt moved into view, Eden saw them laughing together and wished she and Lydia could trade places, for Alex was clearly an accomplished dancer while his nephew moved like a lumbering ox. She greeted the end of the number with a sigh of relief, and when she looked up at Raven, she wasn't surprised to find he appeared equally grateful. When he thanked her, neither his deep voice nor his dark eyes held the slightest hint of warmth, and she thought it a great pity he possessed none of his uncle's remarkable charm.

When Alex Sutton failed to invite her to dance, Eden was more disappointed than she had thought possible. He smiled at her after he had escorted her aunt to the edge of the dance floor, again brushed her hand with a light kiss, but he had then excused himself. Still thinking him quite the most interesting man she had met in a long while, Eden watched him call greetings to others as he walked away. He was obviously a friendly fellow and apparently popular but his nephew looked every bit as uncomfortable as she felt as he trailed along behind him.

"Well, what do you think of him?" Lydia asked excitedly.

"Think of whom?" Eden responded with forced calm, silently praying that despite his earlier lack of discretion, Alex had not revealed how they had met.

"Raven Blade, of course, who else?" Lydia shook her head impatiently. "Lord Clairbourne is childless, so his nephew is his heir. He was raised on Jamaica and his manners are not what they should be, unfortunately, but he will be enormously rich when he inherits his uncle's wealth."

"That can't possibly be soon enough to make marriage to that brooding oaf worthwhile," Eden mused aloud.

"Hush!" Lady Lawton hissed sharply. "Lord Clairbourne has asked to speak with me privately tomorrow afternoon. I think he may want to suggest a match between Stephanie and Raven. While I shall promise to do no more than consider it, I'll admit the prospect is a tremendously exciting one."

"Does Stephanie even know who Raven is? I've never heard her mention his name."

Lydia favored her niece with a triumphant smile. "If she doesn't know who he is tonight, I can assure you she most definitely will by tomorrow."

The following afternoon, Eden and her cousin strolled about the well-tended garden of the Lawton townhouse while Lord Clairbourne met with her aunt. Stephanie had indeed known who Raven Blade was but Eden found her cousin's enthusiastic praise for him difficult to understand. She tried to keep in mind the difference between their prospects for making a good marriage, but even that bias failed to change her view of him. He was remarkably handsome, she could not deny that, but his manner was too forbidding for her to focus on his appearance as Stephanie so easily did. She simply did not like the dark-eyed young man and she did not understand how her cousin could admire someone so lacking in warmth.

Stephanie paused to savor the aroma of a deep, red rose before continuing her steady stream of complimentary remarks. "I think Raven is quite dashing. That he's so dark gives him an air of mystery, don't you agree? He might be capable of almost anything, from the grandest heroics to the vilest treachery. Who can say?"

"Who indeed?" Eden agreed. "Have you ever danced with him?"

"Of course," Stephanie replied flippantly, not recalling how few partners Eden had had. "He danced very well, too. He didn't speak, but I believe him to be the type of man who feels things very deeply and keeps his emotions to himself."

"That's an intriguing possibility." Again Eden smiled, but she had seen nothing to indicate Raven was the sensitive sort. On the contrary, she suspected he deliberately used silence to intimidate people. She had to admit it was an effective technique, for he had certainly succeeded in intimidating her. She turned to look back toward the townhouse, hoping they would be invited to join her aunt and her guest for tea. Lord Clairbourne had merely been kind to her the previous evening, she knew that now, but she had enjoyed his company and was anxious to talk with him again.

There had been no hint of sorrow in Alex's manner, so she wondered if perhaps his wife had been dead a long while. He had not seemed lonely, though, for there was none of the quiet desperation she had seen in men who were. Of course, he was quite attractive and might keep a mistress, as she had heard so many titled Englishmen did. The indecency of that thought made Eden blush, and she realized she had been so lost in her own thoughts she had not heard a word her cousin had said for several minutes.

"I think my mother is being very wise only to consider Clairbourne's offer rather than to accept it. Alexander Sutton is by no means old so it could be many years before Raven comes into his inheritance and there are plenty of other men who have control of their family's wealth now."

"Definitely a point to consider." Eden nearly choked

getting that response out, for clearly Stephanie was merely planning to sell herself to the highest bidder. Her mother had warned her it was a common practice, but until she had met her English aunt and cousin, she had not truly believed it.

When they heard Anna, one of the maids, calling to them, Stephanie hurried toward her but Eden hung back, now doubting she would even be included in the invitation to tea.

After a brief conversation, Stephanie wheeled around, a dark scowl marring the sweetness of her features, "Mother has sent for you," she announced in a foul-tempered hiss.

"For me?" Eden lifted the skirt of her mauve-hued gown as she hurried to reach her cousin. "Why would she wish to see me?"

"How should I know? The only thing which seems clear is that Clairbourne didn't come here today for the reason we had hoped."

Stephanie appeared ready to burst with envy, but Eden was certain her anger was unjustified. "This must be some sort of a silly misunderstanding, Stephanie. I'll be gone only a minute, I'm sure."

The warmth of Alex's smile melted Eden's apprehension the moment she entered the parlor. The light of the afternoon sun was more flattering than the candles' glow at the ball and she revised his age down a few years from forty. Whatever his reason for paying a call, she was happy to see him and returned his unspoken welcome with a dazzling smile of her own.

Lydia shot her niece a sharply disapproving frown which instantly erased that charming smile, but the woman had seen it and could not help but wonder what had prompted Alexander Sutton's surprising call. "I'm glad to see that you remember meeting Lord Clairbourne last night," Lydia began rather stiffly. "He has been kind enough to take an interest in you. He has asked my permission to call on you, and I knew you would be flattered and want to thank him."

"To call on me?" Eden asked in a breathless rush. "Do you mean that you wish to . . ."

Alex could not help but laugh when Eden became too flustered to continue. "I know we had no more than a glimpse of each other last night, but surely I'm not the first Englishman to find you so attractive I would like the opportunity to become a friend." That he was obviously the first was apparent in her startled response, but he was too enthused about the ploy he was attempting to dwell on her dismay.

Eden looked toward her aunt and found her staring with so menacing a glare she knew instantly she had sounded as though she had no breeding at all. "Please forgive me, m'lord. What I should have said is that I am honored you wish to call on me."

"The honor is all mine, I assure you," Alex responded as he came forward to take her hand. "And I insist that you call me Alex."

Lydia watched a warm glow of pleasure fill her niece's cheeks as Alex brushed the back of her hand with a light kiss, and she feared the man's interest in the girl wasn't at all proper. Eden was her sister, Sarah's, only child, and she was attempting to do her best for her. Not that Alexander Sutton had less than a spotless reputation, but still, with the Sinclair family fortune tied so closely to the fate of the Confederacy, Eden could scarcely expect a marriage proposal from an earl. Eden was a beauty, however, and it was only natural that men would be attracted to her. Alex seemed sincere, but Lydia still suspected his motives. He had been a widower for at least ten years so she was certain had he wanted a second wife, he would have wed

27

one long ago. When he mentioned a carriage ride the following afternoon, she refused immediately.

"I hope you will understand, Lord Alex. I simply can't allow my niece to see you without a chaperon."

"Would you like to come with us then?" Alex invited graciously.

"I'm afraid I have my own daughter to consider," Lydia replied far more sweetly. "Stephanie frequently has callers in the afternoon and I can't leave her alone either."

Having listened to Stephanie praise Raven Blade for the last half hour, Eden quickly made a suggestion she knew both her aunt and cousin would approve. "We could take Stephanie with us, couldn't we? And perhaps if your nephew doesn't have other plans, he could join us too."

"What a charming idea, Miss Sinclair," Alex agreed, delighted Eden had found the obvious solution to their dilemma before he had been forced to suggest it himself. "Would you object to the four of us going out together, Lady Lawton? We'll tour the city, and be back in time for Stephanie and Eden to join you for tea."

Lydia hesitated a moment, but not wanting her daughter to miss an opportunity to impress Raven Blade, she reluctantly gave her consent. "That sounds like a pleasant outing, but only if you promise not to be gone more than an hour or two."

Eden noted the grace of Alex's gestures as he and her aunt finalized the plans for the following day. Despite the elegance of his attire and manners, he displayed a masculine strength that she found as appealing as his striking good looks. His deep tan revealed he spent most of his time out-of-doors. His waistline was as trim as his nephew's, convincing her he enjoyed far more active pursuits than many of the wealthy men she had met whose builds more closely resembled dumplings than an athlete's muscled form. He was so handsome she found it difficult not to smile too widely each time he glanced her way, but she was so thrilled that he wished to call on her she could barely contain her joy.

As Alex left Lydia Lawton's, he was pleased his plans were progressing so well. It was now clear to him that Raven needed more strenuous encouragement to court the beauties of London than he had first realized. From what he had seen, Stephanie Lawton was among the most popular. She seemed both charming and sweet, if not as great a beauty as her American cousin. The Lawton family would provide the social ties Raven presently lacked but would most definitely need when he inherited a title. Surely if Raven were to spend some time with Stephanie, he would soon come to see how agreeable a wife she would make.

Yes, Alex decided, all Raven needed was a chance to become better acquainted with Stephanie, and he was determined to provide as many opportunities as were necessary to achieve that goal. The scheme struck him as remarkably clever until he recalled the warmth of Eden's smile when she had first seen him. It had been a long while since he had cared for a woman, or allowed one to care for him. Too long perhaps, but he wanted to be a friend to Eden, nothing more.

As he entered his carriage, he realized a true friend would not involve a lovely young woman in the farce he had just begun. It was Raven's future that was of paramount importance to him, however, and he promised himself he would display no more than a fatherly interest in Eden so that she could not possibly misinterpret his intentions and be hurt. He made that vow several times on his way home, but the memory of Eden's enchanting smile proved impossible to forget. He could not even recall the last time he had seen such an enthusiastic light dancing in a young woman's eyes and it was immensely flattering to think he had inspired it.

"If only," he began regretfully, but he swiftly buried that dream deep in his heart where it could not torment him with desire as he feared Eden Sinclair's spirited beauty would continue to do.

Two

July 1863

Raven had known without making the attempt that it would be useless to argue when Alex had told him they were to entertain Lady Stephanie Lawton and her American cousin for the afternoon. One well-bred young woman was as tiresome as the next in Raven's view, but he soon found himself reassessing his opinion as he watched Eden and his uncle converse. He and Stephanie were seated opposite them in an open carriage that afforded a fine view of Hyde Park, but he was taking little notice of the scenery.

The dark-eyed young man had been startled to learn Eden's father commanded the *Southern Knight,* one of the Confederate Commerce-Destroyers which had been built in England to prey upon merchant ships carrying cargo from the Northern states to European ports. There had been a lively debate at the time the cruisers were built, and he had sided with those who thought England had clearly violated her neutrality by providing ships for the Confederacy, despite the fact they were outfitted with their armaments elsewhere.

Noting the direction of her companion's glance,

Stephanie leaned close and whispered to Raven, "All Eden cares about is that abysmal war. I wish your uncle hadn't encouraged her to talk about it. She'll never stop."

Raven nodded, and tried not to flinch too badly as Stephanie tightened her hold on his arm to the point she threatened to cut off the blood flow. How she could criticize her cousin when she was such a chatterbox herself he did not know, but he restrained himself from making such a rude observation aloud. Stephanie preferred to discuss the parties he found so tedious, but because they had attended all the same fetes, she mistook that for a common interest. He had stopped listening soon after the petite brunette had said good afternoon, but he considered her too self-absorbed to realize he was listening to Eden rather than to her. He liked the seriousness of Eden's conversation, as well as her delightful Southern accent.

Eden could not help but notice Raven's unwavering stare, and while it was distracting, she found Alexander Sutton such an enthralling man it was not overly difficult to ignore his nephew. That Alex owned a fine clipper ship that carried the produce of Jamaica to England and returned with commercial goods delighted her, for it gave them a common bond she had not expected them to share.

"I prefer to remain at my home on Jamaica, and let Raven manage our shipping interests now, but when I was young, I dearly loved the sea."

"Why, what do you mean?" Eden exclaimed, sincerely surprised by his remark. "You are a young man still."

Alex laughed heartily, pleased that she would think so. "In years perhaps, but there are other ways to measure age."

"By what you have suffered, you mean?" Eden inquired sympathetically, for she had not forgotten that he was a widower. "That I can easily understand. Just three years ago I was like every other girl in Richmond: inter-

32

ested only in the latest fashions and which men knew the steps of the most popular new dance. That all seems so frivolous to me now. I'm ashamed that I didn't realize how precious that time was, and make better use of it."

Alex was again wearing gloves, and so was Eden, but he could still feel the lively warmth of her hand as it lay in his. He was surprised she had grasped his meaning so quickly. She was very bright, but unlike many of his contemporaries, he did not feel threatened by her intelligence. "Yes, the concerns of youth are frivolous, but that's only natural and nothing about which to be ashamed. No one grows up so rapidly that they do not spend some of their days foolishly. Besides, every young woman should have pretty clothes and handsome dancing partners. There's nothing wrong in that."

"I know it isn't wrong," Eden agreed with a slight frown. "It's just, well, so trivial a concern when compared to the numbers of men who have lost their lives defending our beliefs."

Raven knew slavery had been only one of the issues that had caused the Southern states to secede from the Union and he was convinced Eden Sinclair would vigorously debate them all if given the opportunity. He had never enjoyed argument for its own sake, however, and did not challenge her to defend her cause. He had overheard a whisper or two about her mother and, growing curious, decided to ask Alex about her family when they returned home.

For now he was content to merely watch the blonde with the luminous topaz eyes, and he found it a more fascinating pastime than he had imagined possible. She was dressed in apricot-colored muslin that day, a splendid shade that complimented her fair coloring while the demure lines of the fashionable outfit were every bit as flattering to her superb figure as her low-cut evening gown had been. The fullness of the sleeves accented the grace of her gestures, which he was amused to see she made constantly as though she considered no sentence complete without that additional emphasis.

The depth of her emotions was so easy to read in her expression, unlike the talkative young woman at his side whom Raven doubted possessed the capacity to feel anything deeply. As their ride continued, he was soon convinced that, for such a brief acquaintance, Eden and Alex had formed an amazing rapport. That worried Raven, for there was no point in the attractive young woman lavishing her affection on a man with no future.

Despite the cleverness of his plans, Alex found himself so captivated by Eden Sinclair's insightful conversation he quite forgot that the purpose of the afternoon's ride was for Raven to become enamored of Stephanie. He was dimly aware of the steady hum of Stephanie's voice, but unlike her more considerate cousin, she did not frequently provide an opportunity for Raven to offer a comment of his own. Alex thought it odd she did not know how greatly most men enjoyed talking about themselves. Not that Raven had such a flaw, but even if he had, he would have had scant opportunity to express himself when Stephanie seldom paused, and even then only long enough to draw a breath.

"Tell me more about Jamaica," Eden encouraged, determined not to make everyone else's mood as gloomy as her own by dwelling on the Civil War. She could easily imagine Alex riding about the plantation as he began to describe it. He explained that he raised sugarcane, ginger, and allspice and deftly managed to convey the impression that his life was not only wonderfully satisfying but exciting as well. She gave his hand a fond squeeze the way her mother had taught her to do when she wished to encourage a man's attentions. When Alex returned it, she blushed prettily at the effectiveness of that ploy.

Much to his own amazement, being with Eden made Alex feel younger than he had in years. He had never seen her so relaxed either. There was none of the tension about her manner now that he had noted at the Carlisles' ball or on other occasions prior to that, for indeed she had caught his eye long before she had joined him in the library. She was simply adorable, so utterly charming he began to wish there could be more than the friendship that had developed so easily between them. That was completely impossible, of course, and the pain of that realization forced him to look away.

Alarmed by the sudden sorrow of his uncle's expression, Raven leaned forward to touch his knee. "Are you all right?"

"What? Oh yes, I'm fine," Alex replied. Then scolding himself for wasting even a second of the time he had to share with Eden, he continued to extol the beauties of his island home.

"Jamaica must be like paradise," Eden mused with another appreciative smile.

"Yes it is, even without a wife to share it," Raven interjected sharply, not realizing how his remark would be interpreted.

Stephanie was so startled by the sound of Raven's voice she ended her monologue in midsentence, but she had not been following Eden and Alex's conversation and had no idea what Raven meant.

Eden, however, gasped sharply, thinking she must have been too forward. She had not said anything about visiting Jamaica, though; she was positive she had not, let alone offered to share Alex's home with him. As her glance locked with Raven's, she felt the same icy chill of apprehension she had experienced at their first meeting.

35

For a man raised in the warmth of a tropical paradise, he had a remarkably cold manner. It was not that his gaze was threatening, it was that he seemed to be looking right through her. To what? she wondered. Did he think she was merely flirting with his uncle and did not approve? She tried to think of some witty response to put him in his place, but when nothing suitable occurred to her, she was forced to remain silent.

Alex was too perceptive not to notice Eden's embarrassment, and while he knew what had prompted Raven's remark, he dared not explain it. "Raven didn't have the benefit of a mother's love while he was growing up and I fear the manners I managed to instill in him are rather few. You're wrong, though, Raven. Every joy is enhanced when it's shared."

"And every sorrow cut in half," Raven added flippantly. He looked away then, cringing at the pain of knowing that Alex had insisted he take a wife not for the pleasure a woman would provide but for the comfort he would need when he was alone. He turned, meaning to call to the driver to stop the carriage so he could get out and walk home, but Alex shot him so murderous a glance he thought better of it. He leaned back, resigned to spending the afternoon with a brunette who would not keep still and a beautiful blonde who was so charming he feared Alex might choose to die in her arms.

When they returned to the Lawton home, Alex let Raven and Stephanie leave the carriage first, then hurriedly apologized again to Eden for his nephew's rudeness. "I have hopes that Raven will take a bride while we're here. Unfortunately, he doesn't share them. If his temper gets the better of him at times, you mustn't think badly of him. He's a fine man, only young and frequently thoughtless."

Enormously relieved to learn that Raven had not been calling her a fortune hunter, or worse, Eden left the carriage with an agile dancing step. When Alex moved far more slowly, she did not question the reason, but took his arm and followed Raven and Stephanie inside the well-appointed townhouse where her Aunt Lydia invited the men to remain for tea. Delighted they would not have to part immediately, Eden decided if Raven continued to be an obnoxious bore, she would simply pretend he was not even there. She was having far too marvelous a time with Alex to allow anything, or anyone, to spoil it.

"Lady Lawton and Eden's mother are sisters?" Raven asked soon after they had bid the young ladies goodbye, hoping his interest in Eden wasn't too painfully obvious.

"Yes, but they are nothing alike," Alex responded. He hesitated a moment, gathering his thoughts before continuing, "It must have been twenty years since I last saw Sarah. She was as lovely as her daughter, enormously popular, and created quite a stir when she chose to wed an American. Sinclair not only owned ships, but built them too as I recall, or at least his family did. It wasn't as though Sarah had eloped with a ship's captain, but she might as well have for all the gossip their wedding caused."

"That explains why Eden is so unlike Stephanie then."

Alex smiled, "They are like night and day, aren't they?"

Raven nodded. "Fair and dark, charming and cloying. I can't abide another minute of Stephanie's company, but your interest in Eden astonishes me. I had no idea you planned to find yourself a bride on this trip."

Alex tried not to react angrily to the sarcasm in Raven's tone, but failed. "If you were not so lost in yourself, you would have noticed Eden has no suitors despite her beauty and charm. I'm sure there are those who recall her mother with other than fond memories, but the real problem is the uncertainty of her family's future. She may be a lovely American heiress today, but who can say how she'll be categorized a year from now? It's obvious too many think the Confederate cause already lost and regard her as impoverished."

"You are avoiding the issue," Raven pointed out with his customary passion for the truth. "Is it merely pity that prompted you to call on Eden, or a desire for something more?" Unable to declare his own admiration for Eden, Raven held his breath as he awaited his uncle's reply.

That impertinent question conjured up a mental image of the delectable Eden Sinclair lying nude upon his bed, and Alex hastily cleared his throat to force such an erotic vision from his mind. "I'm not dead yet, Raven, but I might as well be when it comes to pursuing a beauty like Eden. I have nothing to offer her but the innocent pleasure of an afternoon of sightseeing and polite conversation."

Raven could see Alex was far from content with that, but what choice did he have? Knowing the man had none, Raven was filled with shame for forcing him to say so aloud. "You're right, I've been very selfish. If you enjoy Eden's company, and she is not refusing the attentions of others to see you, then what is the harm in your calling on her? Until I find someone who excites me as Eden obviously does you, then I'll not complain about providing an escort for Stephanie so the four of us can spend our time together."

A slow smile raised the corner of Alex's mouth. Even if it was for completely the wrong reason, Raven had just agreed to continue seeing Stephanie Lawton, and that was too generous an offer to refuse. If nothing else, Raven would surely benefit from the practice of pleasing a cultured young woman even if it was one whose company he did not particularly enjoy. "Perhaps you will find one of Stephanie's close friends more to your liking."

Raven shook his head. "I doubt it, but as long as one of us is enjoying himself, our trip won't be a total waste." He turned away to hide his smile, but he was also looking forward to enjoying more of Eden's company.

In the following two weeks, the foursome spent five more afternoons together. Raven also went to the effort of dancing with both Eden and Stephanie more than once at the three balls they attended while Alex had fabricated an equestrian accident which he blamed for preventing him from dancing more than a waltz or two in an evening. Whenever he did feel up to dancing, it was Eden who was in his arms.

As they arrived at still another lavish party, Raven sighed wearily. He was ready to go home to Jamaica, for while he had not admitted it to Alex, Eden Sinclair was the only woman who interested him, and clearly she preferred his uncle to him. Whenever they danced together, she maintained a refreshing silence which provided a stark contrast to her cousin's incessant patter. Raven considered the seriousness of her nature very appealing, but he found it impossible to confess that to her. He had to be content with merely observing her while she and Alex continued to cultivate the warmest of friendships. It was not in the least bit satisfying to do so, but when Alex's pleasures were so few, Raven would not even consider competing against him for her affection.

By the third time she had seen Alexander Sutton, Eden knew beyond the slightest doubt that she had fallen in love with him. He was thirty-eight and she was nineteen, but women frequently married men many years their senior and she did not think the disparity in their ages too

39

great. He was a marvelous dancing partner, even if he could only dance a time or two rather than all evening as she longed to. He was wonderfully attentive, but had not once contrived to be alone with her again. Just as they had in Richmond, she frequently saw couples disappear into the shadows on the terrace, but Alex had never lured her outside to steal a kiss.

Having had to contend with the affections of impetuous young Southern gentlemen in her early teens, Eden found Alex's failure to demand more than a fondly held hand frustrating in the extreme. She wished she could talk to her mother about him, for she felt certain Sarah would remember Alexander Sutton had she ever met him, but that was impossible, and she could not go to her Aunt Lydia as a substitute.

No, Lydia was totally absorbed with helping Stephanie wring a marriage proposal from Raven Blade's lips, and Eden did not feel close enough to confide in her. Besides, even if she could not remember whom to address as m'lord, Eden was clever enough to realize if she were to marry Alex, she would be the one to enjoy his fortune, while Stephanie might have to wait half a lifetime for Raven to inherit his share of it.

When the perplexed blonde found herself suddenly paired with Raven for the last measures of a lively dance in which partners were changed frequently, she quickly decided he would be the best source of information on his uncle's feelings. His manner had remained too formal for her to consider him a friend despite the time they had spent together with Alex and Stephanie, but she had decided that was simply his way and no longer faulted him for it. Even if he lacked warmth, he was not openly hostile, and while it was a small comfort where he was concerned, it was the only one she had.

When the musicians accented the tune's final note,

Eden continued to hold Raven's hand. "It's gotten so warm. Would you mind strolling outside on the terrace for just a moment? I believe the musicians are taking a break."

"Would you rather I brought you some refreshments?" Raven inquired politely, inordinately pleased that she wished to spend some additional time with him.

"I want to go outside," Eden whispered insistently, and although Raven was startled by that demand, he graciously escorted her out onto the terrace, where numerous other couples stood looking out over the gardens or gazing up at the stars.

"I hope you won't think me frightfully rude," Eden began nervously, "but there is something I simply have to know and there's no one else to whom I can turn. I want you to be completely honest with me. Will you promise to do that?"

Raven's first thought was that somehow she had guessed how greatly he admired her, and not knowing how to respond, he simply nodded. The anguish in her expression was heartbreaking, and he could not bear to think he had caused her even a tiny twinge of pain.

While she did not find Raven's response particularly encouraging, Eden plunged ahead. She took the precaution of making certain no one was standing close enough to overhear her questions then hurriedly asked them. "I adore your uncle, and I can't pretend not to, but he has me terribly confused. He calls on me often but he seems to be no more than fond of me. Is it because he's still in love with his late wife? Or because he thinks my family's fortune doesn't compare with his? I think I could better tolerate his reserve if I understood the cause. He doesn't seem to care for any of the other young women, but is there some reason why he doesn't care more for me?"

41

Raven stifled a low moan and continued to stare down at the distraught blonde, not knowing how to justify his uncle's actions when he dared not reveal the truth. "Come with me," he finally invited, and taking her elbow he guided her to the farthest corner of the terrace to continue their conversation.

"Alex is more than merely fond of you, I'm certain of it," he began.

"Then why doesn't he—"

Raven shook his head, urging her to be still because he knew their absence from the party would soon be noted. "He hasn't meant to give you false hopes."

"He has given me no hope at all—that's the problem," Eden reminded him.

Raven was having a difficult time as it was without her constant interruptions. "Please, Miss Sinclair, I am doing my best to explain," he cautioned her crossly.

"I'm so sorry. Please continue." Eden opened her ivory fan and began to stir what breeze she could but she knew it was embarrassment and not merely heat that had brought a bright blush to her cheeks. As for Raven, the formality of his replies had already convinced her that she would learn nothing of any value from him and she was desperately sorry that she had confided in him. It was only that she was so far from home and had no other options that had made her choose such a brash course of action in the first place.

Raven had always despised lies, and it galled him that he was stretching the truth so shamelessly. He could tell from the proud tilt of Eden's chin that he had offended her, and that had not been his intention. He longed to draw her into a tender embrace and reveal how tragic Alex's fate truly was, but not even a husband and wife displayed that degree of closeness in public. That he could

42

offer neither the comfort of his touch, nor the truth, tortured his conscience badly.

"Alex has no plans to marry again, ever, but you mustn't think him selfish for making such a decision. He has absolutely no choice."

"No choice?" Eden's spirits sank even lower as she attempted to comprehend what Raven meant. Leaning closer, she whispered softly, "Do you mean that he's unable to, well, unable to . . ."

Although Eden left that question unfinished, Raven readily grasped her meaning. If possible, he was even more mortified than she by the subject they were discussing. Alex had used a nonexistent back injury as an excuse not to dance more than a time or two at each party, but Raven could not bring himself to say that he was impotent too. "No, it's not that. He has his reasons, but they are private ones I'm not at liberty to share."

Thoroughly confused, and deeply discouraged, huge tears welled up in Eden's eyes. She turned away in an attempt to hide them, but Raven readily felt her pain. Unable to bear her sorrow in addition to his own, he reached out toward her, but the instant his fingertips caressed her bare shoulder, she stepped away to avoid his touch.

"Please forgive me for bothering you," Eden whispered anxiously without turning back toward Raven. "I realize I've made a complete fool of myself and I would appreciate it if you didn't repeat this conversation to your uncle. I'm certain he would be as badly embarrassed to learn of it as we are that it ever took place."

"Why don't you ask Alex what his intentions are?" Raven suggested in a desperate ploy to provide her with the truth. "I think you have that right."

"Oh no, I couldn't do that. It would only force him to

tell me to my face that he doesn't love me and I couldn't bear to hear that."

That Eden would mention love shocked Raven, for he had not realized her feelings for Alex were that intense. While he thought it quite possible that Alex did love her, he knew the words ought to come from his uncle rather than him. Retreating behind his usual mask of indifference, he stepped in front of her and brought their conversation to a close. "Life is filled with unbearable sorrow, Miss Sinclair. I'd change that if I could, but it's beyond the scope of any man to alter fate."

Eden was uncertain what fate had to do with her and Alex, but she could not bear to continue such an embarrassing conversation another minute. She slipped her arm through Raven's and he escorted her across the terrace, but before they reached the French doors, she looked up to find Alex, Lydia, and Stephanie watching them with glances that ranged from deeply suspicious to openly venomous. Apparently the trio had been observing her and Raven for some time, and clearly they had all misinterpreted what they had seen. Eden attempted to smile bravely and waited for Raven to break the awkward silence, but as usual he kept his thoughts to himself and she felt utterly abandoned.

"It was so warm inside, I feared I might faint," Eden explained with the most innocent smile she could affect. "It's ever so much more pleasant out here. Don't you agree?"

"It is apparently still too warm for you to think clearly. Come, we are leaving now, before the heat causes you to lose your senses completely," Lydia commanded sharply.

Eden had never been treated as a child at home, and to silently take what she considered uncalled-for abuse from her aunt was almost more than she could bear in her current mood. She looked first to Alex, hoping he would protest her making such an early departure, but he continued to regard her with an expression that revealed only a shock and hurt she knew he had no reason to feel. She felt Raven's hand shift to her elbow and realized he was about to propel her toward her aunt. She looked up at him then, and his eyes narrowed slightly in a clear warning to keep still. Obviously he was as badly embarrassed by her behavior as her aunt was, but she thought he ought to have sense enough to know she would never reveal what they had been discussing so intently.

"I'm sorry," Eden finally remarked. "The parties are so much less formal in Richmond, that I didn't realize coming outside for some air would offend anyone."

Lydia Lawton did not respond, she simply turned and left, confident both Stephanie and Eden would follow.

Raven watched the three women depart, and hoped Alex would want to leave also. "It's not what you think," he insisted as he crossed to his uncle's side.

"What could I possibly think?" Alex responded with an uncharacteristic burst of temper. "That you've suddenly taken to seducing comely virgins?"

Raven did not reply, but left instead to summon their carriage. The ride to Alex's townhouse was not a long one, but he found it difficult to keep his thoughts to himself until they arrived home, where any argument they might have could not be overheard. While there was a full staff of servants, Alex always insisted that none wait up for their return so they were quite alone.

Raven refused Alex's grudging offer of a brandy, and followed him upstairs to his room. Alex would have slammed the door in his face, but Raven was too quick for him and pushed his way inside. "Eden begged me not to reveal what we discussed, but I'll not allow you to continue to imagine that was a romantic interlude you saw out on the terrace. Eden took me aside to ask about you.

45

She has my penchant for honesty, it seems, and wanted to know your intentions without having to suffer the embarrassment of asking you such a question."

"My intentions?" Stunned, Alex collapsed into a brocade armchair that promised the only comfort he was likely to find that night.

Raven yanked off his tie and pulled it through his fingers like a rope he intended to fashion into a noose. To have to plead Eden's cause struck him as the cruelest of ironies. "You asked permission to call on her, so she naturally assumed your interest was a romantic one. She cares for you, Alex. She can't help but be confused about your intentions when you've been so attentive, but haven't given her the affection she obviously craves."

"What did you tell her?"

Raven began to pace, his stride long and smooth despite the turmoil he felt inside. "Nothing of any consequence. You're the one who should speak with her. She's obviously taken with you, as I think you are with her as well. It may not be what you planned or expected, but now that it's happened, you must deal with her fairly. You owe her that much, Alex. You know that you do."

Alex closed his eyes and rested his head against the back of the chair. He had had such high hopes for their stay in London, but now he felt only despair. His chest ached, but it was not from exertion, merely from the sad realization of how badly his plan to find a bride for Raven had gone awry. "When Eleanora died, I never thought I'd ever love another woman, and I haven't, not until now. You're right, of course. Eden does deserve an explanation of some sort, although I don't know what I can possibly tell her that will make any sense."

"You must tell her the truth," Raven insisted emphatically. "Everything about Eden is refreshingly honest and real, you can't fabricate some convenient lie for a woman like her. It would be too great an insult."

Alex was too concerned with his own dilemma to recognize how much Raven had just revealed about his feelings. "I don't want her pity," he murmured softly.

Raven came to a halt and turned back to face him. "It will not be pity that she feels, but rage. Rage that so many lesser men have been allowed to grow old while you'll not live past your prime."

Even as a child of eight, Raven had displayed a wisdom far beyond his years. While Alex frequently took pride in the fact he had raised him, there had been many occasions, like this one, when he knew Raven would have grown up to be a remarkable man in all respects even if they had never met. He reluctantly agreed that Eden deserved to hear the truth, as indeed she had in the beginning.

"I'll call on her tomorrow afternoon," Alex announced solemnly. "I know I can trust her to keep the perilous state of my health a secret. It would make my stay here unbearable if the fact I have so little time left were widely known."

"I'm ready to go home now."

"I know that you are, but not yet. There are three million people in London. There has to be a woman for you among them. I'd like for you to look awhile longer."

"As you wish," Raven agreed, but he knew Eden would be so heartbroken to learn the man she loved might not see another summer that she would never notice him. He had known from the outset their trip to London had been a mistake, but each new day convinced him he had badly underestimated the potential for disaster. Alex looked not only troubled, but pale as well, and he could not help but worry about him. "You should go to bed."

"In a moment or two," Alex promised, but once alone

47

he remained seated, trying to understand why the love that had eluded him for so many years had come too late. Until recently he had considered himself a lucky man to have had so much, but after having met Eden, he now knew just how greatly he had been cheated.

Amazingly, that bitter thought brought a slow smile to his lips. Fate might have dealt him a poor hand, but he knew in life, just as in a game of chance, the winner was not always the man with the best cards. On the contrary, it was often the man who relied on his wits rather than luck, and made the most of whatever cards he held.

Alex wanted Eden, and badly. Now that he knew her affection for him also ran deep, why shouldn't they spend what time he had left together? It was a daring thought, and perhaps a selfish one, but the choice, after all, would be Eden's. His mind made up, he rose and began to undress. He would call on Eden just as he had promised Raven he would, but rather than bidding her a tearful farewell, he would offer her all the love that filled his heart. Knowing his beautiful rebel was a woman of spirit and courage, he was confident what her answer to his proposal would be.

Lydia Lawton also waited until she reached the privacy of her own room before she confronted Eden with what she considered not only her shocking lack of discretion, but an unforgivable breach of trust as well. Her voice was low and controlled, for she had no wish to start her servants gossiping about her niece.

"When Lord Clairbourne has been so generous with his time and attention, how dare you repay him by sneaking off with his nephew? And how could you have done that to Stephanie? Raven has been seeing her, not you. Did you think a few moments alone with him would be all you'd need to take him away from her? Is this how you wish to repay us for the kindness we've shown you? I can't believe Sarah didn't raise you to show better judgment, to say nothing of higher morals, than we've seen from you tonight. You have betrayed us all, and I demand to know why this very instant."

When her aunt had finished her scathing rebuke, Eden looked up, the sorrow of her expression still a reflection of her conversation with Raven, rather than a result of Lydia's string of undeserved insults. "My parents raised me to be a lady, and I am one. Raven was my partner when the music ended. I was too warm and wished to go outside. There was nothing more to it than that. It was entirely innocent."

"There was far more to it," Lydia contradicted. "I saw you two standing close, discussing something of obvious importance. Don't insult my intelligence by claiming you were talking about the weather."

As she searched her mind for a reasonable reply, Eden toyed nervously with the fan she still held in her lap. Were she to confess the truth, her aunt would be even more outraged than she was already, so she dared not do that. She would not lie about what she and Raven had been discussing either.

"While I'm half English, many of your customs are foreign to me. If I embarrassed you this evening, I'm truly sorry. I'll apologize to Alex the next time I see him as well."

"I doubt you'll ever see him again," Lydia snapped angrily.

"Not see him, but why?"

Lydia shook her head, amazed Eden did not understand. "No man is pleased to find a woman he admires prefers another man to him. When the other man is his own nephew, well, the shock had to be a most painful one."

"Stop it!" Eden leapt to her feet, no longer able to stoically tolerate her aunt's innuendoes when they now included Alex. "I did not lure Raven out into the gardens intending to seduce him! We were merely standing on the terrace enjoying the coolness of the night air. There is absolutely no reason for Alex to feel hurt by anything that happened tonight and I'm positive Raven will tell him so. I won't listen to another of your malicious lies. I'm going to bed."

Stephanie had been listening at the door, and when Eden stormed by her, she had to lurch out of the way. She was torn then, not knowing whether to follow her cousin or join her mother. Finally she entered Lydia's room. "Mother?" she called out hesitantly. "I'm not certain what we saw anymore, but Raven is not the type a woman can manipulate. He's very much his own man."

"Every man can be manipulated by a clever woman, every last one!" Lydia insisted as she yanked the bell pull to summon her maid. "Eden is exactly like her mother. Exactly, and if her willfulness has spoiled your chances to marry Raven Blade, I'll send her home and I won't mourn if she doesn't survive the voyage. Now go to bed. You've fittings for new gowns tomorrow and I won't have you going out looking pale and drawn."

When Stephanie reached her room, she was shocked to find Eden waiting for her, but she didn't waste a moment before venting the anger her mother had just fostered. "I had believed you to be so enamored of Alex I didn't think you had even noticed Raven. If you have, forget it, because I won't let you have him."

Eden had meant to reassure Stephanie that she had no such intention, but she was not inspired to respond to her cousin's vicious challenge with such a courtesy. "You don't own Raven Blade," she replied proudly, "and you never will." With a satisfied smile, she left her cousin to smolder in a tormenting mixture of jealousy and dismay.

Three

July 1863

Bound for the port, Raven left their townhouse before Alex was awake the next morning. Because he knew neither of them would be in any mood to be entertained the rest of the week, if ever, he had left the message he planned to stay on board the *Jamaican Wind* several nights while he made the final arrangements for the cargo they would be carrying home.

"Home," he recalled fondly, for indeed Jamaica was home to him. He had never felt welcome in London despite his numerous trips there. The city was not only terribly overcrowded but filthy as well, and now that the underground railway was being constructed, there seemed to be twice as much noise and dirt. All in all, he considered it a horrid place, one he would avoid whenever possible in the future.

He was far more comfortable among the colorful folk who inhabited the docks, and in the rowdy taverns that catered to sailors' tastes, than he was being entertained by Alex's elegant circle of friends. He could laugh out loud in a tavern, swat the barmaids on the fanny, and down ale until he passed out if he wished. He could relax completely and be himself instead of the reserved gentleman London society required him to be.

Alex knew how he felt and had taken him to the clubs where gentlemen gambled until dawn, but while the atmosphere was reasonably relaxed at such places, he had not been even remotely tempted to return on his own. He was not averse to an occasional game of cards, nor to playing for high stakes. He simply preferred the company of friends he respected to that of men who maintained their wealth by extorting high rents from the impoverished tenants who populated their estates. They were parasites in his view: living off the sweat of others while the most strenuous labor they ever did was to shuffle a deck of cards. Surely that was no way for any self-respecting man to live no matter how many titles he could claim.

Raven had been born into a hostile world where even a child had to work from dawn to dusk in order to survive. Alex might have rescued him from that wretched environment, but Raven had never forgotten it. He considered men who pursued no useful work, or philanthropic endeavor either, to be insufferably weak and avoided them whenever possible. The problem was, he had been unable to do so for the last few weeks, and as a result, he was eager to return to his ship, where he felt completely at home and where there would be work for him to do that mattered.

He whistled as he strode up the gangplank, and then broke into a wide grin when the mate came running to meet him. "I'm pleased to see you've kept the ship afloat without me," he called out in greeting.

"Aye, that I have, and it weren't no small job either," Randy MacDermott replied. "And what about you? Have you found yourself a bride yet?"

"No, the women here aren't nearly as pretty as the ones

at home." Raven gave the stocky red-haired mate a playful cuff to the shoulder, and then kept their conversation centered on the shipping trade but he had not forgotten that Alex would soon be calling on Eden, nor how sad that meeting would surely be.

When Alex arrived at Lydia Lawton's, she and her daughter were out, but recognizing him as a frequent visitor Anna showed him into the parlor and hurried out to the garden to inform Eden that she had a caller.

"Lord Clairbourne is here?" the astonished blonde gasped.

"Yes he is, miss, and he's asked for you."

Eden was so unnerved she almost forgot to send Anna for refreshments. She had never expected to see Alex that day. That he had come alone frightened her, for after his first visit Raven had always been with him. She wiped her palms on her billowing skirt and prayed he had not come to tell her goodbye.

When Eden came through the door, delightfully pretty in pale blue, Alex was so enchanted by the shyness of her smile he broke into a wide grin. "It's such a lovely day," he began. "Would you show me the gardens?"

For an instant Eden wondered if he were making fun of her desire to visit the terrace at the previous evening's ball, but the warmth of his smile quickly banished that suspicion. "Yes, of course, the flowers are so lovely I spend my every spare minute there. I believe my aunt has roses of every possible hue."

Eden took Alex's arm as they left the house. After a leisurely stroll they made their way to a marble bench shaded by an arched trellis covered with climbing roses. The sweet scent of their bright yellow blooms reminded Alex of the abundance of tropical flowers that perfumed the air on his island home. He was pleased the garden provided a setting as romantic as his mood.

He had rehearsed several versions of his proposal, striving to evoke passion rather than pathos, but Eden's haunting topaz gaze proved terribly distracting. Memories of Jamaica had brought Raven to mind, and because his hopes for his nephew were a primary concern, Alex decided to begin with him.

"I told you that I had hoped Raven would take a bride on this trip, but I didn't tell you why."

"It's not for the usual reason?" Eden asked, greatly relieved he had not spoken about last night. She was delighted he had chosen to ignore the unfortunate way the evening had ended. Clearly he was as fine a gentleman as she had thought, and if he could pretend the incident had never occurred, she would follow his example.

"The usual reason?"

"Well, yes, to have a woman to love, a woman with whom to have children and share the rest of his life."

"Yes, for those reasons certainly, but there's another consideration in his case."

This time Eden remained silent. Alex was frowning slightly, an expression he seldom wore, and while she was extremely curious, she thought better of interrupting him again.

"You mustn't tell anyone what I'm about to tell you, Eden, not your aunt, nor Stephanie, nor anyone else."

"You have my word on it." The puzzled blonde sat forward slightly, greatly intrigued by the secret he wished to confide. She had never seen him in so serious a mood and could not suppress a small shiver of dread.

Seeing that he had frightened her, Alex took her hand and patted it lightly as he spoke. "The men in my family have all been bright and handsome, but unfortunately none has been blessed with a long life. I am the first to live past the age of thirty-five. That's why I'm so eager for Raven to take a wife now, so that I can meet her. I'm thirty-eight, Eden, and I haven't much more time. I may appear strong, but I'm not. At any minute my heart may cease to beat. Quite frankly, I'm always amazed when I awake each morning, for I never really expect to survive the night."

Alex's skin glowed with a healthy tan, and his blue eyes were so bright and clear she did not understand how he could possibly be in imminent danger of death. "That can't possibly be true," she protested immediately. "It just can't be."

Alex placed her fingertips on his wrist. "This should be proof enough for you," he murmured confidently. "What do you feel?"

At first she felt nothing at all, then finally she did detect a faint pulse but it did not echo her own. Instead, it was an erratic rhythm that caused her eyes to widen in dismay. "Oh Alex . . ."

Alex raised a fingertip to her lips to still whatever burst of sympathy she was about to make. "Yes, I know, it's a shame but there's nothing we can do about it. We have a decision to make, Eden, one of the most important of our lives. I've enjoyed your company more than I have ever enjoyed any other woman's, but it wasn't until last night that I realized it was possible for us to become more than affectionate friends."

As he grasped both of her hands in his, Eden felt certain Raven had betrayed her confidence. Because Raven had not impressed her as having any tact, she was certain he had done it poorly too. Deeply embarrassed that Alex knew how she felt about him, her cheeks filled with the heat of a bright blush.

While that show of demure innocence was charming, Alex was too anxious to hear her reply to his proposal to waste any more time in getting to it. "I've made the mistake of doing the thinking for the both of us, Eden. I thought since I couldn't offer you a long, as well as a happy life together, I should keep my feelings to myself. But if you love me as dearly as I love you, then we ought to seize whatever time we can have together, without any regard for the precarious state of my health. We ought to live each and every day to the fullest, and never worry about what tomorrow might bring.

"I would be deeply honored if you would become my wife. I know what I've said has probably shocked you. If you want some time to consider whether or not you want to marry me, I'll try and be patient, but I hope you won't keep me waiting too long. Please believe me, if your answer is no, I'll understand why and we'll simply go on as before. I'll be your escort whenever you need one but you must never tell anyone that I'm not as well as I look. Pity is the last thing I want from anyone, and most especially not from you."

That Alex had possessed the courage to propose, after giving her a good reason to refuse him, made Eden love him all the more. "No one is guaranteed a long life, Alex. I might be trampled by a team of runaway horses tomorrow, or trip and drown in my bath. I could catch cold and die of pneumonia within a week. Or I might come down with typhoid and die like Queen Victoria's dear Albert. Just because I'm healthy today doesn't mean that I'll be alive tomorrow."

"Accidents happen, people fall ill," Alex agreed with a shrug. "I'll concede that, but my death is inevitable, Eden. You mustn't delude yourself with false hopes."

"Everyone's death is inevitable," the determined blonde replied.

"What are you saying?" Alex studied her expression closely, hardly daring to hope that she meant what he

57

thought she did. He had never thought any woman would willingly choose to share his life when the end was so near. That a young woman as lovely as Eden would even consider such a grim prospect both thrilled and astonished him.

Eden knew her aunt would have a hysterical fit at the boldness of her response, but that did not prevent her from making it. "I had friends who married young men knowing they might not survive the War. That didn't concern them. All that mattered was that they would spend whatever time they had together. I know I'm not a proper bride for an earl. I'm only half English, but I love you, Alex, and I'd be proud to be your wife whether it's for fifty years or only one."

The sincerity of that heartfelt compliment brought a low moan to Alex's lips and he nearly crushed Eden with the enthusiasm of his embrace. He kissed her then with all the passion he had thought he would never again express. He kissed her again and again until they were both so breathless he had to draw away.

"I don't think we ought to waste any time being engaged," Eden suggested persuasively. "Do you know an Anglican priest who can perform a wedding ceremony this afternoon?"

Alex could not help but laugh at her enthusiasm for their marriage. "All of London will be talking about us for weeks, if not years to come. You realize that, don't you?"

"So what? If they have nothing better to do than to gossip about two people who fell in love, then they aren't worth worrying about."

"That sounds like something your mother might have told you."

"No, she never said that, but you're right, she might have. She married the man she loved regardless of how greatly that decision shocked London society. I hope there's an opportunity for you to meet him. My father is a wonderful man."

"I'm sure that he is," Alex agreed. Seeing Anna coming their way with a tea tray, he sat back to put a more respectable distance between them. "Let's have tea, then you can pack a few things and we'll find a priest who has as romantic a nature as we do."

Eden waited until Anna had returned to the house before she kissed him again. "I love you so much, Alex. You'll never be sorry you married me. Never."

"I promise you'll never be sorry either, Eden. I'll make our entire marriage a honeymoon." That he had ever imagined a friendship as warm as theirs could remain a chaste one struck him as absurd now. Still, he could not help but feel a tinge or two of guilt. "I'm being very selfish, but I swear I can't help myself."

"Selfish?" Eden shook her head, "You are the warmest, most sympathetic man I've ever met. I doubt you are ever selfish." Not about to allow the man to have second thoughts, Eden rose and, taking his hands, pulled him to his feet. "Come upstairs with me. I'll need your advice about what to bring."

"That wouldn't be at all proper," Alex protested, but his grin was too wide for Eden to mistake his mood.

"Neither is eloping, m'lord." With a throaty giggle, Eden led him inside but she took care to walk up the stairs very slowly so as not to tire him.

It was after dark by the time they arrived at Alex's townhouse. He had had no difficulty arranging for a special marriage license and, with that in hand, had easily persuaded a young priest to perform a marriage ceremony without the required reading of the banns. It had been the most exciting afternoon he had spent in a long while, but he was too happy to allow the resulting fatigue to spoil his wedding night.

He dismissed his servants for the evening immediately after he and his bride had finished the sumptuous supper his cook had gone to great lengths to prepare. He felt slightly tipsy although he had had only one glass of wine.

"I want to take you home to Briarcliff, my estate in Devon. We can spare a month at least before having to make the return voyage to Jamaica. I think it will do Raven good to be on his own for a while. Maybe without my constant urging, he'll fall in love too."

Eden laced her fingers in her new husband's as they started up the stairs. She had expected Alex to send for Raven so he could attend their wedding, but she had been relieved when he had not wanted to wait for the young man to be found. Somehow she did not think Raven would approve of their marriage, and she was grateful to have avoided what could have easily been the most embarrassing of scenes. That she would not have to face him for a month pleased her. Surely that would provide ample time for him to accept his uncle's marriage.

"Can we leave first thing in the morning?"

Alex rested his hand on the banister, for he could not climb stairs and talk at the same time. "Do you want to stop by and see your aunt and cousin before we go?"

Eden pursed her lips thoughtfully. She had left her aunt a note, even though it seemed a cowardly thing to do. "I'd rather not. I don't want anyone to spoil our happiness, least of all Lydia and Stephanie. They're both very fond of you, but I know they'll take exception to the haste of our marriage."

Understanding her concern, Alex continued on up the stairs and waited until they had reached the landing to reply. "I wish there had been time for us to plan an enormous formal wedding, a lavish reception, and the most exotic of honeymoons. You've given up a great deal to marry me, and I hope you won't soon regret it."

Eden wondered if Alex were recalling his first wedding, and his first wife, but dared not ask when she wanted his thoughts focused solely on her that night. "My family and friends are all so far away and I would have missed them terribly had we had a large wedding. If anyone asks why we chose to elope, let's blame it on the War. We'd be believed, don't you think?"

"The War? Why yes, of course. That's positively brilliant, Eden. We chose to elope because your country's at war." Alex was pleased beyond measure to have so logical an excuse for a completely illogical elopement. He led her into his bedroom rather than the adjoining one where she had bathed and dressed before supper, and then made what he hoped was not too gruesome a request.

"It's customary for the husband to visit the wife's bedroom, but I don't want to run the risk of dying in your bed." He paused an instant, half expecting Eden to protest his mention of death as Raven always had, but instead she nodded in agreement.

"I understand. That I will someday be a widow will bring sorrow enough, I don't want to be the subject of crude jokes about the manner in which you died."

"Precisely." Alex pulled her into his arms and hugged her tightly. "I've felt so terribly alone, and to find that you understand my concerns so readily is a great comfort to me."

Eden relaxed against him, grateful that they could now display their affection for each other openly, but she was as deeply concerned about her new husband's health as he was. "Alex, if making love will be too strenuous for you, if you truly do fear dying in my arms, we could simply sleep together and be close in ways other than the merely physical."

Alex stepped back so he could study her expression, but he had a difficult time containing the amusement her question had prompted. "Life is filled with difficult choices, Eden. Somehow I think you're already aware of that. If I stayed in bed, alone, and did nothing more strenuous than sip soup and tea, I could probably prolong my life. But what kind of life is that to live? I would rather be a real husband to you for six months, than no more than an affectionate friend for a year. Isn't your choice the same? Wouldn't you advise me to live whatever time I have left as fully as I possibly can?"

Eden replied not with words, but with a kiss so filled with love he could not mistake her answer. She was a vibrant beauty, and it was that very quality that had attracted him to her in the first place. She was as eager to live life fully as he was, and while their time together would be heartbreakingly brief, he planned to make certain she did not regret a second of it. He trailed sweet kisses down her throat and across the luscious swell of her bosom, peeling away her white satin gown with the expertise of a man well schooled in the art of seduction. He knew he would have to rely upon finesse rather than stamina, but vowed not to disappoint her.

Eden had never expected to marry that day, but fortunately her mother had long ago provided her with all the information any bride would need. She knew exactly what would happen, but she also knew there was far more to making love than the act that would make her Alex's wife. It was instantly plain from his adoring kiss and tender caress that he knew it too. He was no ardent boy intent upon sating his own lusts with her body. He was a lover of extraordinary insight and skill and she loved him all the more for it.

When a few minutes later Eden found herself lying nude across his bed, she could not recall precisely how he had managed to remove all her apparel without her assistance, but she thought him extremely clever for doing so. When he reached toward the lamp at the bedside, she objected. It was already turned down low, and she thought the soft light provided precisely the romantic glow a wedding night required. "Leave the lamp as it is," she requested in a seductive whisper.

Alex considered Eden's beauty of the most exquisite sort, and had no objection to feasting his eyes upon her all night, but he had thought she would prefer to have the room dark. "You are not embarrassed?"

His bed had already been turned down in preparation for the night, and Eden raised the corner of the sheet to demurely cover her breasts. "I didn't realize I should be."

"I didn't mean of your own body, but of seeing mine."

Eden took a deep breath before assuring him that was not the case. "You're a very handsome man, Alex, lean and fit. Why wouldn't I find you attractive?"

Alex had already slipped off his coat and waistcoat and sat down on the side of the bed as he began to unbutton his shirt. "Men's bodies are very different from women's. I know some brides find that discovery frightening."

"I've seen nude men. The sight doesn't disgust me."

Alex's mouth fell agape, for it had never occurred to him she might not be a virgin. Not that it mattered to him when he loved her so dearly, but it was a shock just the same. Unable to think of any way to reply to such a startling confession, he concentrated on unbuttoning his shirt, but fumbled so badly with the buttons he made very slow progress.

"Alex?" When he failed to immediately look up, Eden began to giggle. "I'm not in the habit of cavorting with nude men. Is that the way that sounded? I worked tending the wounded before my parents sent me here to London. That was the primary reason they insisted I leave Richmond. They felt I had seen too much bloodshed for one so young. The boys who were dying were no older, though, so I thought their decision was very unfair. Had I been their son, they would have let me fight, but they didn't want their daughter touched by the horror of the War."

Alex was ashamed for doubting her virtue for even a moment but thought better of admitting that aloud. "That's ironic, isn't it? That your parents sent you away to escape the horror of death when all they succeeded in doing was—"

Eden stilled his words with her fingertips. "No, not another word about death tonight. Tomorrow in the sunshine, on the way to Briarcliff, we can talk about it as long as you like, but no more tonight."

Alex took her hand and placed a kiss on her palm. "You are a priceless treasure, Eden, truly you are." Readily agreeing to her suggestion, he left the bed to search among the bottles of cologne atop his chest of drawers. When he returned, he was holding a lavender bottle made of delicate hand-blown glass. It was fashioned in the oval shape of a newly opened rosebud and its stopper was topped by a hummingbird that had paused in flight to savor the flower's nectar.

Eden could not recall ever seeing anything quite so exquisitely beautiful. "Is that perfume?" She had brought along her favorite scent, but thought perhaps the lovely bottle contained a fragrance he preferred.

"This has a pleasant scent, but it's not perfume," Alex explained, but he could think of no way to describe the exotic liquid's true value. Setting the stopper by the lamp, he shook the bottle, and capturing a few drops on his fingertips, he spread them on Eden's lips. "Do you like the taste?"

Eden ran her tongue over her lips, then smiled at their sweetness. "It's more delicate than honey, or maple syrup, but it's very good. What is it?"

"Merely an oil to use for massage." This time Alex pulled away the sheet so he could spread a thin coat of the pale liquid on the tip of Eden's right breast. When he leaned down to lick it off, she ran her fingers through his hair to press his face close.

"Is that how to give a massage?"

Alex's answering chuckle was low in his throat. "It's how I like to do it." He sat back then, quite pleased with the way the evening was progressing. He could recall his first wedding night vividly. Eleanora had been so shy he had had to ply her with brandy for half the night before she had gotten in a sufficiently loving mood to allow him to consummate their marriage. In time she had become an affectionate wife who always pleased him, but she had never been as delightfully wanton as Eden already appeared to be.

Eden's lips began to tingle slightly and she licked them again. She watched Alex rub the sweet-tasting oil on his own nipples and understood what he wanted her to do when he placed his hand on her shoulder to draw her near. The coarse curls which covered his chest were still as dark as his hair had once been. They tickled as she pressed her mouth to his flesh. His skin was warm, and she began to feel a delicious heat filling her own body as well.

Alex shed the last of his clothing, then continued to play a teasing game with the scented oil. While its full effect wasn't noticeable for several minutes, Eden soon learned it left a trail of fire wherever it touched her skin. It was merely a drop or two at first, on her earlobes, at the base of her throat, again on the flushed tips of her breasts, and each time he kissed the slippery substance away, she would repay the favor in kind.

She soon felt so dizzy she was sorry she had not allowed Alex to extinguish the lamp, for the room's furnishings seemed to be spinning around the bed at a most alarming rate. She had sipped her wine slowly all through supper and knew she had not been inebriated when they had walked up the stairs, but she could not understand what had happened to her now. She had never felt so light-headed, and yet at the same time her senses had grown painfully acute.

She closed her eyes, hoping to shut out the distracting visual images that surrounded her but found that self-imposed darkness only increased her dismay. She now felt as though she were falling, slowly sinking into the most delicious sensation she had ever experienced. Alex's touch was soft and sure as he parted her thighs, and before she could tell him not to spread the oil's tormenting heat in so intimate a place, he had already done so. It did not burn her delicate flesh, but the effect of the fiery potion was immediate. It created a craving for release that overwhelmed the last of her reason. She called out to him, but all that escaped her lips was a breathless plea for a fulfillment of the night's spiraling journey into pleasure's core.

She tried to open her eyes, even though she feared Alex would be no more than a blur, but she could not manage even so simple a feat. Remarkably, in her mind's eye she could see them both sprawled across the bed, the neatly ironed bedclothes now tangled beneath their oil-slickened bodies. She had never had the opportunity to observe a couple making love, and while she knew she could not possibly be watching herself and Alex, that was who she saw.

She watched the fascinating scene unfolding in her mind and at the same time she could feel Alex's fingers slide inside her, preparing a slippery path. He had already awakened the most primitive of human needs and she clutched his shoulders, urging him to finish what he had begun. She saw him shift his weight, and watched the muscles ripple across his back as he positioned himself above her. When he hesitated a moment, she noticed they were a striking pair, for he was dark while her usually creamy skin was flushed with a rosy glow that extended from her cheeks to the tips of her toes.

In the next instant she felt the blunt tip of his manhood brush against her, but he retained the same languid rhythm that had marked his gestures all evening. After his first shallow probings, he began to plunge deeper with each new thrust, but with deliberate care he withdrew each time he felt her grow tense. As relentless as the rising tide, with every new approach he filled her more completely until finally he lay fully contained within the warm channel that he had taken such care to prepare. That her body had accommodated his so easily convinced Eden she had been born to be his mate. That it had been Alex's clever use of the exotic oil that had permitted them to join so easily did not occur to her.

Eden slipped her arms around Alex's waist as she returned his deep kisses. He seemed content, but she knew there had to be more to making love, and impatient to discover it, she rolled her hips against his, silently demanding that he continue and show her all there was to see and feel. This time he abandoned his cautious pace, and lost himself in the wonder of her eager acceptance. She felt the rapture she had craved swell within her, and poised on the edge of paradise, she lunged for it. Her graceful writhing drove Alex to increase the speed of his deep thrusts until the blinding moment of ecstasy overtook him with a convulsive shudder that echoed hers in endless ripples of joy.

A long while passed before Eden became aware of Alex's weight, but she found it very pleasant to be pinned beneath him still. She could feel the warmth of his breath against her throat and cuddled close. She ruffled his soft silver hair and decided her mother had been right: there was nothing more glorious than being with the man you loved.

As they left for Briarcliff the next day, Alex sent his cook's son to deliver a message to Raven. It took the poor lad a long while to locate the dock where the *Jamaican Wind* was moored, and then he had to wait for more than an hour for the captain to return from an errand.

Recognizing both the messenger and the heavy vellum stationery, Raven ripped open the envelope, afraid it contained bad news, but not in his worst imaginings had he envisioned the hastily scrawled note would announce an elopement. Stunned, he handed the boy a generous tip for his trouble and sent him on home. He then retreated to the quiet of his cabin, where his temper swiftly erupted into a blazing fit of fury.

"The diabolical witch!" he shrieked, for he could make no sense of what had happened. As far as he knew, Alex had meant to be honest with Eden about his heart condition. How could he have married her instead? Alex was not the type of man to make spur-of-the-moment decisions. All his judgments where well thought out and sound. Raven was positive there was no way he could have been the one to suggest marriage. No, it had to have been Eden's idea.

She was a rare beauty, and obviously bright, but he had not even suspected she possessed a character so devoid of morals as this ridiculous elopement proved her to have. Had she enticed Alex into marriage by promising to make his last days happy? Or had she simply seduced him then demanded he offer marriage? What had the bitch done to talk Alex into a marriage that could not possibly endure?

"She'll kill him," he swore under his breath. "As surely as putting a pistol to his head, she'll kill him with that luscious body of hers."

Unable to shake that hideous thought, Raven paced his cabin with an anguished stride. He knew Alex was no fool. If what he wanted was a gorgeous bride who would probably not mourn his passing more than five minutes before she began to count his money, then he would not interfere. He would not criticize her as long as Alex lived, but the instant the dear man was buried, he would vent every last ounce of his anger on his widow.

It might be impossible to prosecute Eden for murder, but he would never allow her to forget that she had hastened Alex's death. Every time she lured Alex to her bed, she would be shortening his life, and no matter how loudly she protested her innocence, Raven would call her a murderess.

Four

July 1863

They would not meet again, so Raven had not bothered to remember the petite brunette's name. She was pretty, and her figure possessed alluring curves, but the pleasing nature of her appearance had had no effect on the blackness of his mood. Her conversation consisted of the adoring praise he had come to expect from her kind. He was not really listening to her, and could not have said what sort of personality she had. He was all too aware of her heavy perfume, however, for it filled the garishly decorated room with a near suffocating stench. It was too late to rise from her bed to fling open the window, but Raven wished he had had the foresight to do so when he had first stepped across the threshold.

As the agile brunette moved astride him, her shiny, black ringlets swayed across her pale breasts, but Raven failed to notice the stark contrast between her ebony hair and fair skin that other men found so appealing. Her nipples were the color of milk chocolate but he had not been tempted to sample their taste. Instead he reached up to roll the tips between his fingers until they became taut buds.

Responding to the tenderness of his touch, the girl licked her lips suggestively and began to move her hips with a sensuous rhythm to bring him to climax again. He was a lusty man, but she was confident she could satisfy his every need. She thought him extraordinarily handsome, and told him so repeatedly, but his expression remained disappointingly remote. Not discouraged, she began a circular motion that brought their bodies together in a new and, what she considered, even more exciting way.

Raven continued to fondle her breasts, but the warmth of the brunette's skin did not make him feel any less alone. Tall and well built even in his early teens, he had often spent an idle afternoon in a whore's bed, and none had ever guessed how young he was. The thrill of being with a woman had been enough then. Now he possessed the same strong sexual appetite and stamina, but the release he found joining with strangers, no matter how pretty, was no longer half so sweet.

He felt the first stirrings of ecstasy fill his loins and dropped his hands to encircle his companion's waist. He controlled her motions then, forcing her to slow down to make the feeling last until he could no longer restrain the force of his passion. He let it wash over him then, felt his body grow tense at the instant his seed shot forth, but the peace he had hoped to find with a woman again eluded him.

"I did not please you?" the brunette asked, puzzled when Raven swiftly left her bed.

Pausing at the washstand in the corner, Raven scrubbed hurriedly before pulling on his clothes. He did not want any reminders of the time he had spent with her and wished he could have taken a hot bath to thoroughly remove her sickeningly sweet scent from his body before he returned to his ship.

71

"Did you hear me complain?" he asked gruffly.

"No," the brunette replied. "I did not hear you say anything at all."

Once dressed, Raven jammed his feet into his boots, then tossed a generous amount on the rumpled bed. "I didn't come here for conversation."

As he reached the door, the brunette rose up on her knees and called out to him, "When will you come back to see me?"

Never, Raven thought to himself, but he left the room without dashing her hopes with that bitter farewell.

It had been only a week since Alex and Eden had left for Briarcliff, and Raven had lost count of how many pints of ale he had drunk and how many women he had paid for what passed for affection in all too many sailors' lives. He had not returned to the townhouse, nor had he sent anyone to collect the mail. He thought it likely several invitations must have arrived, but he did not care enough about anyone he had met to attend the last of the season's parties now that Alex was not there to insist that he go.

Alex enjoyed himself everywhere he went, but despite his constant encouragement Raven had never been able to match his uncle's keen appreciation of life. Their personalities were entirely different, of course, and always had been, but it pained Raven that he had been unable to master Alex's talent for savoring the moment. His nature was far more serious, but his mood had seldom been as gloomy as it had been since Alex's elopement.

Wisely, his crew had stayed out of his way; unfortunately, Stephanie Lawton was not nearly so clever.

Soon after Raven had returned to his ship, Stephanie alighted from her family's carriage and with an unladylike haste, dashed up the gangplank. Raven ignored Randy MacDermott's snicker and strode across the deck to meet her, but before he could greet her properly, she grabbed his hands and began an insistent plea.

"Is there a place where we might talk in private? Your cabin, perhaps?"

Alarmed by that request, Raven stared down at the brown-eyed girl, wondering why he had not instantly realized how closely the brunette with whom he had spent the better part of the afternoon resembled her. "I'm not accustomed to receiving young ladies for tea. My quarters can't possibly be grand enough to entertain you, Lady Stephanie."

Frustrated by the coolness of that response, Stephanie's voice took on a petulant whine. "We've got to talk about what's happened, and we need some privacy to do it."

Recalling all too vividly the disastrous result when Eden had made that same request, Raven shook his head. "I'll escort you home. Your carriage will have to be private enough."

Stephanie bit her lower lip to stifle a moan of disappointment as she turned to look toward her carriage. The gleaming black vehicle would indeed provide privacy, but she was not at all certain the journey home would be long enough for what she wished to accomplish. Hoping to make the best of the time they spent together, she smiled coquettishly as she turned back toward Raven, but when his expression failed to become more sympathetic, she gave up as futile the effort to speak with him there. Resigning herself to letting him have his way, she took his arm for the walk down the gangplank and returned to her carriage. When Raven was comfortably seated across from her, and their journey underway, she began to confide in him.

"I know you must be as dreadfully embarrassed as we are by Eden and Alex's elopement. Mother and I may never recover from the shock. I'm certain you can imagine how difficult this is for my dear mother to bear. Her sister created the same scandal twenty years ago, and now Eden has followed in her mother's footsteps and given no thought to her relatives' feelings. Oh, we've gone to all the parties as though nothing were amiss, but we can't help but hear the gossip. To elope is so dreadfully common, don't you agree?"

Common was not the word that came to Raven's mind, for in Alex's case he considered it madness. He took a perverse pleasure in arguing with Stephanie, however. "I always thought elopements were regarded as romantic."

"Perhaps it is when a chambermaid runs off with a chimney sweep, but surely not in this case."

"An earl is not allowed to be impetuous?" Raven taunted with a sly grin. He knew he should have been agreeing with Stephanie since he was as outraged over the haste of his uncle's marriage as she was, but he simply could not stop himself from taking the opposite view just to spite her. They might have spent many hours together, but he had not developed any warm feelings for the self-centered girl.

"Of course an earl is allowed to be impetuous if he is in love," Stephanie admitted reluctantly, "but there are far more acceptable ways to go about it." She was dressed in dark blue, and nervously brushed a bit of lint from her skirt before looking up at him.

"Is that all you wished to say to me, that you are embarrassed by the gossip my uncle's elopement has caused? If so, there is absolutely nothing I can do to help you. The damage has already been done and you'll simply have to live with it."

Clearly Raven thought her complaint too trivial to merit mention, but Stephanie did not. She was bright enough not to belabor the point with him, though. "No, that was not the primary reason I wanted to see you." She reached out to pat his knee lightly, but drew her hand away when she felt him flinch. "I, that is, my mother and I, have missed seeing you. We thought if you were unwilling to attend the Russells' ball this evening alone, that you might consider going with us. I'm sure you're not the type of man to allow gossip to determine your actions."

"Is that a dare?"

Stephanie now found herself flinching under Raven's menacing stare. Until that very moment, she had always thought the darkness of his coloring lent him a wonderfully appealing air of mystery. Now she wished his eyes were not as black as coal when it made his thoughts impossible to read. "No, not at all," she insisted when she had recovered her poise. "It's merely that both our families are involved in what appears to be the season's most delicious scandal and I thought we could comfort each other."

"I'm not in need of comfort," Raven declared firmly, or at least not the type of comfort that she could provide he did not add.

Stephanie fussed with her kid gloves, tugging on them as though their fit were not superb. "I have missed you," she whispered, silently praying he would reply with something sweet even though he had never used even the slightest endearment with her. When Raven appeared to be too astonished by that confession to say anything at all, she quickly moved to his side and threw her arms around his neck.

"Oh Raven, don't you have any tender feelings for me? I'm so fond of you and I don't want the gossip Eden and Alex's elopement has caused to keep us apart any longer."

Raven turned his head quickly and her wet kiss slid off his cheek. Disgusted she would be so forward when he had given her no indication he would welcome such an affectionate display, he took a firm hold on the distraught young woman's shoulders and forced her away. "Stephanie, please. I can understand why you're upset, but it really has nothing to do with me."

"But it has everything to do with you!" she exclaimed, the carefully constructed façade of her ladylike demeanor now ripped to shreds. "You enjoyed my company, I know that you did. Now Eden has ruined our chances to find happiness together, and I'll never forgive her for that. I wish she had stayed in Richmond where she belongs. She ruined all our lives by coming here!"

Stephanie's hysterical accusations failed to move Raven. He eyed her coldly as she withdrew a lace handkerchief from her reticule and continued to sob as though she had suffered some terrible tragedy. She obviously blamed Eden for the embarrassment she and her mother had suffered and despised her for it. While he still doubted Alex would have thought of eloping on his own, Raven was repelled by Stephanie's spiteful condemnation of her American cousin. Not about to take Eden's side, however, he remained silent until they reached the Lawton home. He then escorted Stephanie to her door, but when he refused the loan of her carriage to return to the docks, she again grabbed his hand to detain him a moment longer.

"I could come to your ship again tomorrow. If only we could be alone for an hour or two, I know you'd realize how much you really care for me."

Stephanie was quite blatantly offering herself to him, but Raven was merely annoyed rather than intrigued by the possibility of making love to her. An affair with her would not provide the escape he sought when she would undoubtedly demand marriage in exchange for her favors. Perhaps she was attempting to lay the same trap Eden had, but he was far too cautious a man to be caught as easily as Alex apparently had been.

"I think we should count ourselves fortunate if we never

meet again, Lady Stephanie." Raven reached around her to open the front door, and placing his hand in the center of her back, he propelled her into her home. He pulled the door closed behind her and turned away, hoping that a long and tiring walk would help him to get a better night's sleep than he had had in a long while.

Lydia heard her daughter race up the stairs and slam her bedroom door. Curious as to the cause of that dramatic return, she looked out the window in time to see Raven striding down the walk. His features were set in a sullen frown and she guessed instantly what Stephanie had done. Hurrying to her room, she found her daughter lying across her bed, convulsed with tears.

"Have you taken leave of your senses?" Lydia began in the harsh tone she reserved for criticizing her only child. "Of what possible use is Raven Blade to us now? Do you think I would allow you to marry him now when it will be Eden who will be running Alex's household? I was a fool not to realize that Alex could be tempted to remarry. He could have been yours if only we had guessed how vulnerable he was before Eden did."

"But I don't love Alex," Stephanie insisted in tear-choked gasps. "Raven is the one I want."

"So you paid him a call at his ship?" When Stephanie did not reply, Lydia assumed that she had guessed the truth. "I'll not have you down on the docks chasing after men who haven't the manners to call on you here. You'll not leave this house again without a responsible chaperon. You knew better than to throw yourself at men before Eden came here to live. Your actions today are clearly the result of her influence rather than mine."

"I'm nothing like Eden!" Stephanie shrieked. "I hate

her, I hate her! Raven would have married me had she not interfered, I know that he would have."

"Forget the man. He's of no consequence now. Rest with a cold compress on your eyes until it's time to dress for the Russells' ball. We've already wasted too many nights on the wrong man. We can't waste tonight as well."

"I don't want to go to the Russells'," Stephanie complained in a hoarse sob.

"You'll not only be there, you will be so charming none of the other girls will receive even half the attention that you do. We must begin to use the scandal Alex and Eden have created to our own advantage. You will not only draw attention, but use it to increase your popularity. Now stop carrying on so. There may be few men who are as handsome as Raven Blade, but you know which ones can equal the Clairbourne fortune and it's one of those men you must enchant now."

Stephanie had been tutored from the cradle to know she had to marry well, not only to ensure a comfortable life for herself but to uphold her family's reputation. Because her mother's plan offered the only way to salvage the pride she had sacrificed in declaring her feelings to Raven, she gave in and wiped away her tears. "Yes, Mother. I'll go tonight, and I'll try to impress everyone."

"You'll not merely try, my dear. You'll succeed." Lydia closed Stephanie's bedroom door behind her and returned to her own room. She needed to take a nap herself after that scene. With Eden now a countess, Stephanie had to do at least as well. Lydia simply would not allow Sarah's daughter to outshine her own. As she drifted off to sleep, she ran through a mental list of eligible bachelors until she was satisfied there were several who would find her daughter absolutely irresistible that night. She was determined that they would soon have another wedding in the family, and this time an appropriately elaborate one that would be the envy of all her friends.

It was dark by the time Raven reached the *Jamaican Wind*. He went to his cabin to clean up before supper, but found he had little appetite despite the long walk Stephanie had caused him. At every party he had attended, she had always been surrounded by eager admirers so he could not honestly believe she had actually missed him.

He had not missed her at all.

It was Alex he missed, but he knew he would have an even more difficult time adjusting to his uncle's return when his bride would always be by his side. Alex and Eden had been so close a couple before their marriage Raven was certain they would have no time for him now that they were husband and wife. He wasn't jealous of Eden, he refused to call it that. He was merely apprehensive about being around her when it would be so difficult to keep his suspicions about her motives to himself. He had never been noted for his tact, but he had vowed not to reveal his opinion of Eden rather than upset Alex by voicing his doubts about her aloud. That was a promise he intended to keep, but he feared it might prove to be the most difficult challenge of his life.

Glancing around his cabin, he knew he should move his belongings into the smaller quarters Alex usually occupied so that the newlyweds could enjoy the more spacious captain's cabin. It would be a generous gesture on his part, so he decided to do it, but not yet. Now he needed the space to pace, to stretch his legs on the nights when he could not sleep. There would be time enough during the next two weeks to trade cabins.

"Two weeks," Raven whispered. He was so anxious to

return home that a two-week delay seemed like an interminable wait. On the other hand, he knew that was not going to be nearly enough time to prepare himself to face Eden again.

He stretched out on his bunk and propped his head on his hands as he finally allowed his thoughts to dwell on her. He had no way of knowing what had been clever pretense and what had been real, but from the night they had met, she had had eyes only for Alex. Raven knew he was handsome, he heard it often enough from women, but Eden had never given him more than a passing glance. Whenever they had danced together, she had always seemed preoccupied, and relieved when the music ended and they could part.

Was her clear preference for Alex based on his wealth? Or was it possible Eden actually felt something for the man? He could not bear the thought she had married Alex for his money and not for the charming man he was. That was too cruel a trick to play on any man, no matter what the gain, but try as he might to analyze her actions, Raven still could not understand why Alex had married her. It was a question that plagued him both day and night. Why had Alex chosen to wed when he had so little time left to live? Why would any man inflict the pain of widowhood on a woman, no matter how irresistibly young or pretty?

When a familiar ache filled his chest, Raven finally recognized it as the painful loneliness he had endured as a child. With Alex's elopement, the desolation of being alone had returned with full force. "My God," he moaned softly. It had been nearly twenty years since Alex had taken him in but now the wretched memory of the shabbily dressed orphan he had once been tortured him as though he had never found a loving home with a kind and generous man.

With his usual thoughtfulness, Alex had urged him to

use the joy of marriage to dull the pain that his death would surely bring. That the only young woman who had caught his eye was now his aunt struck Raven as the cruelest of jokes. Fate seemed determined to kick him right back into the gutter but he was equally determined to continue his escape from the lowly circumstances of his birth. One day, and he dreaded all too soon, he would be the Earl of Clairbourne, and he planned to wear that title as proudly as Alex always had. That he would have to face his future alone on that day did not frighten him, and he refused to wallow in sorrow while Alex was still alive.

Determined to overcome the tormenting sensation of isolation that threatened to overwhelm him, Raven left his cabin, and went to find Randy. The mate was always eager to go in search of a good time, and while Raven knew getting drunk again would only serve to blur his pain until morning, he needed sleep too badly to care.

Three days later, two letters arrived from Alex. They were hand-delivered by a groom named Peter Brady, who had a sweetheart in London and was always eager for an excuse to travel into the city. He handed over the two envelopes bearing Alex's crest with so wide a grin Raven knew instantly they could not possibly contain bad news.

"I trust all is going well at Briarcliff," the tall captain inquired of the groom.

"Much better than that, sir," Peter informed him with a hearty chuckle. "None of us has ever seen his lordship so happy, and his bride is such a dear young woman we have all come to love her."

Unable to reply to that unwanted piece of news with a polite response, Raven tipped Peter and sent him off to a nearby tavern for an hour to give him time to read the letters and answer them. Once seated at his desk, he found

81

the envelopes were marked with numerals to indicate the order in which they were to be opened. Curious as to what sort of messages they contained, he slit open the first and found it to be a request to increase the amount of munitions they were carrying home. They had already loaded gunpowder, but Alex wished him to double the amount, and to purchase as many Kerr five-shot revolvers and Enfield rifles as the London Armoury could provide, along with as much of the appropriate ammunition as possible.

Raven thought the Confederacy was probably still desperately short of arms since the South had lacked munitions factories at the start of the War and had had to rely on blockade runners to supply their needs from European manufacturers. Was that what Alex intended to become, a blockade runner?

"No," he answered himself aloud. "It is what Eden wants him to become!" Her plan was immediately clear. The first time Alex had mentioned he owned a clipper ship, Eden had been keenly interested in hearing all about it. Both he and Alex had assumed that was due to her family's shipbuilding interests, but such a conclusion now seemed shockingly naïve. She had made no secret of the fact her father captained the *Southern Knight,* and now it seemed she planned to use her husband's wealth and ship to keep her beloved Confederacy supplied with arms.

Raven drummed his fingers on his desk in an anxious rhythm as he weighed the wisdom of granting Alex's request. It soon became apparent that he had no choice but to comply or he would make Alex appear to be an ineffectual fool in his bride's eyes. He had never questioned Alex's purchase orders in the past but he had never had reason to either. He would visit the London Armoury, and buy whatever he could, but he would not pretend to Alex he was pleased about what he intended to do. Tossing the letter aside, Raven opened the other one and found its contents even more disturbing.

Alex had written not to explain his elopement, but to praise the beauty and grace of his bride. He described the days they had spent together in rapturous detail and swore they were the best of his life. It was the last two paragraphs, however, that tore Raven's heart in two.

"You have been the best friend I have ever had, and I was proud to name you as my heir," Raven read aloud. "I beg you to look after Eden when I am gone. She is so wonderfully generous with her love that I cannot bear to think of her spending the rest of her life alone when what she deserves is the endless bliss she has given me. Please help her find a second husband who is as fine a man as you, a man who will cherish her love for the treasure it truly is.

"You know how badly I want you to find a bride as precious as Eden. Don't let anything deter you from that quest. I don't want either of you to be alone and I pray the future will bestow many blessings on you both."

There was a postscript mentioning several gifts he had neglected to include in his will, but Raven's eyes were too filled with tears to make out the details. He slumped back in his chair, certain he understood the true purpose of Alex's letter, even if it had not been stated in so many words: Should he and Eden fail to fall in love with others, Alex was giving them his permission to wed. It was a heartbreakingly generous thing to do, but overwhelmed by the sorrow that had prompted Alex to make such a suggestion, Raven sent Peter back to Briarcliff with no more than a verbal acknowledgment that Alex's letters had been received.

Five

Raven waited until two days before the end of Alex and Eden's month-long stay at Briarcliff before he began to move his clothing out of the captain's cabin. Alex had left nothing in his quarters, so the process was a relatively simple one he would have completed before noon had Peter Brady not interrupted him. This time the groom was in tears and the envelope he handed Raven bore Eden's feminine handwriting rather than Alex's bold script.

"Is Alex dead?" Raven asked without needing to open the letter.

Peter nodded, then pulled out his handkerchief and blew his nose. "He and his bride were down in the lower pasture watching the colts that were born last spring. I heard her calling for help, but by the time me and John reached them, Lord Clairbourne was already dead. We'd spoken with them a few moments before when they'd walked by the stables. They were always outdoors, liked the sunshine they said. I wasn't around then, but those who were said his lordship's father died just as sudden."

Badly shaken, even though he had known Alex's untimely death had been inevitable, Raven sank down on the

84

bunk as the groom began to praise Alex as the finest man he had ever known. "Yes, he was that," Raven readily agreed.

Peter was not ashamed to weep openly, but Raven stubbornly refused to give in to tears even though the powerful emotion that threatened to prompt them stung his eyes and filled his throat with a painful knot. Swallowing hard, he knew he would spend the rest of his life grieving for Alex, but he intended to do it in his own way.

Seeking to distract himself from the sound of Peter's heartwrenching sobs, he ripped open the message Eden had sent. It was brief, but a more poignant plea than he had expected from her.

Dear Raven,
    My darling Alex is dead. Please come to Briarcliff. I need you desperately.

                                     Eden

The enormity of what they would both need was more than Raven could bear to contemplate in depth, but clearly Eden expected him to help bury her late husband. To refuse to attend Alex's funeral was unthinkable. It was more than a hundred miles overland to Briarcliff, and while it was a pleasant journey when made by carriage with the nights spent in inns, the need now was for all possible haste. When Raven questioned Peter, he discovered the groom had ridden a succession of rented horses at a wild gallop to reach London in under two days, but Raven was confident he could sail the *Jamaican Wind* into Lyme Bay below Briarcliff in well under that time. Calling for the mate, he explained what they had to do and why.

Randy MacDermott had seen Peter's downcast expression when he had come on board, but he had not suspected the groom's errand had been of such a tragic nature. "How did it happen?" he immediately wanted to know.

"Assemble the crew, and I'll tell you all at the same time. I know there are several men on shore, but we've no time to send anyone out to find them. We'll just have to leave word that we'll return in a few days. We haven't received everything I ordered from the London Armoury, so we'll have to come back to load the balance anyway."

Randy stared at Raven, his expression a mask of confused disbelief. "Alex is dead, and you're concerned about the cargo?"

"No!" Raven denied hotly. "I don't give a damn about the cargo, but I'll not leave munitions Alex paid good money to buy sitting on the dock. Now hurry and assemble the crew as I asked."

Randy knew Alex and Raven had been close, and he could not understand why Alex's sudden death had not had the same devastating effect on Raven as it had on him. Raven was not an easy man to get to know, but Randy had always thought he knew him as well as any man did, until now. Now he was looking at an aloof stranger who had just given him an order he quickly obeyed.

Far from immune to the sorrow that flooded Randy's eyes with tears, as he went up on deck Raven felt as though he were the one who had died. He mouthed the words he knew his crew would be deeply saddened to hear, but kept himself from reacting to their chilling effect. He dug his fingernails into his palms and forced his own grief down deep inside his soul as he watched the grown men who had served Alex before him cry like motherless babes.

Shocked and filled with dismay, the crew asked questions Raven answered as truthfully as possible, but he did not admit Alex had not been in as good health as they had all assumed. Heart trouble ran in the family, was all that he would reveal. When a melancholy silence settled over the crew, Raven nodded to Randy and the mate began the series of orders that would get them under way. Readily understanding the need to reach Briarcliff as soon as possible, the men dried their eyes on their shirtsleeves and ran to their places.

Peter had left the last horse he had ridden at the nearest livery stable, and never having sailed, he grabbed the rail and hung on with a frantic grasp as the sails were unfurled and the *Jamaican Wind* pulled away from the dock. On any other day, he would have been teased unmercifully by the crew, but now no one felt up to making jokes.

As swift as she was beautiful, in full sail the *Jamaican Wind* was a glorious sight. Raven set a course that kept them close to the coast as they passed through the English Channel, and with the entire crew working to speed their way, they were able to drop anchor in Lyme Bay the following afternoon. It had been three days since Alex's death, and they all hoped they had not arrived too late to attend the dear man's funeral.

Approaching the house from the sea, Raven recalled the first time he had visited Briarcliff. The elegant stone mansion had looked like a castle to a child of eight, and he had asked Alex if he were a king. Alex had laughed, tousled his curls, and told him it was a drafty old place he did not like half as much as his home on Jamaica, but Raven had still believed Briarcliff to be a palace fit for a king.

Peter Brady followed Raven up the worn stone path. The groom had insisted upon carrying the captain's valise, and had volunteered to return to the *Jamaican Wind* to inform the crew of the funeral plans once they had learned them. "Lady Clairbourne wanted to wait for you. I hope that we've arrived in time."

"We'll hold a second service if we've missed the first," Raven assured him.

Peter had never heard of anyone having two funerals, but he dared not question Raven's remark. When they reached the terrace, the captain turned back to survey the grounds of the impressive estate that now belonged to him, but Peter saw only sorrow in his dark eyes, rather than a warm glow of pride. Thinking perhaps he wished to be alone for a moment, he stepped by him.

"I'll take this on up to your room, m'lord."

"What? Oh yes, thank you." Raven was unaccustomed to being addressed in that fashion, and needing some time to get used to it, he was indeed glad to have a few moments to gather his thoughts before entering the house. He stood with his hands clasped behind his back, his gaze focused on the *Jamaican Wind* anchored in the bay. He had always felt more at home on the sea than on land, and despite what he knew would be an entirely new set of responsibilities, he did not want his life ever to change.

Startled by the sound of Eden's voice, Raven wheeled around to find her running toward him. She was dressed in a gray gown she had worn for one of their afternoon outings, but his opinion of her was so low, he was not surprised to find she had not chosen to wear black as any other newly widowed woman surely would have.

"Eden," was all he managed to gasp before she threw herself into his arms.

"Oh Raven, I knew you'd not disappoint me!" Eden hugged him tightly, enormously relieved and reassured by his presence. She closed her eyes and held on to him for a long moment, grateful for his warmth when she felt chilled clear to the bone.

Raven was shocked by the enthusiasm of Eden's greeting until he remembered that she had always been a far more demonstrative person than he. Certain they were being observed from the house by the servants, and possibly a great many people paying sympathy calls, he responded by enfolding her in a light embrace and patted her back with what he hoped would pass for a soothing rhythm.

To his utter dismay, he immediately discovered the sensation of holding the fair beauty was far more pleasurable than merely dancing with her had been. She was pressing her whole body against his as though he were her dearest relative, and even though he was appalled by her boldness, he had to fight the nearly overwhelming impulse to cling to her just as tightly.

Her perfume was a light floral scent that not only clung to her somber clothing but also graced her tawny hair. As she lay her head against his chest, her upswept curls brushed his chin like a silken caress, sending his senses reeling. He was unable to draw a breath for a moment as with a lover's grace Eden swayed against him. Appalled by the speed of his body's predictable and, he was certain, totally inappropriate response, he forced himself to grasp her waist firmly and pushed her an arm's length away.

"Forgive me," Eden begged, for a few seconds as disoriented as Raven. The usually aloof young man's embrace had been so like that of her beloved husband that she knew she had lingered in his arms far too long. Not ashamed to admit how badly she needed his comfort, however, she attempted to smile as bravely as she had all day.

"Would you like to sit with Alex for a while before I tell them to close the coffin?" she asked considerately.

Not even tempted to spend a few minutes alone with

the dead man, Raven shook his head. "No, thank you. I want to remember him as he was."

Eden took Raven's arm as they started toward the double doors that led into the house. "I wish I had been able to do that but he died in my arms. One minute we were laughing together, and in the next he was gone. Did Peter tell you what happened?"

"Yes." Raven knew it would be polite to inquire how she was getting along, but the answer was too obvious to merit wasting his breath. Eden was doing beautifully. He stood by her side as she calmly gave Jonathan Abbot, the butler, the order to close Alex's coffin and see that it was promptly delivered to the church in Exeter. Apparently she had been awaiting his arrival, and now saw no reason for further delay. Raven reminded himself that Alex had been dead for three days, but still Eden's haste to have the funeral struck him as unseemly.

Eden slipped her hand into Raven's as they took their places in the first pew. The church was filled to overflowing with sailors, townspeople, servants, and tenant farmers. It was an unusual gathering but she had known most of Alex's close friends would be in London and unable to reach Briarcliff in time to attend the service. She was pleased that so many others who had known and admired her husband had wanted to be with him now.

They knelt frequently for prayers during the service, but she did not release Raven's hand. Unlike Alex's, his palm was calloused, evidence of his active life at sea, and she found that sign of physical strength immensely comforting. Alex had never been strong, despite his zest for life, but she needed the strength his love could no longer provide and drew it from Raven.

She and Alex had not discussed his funeral, but Eden

was pleased when Robert Boyer, the priest who had known him for many years, was able to provide a moving eulogy. She had wondered if Raven might not wish to give it himself, but thoughtfully did not force him to refuse when he did not make the offer voluntarily. She knew him to be a very private person who kept both his thoughts and feelings to himself. Respecting that right, she sat by his side, too numbed by grief to weep, and said her own goodbyes as silently as he.

That Eden kept running her thumb across his palm nearly drove Raven to distraction and finally he grasped her hand in both of his to make such an intimate gesture impossible to continue. Had the woman no idea what she was doing to him? he wondered. Didn't she care? Or was she deliberately trying to seduce him just as she must surely have seduced Alex? That struck him as the most obvious explanation but didn't she at least have the decency to wait until Alex was buried to do it?

When it came time for the pall bearers to carry Alex's coffin to the adjacent cemetery, Raven leapt to his feet, eager for the excuse to be among the first to leave the church. The service had been a fitting tribute to Alex's memory, but as deeply aware of Eden's presence as he was of the tragedy of the occasion, Raven had seen and heard little of it. Now he just wanted to get outside where he would be able to breathe deeply without filling his lungs with the incense-laden air that reminded him all too vividly of the smell of death.

Alex's grave had been dug next to Eleanora's, but until they began to lower his coffin into the ground, Raven had not remembered that she had been buried in the Clairbourne family plot. Her grave was marked by an exquisitely carved marble angel, and he wondered what sort of headstone Eden had requested for Alex. Certain it would be inappropriate no matter what she had chosen, he decided to cancel her order and place one of his own.

When the priest had completed the graveside prayers, Eden stepped forward to toss the first handful of dirt into the grave, but her expression gave no hint of her despair. Heartbroken that she had lost the husband she adored so shortly after their wedding, she nevertheless managed to survive the afternoon without breaking down in front of the people who followed her back to Briarcliff to offer their condolences. She did not want her behavior to reflect poorly on Alex's choice of an American bride, but nothing in her young life had prepared her to survive such a tragic loss, and while she hid her pain bravely, she doubted it would ever go away.

Randy MacDermott had not met Eden before that day, but he was impressed not only by her rare beauty but also by her strength of character. "She's got plenty of courage," he remarked to Raven. "She must have made Alex a fine wife."

Raven was relieved when Randy seemed to find a noncommittal nod reply enough to an opinion he knew he would never share. All around him he heard people whispering the same admiring comments but in his view Eden was merely indifferent rather than stoic. At least she had frequently been drawn away from his side, but whenever she was near, he was disgusted with himself for being all too aware of her disarming femininity.

When finally the last of the callers had departed, Raven doubted he would be able to keep his opinion of Eden to himself, but she surprised him by excusing herself immediately. Grateful to be relieved of the agony of her company, Raven told Abbot he did not wish to be disturbed. He opened a bottle of Alex's blackberry brandy that was made from the fruit of Briarcliff vines, and settled himself down in the study to be alone with his memories.

He wasn't certain when Alex had first told him about his heart condition, but for a long while he had refused to believe anything could possibly be wrong with the man who had raised him. Wisely, Alex had not belligerently forced him to face the pain of that reality, but that kindness did not make the sorrow Raven felt now any easier to bear. Every step of the way he had fought coming to terms with the fact Alex would never grow old, but he had not expected the last time he had seen him to be the last. He wished now that he had not insisted that Alex tell Eden the truth, but there was no way to take back their final conversation, nor the disastrous elopement to which it had led.

Raven had gotten only a few hours' sleep the previous night, and soon the warmth of the brandy and the solitude of the early evening combined to make him so drowsy he gave up his maudlin reverie in favor of going to bed. Not finding his valise in the room he always used, he wondered where Peter had taken it. He would not need clean clothes and his razor until morning, but he did not want to have to roam the halls looking disheveled then. After all, he was now an earl, and surely an earl did not greet a new day by prowling about his mansion searching for his clothes.

Thinking it possible Peter might have mistakenly put the valise in Alex's room, he went there first. The door was unlocked, a lamp burning on the chest of drawers illuminated the room, and just as he had supposed, his valise sat on the floor at the end of the bed. It was not the scuffed leather satchel that immediately caught his eye, however, for the fact that Eden was sound asleep in the magnificent mahogany bed shook him clear to the marrow.

He closed the door quietly behind him, and as he approached the bed, the thick Aubusson carpet muffled the sound of his footsteps. Eden was smiling sightly, obviously lost in the sweetness of her dreams, and Raven could not help but wonder what she was doing in her late husband's bed. Then a truly wicked thought occurred to him. The bed no longer belonged to Alex; it was now his.

Was that Eden's plan, to welcome him to Briarcliff as no one else could? Considering that likely, he brushed her long curls aside and leaned down to peer at her closely. He was not surprised to find her complexion was as flawless as it appeared from a few steps away, but there was no sign of tears on her lashes or cheeks. Plainly she was no heartbroken widow who had cried herself to sleep in her late husband's bed. She was a clever vixen lying in wait for the next man to come along.

Raven went back to the door, locked it, and secured the one leading to the adjoining bedroom as well. He then began to undress with deliberate care, slowly peeling off the fine clothes he had worn for Alex's funeral. He wanted Eden to open her eyes and watch him, but she continued to sleep as though her conscience were as pure as her snowy white nightgown.

Wanting to be able to watch her expression when she did awaken, Raven left the lamp burning low. Now nude, he raised the covers and joined Eden in the comfortable bed. She shifted her position slightly, but continued to sleep as he slipped his left arm beneath her shoulders to pull her into an easy embrace. Her hair again fell across her face, and as he combed it through his fingers, he could not help but marvel at its softness. She was the most alluring of women but now he no longer had to fight her appeal. She might have laid a trap for him, but determined she was the one who would be caught, he lowered his mouth to hers.

Exhausted by the ordeal of Alex's funeral, Eden was slow to wake. She did not feel the pressure of Raven's lips until his kiss grew demanding. Forgetting for a moment that she was now a widow, she raised her hand to his nape, thinking it was again Alex who had joined her in bed. She opened her mouth, curled her tongue over his, and pressed against him. Wanting all he could give, she waited as she always had for him to be the first to draw away.

Even fully aware of his inexplicable weakness for her, Raven was stunned by the effect of Eden's adoring kiss. He seldom bothered to kiss the women with whom he spent his time, but Eden's affection was so delicious he paused only long enough to draw a deep breath before capturing her mouth anew. He slipped his right hand beneath her gown and traced the length of her thigh with a gentle caress. Her skin was soft and smooth, as seductively warm as her kiss, and impatient to feel her body next to his, he ended their second lengthy kiss to help her remove her gown.

The force of Raven's insistent tugs on the soft folds of her nightgown brought Eden fully awake, but her vision was obscured as he pulled it off over her head, and she didn't realize it was he until he had tossed it aside.

"Raven!" she gasped, and grabbed the sheet to cover her bare bosom.

That she could look so shocked merely amused him, "Who did you think you were kissing?" he asked, but before she could reply, he leaned down to kiss her again.

Fully aware that she had responded to his kisses in a wanton fashion, Eden was mortified by the handsome young man's question, and struggled to push him away. "I was asleep. I didn't know who you were."

"You'll admit that any man will do?" He broke into a wide grin when her bewildered topaz gaze grew wider still.

"No, certainly not," she argued weakly, completely dazzled by his smile. She had never really seen him smile before, and she was stunned by how greatly that expression enhanced his already handsome appearance. Forcing her gaze from his face, she finally took note of the black curls that covered the broad expanse of his bare chest. Instantly certain he was as naked as she, she tightened her grip on the sheet to a frantic clutch.

Raven had helped her to bury Alex only that afternoon—how could she tell him that it was Alex she had thought she had kissed? Coming out of her dreams, she had been aware of the spicy scent of her husband's cologne, and tasted the flavor of his brandy. It had been Alex, she realized with a jolt of recognition, or his ghost, for surely a man who had always displayed Raven's reserve could not possibly have kissed her as passionately as her husband had.

Eden continued to eye him with an astonished stare, but when she failed to speak, Raven seized the opportunity to kiss her again. Leaning across her, he forced her down into the feather pillows. For the briefest of instants she stiffened in his arms, then with a low moan of surrender from deep in her throat, she raised her arms to encircle his neck and made the kiss her own. She's lovely bait for a trap, Raven recalled dimly, but he wanted Eden too badly to worry over the possible danger to himself.

Raven had always worn the same cologne as Alex, Eden's numbed mind dimly remembered. That his kiss was flavored with blackberry brandy, as Alex's often was in the evening, was not remarkable either. But having mistaken him for Alex, she now found it impossible to accuse him of taking advantage of her as she knew she should. Instead she longed for him to make love to her when he was so like Alex she could not tell the difference between them when she closed her eyes.

That was Eden's last rational thought. It was Alex she loved, Alex she wanted to cherish with love's most beautiful expression, and caring not at all what Raven's thoughts might be when hers were so full of her late husband, she gave herself to him with the same uninhibited passion she and Alex had always shared.

Raven felt Eden's hands moving over his shoulders, then his back, her fingertips lightly tracing the muscular planes before sliding down his spine. Her touch was as provocative as her kiss. He had always regarded kissing as a bothersome prelude to far more sensual pleasures, but he realized now that was merely because he had never kissed Eden. He could not take his mouth from hers, and it was not simply that her taste was indescribably sweet. It was because of the abandon with which she welcomed each thrust of his tongue and returned it until he was certain she knew his mouth as well as her own.

Gradually Raven became aware of the distinct possibility that he had never really made love before, for Eden affected his emotions far more strongly than any of his previous partners ever had. He did not know how many women there had been, too many perhaps, but the physical release they had given him had never been preceded with such loving affection as this.

While he was no longer able to fight the attraction he had always felt for Eden, Raven still could not forgive her for enticing Alex into marriage. They were two entirely separate considerations in his mind, one purely pleasure, the other unbearable pain. For now he intended to take every joy she could provide, and later he would allow his anger free rein.

Lost in her own precious memories, Eden lay bathed in the heady enchantment of her husband's affection. Her whole body felt gloriously alive, as sensitive to his touch as she had been on their wedding night. As always, he did not rush her, but instead allowed her to lead him ever deeper into the magical beauty of love. When at her urging he finally brought their bodies together as one, it was with the same exquisite tenderness he had always shown. He moved slowly, allowing her need for him to heighten until she clung to him, her motions mirroring his until they were both consumed in a heated rush of ecstasy. As that rapturous sensation began to ebb, they remained together still, their arms and legs entangled in a lovers' embrace.

When Raven could again draw a deep breath, he began to cover Eden's flushed cheeks with adoring kisses. Her lashes fluttered slightly, and then she opened her eyes. She looked up at him with a gaze that held both puzzlement and sorrow.

"Alex?" she whispered softly, devastated to find her beautiful fantasy was at an end.

"Alex is dead," Raven replied, and as he spoke those words, the anguish that he had successfully suppressed until that moment suddenly became an unbearable burden. Overwhelmed by the pain of his grief, he buried his face in Eden's silken curls and wept without shame for the man who had shown him the only love he had ever known.

As responsive as when they had made love, Eden held Raven tightly and murmured every comforting phrase she had ever heard. She knew only too well how much it hurt to have lost Alex, and she didn't want him to have to suffer that excruciating pain alone. Somehow they had to find the courage to survive the loss of the man who had meant so much to them both. While she had not thought it would be Raven who would need her strength, she nonetheless gave it unsparingly until he at last fell asleep in her arms.

Her lips brushed his black curls with a goodnight kiss, but when Eden closed her eyes, it was again the soft silver sheen of Alex's hair and the bright blue sparkle of his eyes that filled her dreams.

Six

August 1863

When Eden awakened late the next morning, Alex's bedroom was awash in bright sunlight. Enjoying the view of the garden below, Raven was leaning beside one of the leaded windows that framed the massive bed. Arms folded across his chest, he appeared more relaxed than she had ever seen him, and infinitely more attractive. His damp curls glowed with a blue-black sheen and his well-chiseled features were bathed in golden light. He was dressed in tight-fitting black pants and a white shirt, whose loose folds concealed what she now knew to be well-muscled shoulders and arms.

Although Raven felt the warmth of Eden's gaze, he did not turn away from the window before announcing calmly, "We'll have to marry."

Badly startled by that greeting, Eden sat up slowly. Her nightgown lay across the bed within easy reach and she hurriedly pulled it over her head then brushed back her tangled curls. "Raven," she began hesitantly, certain they would never have a more important conversation, and therefore selecting her words with care, "Last night, well, neither of us was thinking clearly and—"

"I won't argue with that," Raven agreed, but he appeared more amused than upset by it.

Choosing to ignore the smile that tugged at the corner of his mouth, Eden continued in an effort to gain control of what she regarded as a most unfortunate situation. "Good. To offer marriage is wonderfully generous of you, but it really isn't necessary."

As Raven turned to face her, his dark gaze took on its familiar mocking gleam. "You misunderstood me. I didn't offer a proposal you could accept or decline. I said we'll have to marry, today if Robert Boyer will agree to perform the ceremony. Under the circumstances, I'm certain he'll understand why we don't wish to invite any guests other than the required number of witnesses."

Absolutely mortified by his plan, Eden's mouth fell agape, but she quickly recovered and began to argue. "I've been a widow only four days, Raven. To even mention marriage, let alone insist upon it, is so totally inappropriate that—"

This time Raven interrupted her with a rueful laugh. "Not after last night it isn't."

In no mood for levity, Eden clasped her hands tightly in her lap and continued as though he had not spoken. To use Raven as a substitute for Alex had been inexcusable, but she refused to compound that error by rushing into marriage when she barely knew him. From now on, she would have to keep her eyes open so no matter how good Raven smelled or tasted she would be able to remember exactly who he was.

"We both loved Alex," she explained with deliberate care. "It's only natural that our grief drew us together. We'll just have to be more careful from now on so that our emotions don't get the better of us ever again. Neither of us is to blame for what happened last night, so we needn't

100

allow guilt to force us into what would surely be the worst of marriages."

Mystified by that dreary prediction, Raven moved to the side of the bed. "What is it you're after, Eden? When I found you in my bed last night, I thought it was me. I can't believe you've changed your mind. Not after—"

"Your bed?" Eden cried out incredulously. "This is Alex's bed, our bed. Not yours."

"No, it's the earl's bed, and I want you to share it with me every night we're at Briarcliff." Regardless of the ridiculous things Eden was saying now, Raven was positive of that. She had awakened a need within him he had not even suspected he possessed and he intended to have her satisfy it as often as humanly possible.

This was the Raven Eden knew only too well—a cold, arrogant young man whose dark glance had always frightened her. The issue at hand was far too important for her to give in to those fears, however. "You have no right to talk to me like that."

Eden grabbed ahold of the covers and flung them aside, meaning to leap from the bed, but Raven quickly sat down beside her to block the way. She then had to struggle to pull her nightgown down past her hips but that failed to make her feel sufficiently clothed for a heated argument with him.

Raven considered that tardy show of modesty as puzzling as what he regarded as her feigned show of indignation. Eden had such lovely legs, he was sorry she had covered them. Or was she only teasing him? Expecting a trick, he leaned across her and dropped his right hand to the bed to brace his weight. He had her caught between his arms then, and she could not move off the bed in either direction.

"You were willing to surrender your rights last night,

Lady Clairbourne. Why do things seem so different to you by the light of day?"

Angered by his aggressive pose and insulting question, Eden shrank back against the carved headboard. "I want you to leave. I'm not in the habit of carrying on lengthy conversations with men before I've left my bed."

Certain she was teasing him now, Raven's expression softened as he reached out to trace the curve of her cheek with his left hand. "We needn't talk if you don't want to."

Eden swallowed hard, but that failed to alleviate her growing sense of alarm. She had never felt comfortable around Raven, and at last she realized why. It was not merely the darkness of his coloring that signaled danger, but the fact he radiated an aura of sensuality that was so strong she doubted any woman would be immune to it. A clear challenge had always been reflected in his glance, the pride of his posture, the insolent curve of his taunting smile, but she had been too innocent to understand it for what it truly was. Alex had taught her a great deal about the relationship between a man and woman, but it had been with a loving perspective. What she now recognized in Raven was merely the primitive power of raw desire.

She could not draw a deep breath until Raven dropped his hand, but then his actions became as suggestive as his words as he began to unbutton his shirt. Appalled by the boldness of that gesture, Eden reached out to stop him.

"Raven, this is ridiculous! Last night was a regrettable mistake that mustn't ever be repeated. Can't you understand that?"

"No, this is all I understand." Raven leaned toward her, his mouth opening slightly as his lips drew close to hers.

Paralyzed by the same fascination that exists between helpless prey and a sleek predator, Eden watched Raven's eyes close, the black fringe of his lashes becoming dark crescents against his bronze skin. Freshly shaven, his cheek felt as smooth as her own when she raised her hand in a feeble effort to turn his face away. Raven caught her wrist, placed a tender kiss on her palm, then pressed her open hand against his chest. His heart was beating with a slow, steady rhythm, in contrast to her own, which seemed to pound louder and louder in her ears until the sound drowned out the voice of her conscience and she heard only the sweet song of desire.

Raven's lips found hers then, soft, yielding, as tempting as he had remembered while Eden thought only that while he no longer tasted of brandy, his kiss was every bit as intoxicating. Her fears of him instantly forgotten, she made no effort to escape his embrace now, and let her hand slide down his chest, gently combing the crisp black curls that tapered to a thin line at his navel. She could not remember why they had been arguing when all she had to do was close her eyes and Raven was magically transformed into Alex. Dear, dear Alex, whose kisses had always been gentle, and overflowing with love.

It was her passions he had wanted to arouse, but Raven was sufficiently captivated by the sweetness of Eden's surrender to allow her to set a relaxed pace. With her help, he shrugged off his shirt. Her nightgown then followed it to the floor. Had he known they would be making love again that morning he would not have bothered to dress but he quickly cast the rest of his clothing aside so nothing hindered his appreciation of the velvet softness of her skin. He pulled her close, aligning their bodies so that the fullness of her bosom fit snugly against the hard planes of his chest.

Despite Alex's encouragement, Raven had never thought he needed a wife, but he now intended to bed Eden as often as it took to convince her they had to wed. He felt the pale flesh of her supple body warm beneath his caress, and knowing she would not try and elude him

103

now, he relaxed his hold on her. The smooth swell of her breast fit perfectly in the gentle curve of his hand and he leaned down to moisten the delectable pink tip with his tongue. He had never wanted to suck at another woman's bosom like an adoring child, but as Eden enfolded him in her arms, pressing his face close, he found the long forgotten instinct too powerful to suppress. He wanted all of her, in every way a man could take a woman, but when he brought their bodies together, he knew the oldest way would do for now. Eden was a uniquely fascinating female and it pleased him to think he would have a lifetime to enjoy her charms.

Had Raven attempted to force himself on her, Eden would have fought him with her last ounce of strength, but she simply did not have the will to fight his subtle seduction. He was not demanding, nor possessive. He was slow, and so gentle he drew forth emotion in endless waves of delight. Filled with the most exquisite of sensations, she again sought to recapture the love she had thought lost to her forever, and in Raven's arms it was so easy she had no will to resist. In her mind, it was Alex who again shared her bed and it was his name that echoed in every beat of her heart.

Raven had never been with a woman he had not paid. When he again felt Eden's climax shudder clear through her, he realized the squeals of ecstasy he had so frequently heard had been no more than the carefully rehearsed response a whore's profession required. He had mistakenly believed he had known all there was to know about women, but now he realized he had merely been trained to accept an artfully acted lie. Making love with a whore was no more exciting than walking through the steps of a dance without the music, and yet he had believed that was all any man ever felt.

How could I have been such an ignorant fool? he asked

himself. It was no wonder he had become bored with women when none had cared for anything but his money and he had cared even less for them. With Eden he felt reborn, and the pleasure he found in her arms was so intense the blissful calm that followed was the most perfect peace he had ever known. He was floating on that dreamlike cloud now, and wanted it to last forever. He shifted his position to spare Eden the burden of his weight, but continued to hold her cradled in his arms. He combed her tawny tresses through his fingers, more content than he had ever been.

"Today, Eden," he whispered softly.

The sound of Raven's voice jarred Eden badly. Devastated by how swiftly her memories of Alex had led her astray, she rose up on her elbow and forced herself to look at her dark-eyed companion. When he responded with the rakish grin that had been her undoing the previous night, she was overwhelmed with the worst feelings of shame and remorse she had ever experienced, or had need to. Gathering the sheet to cover herself, she sat up as she began to cry.

"This isn't your fault. It's entirely mine, but I can't marry you. I'm still in love with Alex. His memory is precious to me and deserves the greatest respect." She fell silent then, unwilling to confess how badly she had used Raven when she knew he would surely be deeply hurt by it, if not so outraged he might promptly strangle her. She had no choice but to let him think she was completely devoid of morals, but it was better than telling him the truth when he would despise her for it.

Dismayed, Raven watched Eden sob as though her heart were broken, but when he tried to pull her back into his arms, she cried even louder and pushed him away. He had had a month to fume over the way she had enticed Alex into marriage. He knew exactly what she was and he was certain that, even though she would undoubtedly also be marrying him for his wealth, he would get his money's worth. What he could not understand was why she was pretending to be so upset by what had transpired between them when it had felt so good.

"You certainly have convenient limits to the way you plan to respect Alex's memory," he chided.

Sickened by the truth of his words, Eden turned aside, buried her face in her pillow, and continued to weep for the husband she had lost and, to her everlasting shame, the desire she could not control.

Having had enough of her tears, Raven rose from the comfortable bed and dressed for the second time that day. He then went to the valise that now lay open at the end of the bed. He sorted through his clothes until he found Alex's letters. He had brought them intending to wave them dramatically while he told Eden exactly what he thought of her, but they would serve a different purpose just as well. Selecting the second one, he carried it over to the bed.

"Alex wanted us to be together, Eden. Here, read this, you'll see what I mean."

Even through her tears, Eden recognized Alex's handwriting. She reached out and took the letter in a reverent clasp as she again sat up, but she needed a moment to compose herself sufficiently to read it.

Raven moved back to the window. He could make out the masts of the *Jamaican Wind* in the distance, and as always the sight of the graceful ship filled him with pride. "I'd like to leave for home within a week. There will be too great a risk that we'll run into hurricanes if we delay any longer."

"Home to Jamaica, you mean?" Eden was running her fingertips over the neatly penned lines of Alex's letter, not yet focusing on the words.

106

"Yes. Alex meant to take you there. You'll be going with me instead."

Eden smoothed out the single sheet of stationery, then read the letter twice. She was deeply touched by Alex's glowing description of their life together as well as his hopes for her future happiness. As perceptive a person as Raven, Eden also understood the message that was only implied in his words. "Alex was a dear and thoughtful man, and I'm certain he didn't mean this subtle hint that we might one day marry as an order."

Twenty-four hours earlier Raven would have agreed, but now it served his purpose to honor Alex's last request. "I would have liked to have discussed the matter with him, but Alex knew me far better than you do. He knew I would have rebelled at such an order, while his gentlemanly plea is impossible to refuse."

"I can understand how he would have been concerned about me, but what about you, Raven? You were the one who was supposed to find a wife this summer. Have you been seeing anyone besides Stephanie this last month?"

Raven stifled a derisive snort at the last possible second, and shook his head instead. "I've no interest in your cousin, nor any of the other young women I've met."

"Stephanie will be heartbroken to learn that. She's very fond of you."

"Stephanie is a . . ." Raven paused as he searched for an appropriately descriptive term that would not also apply to Eden.

Eden recognized his sullen frown as clear evidence of the foulness of his mood. "You needn't say it. It's obvious you aren't as attracted to her as she is to you."

"I despise the bitch!" Raven took a step toward the bed, tempted to tell Eden what Stephanie thought of her, but decided against it when he saw Eden's eyes widen with horror.

107

"I'm nothing like Alex, Eden. You might as well get used to that now. He always displayed the best of manners while I won't pretend a respect I don't feel. The only reason I even spoke to Stephanie, let alone spent any time with her, was so that Alex could be with you. I know he hoped that I'd find her attractive but I didn't. She just never shut up long enough to notice I didn't hear a word that she said."

"You despise pretense, but were willing to pretend to help Alex?"

Raven's frown deepened as he realized she had a valid point. "That is a contradiction, isn't it?"

"Alex thought the world of you too, Raven. It's understandable that you would go to any lengths to help each other."

Eden was now speaking with him so calmly that Raven decided to push for whatever advantage he could gain. "What did he tell you about me?"

As always, Eden found it difficult to think when Raven's dark glance pierced her defenses with such ruthless ease. She looked down at Alex's letter instead. "He always spoke of you in the most glowing terms. He could not have been any more proud of you had you been his son rather than his nephew. Surely you must know that."

Alex hadn't told her the truth about him, Raven immediately realized. Like everyone else, Eden believed he was a blood relative. That was the greatest pretense of all, but a necessary one he would not end. "Yes, I did. That's why I intend to take care of you as best I can. It's what Alex wanted, so it's what I want as well."

"And what I want doesn't matter?" Eden asked shyly.

Raven clasped his hands behind his back as he began to discuss her options. "Have you made some plans of your own?"

"Well no, not yet."

"I thought not. You can continue to live here, of course, although I imagine you would be unbearably lonely without Alex's company. The owners of the neighboring estates spend most of their time in London, but there's always a chance they might remember to invite you to come for tea when they're at home. The fact that you're an American is unfortunate, because you'll be considered an outsider by many even though you are Alex's widow and he was quite popular. If you decide to stay here alone, I'll leave you a list of the men who can be expected to call. Most will have titles as old as Alex's, but they're in need of funds and will court you for your money."

"Raven," Eden begged with an anguished glance. "Are you always so suspicious of people's motives?"

"Of course. England is full of men with more prestige than wealth and you can expect every last one to try and impress you. Briarcliff now belongs to me rather than you, however, and while I will naturally provide for you as generously as Alex would have, if you remarry, that support will promptly end. The more intelligent of your suitors should realize that fairly quickly and ask you to invest in their schemes with no real intention of ever marrying you."

"Am I supposed to thank you for that kind of advice?"

Raven regarded her perplexed expression with a knowing smile. "If you don't now, you will later. Would you rather return to your aunt's house in London? if so, I really must warn you that your aunt and cousin didn't take your elopement at all well. Apparently they feel you've disgraced them somehow, and they've been badly hurt by the gossip."

"Oh no, I knew they'd be upset, but I thought by this time . . ."

"No. If anything, I'm afraid time will only magnify their distress. If only your country weren't at war, you could return home to Virginia. That's quite impossible under the circumstances, however. The effectiveness of Confederate raiders like your father's have made passenger travel between Europe and America too dangerous to consider. It looks as though the War might continue for many years, so it may be a long while before you see your parents again."

Eden nodded. "Yes, I know that. They sent me to Aunt Lydia to keep me safe. I'll not ignore their wishes by risking my life to go back."

"That's very sensible of you," Raven agreed in his most persuasive tone. "You really should think of yourself as Alex's widow rather than your parents' child anyway. His home was on Jamaica. I know he told you about it. It's not only a beautiful place to live, but one free of the tiresome constraints of London society. You would have been happy there with him, and I think you already know how happy you'll be there with me."

Eden's cheeks filled with a bright blush at the suggestive nature of that comment. "You make it sound as though my only choice is to marry you."

"No, there is another choice I've not mentioned."

"Really?" Eden asked with a delighted smile. "What is it?"

Raven knew it was unkind to dash her hopes, but did so quite willingly. "You can remain with me without the benefit of marriage. If you'd rather be my mistress than my wife, then I'll still treat you well. You can simply refer to yourself as Alex's widow and no one will question your presence in his home, or rather, my home."

It was the arrogance of that offer that infuriated Eden. "I am Alex's widow, I'd not just be calling myself that. Why couldn't I go to Jamaica if it's such a wonderful place? I could live there until the Civil War ends and then I could return home to Virginia."

Raven sat down on the side of the bed, slipped his fingers through Eden's wild mane of curls, and pulled her close for a kiss he did not end until he felt the tension that had filled her melt away. That she had as little resistance to him as he had for her seemed perfectly natural to him, and confident he would eventually bend her will to his, he sat back slightly.

"This is an enormous house, and yet we slept in the same bed. You'll not be able to avoid me on board the *Jamaican Wind,* and I doubt you'll even want to. Once we reach Jamaica, you'll be so accustomed to sleeping with me, you'll never want to be alone. I expect we won't be able to keep the depth of our relationship a secret for long, but if you feel you can survive the resulting scandal, so can I.

"You know what you are as well as I do, Eden. You're the kind of woman who enjoys being with men. There's no reason for you to be ashamed of it. Just accept it. We'll be going to Jamaica as lovers. Whether or not you'll also be my wife is up to you. It's what Alex wanted. It's what I want. It ought to be what you want as well."

Eden stared into Raven's eyes, searching for some glimmer of hope that what he said was untrue, but all she saw was the confidence that marked all his actions. He was wrong, though, for he was not the one she could not resist. It was the ease with which he brought Alex back to life that captivated her.

"Please," she whispered. "I need time to think things through. Losing Alex, the prospect of making a life with you, it's all coming too fast. Don't ask me to make any decisions today. I need more time."

Raven responded with another possessive kiss. "You know I could keep you in that bed all day and make you agree to anything I want, don't you?"

Eden nodded. She missed Alex so badly she could not

fight the way Raven made her feel. "Please don't," she begged softly.

This time when Raven pulled her into his arms, she rested her head on his shoulder. He brushed her hair aside and patted her bare back lightly, glad that she could not see the width of his smile. "You'll have to make up your mind by the time we leave for Jamaica, because once we set sail, there will be no way for us to marry. I can give you only that long to make your decision."

"What about Alex's townhouse?" Eden remembered suddenly. "I could live there!"

That he had completely forgotten about the place annoyed Raven no end, but he didn't allow his disgust at that oversight to show in his expression when Eden sat back to face him. "I'm afraid you'd encounter even worse problems in London than here. Your aunt's circle of friends would shun you for embarrassing her while the men interested in your wealth would simply find it more convenient to call on you there. You would be alone except for the servants, and while they are a competent group, they aren't fit company for a lady. No, I wouldn't feel right about leaving you alone in London and I'm certain Alex wouldn't approve."

"He'd not approve of my being your mistress either."

"That, Lady Clairbourne, is entirely up to you. I've offered marriage, but if you refuse . . ."

He left the consequences unspoken, but Eden understood. They were not even friends, but she would not be so foolish as to try and convince herself she could stay away from him. She felt utterly defeated, trapped, and then realized he must feel the same way. "I still think this is unfair to you. You should choose your own bride, not take me because Alex hoped that we might one day wed."

Raven wondered if it were merely the unusual topaz shade of her eyes that made her glance appear sincere, but she looked truly troubled. He placed a light kiss on her forehead, and rose to his feet. "I owe Alex a great deal, but had he married Stephanie, I wouldn't have shown her that letter."

"But Stephanie could have just gone home to her mother."

Raven shrugged, "I suppose that's true, but I don't regard marrying you as an obligation I've no choice but to honor. I can think for myself, and I'll never do anything I don't truly want to do just because someone else thinks I should."

"Not even Alex?"

"No, not even Alex. Now let's not discuss the issue anymore today. I want to visit all the tenants. Alex never raised their rent and I want to assure them that I won't either. I think the men who have grown wealthy by charging industrious peasants exorbitant rents ought to be prosecuted as criminals. I don't want any of the people who've spent their whole lives on this estate fearing I'll ever show that type of greed."

"That's very generous of you."

Unable to accept Eden's compliment graciously, Raven ignored it. "Will you be all right today on your own?"

Eden felt not only tired, but sick to her stomach. Certain that discomfort was due to mental rather than physical anguish, she attempted to smile bravely. "Yes. You needn't worry about me."

Eden waited until Raven had left the room before again donning her nightgown and leaving the bed. Still clutching Alex's letter tightly, she carried it into her room and put it away so that it would not become lost. She just wished Alex had told her he would like her to marry Raven so the suggestion would not have come as such a dreadful shock.

"Oh Alex, I miss you so," she murmured to herself.

113

As she bathed and dressed, Eden forced herself to concentrate on the tenants' welfare. She wanted Briarcliff to always be the beautiful estate Alex had loved and she was grateful that Raven obviously had the same goal.

Raven returned to the manor in time to join Eden for tea. She provided only a vague reply to his inquiry about how she had spent her day, but she looked pale and drawn as though it had been a very difficult one for her. That surprised him since she had buried Alex with such ease. Meaning to dress for dinner, they started up the broad staircase together, but Eden stopped to admire the portrait of Alex that hung on the landing.

"There's a far better likeness of him in our home on Jamaica," Raven told her.

"Really? I'm very fond of this one."

Alex had been only twenty-five at the time but his hair had already begun to turn gray. Raven glanced up the stairway. All of Alex's ancestors had been handsome, and all the portraits were of them in their twenties since none had lived to any great age.

"Raven?"

"Um?"

"How old are you?"

"I'll be twenty-seven in November." When Eden looked back at Alex's portrait, he understood the full import of her question. "I didn't inherit the heart condition that killed him. Is that what worries you?"

Eden sighed softly, "I hadn't thought about it until just this minute. I'm sorry, I hope that doesn't sound ghoulish."

"Not at all. It's a very sensible question since we'll undoubtedly spend the rest of our lives together."

"You've not given me even one day to consider my options," Eden reminded him. "Please don't rush me." Raven did not look pleased by that request, so she hurriedly changed the subject. "Why is there no portrait of Eleanora here?"

"Alex had only one of her and he took it to Jamaica. You'll see it there."

Exasperated that he had again taunted her about her decision, Eden gave up on their conversation but she was very curious about what sort of a woman Eleanora had been.

As they continued on up the stairs, Raven made no effort to hide his smile, and with the promise to rejoin her soon, he left her at her door.

Seven

Eden wore a gown of ice blue satin to dinner that night. Raven recalled seeing her in it at one of the balls they had attended. It was stunning, but once again he wondered at her choice of attire. When they entered the dining room, he helped her take the first seat on the right, then slid into what had always been Alex's place at the head of the table.

"Do you not own a black gown?" he attempted to ask without sounding critical.

"Why no, I don't. But Alex asked me not to wear black for him. He wanted me to always wear the pastel colors he thought so pretty."

Raven had no way of knowing what Alex had told Eden, but because that did sound like something the gracious man might have said, he didn't question her any further. Her wardrobe was a minor point when Raven considered the fact he had absolutely no idea of the content of Alex and Eden's conversations just prior to their elopement or during their brief marriage. If Eden realized that, then surely she would use it to her own advantage and cleverly fabricate all kinds of convenient things Alex might have said whenever she wished to make a point.

116

It was a disturbing thought, but if she and Alex had talked about something so insignificant as her wardrobe, what could they have failed to discuss? Realizing there were several important questions he ought to ask, Raven waited until they had finished their soup to respond.

"You knew all the while, then, that Alex didn't have long to live?"

Eden was amazed by that question when she thought the answer had to be obvious. "Yes, of course. He told me before he proposed. The shock would have killed me when I lost him had I not known that each day we spent together might be our last. Perhaps we were overly optimistic under the circumstances, but we'd hoped to measure the length of our marriage in months or possibly years, rather than days. Didn't you realize that I must have known Alex's heart wasn't strong?"

Raven shrugged. "I knew Alex meant to tell you, but I wasn't certain that he actually had." After all, the last time he had spoken with him, he had gotten the impression that Alex meant to tell her goodbye.

Determined to defend herself, Eden could not let that comment go unchallenged. "Then you must have thought me the most unfeeling of women."

Raven had a great many opinions about her, but few he cared to share. "You always struck me as being very serious-minded. When you learned of Alex's illness really doesn't matter. I knew you'd be able to cope with his death."

The coldness of that remark jarred Eden badly. If Raven truly thought her more unfeeling than brave, she did not want him to hold such an insulting misconception a moment longer. "I'll miss Alex for the rest of my life. That I'm not so sick with grief that I can't leave my bed doesn't mean that his death didn't affect me very deeply."

The threat of tears made her amber eyes glow with an

117

appealing golden light. That she was a great beauty was a fact of which Raven was already fully aware, however. He reached over to take her left hand. Alex had given her a magnificent diamond and ruby ring, which Raven caressed lightly with his thumb as he began to smile. "Anytime you wish to take to your bed, let me know, and I'll be happy to console you there."

"You bastard." Eden yanked her hand from beneath his and rose to her feet so rapidly she nearly toppled over her chair. She fled the elegant dining room, unable to give him the tongue-lashing he deserved, but the minute she reached the privacy of her room, she gave vent to her rage. She blasted Raven with every despicable name she had ever heard shouted in her father's shipyard, but that failed to erase her guilt over the ease with which he had already shared her bed.

She had used the handsome young man shamefully, and that was something she knew she would never be able to forgive herself for doing. That Raven would pounce on an opportunity to remind her of that horrible indiscretion was equally unforgivable, however. Despite his devotion to Alex, Raven had proven himself to be arrogantly self-centered. Clearly he cared only about himself.

A new torrent of tears began to stream down Eden's face then, for all she truly cared about was Alex, and her darling Alex was gone.

Eden's parting insult stung Raven far more harshly than she could ever have guessed, but he did not let it show. Instead, he continued to enjoy the excellent meal. He gave no excuse for Eden's sudden departure from the table to the footmen who brought in the remaining courses. Instead he made a point of savoring every last crumb and sending his compliments to the cook. He then went out for a stroll in the garden before entering the study, where he sat and sipped brandy for a good long while.

He liked the fact Eden was such a high-spirited woman, but he saw no reason for her to constantly resort to tears to justify her actions when her motivations were all so clear. She had to have known even a brief marriage to Alex would leave her wealthy should her family suffer irreversible losses in the Civil War.

Women were expected to protect their futures with marriage. He would not condemn her for that. It was the fact she had taken advantage of Alex's love for her that galled him, for in doing so she had undoubtedly hastened his death. Even if she had shortened Alex's life by no more than an hour, he intended to make her pay for that crime.

Raven felt neither sad nor lonely that night, merely determined. He knew precisely what he wanted from Eden, and certain she had had sufficient time to calm down and provide it, he went upstairs to find her.

His bed had been turned down, but it was empty that night. He had expected as much, however. When he tried the connecting door between his room and Eden's, he found it locked but that presented no problem to a man who had been raised in the house. All the doors could be unlocked with a single key, and he had several.

When he walked into Eden's bedroom, Raven was disappointed to find her already asleep. Her blue gown had been replaced in the wardrobe; indeed, there was nothing out of place, no feminine clutter in sight. If she had carelessly tossed her clothes about, then one of the maids had seen that the fine garments did not remain on the floor.

Unlike the previous night, Eden was hugging a pillow tightly and her brow was puckered in a troubled frown. Clearly her dreams were not sweet tonight.

"Guilty conscience, my pet?" Raven called softly, but

Eden did not stir. He removed his clothing, laid it over the bench at the dressing table, and again joined her in bed. He had said they would share his bed each night, but he was in no mood to argue over which room they slept in as long as they were together.

He drew her into his arms and nuzzled her sun-kissed curls, grateful she did not braid her hair at night as so many women did. She felt delightfully warm and relaxed, and as he pulled her close, her body conformed to the contours of his as easily as spoons fit together in a drawer.

"Eden?" he whispered, wondering if he would again have to kiss her awake. She snuggled against him, but the deep, even rhythm of her breathing did not change. Raven rose up slightly and found her expression had become the sweet smile he had often seen her wear with Alex.

Certain Alex would not approve of his method for convincing Eden they should marry, Raven lay back down. In all his life he had never trusted anyone as he had Alex. He had never known him to make even the smallest error in judgment. Had marrying Eden been his single mistake? A deadly mistake he had suggested Raven repeat?

It was a sobering thought but it did not prevent Raven from hugging Eden even closer. He knew he could again turn her anger to passion, and the pleasure they would find together would be just as deep, but now he wanted it on his own terms. She was his now, and he meant for her to realize it, to eagerly await him in his bed rather than to hide in her own.

Was she again teasing him? Had she wanted him to kick in her door and drag her off by her hair? That was just ridiculous enough an idea to appeal to her, but not to him. He liked being able to hold her close, to sleep with her, and for that night at least, it would be enough. If she wanted to tease him, she would soon learn he would repay her in kind. Thinking he had won this latest battle between them, Raven closed his eyes and went to sleep confident he was clever enough to get the better of her every time she defied him.

It was still long before dawn when Eden awoke. Frightened at first, she soon realized it was Raven who held her wrapped in a confining embrace, but she dared not risk waking him by struggling to break free. Instead she lay still. When the initial fear the discovery of his presence had caused passed, she began to relax and then did not find lying in his arms unpleasant.

His breath was very gentle as it caressed her cheek, warm and comforting. She had been terrified she would awake some morning to find Alex had died during the night, but she had no such fears with Raven. He radiated strength from every pore. The man would probably live to be one hundred. The question was, did she wish to spend those years with him?

A firm *no* came swiftly to her lips, but their relationship was far too complicated for a simple *yes* or *no* to change things between them. Since she was Alex's widow, their lives would be linked forever. Unless, of course, she married someone else and never saw him again. She had spent most of the day contemplating Alex's thinly veiled hint that she and Raven marry. That Raven was Alex's choice was not the only point in his favor, however, but the ease with which the virile young man could make her forget who he was was too painful a fact to face, even in the dark of night.

When Eden awoke for the second time that morning, she was alone. At first she thought the memory of Raven's presence might have been only a vivid dream, but the

121

spicy scent that clung to her pillows dashed that hope. She and Alex had never shared her bed. In fact, that was the first night she had ever spent in it, but the fragrance that teased her senses was definitely Alex's.

"Raven's," she reminded herself aloud, determined not to confuse the two men ever again. She sat up quickly when she noticed the door between their rooms was standing wide open. She knew she had locked it, but Raven had obviously not respected her privacy enough to leave it that way.

Slipping out of bed, Eden crossed to the doorway, and peering inside the next room, she found Raven standing in front of the washstand shaving. Bare to the waist, he looked not only disgustingly fit, but handsome as well. His broad shoulders and back were deeply tanned and his muscular torso tapered to a slim waist. As usual, he was clad in black pants. Alex had worn a variety of grays, browns, and blues, but not Raven. His wardrobe appeared to be just as extensive, but the majority of his garments were as dark as midnight.

"I think you must wear black more often than Mr. Lincoln," she called to him.

Raven was not startled by the sound of her voice for he had seen her in his mirror and had been waiting for her to speak. He took the time to wipe off the last traces of shaving soap before turning to face her. Her lace-trimmed nightgown covered her lovely figure with modest folds, but the casual disarray of her long curls gave clear evidence of the wildness of her spirit. It was the allure of the untamed side of her nature that drew him to her now.

"Mr. Lincoln has good reason to wear black, and so do I."

"I think we have already had this argument," Eden replied with forced calm, not wanting to again have to justify her choice of clothing. She was now sorry she had not waited until he had donned a shirt before she had spoken.

Raven walked toward her with a slow, measured stride. "Then let's not have it again. What sort of headstone did you order for Alex?"

Eden's gaze swept over his bare chest before coming to rest on his dark eyes. She had been about to demand he stay out of her bed, but she suddenly suspected he would deny he had ever been there. Because Alex was a far safer subject, she answered his question. "I waited to discuss it with you."

Raven was surprised, but pleased by that. "Do you want to come into Exeter with me? I'm sure the stonemason can create any design we suggest, but I want it to be as beautifully crafted as Eleanora's angel."

"Do you know the man?"

"No," Raven admitted, "but I'll make certain he does his finest work for Alex."

"I know that you will. I'd rather stay here, though. I trust you to choose something handsome for Alex." She hesitated a moment, then rushed ahead. "Even though he's buried beside Eleanora, would you think it terribly selfish of me to request the phrase 'Beloved Husband of Eden'?"

Of all the possible inscriptions, Raven could not think of a less likely one, but recalling Alex's adoring praise for his honey-eyed bride, he could not refuse. "You were his wife, Eden. If that's what you want, then I'm sure it can be done."

"Thank you." Wanting only to get away from him before their conversation deteriorated into another bitter argument, Eden wished him a good day, then closed her door.

Raven had difficulty stifling a deep laugh when he knew Eden had to know he had spent the night in her bed.

He found it highly amusing she had not mentioned it. Whistling softly to himself, he decided his strategy was working. In as good a mood as could be expected, he completed dressing and left for Exeter.

At first Eden had been relieved Raven would again be away for most of the day, but she soon grew restless on her own. It was a short step from that point to despair. She and Alex had never run out of things to do. Since his death, she had had more than enough to keep her busy, although she would have preferred never to have had to arrange for his funeral. Now she found herself wandering aimlessly through the halls of Briarcliff with nothing to occupy her mind but thoughts of the husband she had lost.

Raven had also thought he would appreciate the time alone, but he had not even reached Exeter before he wished he had insisted that Eden accompany him. After all, she was Alex's widow. While it had been thoughtful of her to wait for him to select a headstone, it now struck him as a task they should have shared. Bored and restless on his own, he vowed not to make the mistake of leaving her behind ever again.

By the time he had returned to Briarcliff, Raven was so anxious to see Eden he raced up the stairs and did not slow his pace until he had charged through his room and into hers. Finding it empty, he cursed like the sailor he was, and tore back down the stairs. When he could not find her in any of the rooms where she might be expected to be, he sought Abbot's assistance.

"I believe Lady Clairbourne is in the garden, my lord. She usually spends the afternoons there."

Raven waved his thanks to the butler as he sped out the double doors. The terrace overlooked the garden, but a hurried glance revealed Eden was not seated on any of the shaded benches. Frustrated by his lack of success, Raven was about to return to the house to tell Abbot to send the staff out to look for Eden when he sighted a patch of apricot on the distant cliff.

Recognizing the pale color as the shade of one of Eden's favorite gowns, he could think of only one reason for her to have strayed so far. Terrified she was about to throw herself to the rocks below, he prayed he could reach her in time to prevent such a horrible tragedy. Skirting the winding paths of the garden, he vaulted the low hedges and flowering shrubs in a mad dash to save her life. He had never run so hard, but the lawn that extended between the end of the garden and the cliff's edge seemed a mile wide even though he nearly flew across it.

The sound of the surf kept Eden from hearing Raven's wild approach until he was within a few yards of her. She turned then, and delighted to see him after a long and trying day, she welcomed him with a bright smile before pausing to wonder why he was in such a great hurry.

Raven had expected hysterical tears and defiant screams, but when Eden smiled as she turned to face him, he knew immediately suicide had not been on her mind. Feeling like a complete ass, he slid to a bone-jarring halt, then had to lean forward and rest his hands on his knees while he struggled to catch his breath.

Thinking he must have some sort of terrible news, Eden ran to Raven's side. "What's wrong?" She was tempted to reach out and touch his curls, but stopped herself.

"Nothing," he managed to assure her between deep gasps. Horribly embarrassed, he straightened up as quickly as he could, but his breathing was still labored.

"Well, something dreadful must have happened or you wouldn't have run out here like that," Eden prompted as she reached out to take his arm. "It isn't the War, is it? Has there been news of the War?"

Raven held up his hand in a plea for patience, and in another moment he was able to speak. "I didn't hear any news from America. It was just that I saw you out here on the cliff, and I was afraid that you were about to do something desperate."

Eden didn't understand. "What are you talking about? What could I possibly do out here?"

That she didn't see the obvious appalled him. "I thought you were about to leap off."

Raven still looked so terribly upset that Eden didn't doubt his words. She thought him absolutely daft for thinking such a thing, however. "Oh Raven, where did you ever get such an absurd idea?" She couldn't help but giggle then, and she was grateful she had him to hold on to when she could not control the riotous peals of laughter that bubbled up from deep inside her.

That he had exhausted himself racing to rescue her when she had not been in any danger was bad enough, but that she would ridicule him for it was more than Raven could bear. Infuriated with her, he grabbed ahold of her upper arms and lifted her clear off her feet.

"Don't you ever laugh at me again!" he shouted in her face. "Don't ever make that mistake again!"

Dangling in midair, Eden was aghast to find he did not think the situation as humorous as she did. His dark eyes were aglow with the fury of his rage and she clung to his lapels, terrified that he might be angry enough to fling her off the cliff himself.

"I wasn't laughing at you," she argued in a frantic whisper.

Raven watched her eyes fill with tears, and certain she was no longer in any mood for laughter, he placed her on

126

her feet. "Women have killed themselves over a lost love. You must know that's happened."

When he released her, Eden backed away. "Is that what you feared, or what you were hoping for, Raven? You're not the only one who despises pretense. Just forget that Alex hoped we might marry. There's no way I'll ever marry you when it's plain you'd rather see me dead!"

Raven clenched his fists tightly at his sides but he didn't follow Eden when she ran away from him. She might have called him a bastard and laughed in his face but he certainly did not wish her dead. No, he wanted her very much alive, and if she had not fled from him when she had, he knew in another instant he would have pulled her down into the grass and taken her right there.

He waited until she had reached the terrace before turning away and walking to the edge of the cliff. He waved to the men on the deck of the *Jamaican Wind* and decided since he had come that far he might as well go out to the ship. A few hours spent with Randy would undoubtedly put him in a better mood, and it would also give Eden the time to realize how ridiculous her accusation that he wished her dead truly was.

Eight

August 1863

Eden did not dress for dinner. She remained in her room stubbornly determined to again make Raven dine alone but that plan was foiled when he did not return to Briarcliff. His failure to do so confused her as he had not impressed her as the type of man to turn tail and run.

Then a truly horrifying thought occurred to her. What if he had sailed for London on the *Jamaican Wind?* He had certainly been angry enough to abandon her. Had he actually done it?

Not willing simply to fret over such a dire possibility, Eden rang for a maid. By the time the girl reached her room, she had a note written for Abbot asking him to ascertain immediately whether or not Raven's ship was still lying at anchor in Lyme Bay. She waited at her window, thinking whomever Abbot sent would be carrying a lantern, but a knock at her door soon drew her away from her vigil.

Abbot had come in response to her note, and the white-haired butler appeared to be baffled by her request. "Lady Clairbourne, if the ship is in the harbor, is there a message of some kind that you wish sent out to it?"

Other than to tell Raven to go straight to hell, Eden could not think of anything. "Why no," she attempted to answer calmly, "I just wondered if the ship had sailed on the evening tide."

"Lord Clairbourne would not leave without informing you of his intentions," Abbot assured her.

Eden took the precaution of glancing up and down the hall, and seeing no other servants about, she hurriedly drew Abbot into her room and closed the door. "I know Alex trusted you, and I trust you as well. Raven and I are not well acquainted, and constantly misunderstand each other. How would you describe his character? I know Alex thought very highly of him, but I find it extremely difficult to hold such a generous opinion."

To ask a butler for a personal comment on his employer was irregular, to say the least, but in the past month Abbot had found Eden's unassuming charm so delightful he was not offended by her request and responded in a fatherly tone. "I have known Raven for nearly twenty years, my lady, and he has never given anyone reason to criticize his behavior. He is a fine man, and very young for the heavy load of responsibilities he bears. These are difficult times for all of us who loved Alex. If a problem exists between you two, it is doubly unfortunate coming now when each of you is suffering so badly from grief."

Ashamed to think what he said about Raven might well be true, Eden was so embarrassed she had to turn away for a moment. It was clear to her then that she had had no real cause to accuse Raven of wishing her dead. He had simply frightened her half out of her wits, that was all, and perhaps it had been rude of her to laugh at him for thinking her about to attempt suicide. They had again made a complete mess of things, but she did not think she was the only one to blame. Not wanting to keep Abbot from his duties while she pondered her problems, Eden moved to the door and opened it for him.

"Thank you for being as good a friend to me as you were to Alex."

"What about the ship?"

"It must be there. Please don't send anyone out to look."

Eden still wore a troubled frown, and Abbot hated to leave without having lifted her spirits. "Would you like the cook to send up some supper on a tray? I believe there's roast pheasant tonight."

Eden's mouth began to water at the thought of the succulent bird. "Would you please? I'd rather not go down to the dining room, but I know I'll soon regret not eating if I don't have something. Pheasant sounds wonderful."

Hoping he had been some small help to her, Abbot hesitated at the door. Eden was lovely, but very young to face the future alone. Realizing it was Raven's place to offer counsel to her rather than his, he wished her a good evening, but he gave sending his own note out to the *Jamaican Wind* careful consideration before deciding to leave well enough alone.

Eden awakened frequently during the night, and each time she got up and looked in the adjoining room to see if Raven was in his bed. She would not have joined him, but it would have put her mind at ease to find him there. Morning arrived before he did, and she did not feel as though she had slept more than a few minutes. When she sat down at her dressing table to brush her hair, the dark circles beneath her eyes provided clear evidence that she had not.

Condolence letters had not yet begun to arrive from London, but as she ate a few bites of breakfast, Eden began to look forward to receiving some as writing replies would give her something useful to do although it would not be at all pleasant. With no mail to answer as yet, she went into the library in search of something to read. She found several novels with appealing titles, but when she sat down with one, she could not concentrate for more than a paragraph or two before her mind began to wander and she left the book lying open on her lap.

When Alex had been alive, being a countess had never been dull, but now the whole day stretched before her without a single responsibility to occupy her time. Abbot ran the house so beautifully that there was not a speck of dust on the furnishings nor a bit of tarnish on the silver.

The cook was extraordinarily talented and prepared delicious meals from the wide variety of livestock and produce grown on the estate. Eden had always been busy at home, and even at her aunt Lydia's she had managed to find useful things to do. But Briarcliff ran itself, and she did not feel needed there.

The day was again bright and warm, but a sleepless night had left her without the energy to go out for a ride. "No one should be widowed at nineteen," she whispered softly to herself.

Raven heard the sound of Eden's voice, if not her words, and not wanting to interrupt a conversation, he peeked into the library to see to whom she was speaking. Finding her alone, he walked on in. "I thought it would be better for both of us if I remained on board my ship last night. If you've nothing better to do than talk to yourself, why don't you come upstairs and help me sort though Alex's things? Once we get that chore done, we can leave for London."

Raven was in his shirtsleeves, his coat slung over his shoulder. Well-groomed as always, he looked rested and eager to get to work. Eden, however, felt completely drained. "Do you actually consider that an adequate apology after the way we parted yesterday?" she asked.

"On the contrary, I think you owe me one," he countered smoothly.

Rather than argue with such an obstinate man, Eden slammed her book shut and rose to her feet. Knowing she lacked the interest to complete the novel, she replaced it on the shelf, and then preceded Raven out the door. "Alex had such a beautiful wardrobe. Can you wear any of his things?"

Surprised Eden had merely ignored his request rather than angrily persisting in her demand for an apology, Raven frowned slightly as he caught up with her. "No, I outgrew his clothes in my teens. The fact I was several inches taller threw everything out of proportion."

"Yes, I understand. Do you want to give his clothes to the poor then?"

"No, there are men on the staff who can use a new suit of clothes."

Eden didn't argue as her father had frequently passed his clothes on to their servants and it was a common practice. When they reached his room, she went to the wardrobe and began looking through her late husband's suits, making certain nothing had been left in the pockets while Raven chose to sort through the contents of the dresser.

That Raven had again assumed she would be leaving Briarcliff with him annoyed Eden no end, but she had spent enough time by herself since Alex's death to know she ought not to remain there. She would have liked to have been asked what she planned to do though rather than told, however.

Raven had not noticed that Eden did not look well, and he was grateful for her silence as he looked through the assortment of tie pins, shirt studs, and cufflinks in Alex's jewelry case. Finding the gold signet ring bearing the Clairbourne crest that his late uncle had occasionally worn, he tried it on. He liked the way the heavy gold ring felt on his hand and decided to wear it. He then set the small velvet case atop the dresser, and opened the next drawer.

The hummingbird-topped bottle tucked in the corner immediately caught his eye. He picked up the delicate glass container, removed the stopper, then tasted a drop of the fragrant oil. He recognized the damiana instantly, and turned toward Eden. "Do you know what this is?"

Eden looked up, and began to blush when she saw what he was holding. "Yes, and the bottle is so very pretty I'd like to keep it if you don't mind."

"Did you and Alex use this often?" he asked, barely able to keep his temper in check.

"That's really none of your business," Eden replied, unwilling to discuss the intimate details of her marriage with him.

Raven crossed the room in two long strides. "An aphrodisiac this potent leaves a healthy man as weak as a babe. Didn't you realize what it would do to Alex?"

What little color had been in Eden's cheeks faded instantly. "You mean it was harmful?"

"Harmful? For the love of God, Eden, it probably killed him!" Incensed by the stupidity of her question, Raven hurled the exquisite bottle against the far wall with a force that shattered it into a thousand shimmering bits. What little oil it had still contained splattered across the burgundy silk wallcovering leaving a dark stain trailing narrow rivulets that slid slowly to the floor.

Raven was every bit as enraged as he had been the previous afternoon and Eden was terrified not only by the hostility of his expression, but also by the harshness of his words. "He couldn't have known that, Raven, or he would never have used it."

"You must know what it does, so you can't possibly be so stupid as to believe that," Raven scoffed. He lowered his voice, taunting her anew, "It makes a person dizzy, makes everything seem like a fabulous dream where making love provides pleasure so intense it's nearly pain. It also makes the heart race wildly until—"

"Stop it!" Eden screamed as she clamped her hands over her ears. She knew very well that the oil heightened the senses until reality was lost in a cloud of desire, but could its effect overwhelm a heart that already had to struggle to beat?

Raven grabbed her wrists so she could not block out his words. "You never thought about it, did you? Your only concern was how wonderful it was to be with Alex when all the while he was risking death to please you!"

"No!" Eden screamed. She tried to get away from Raven, to flee the room, to escape the horror of his words, but he refused to release her. He was so strong he needed only to tighten his grip on her wrists and he again lifted her off her feet. Crushed by the brutality of his accusations, Eden swiftly became hysterical. She had been able to accept Alex's death with a calm resignation, but not under the circumstances Raven described, not if her passion for her husband had hastened his death.

Knowing the walls of Briarcliff were so thick they would muffle her cries, Raven let Eden shriek until she grew hoarse. His worst suspicions confirmed, he braced his feet and continued to hold her firmly, waiting for her to admit the responsibility for what she had done.

Bent on escaping him, Eden thrashed about so wildly her hair came loose from the bun at her nape. Her curls flew about her head, blinding them both with a veil of silken tresses. She tried to kick him, but her feet became entangled in her slips and she did no damage to his shins.

Raven did not shake Eden, nor slap her. He merely held her while she struggled and drenched him with her tears. When she had first begun to sob, he had felt a surge of triumphant satisfaction but as she continued to fight his grasp and wept past the point of exhaustion he grew concerned, and then alarmed.

"Eden," he called, pulling her against his chest but she shrank away from him. He knew her to be high-strung, but now feared in his quest for an admission of guilt he might have pushed her into madness. Gathering her up in his arms, he carried her to the bed. Her full skirts and crinolines presented a bothersome nuisance that blocked his way so he hurriedly removed her gown and the layers of starched cotton slips beneath it.

Clad now in her chemise and pantalettes, she was much easier to handle and he forced her down on the bed and stretched out beside her. She had given him something precious in the times they had made love. He had only wanted her to see the truth, not to destroy her. He covered her tear-streaked face with kisses, smoothed her hair away from her eyes, and murmured the tender promises of a lover until at long last her racking sobs became no more than soft whimpers of despair.

As always, Raven had confused Eden completely. He had broken her heart with his mean accusations, and yet as his lips caressed hers lightly, she felt only desire rather than hatred. Too hurt to logically contemplate the puzzling change in his mood, she longed to be held rather than cursed. She wrapped her arms around his neck and again responded to his affection with kisses so deep they left him craving much more.

His passion loosed with anger, Raven eagerly accepted Eden's unspoken invitation. He removed her lace-trimmed lingerie with a few savage tugs, flung his own clothes far and wide, and then returned to her arms with a cry of surrender that echoed hers. He knew he had thoughtlessly pushed her to the edge of reason, but now he hoped to undo that damage in the only way he knew how.

This time Eden had no illusions about what she was doing or with whom. She kept her eyes wide open, although Raven closed his to savor the beautiful sensations her loving created. Fully awake, she felt Raven's strength rather than Alex's tenderness, the exuberance of his youth rather than the masterful seduction of a mature lover. Cursing her own weakness, she wanted it all and she returned Raven's fiery passion as though it were her natural right. Seductive, alluring, with a wanton abandon she drew Raven into a union that was as heated as the flames of her own private hell.

Wanting to prolong this passionate yet strangely bittersweet encounter, Raven plunged deeply then lay still within her. He held Eden's face cupped tenderly between his hands as he searched her expression for the acceptance he sought. Her topaz gaze had always held a hint of wildness, but now it was darkened with desire. Certain she wanted him as badly as he wanted her, although he knew she would never say so, he began to move, striving to again make their union as perfect for her as it was for him. He held back the full force of his desire until he felt the waves of her climax begin to contract around him. He buried himself deep inside her then, and did not relax his loving embrace until she had fallen into the peaceful sleep of an untroubled child.

Raven did not disturb Eden's rest until Reverend Boyer responded to his summons in the late afternoon. He then awakened her gently, wrapped her in a silk robe, and sent her into her own room where a maid was waiting to help her bathe and dress. He gave her no clue as to his purpose until she was again as beautifully groomed and dressed as was her custom. He had laid out the ice blue gown, and he was delighted when she accepted his choice rather than defying him. After thanking the maid for her assistance, he dismissed her and drew Eden into his arms.

"I arranged for a marriage license while I was in Exeter yesterday. I also informed the priest that it was Alex's wish that we wed. I told him our grief has made us too dependent upon each other to live apart for any length of time, and that we ought to be allowed to wed without observing any further period of mourning. He was shocked by my request as you might well imagine, but I convinced him that our reputations would be sacrificed whether or not we married, and he could not in good conscience condemn us to a life of sin."

Despite her lengthy nap, Eden's head ached so badly she could scarcely understand Raven's words. "Sin?" she repeated softly, thinking what she had done to Alex was a far greater sin than what had transpired between her and Raven.

"No one will dare say what exists between us is sinful when we are husband and wife," he assured her. When Eden did not respond, Raven was grateful she appeared to be too distracted to argue with his plan. He slipped his arm around her waist and escorted her downstairs, where the entire staff, along with Randy MacDermott and several other members of the *Jamaican Wind*'s crew, had gathered in the drawing room to witness the ceremony. If any thought the wedding of a newly widowed woman to her late husband's heir ill advised, they kept their thoughts and comments to themselves.

At her wedding to Alex, Eden had felt a delicious excitement that had been impossible to contain, but now with Raven by her side, she was overcome with the pain of grief and despair. Only dimly aware of the significance of the proceedings, she had to be prompted to give the appropriate responses. While in reality lasting only a few minutes, in Eden's pain-numbed state the ceremony appeared to consume hours and she found it increasingly difficult to remain standing. When Raven slipped his arm around her waist to provide support, she looked up at him but was unable to convey her gratitude with a smile.

Expecting Eden to faint at any second, Raven did not merely clasp her waist, but instead took a firm hold on the smooth satin of her gown so he could keep her on her feet until the priest pronounced them husband and wife. When that moment finally arrived, he breathed a deep sigh of relief that his pale bride was still conscious. At least her eyes were open, but she scarcely seemed to see the people who came forward to wish them well. The mood of the small gathering was subdued as could be expected with Alex's passing so recent, but still, there was not a guest present who did not appear far happier than the bride.

"We'll not leave Briarcliff for a day or two," Raven told Eden as they returned to his room that night. During dinner he had done his best to be as charming as he knew Alex must have been on their wedding night, but feared he had failed miserably. Eden had tasted each of the courses, but he doubted she had swallowed more than a thimble full of food the entire meal.

Her occasional responses to his conversation had been appropriate, if brief, so he knew she had at least been listening to him, but she had not glanced his way once. She had been in better spirits at Alex's funeral than she was that evening, and he knew he was to blame for the blackness of her mood.

"I looked through your wardrobe this afternoon while you were sleeping to judge how much there was to pack.

Several of the gowns I remember seeing you wear are missing. Did you leave some of your things at your aunt's?"

What an odd question, Eden thought, for the size of her wardrobe was of no consequence to her. "Yes, the majority of my things are there, if Aunt Lydia has not given them away." Eden could not even glance toward the bed without wincing, and terribly uncomfortable in the room, she started for her own.

"Where are you going?"

"I can't stay here," Eden responded with a shudder.

Her tone held more spirit than he had heard since their confrontation that morning, and rather than being insulted, Raven was relieved the damage he had done had not been permanent.

"Are you objecting to this room, or to me?" he asked as he followed her toward her door.

Her hand resting upon the doorknob, Eden turned to face him. She remembered the night they had met. He had been dressed in elegantly tailored evening clothes as he was now, but it had not been the attractiveness of his appearance that had impressed her. It had been the chill of his glance as he had dismissed her with no more than a nod. Now that aloof stranger was her husband.

"Both," she replied truthfully.

Raven halted his advance in midstride, but his pose was relaxed rather than threatening. "The room we can change, but if that's not the only problem, just what is it you want?"

Eden took a deep breath and let it out slowly. "I want to be by myself."

"On our wedding night?" Raven was barely able to ask before breaking into deep chuckles.

Eden considered his laughter as out of place as he had thought hers was on the cliff. "I can understand why we had to marry, but this isn't the way newlyweds ought to feel."

"How do you know how I feel?" Raven asked in a far softer tone.

"I know you think I killed Alex," Eden responded. "So I can't imagine you feeling anything but loathing."

Raven could not deny the first part of her accusation, but he most certainly did not loathe her. That was a contradiction that he could not justify even in his mind, let alone aloud to her. He had thought her a lovely opportunist and he had wanted to make her pay for her selfishness. Clearly he had gotten his point across, but he could not take any pride in the accomplishment. The anguish in her eyes was too real. He had never deliberately hurt another person as he had Eden, but there was no way he could take back what he had said. Even if he offered an apology, she would never forget that bitter attack nor the fact he had made her face a truth she would never have seen for herself.

"If you would be more comfortable in your own room, I won't keep you," he finally offered graciously, sorry he had not thought of the consequences before he had forced her to accept his view of Alex's death.

When Eden closed the door behind her, Raven held his breath, waiting for her to turn the key. When she did not, he broke into a sly smile. He went downstairs for a bottle of Briarcliff's superb blackberry brandy and two delicate crystal snifters. He then returned to his room and waited until he was certain Eden had had ample time to prepare for bed. He then rapped lightly on her door, but entered her room before she had time to respond. She was seated at the dressing table, wearing the nightgown he had removed from her slender figure twice, and brushing her hair.

"I thought a brandy would help you sleep."

140

Eden watched him approach in the mirror. He'd shed his jacket and waistcoat, and unbuttoned his shirt clear to the waist. She knew the brandy was merely an excuse to speak with her again, but she lacked the emotional strength to send him away. "That's very thoughtful of you, but I've never cared for brandy."

Undaunted, Raven placed the two snifters on the dressing table. "I'll give you only a drop then." He poured her no more than a splash, but was far more generous with himself. After recorking the bottle, he took a long sip then set his brandy aside.

"Will you let me brush your hair?" When she appeared to be reluctant to relinquish her silver-handled brush, he took it from her hand. "Did Alex like to do this?" He drew the brush through a long tawny curl, then wound the end around his hand. "Well, did he?"

"Yes."

"Just close your eyes and pretend I'm Alex then."

That was a suggestion Eden had never expected to hear from him. That she had already played such a dangerous game on more than one occasion was a secret she intended to take to her grave. His hands caressed her back gently as he continued to brush one curl at a time and she could not suppress a shiver. She was not cold, merely all too aware of him.

"You don't know what you're asking," she replied in a breathless rush.

"Oh but I do," Raven argued. "You may find it difficult to believe, but I want our marriage to succeed. I know you don't love me, but that hasn't kept us from achieving a degree of closeness many couples never share. I know you'll not forget Alex anytime soon, if ever, but if it would make being with me easier to bear, I won't mind if you pretend that's who I am. I'd be flattered actually."

Eden studied his expression in the mirror, and was

amazed to find he looked sincere. He appeared to be giving his full concentration to his task, but she knew that was merely what he wanted her to believe. He was awaiting her reply with an anxiety he hoped she would not notice, but she did.

"No, I won't ever do that, Raven. If I were to pretend I was with Alex, it would cheat us both. We may have been drawn together by circumstance rather than love, but we ought to be honest with each other."

"And if I am too honest?" Raven asked, certain he already had been.

Eden could think of no way to reply to that question without reopening the gaping wound of Alex's death. She took a sip of her brandy to fill the awkward silence her failure to respond created but the deep purple liquid failed to ease her troubled mind, or her badly aching conscience.

Raven kept working until her hair shone with soft, golden highlights. It was torture to touch her, and to keep his emotions under control when he wanted so badly to glory in the feelings she aroused within him. He may have condemned her behavior in the past, but he wanted their future to be the best he could possibly make it. Finally he lay the brush on the dressing table, and bent down on one knee beside her so his eyes would be level with hers and she could no longer avoid looking directly at him.

"I know you must have beautiful memories of another wedding night, but this is the only one I'll ever have. Please don't ask me to sleep alone."

His earnest gaze was somehow loving that night rather than intimidating, but again Eden found it difficult to reply. She did not feel like a bride, but like a very recent widow. In fact, she had felt like a spectator at their wedding. Their vows had had a hollow ring, as though strangers were speaking them. She knew Raven was now her husband, but she had never felt less like a wife. He was

142

not demanding that she share his bed, as was his right, however. He was asking politely and that was more consideration than she had expected to receive from a man who was as hot-tempered as he.

She reached out to caress his cheek, and he drew her palm to his lips. That familiar gesture reminded her that they were already lovers. When she had shared the most intimate part of herself with him, how could she turn him away? "I did not think you would want me," she whispered as she set her snifter aside to free both her hands.

Raven was unused to justifying either his actions or his emotions to others, and he could not begin now. "No matter how bitter our arguments become, I will always want you," he responded instead.

"You deserve a wife who truly loves you, Raven. Someone like Stephanie who thinks you're the most dashing man she's ever met."

Raven stood and took Eden's hands to draw her to her feet. He toyed briefly with revealing she had been the only woman in London who had appealed to him, but quickly discarded the idea. He did not want to sound like some pathetic schoolboy suffering from unrequited love.

"You already know what I think of your insipid cousin, so don't mention her name to me again. Surely you must know that the wealthier a couple is, the less likely they are to marry for love," he commented as he skillfully edged her toward the bed. "That does not mean that we can't be happy together."

"Oh Raven, don't you know anything about love?"

"Only what you have taught me," he replied with rare candor. He did not give Eden time to respond, however, before he captured her mouth for a long, slow kiss that stilled all objection to their marriage. He would not leave her alone to brood over Alex's death when he was alive and in such dire need of her affection. He scooped her up in his arms and began to turn in a slow circle as he deepened his kiss.

After a moment's hesitation, Eden flung her arms wide, increasing the effect of his seductive spin. She had been so thoroughly depressed she did not think she would ever recover, but Raven had raised her spirits with his playful, and totally unexpected, antics. It was completely out of character for him and yet it was so spontaneously joyful that she did not question what had prompted him to behave in such a carefree fashion.

By the time Raven laid Eden across her bed, and collapsed beside her, they were both dizzy and convulsed with laughter. Breaking into a happy grin, he kissed both her cheeks then paused to judge her reaction before leading her any further.

"I'd never really seen you smile until a few days ago." Eden was still amazed by how drastically his marvelous grin altered his appearance. "It makes you so much more handsome."

Raven caressed her cheek with his fingertips, delighted her face was flushed with the warm glow of happiness. "Why Lady Clairbourne, are you saying that I'm dashing?"

"Oh yes, very dashing indeed," Eden admitted without the slightest reluctance.

Raven knew how easily flattery poured from her lips, but he was in too good a mood to call her a liar. Instead, he kissed her soundly. They had each had the worst of days. Only that morning their emotions had been plunged to the depths of despair, but now their moods bordered on rapture. Raven wanted to take them higher still and began to make love to her with an adoring grace. His strength now tempered with a gentle restraint, he kissed and caressed her until she was so totally his they became truly one. He did not know or care if he had replaced Alex in her mind, but he knew no one would ever take her place in his heart.

Eden gloried in Raven's affection. She drank in each of his brandy-flavored kisses and never once forgot who he was. He was not Alex, but his loving was so beautiful in itself that it no longer mattered. She could give herself to him with the hope that in time they would grow to love one another. She had not thought Raven capable of such tender emotions, but now that she had felt him express them, she had proof that indeed he could.

She ran her fingers through his thick curls to hold him close as the last shudders of ecstasy throbbed through his sleek body. She had asked him to take things slowly, to give her time, but he had responded by making her his wife with a speed she knew was even more shocking than her elopement had been.

When he wrapped her in his arms, and rolled over to bring her up on top of him, she was so completely relaxed she fell asleep with her head pillowed on his chest but no dream, no matter how blissful, could compare with the charming reality she had found in Raven's arms.

Nine

August 1863

Eden's mood was again a somber one the following morning, but Raven was so pleased with the way their wedding night had gone he attempted to lift her spirits.

"Do you like to ride?" he asked as she finished her last bite of breakfast.

"Yes, very much," Eden responded softly. "Do you?"

"Not particularly, unless I'm out to race or hunt," Raven admitted readily, for sedate rides through the countryside had never held enough excitement to keep him amused. "There are still a few more tenants I need to see before we sail for home. If you feel up to it, I'd like to have your company."

Eden was tempted to offer an excuse, for indeed she had never felt less like riding, but Raven's smile was so inviting, she feared she might insult him if she refused. Thinking that a poor way to begin their marriage, she agreed. "May I have a few minutes to change my clothes?"

"Take all the time you like. I need to speak with Elkins, the overseer. I'll meet you at the stable."

"I won't keep you waiting," Eden promised.

As they rode about the estate that morning, Eden kept Raven under close observation. Although she attempted to keep her frequent glances discreet, he captured far more of her attention than the tenants. That he not only called the men by name, but also knew each wife and child, impressed her most favorably. She felt certain she had met all the tenants at one time or another since coming to Briarcliff, but she was embarrassed that she could not recall a single name. Fortunately, she had only to repeat Raven's greetings and add a word or two of her own.

They had visited half a dozen of the farmers who rented land on Briarcliff before Raven drew his bay gelding to a halt. "Have you had enough?"

"Why no, I'd like to see everyone. I know they all came into Exeter for the funeral and I want them to know I appreciate their being there."

"They know," Raven assured her.

Outdoors, Eden did not feel nearly so apprehensive around Raven. The morning was warm, without a hint of the coming fall. The last time she had toured Briarcliff she had been with Alex, though, and the memory of that day flooded her eyes with a sudden rush of tears. Embarrassed, she quickly wiped them away. "We ought to go."

"Just a minute." Raven drew his mount alongside the small black mare he had chosen for her. "The next man, Paul Jessup, is a bit of a problem. Elkins told me that he drinks more than he should, and while his wife has never complained to him, he thinks Paul abuses her."

"And Elkins lets him get away with it?" Eden asked, clearly upset. "I don't believe Alex knew about it. Or if he did, he didn't tell me."

"No, Elkins didn't want to bother Alex. That's another problem. Elkins has been the overseer here for thirty years. His wife died several years ago, and Alex didn't want to mention retirement to him for fear he'd just lie down and die as well."

"Oh my goodness. It seems we have two problems rather than one, doesn't it?"

Raven could not help but smile at the thought of the two of them attempting to set everything right at Briarcliff. "Let's handle Jessup first. He gets in his crops and pays his rent on time. It can be argued that his personal life is his own business. He may be a mean bastard, but at least he provides a home for his wife and children."

"That's not enough, Raven."

"Do you want to tell him to go?"

"No," Eden admitted reluctantly. She wished she knew how Alex would have handled Jessup, but they had been so engrossed in each other they had not once discussed his tenants. "My mother had a maid whose husband beat her once. Maribelle came running to us for help and my father went over to her house and told her husband that if he even so much as raised his voice to Maribelle again, he'd . . ." she paused then, unable to recall just what the threat had been.

"He'd what?"

"I don't remember," Eden admitted with a frown. "But it must have been something truly horrible because the man never gave Maribelle a reason to complain again. Surely Mr. Jessup must know that he can do better here than anywhere else so he'd not want to leave. Maybe all we'll have to do is threaten to evict him."

"No matter what we threaten, it will be Elkins who'll have to carry it out," Raven reminded her.

"Then tell him that his will be the first home we'll visit when we return to Briarcliff next summer." Then as a sudden afterthought she asked, "We will be coming back, won't we?"

Raven broke into a wide grin. "If that's your wish, Lady Clairbourne, then I'll be happy to bring you back."

Eden had never expected Raven to be such an agreeable husband. Finding it difficult to accept the fact that he was now her spouse, she looked away quickly. She could not actually recall agreeing to marry him. It had not been a conscious decision, at any rate, but now that she considered the question in retrospect, it seemed as though becoming Raven's wife had been her only choice.

As he had been quick to point out, she had had nowhere else to go. To have remained with him as his mistress was unthinkable. That would have disgraced not only her, but her parents and Alex's memory as well. Considering the scandalous way she and Raven had behaved since Alex's death, marriage had been their only moral option.

Eden could justify their hasty wedding in her mind, but her heart still ached with the fear she had done something dreadfully wrong. Her only comfort was the hope for their happiness that Alex had expressed in his letter. Alex had been so loving and kind, she knew he would not disapprove of what they had done, even if the rest of the world did.

Raven watched Eden's expression grow increasingly forlorn, and tapped his mount's flanks lightly with his heels. "Come on, Lady Clairbourne. We need to deal with Jessup's problems rather than dwelling on our own."

Shocked to think the handsome young man could read her mind so easily, Eden sat up proudly and forced herself to smile as they continued on down the tree-lined lane. The tenant farmers had yet to learn of their marriage, and she hoped it would not become common knowledge until they had sailed halfway to Jamaica.

As they approached the Jessups' cottage, Raven decided to seize the opportunity to deal with Paul in a manner that would favorably impress Eden. Clearly her sympathies lay with Mrs. Jessup, and he did not think it would be too difficult to convince Paul that he ought to treat his wife more kindly than he had in the past.

Raven dismounted in the yard, and went to the door while Eden remained by the gate. At his knock, a little girl in a tattered dress opened the door only far enough to peek out, then called for her mother. Isobel Jessup did not appear for a long moment, but when she did, the ugly purple bruise on her right cheek was confirmation enough in Raven's mind that the rumors her husband mistreated her were true.

Isobel's pale blue eyes filled with tears as she looked up at Raven. She knew who he was, but she had never spoken with him. She could not imagine why the new lord of the manor would call at her home, and frightened he had come to tell them to leave, she grabbed for her daughter's hand and pulled her close.

At the other tenants' homes he and Eden had been welcomed so graciously, Raven had not expected to encounter the stark terror that filled Isobel's eyes. "Mrs. Jessup," he began with the most charming smile he could display. "Lady Clairbourne and I will soon be leaving Briarcliff, and we wanted to speak with all our tenants before we leave. Is your husband working nearby?"

"Yes, that is, I think so," Isobel replied in a hoarse whisper. She then bent down to speak to her child, "Mary, go find your father."

As the little girl darted out the doorway, Raven turned to Eden, hoping she would realize he was not to blame for the woman's obvious fright. When Eden gestured for him to come to her, he went back to help her dismount.

"I think things may be even worse here than Elkins imagined," he confided softly.

Eden nodded, then lifted the skirt of her dark green

riding habit and started toward the cottage. "Mrs. Jessup," she called out with a friendly smile.

"Lady Clairbourne," Isobel managed to mumble. She sent an apprehensive glance over her shoulder, certain her home was not nearly fine enough to invite a countess to come inside.

As well as obviously battered, Isobel was painfully thin, but Eden continued to smile as though nothing were amiss. "The morning is so lovely, we're hoping to be able to see everyone on our ride. We can stay only a few minutes so please don't think you must invite us to remain for tea." She bent down to enjoy the fragrance of the single bloom on the withered rose bush that grew beside the door. "I love roses, they remind me of home."

Isobel stared at Eden, her confidence rising when she realized the lovely young woman's smile was genuine. "Roses need more care than I can give them," she apologized, surprised the old bush had again produced a few buds.

"Yes, they are as demanding as children," Eden agreed.

Raven had had frequent opportunities to observe how effectively Eden had charmed Alex. That she could also put a frightened housewife at ease did not surprise him, but it did serve to remind him that he ought to remain on his guard where she was concerned. He listened attentively as, with Eden's encouragement, Isobel shyly described her family as consisting of Mary and four sons who were old enough to help their father in the fields. He thought Isobel might have been a pretty woman once, but the years, as well as Paul Jessup, had not treated her kindly.

Paul soon arrived home accompanied by four scrawny boys in worn and patched clothing. Unlike the rest of his family, who were all quite thin, the man had a brawny build, but was of only average height. Certain he could beat him handily if their conversation came to blows, Raven greeted him as warmly as he had the other tenants and then took him aside so his remarks would not be overheard. Cleverly, he positioned himself so that his back was toward Isobel, Eden, and the children.

"I have no intention of raising the rents Alex set," Raven began, and certain he had Paul's full attention, he lowered his voice as his tone took on a decidedly threatening edge. "But there are conditions you must meet if you wish to continue living here."

"What sort of conditions?" Paul asked with a surly frown.

"I know that you earn a good living, and in the future I'll expect you to spend your money far more wisely. You're the only one here who doesn't look half-starved so it's time you started putting more food on the table. Your wife and children ought not to be clothed like beggars either. Once you put your mind to it, I'm certain you can find a great many things your family needs more than you need to drink yourself into a stupor every night."

Insulted, Paul took a step backward, "The way I spend my money is my own business."

"Not if you want to stay here it isn't," Raven assured him. "There's nothing lower than a man who'll strike a woman and I'll not rent land to you unless you mend your ways. Out of consideration for your wife and family, I'll allow you to remain here, but only on my terms. Make your choice now, because if you're going to leave, it has to be by noon tomorrow."

"Tomorrow!" Paul gasped. "But what about the harvest?"

"You can forget this year's harvest," Raven threatened coldly. Legally, he knew he had no right to throw Jessup off his land when he was not delinquent in his rent, but Raven also knew the man lacked the means to fight the eviction in court. Although he had no respect for land-owners who did not treat their tenants well, in Jessup's case he was prepared to make an exception.

"Make your choice carefully, Mr. Jessup, because if you give me your word that you'll meet my terms but do not, the next time I come to Briarcliff I'll take great pleasure in making you beg for the mercy I'll never show."

Paul Jessup tried to tear his gaze from Raven's but lacked sufficient willpower to do so. He saw the terror of his own expression reflected in the black depths of the young earl's eyes and knew instinctively that Raven was a man of his word. "Every man takes a drink now and then," he whined, "and a good slap don't hurt a woman."

Raven shook his head. "You still don't understand. If you choose to stay, I'm going to leave word at every tavern in Devon that you've bought your last drink, Mr. Jessup. As for your wife and children, you're going to escort them to church every Sunday where they'll be able to show off their new clothes. If every last one of them does not look well and happy, I'm going to hear about it. For every mark you put on them, I'm going to put ten on you, and I'll use a cat-o'-nine-tails to do it."

Paling at that terrifying thought, Paul jammed his hands into his pockets, and tried to think of a way to salvage his pride. The tenants on Briarcliff did far better than those on any of the neighboring estates. The land was fertile, and the rents cheap. Perhaps he did spend a bit too much on whiskey, but that was no reason to throw him off the land he had farmed for twelve years. As for Isobel, as he saw it she deserved a good slap now and then, but it would not be worth it if he got whipped for it later.

"What's your choice, Jessup?"

There was only one that Paul could see. "I'll stay."

"On my terms?"

"Yes!"

"Good." Raven put his arm around Paul's shoulders and walked him over to his wife's side. "I'm very impressed by the changes your husband is about to make in his life, Mrs. Jessup. This will be the first home I'll visit the next time I'm here." As he had at the other cottages, Raven took a moment to place coins in all the children's hands, then took Eden's elbow and guided her back to her mare.

As they rode away, Eden glanced back to wave at Isobel, while Paul glowered and the five children danced about tossing their coins in the air. "What did you say to Jessup?"

Raven briefly recapped their conversation. "I'll make certain that none of the local taverns will serve him, and Reverend Boyer will keep an eye on his family when they come to church. I'll be sure to hear if things aren't going well, and Jessup knows it."

"And you really will do something about it?"

"You don't believe me?" Raven asked in surprise. "Perhaps I should go back and break Jessup's nose or his jaw just to make certain he doesn't have any doubts."

When Raven began to turn his horse around, Eden reached out to grab his sleeve. "Raven! You can't break the man's nose in front of his children!"

"Otherwise you do think I should do it?"

"No!"

"I wish you'd make up your mind," Raven teased with a broad grin.

Eden was exasperated with him, yet she couldn't help but laugh too. "Thank you for not simply ignoring the Jessups' problems. I'm sure a man who drinks to excess and beats his wife must be a coward so he'll not want to cross you."

"Let's hope not or I will make him sincerely sorry."

The rest of the morning's visits went very well. Raven

noticed Eden studying him on several occasions when she thought he wasn't looking and considered that a good sign that he had piqued her interest and perhaps even won a bit of admiration. If he had also improved the lot of Isobel Jessup and her children in the bargain, then so much the better.

At Raven's insistence, Eden rested all afternoon and at dinner she was a far more attentive companion than she had been the previous evening. While she was not nearly as animated as she had always been with Alex, she replied to each of his efforts at conversation with polite interest. He appreciated that courtesy as it gave him hope for their marriage despite the fact he knew she undoubtedly still held grave reservations about the wisdom of it.

As they climbed the stairs to prepare for bed, he did his best not to rush her, but he wanted her so badly he had to fight the impulse to sweep her up into his arms and carry her into his room. Instead, he walked her to her door.

Eden entered her room, and then glanced back over her shoulder. Raven was still standing in the hall, his expression one of such open desire it was almost painful to observe. As he had spoken with their tenants that day, she had seen him display a compassion she had not known he possessed. She hoped that all the discoveries she had yet to make about him would be as good. With an enticing smile, she extended her hand.

"We've only been married one day, Raven. Surely you did not plan to leave me alone tonight."

Raven's heart was pounding so loudly in his ears he wasn't at all sure what Eden had said. What he did understand was the sweetness of her smile and the tenderness of her welcoming gesture. He closed her door behind him, and drew her into his arms to begin what he now knew would be another night of the most incredible pleasure he would ever have. That he did not trust Eden, nor her motives for being such a devoted wife, was the farthest thing from his mind.

Ten

August 1863

Eden stood beside Raven at the port rail as the *Jamaican Wind* sailed out of Lyme Bay. Silhouetted against the morning sun, Briarcliff seemed to glow with a majestic light. As the pale gray stone mansion slowly faded in the distance to no more than a sparkle on the cliff, a lump came to Eden's throat that she could not dislodge. She had spent the happiest month of her life there. She had also buried the dear husband who had made those four brief weeks so memorable.

"I have to go below," she apologized hastily before turning away.

Concerned, Raven laid his hand on her arm. "Are you not feeling well?"

"No, I'm fine. I'm merely tired is all," Eden assured him, but after only a few minutes' rest in his cabin, the anguish of her memories was replaced by an annoying sensation of queasiness. Certain she would feel much better in the fresh air up on deck, she rejoined her new husband.

Raven took Eden's hand and pulled her close. "Did you miss me so terribly that you couldn't stay away?" he asked with a teasing grin.

Too nauseated to appreciate his humor, Eden gulped in the sea-scented air and shook her head. "I needed some air. I never used to get seasick, but I haven't truly felt well since, since . . ."

When she hesitated, Raven readily gathered from her tortured expression what she found impossible to say. "Since Alex died?" he offered softly. "It's no wonder. There are times when I can almost forget we've lost him." He paused a brief instant, as though certain she knew precisely which times those were. "Neither of us will ever forget him, but in time we'll be able to talk about Alex without becoming so badly depressed."

People always said sorrow became easier to bear with time, but Eden doubted that would be true in this case. She was grateful Raven had such an understanding attitude, however, and gave his arm a warm squeeze. She was embarrassed by how badly she had misjudged him. There was far more to the man than the unfavorable impression she had initially formed based solely on his darkly menacing good looks. Why hadn't she had the wisdom to see that?

"I feel better already," she remarked with a shy smile. "Thank you."

"For what?"

"For understanding why I can't always be happy."

Eden's expression was so appealingly innocent Raven could not resist leaning down to kiss her. He kept her by his side for the remainder of the morning, then after they had eaten a light meal at noon, he insisted she take a nap so that she would not become overtired. When he returned to the deck alone, Randy MacDermott approached him almost immediately.

"I think our long friendship gives me the right to speak," he announced with a cocky self-assurance. "I had thought her brave, but it sickens us all to see Lady Clairbourne so comfortable in your arms when Alex has been dead only a week."

Infuriated that the mate thought he had the right to offer such a personal comment, Raven immediately reacted with a hostile glare. He knew he had shocked his friend when he had asked him to be his best man, but he had expected whatever criticism there might be of their hasty marriage to be directed at him rather than Eden. Randy's remark presented an unfortunate eventuality he had not foreseen and that failure alone was enough to anger him.

"Do you realize that duels have been fought over remarks less offensive than yours?" he replied in a challenging hiss.

"Duels?" Randy gasped hoarsely as he began to back away.

"Yes," Raven continued in the same threatening tone, "Lady Clairbourne is my wife and I'll not tolerate a single word spoken against her. How could you have thought otherwise? I don't want to hear another such comment, ever. If I see so little as a frown directed toward my wife, I'll flog the man who wears it and that includes you."

Randy cursed his own stupidity in speaking his thoughts aloud, but he could not help himself. "I meant only to warn you," he insisted.

"Warn me? Of what?"

"Of the type of woman she is. Just look how quickly she betrayed Alex's memory."

When Raven took a step forward, Randy took another step back. Raven then reached out and grabbed the mate's shirtfront to draw him close. "She is a lady," he reminded him coldly. "She hasn't betrayed anyone and she is to be treated with the utmost respect at all times. Our return trip to Jamaica will be the most miserable voyage of your life if you fail to remember that."

Raven had expected gossip aplenty from outsiders, but not from his crew. That Eden was relaxed around him was a source of great pleasure to him and he would not keep his distance to satisfy some ignorant fools' concept of propriety. Damn it, Eden was his wife, and he did not care who knew it! He released Randy with a rude shove and turned his back on him, their conversation over as far as he was concerned, and the mate wisely chose to retreat.

Peter Brady was standing not ten feet away and Raven knew he had to have overheard his argument with Randy. The groom had sailed with them and would ride back to Briarcliff in order to return the mounts he had rented when he had carried the news of Alex's death to London. Rather than ignore the man's presence, Raven walked right over to him. "Does the staff at Briarcliff harbor as uncharitable feelings about my marriage as my crew does?"

"No, my lord, I heard naught a word said against either you or Lady Clairbourne. Briarcliff is your home. None of us would speak ill of you there."

Peter looked so badly embarrassed, Raven dismissed him immediately. Unlike sailors, who could seek work on another ship, the staff of Briarcliff considered the estate their home as well as his. He knew they would not dare criticize his actions for fear of losing their positions, and Peter's words had not been in the least bit reassuring.

When Raven joined Eden in his cabin for supper that night, he was still preoccupied with the dark thoughts Randy's ridiculous criticism had raised. Other than a few distracted smiles, he offered little in the way of company. A loner by nature, he was content without conversation, but he knew he ought to try and make Eden feel welcome on board his ship. He was just not up to making the effort that night.

Eden thoughtfully waited until Raven had finished his

meal before she reached out to take his hand. "Tell me what's wrong," she asked invitingly.

"What could possibly be wrong?" Raven replied with a befuddled frown.

"A problem with the ship or crew perhaps? I'm certain that I know enough about sailing to understand whatever is troubling you."

Raven rejected that offer with a disparaging chuckle. "I doubt there's a captain worthy of the name who seeks advice from his wife on the running of his ship."

Eden had not meant to put Raven on the defensive, and tried to explain herself more clearly. "I'm not offering to give you advice. I merely wanted to give you an opportunity to share your problems with me. I'll be happy to listen, even if I'll not be able to provide any answers. I realize you're not accustomed to discussing your day with a woman, but that doesn't mean it's not a good idea."

Raven studied Eden's face closely as she spoke. As usual, her guileless topaz gaze made her appear sincere in her offer to be a sympathetic companion, but he could scarcely reveal that his crew lacked the intelligence or manners to appreciate her spirit. They did not see her as a woman who had pledged her loyalty to him, but as one who ought to still be in the deepest mourning for Alex. Because she had begged him for more time herself, he would never repeat their complaints to her since she would undoubtedly feel they were justified.

There was another problem which had been weighing heavily on his mind, however, and he decided now was as good a time as any to discuss it. "I've no problem with the ship, but there is something else that's been bothering me."

"What is it?" Eden inquired eagerly, delighted she had convinced him to confide in her.

"Alex asked me to order all the Enfield rifles and Kerr

161

revolvers I could get from the London Armoury. What sort of plan did you two hatch to get them to the Confederacy?"

Astonished by that absurd, if calmly asked, question, Eden's mouth fell agape, but she quickly caught herself and recovered. "I've no idea what you're talking about. Are you positive Alex wanted you to buy guns?"

"Do you want to read that letter too?" Raven's question was accented with the defiantly arched brow she had seen all too often.

"No, I believe you, but honestly I've no idea what Alex's plans were."

"Oh come now," Raven continued in the same skeptical tone. "Alex had little interest in your country's civil war until he met you. With my own ears, I heard you bemoaning the fact England had failed to become the South's ally. Most of the rifles have already been loaded and we'll take delivery on the rest and the revolvers day after tomorrow. I'll honor Alex's promise to you to provide arms, but you'll have to explain how they're to be delivered as I'll not risk my ship nor the lives of my crew attempting to run the Union's blockade of Southern ports."

"Raven, I have absolutely no idea what Alex planned to do!" When the dark-eyed young man's cold stare did not waver, she slammed her clenched fist down on the table for emphasis. "Why are you doing this to me again? You can be so wonderfully considerate at times, and then you turn around and accuse me of some preposterous act like contemplating suicide, or willfully endangering Alex's life, or masterminding a plot to supply weapons to the Confederacy. If all I'd wanted was guns, I would have brought gold with me to buy them when I came to England and they would have been purchased and shipped last fall. I'd certainly not have waited until I married, which I never expected to do, and asked my husband to support the Confederacy with his wealth."

Raven had pushed her as far as he dared as he did not want to ever see her hysterical again. Her face was flushed, her breathing a trifle too rapid, and he lowered his voice to a soothing whisper so as not to upset her any further. "I know that I tend to be a great deal more direct than good manners generally allows, but we are husband and wife and I think we should always be honest with each other."

"So do I, and I have always told you the truth," Eden protested, "but unfortunately I have no control over whether or not you believe me. In this instance it should be obvious that if I'd known about the guns, and had a means to deliver them, I'd tell you. Why would I deny it? That doesn't make any sense at all. I worked in one of the hospitals in Richmond before my parents made the decision to send me to live with Aunt Lydia. I saw too many boys die because the only weapons they had were the rusty old muskets they'd brought from home when they enlisted." Eden choked on her tears at the sadness of that memory, and held up her hand in a silent plea for a moment in which to compose herself.

"I'm sorry. Alex and I talked about this too," she then revealed. "But I never asked, nor expected, him to take matters into his own hands."

Unmoved, Raven's frown did not lift. "I'll admit your outraged denials appear very convincing, but they simply don't match the facts, Eden. Alex managed his investments cautiously. It was precisely because he was such a prudent man that the Clairbourne fortune multiplied so rapidly during his stewardship. He would have been the last man on earth to begin dealing in munitions on his own. He had to have begun such an enterprise to please you."

"Perhaps he did," Eden admitted reluctantly, fearing Raven would be quick to use that admission against her. "We talked about the War frequently, but I swear I never asked him to contribute to our cause."

"Are you suggesting he meant to surprise you? Could he have planned to say something like, 'Oh by the way, my darling, the hold is filled with arms for your beloved Confederacy'?"

Raven had not only given a perfect imitation of Alex's voice, but he threw in one of her late husband's gestures as well. That he had done it so easily both frightened and appalled Eden. "How dare you make fun of what Alex and I shared? We loved each other desperately. Can't you understand that? Alex might have done any number of things in hopes of pleasing me, but I did not ask him to purchase weapons."

Raven already knew his attitudes toward Eden were contradictory, but that was not surprising when his feelings about her were ambivalent at best. He was enchanted with the seductive side of her nature, for the abundant affection she wantonly provided gave him the greatest pleasure he had ever known. It was her intentions that he did not trust. At best, he saw her as selfishly putting her own needs before Alex's. At worse, she was a manipulative bitch who had maliciously hastened his uncle's death to fill her own purse, or the Confederate treasury. Somehow that struck him as being an even worse crime.

"I was not making fun of Alex," he denied hotly. "All I'm trying to do is get to the bottom of this. But to save us both any further frustration, let's drop the subject of why Alex chose to become an arms dealer, and decide how we're to get the blasted guns to your people."

Eden sat back in her chair, for once her gaze as suspicious as Raven's. "What is it you want, a list of sympathetic Englishmen in the Caribbean who might be inspired to deliver the guns for a cut of the profits?"

"I already know who's running the blockades, Eden," Raven responded with another derisive shake of his head. "I'm not trying to trick you into betraying them."

"I've been away from home for nearly a year. I know only what's been printed in the London papers, and that's not in sufficient detail to make any such plans."

Realizing he was getting nowhere, Raven excused himself, got up from the table to pour himself some of Briarcliff's blackberry brandy, and brought one back to the table for Eden. "Alex could be counted upon to help anyone who needed it. Even if you did not specifically ask him to provide weapons, your enthusiasm for your cause would have prompted him to do it. What we need to do now is figure out a way to recover Alex's investment and see the Confederate troops get their much-needed arms."

Eden wiped her eyes on the back of her hand before responding. "You'll not take back your allegation that I somehow influenced Alex to buy the guns?"

Raven was thoroughly exasperated with her protestations of innocence, but he remained unconvinced. "Let's not argue the point any further. We've already paid for the guns, regardless of how the purchase came about, and the real problem is how to unload them at a profit."

"Are you always so practical?" Eden asked in a stunning imitation of the sarcastic tone he resorted to so often. She was certain she would never understand him. He had insulted her deeply, but rather than apologize, he simply wanted to discuss how they would turn a profit on what he had chosen to view as a business deal rather than a noble effort to aid the Confederacy. In her opinion, leaping over issues in such a fashion was no way to settle them. It was plain in his expression that he did not believe a word she said, and she was swiftly learning that he hurt her far too often for her to trust him.

"Always," Raven replied proudly, for he considered the practical aspects of his nature a valuable asset. "Do you feel up to going up on deck for a few minutes? Perhaps some fresh air will inspire some much-needed ideas."

Although she had slept all afternoon, Eden still felt weary. "No, I'd rather just go to bed and continue this discussion at another time," she suggested, although she doubted Raven would ever be in a more reasonable mood. Now in a terrible mood herself, she longed to be left alone. The taste of the blackberry brandy brought back the most erotic of her memories, and she wanted to be alone with them.

"Alex must have had his own cabin. Would you mind if I used it tonight?"

"Yes, I most certainly would. Have you forgotten what I said on our wedding night? I don't care how bitter our arguments become, I'll always want you."

Eden took another sip of brandy to stall for time, but could think of no way to change Raven's mind. "You are a very strange man, Raven."

Both pleased and puzzled that she had spoken in such a reasonable tone, Raven took a deep breath, and let it out slowly. "Strange? I've been called many things, but never that. In what way do you consider me strange?"

"You seem to think you can insult me in any way you choose and then be welcome in my bed."

"The only bed available tonight happens to be mine, my lady, and I'll always do my best to make you feel welcome in it."

Eden looked up at him, and rebelling against the smugness of his smile, both her gaze and expression became defiant. "And if I do not choose to be made welcome?"

Raven broke into a wide grin. "I'll consider it a challenge to change your mind, and you already know how easily I can do it," he bragged confidently.

Disgusted with that boast, Eden refused to back down. "There seems to be only one thing about me that you like, and you can get that elsewhere."

Raven took the precaution of setting his brandy snifter down on the table before he stepped to Eden's side and yanked her to her feet. Holding her pressed tightly against his chest, he emphatically refused that insulting suggestion. "You are my wife, Eden, and I will be as faithful to you as Alex would have been. Would you have refused his affection, or told him to sleep with whores?"

Shocked that he would compare himself to Alex, Eden turned her head away. "He loved me," she reminded him. "It's plain that you never will."

"Never is an exceedingly long time."

"Not nearly long enough where you are concerned," Eden vowed darkly.

As disgusted with her as she was with him, Raven dropped his hands to his sides, then turned and went out the door. He closed it softly behind him, but he was seething all the same. He was well aware that he lacked the warmth to inspire the devotion Alex had always received from women, but if Eden thought she could shut him out of her bedroom, she would soon learn just how mistaken she was.

Eden grabbed for the back of her chair to steady herself, but that did not serve to stop the dizziness that had enveloped her when Raven had jerked her to her feet. From her past experience with him, she thought him far too proud of his talents at seduction to force himself on her, but the thought of having to make love with him later that night truly sickened her. He cared nothing for her—she was merely convenient, that was all. That he had once

167

served exactly the same purpose for her was more than she could bear to admit.

The return voyage to London was an easy one. Raven was not needed on deck but he remained there until midnight anyway. He had never struck a woman, and had no intention of beginning with his wife, but as long as he was angry enough to strangle her, he wisely stayed away. When he at last returned to his cabin, Eden had been asleep for several hours. He had half expected her to hurl the bottle of brandy at him as he came through the door, and it was a relief to find she had not waited up to confront him anew.

As he undressed, Raven was sorry their second day of marriage had not ended on a better note. Not expecting her to deny all knowledge of the order Alex had wanted placed with the Armoury, he had again made the mistake of speaking his mind without considering what Eden's reaction would be. Damn it all, he swore to himself, a man ought not to have to watch every word that he spoke to his wife.

As he eased himself into the cabin's single bunk, he considered his crew's opinion dead wrong. To them Eden might have appeared to have switched her affections to him with shocking speed, but in reality she was still Alex's wife, and it seemed now that she always would be. He had not wanted a wife, and now it seemed to Raven that fate had granted his wish in the cruelest of ways.

Saddened by how poorly they were getting along, he drew Eden into his arms and made himself as comfortable as possible without waking her. He wished she were half as warm and pliant when she was awake as when she was asleep. Even in her dreams her pose was such a graceful one he could not help but want to snuggle close, but it was a long while before he fell asleep when he dreaded what the next day would bring.

Eden awakened as Raven left the cabin the following morning. He had closed the door quietly, but she had still heard it swing shut. She sat up slowly, but the nausea that had plagued her the previous morning returned in a sickening wave that sent her right back to the comfort of the blankets and pillows. After lying still for a moment, the feeling abated slightly, but she was positive it was not the rolling motion of the ship which had upset her stomach for she now recalled that the same queasiness had greeted her upon waking several mornings at Briarcliff. She had blamed it on her grief then, and Raven's stubborn persistence in occupying her bed, but now she recognized that might not be the case.

She could think of only one likely possibility that would cause a woman to feel so wretched upon awaking. She and Alex had made love often during their brief marriage, but they had not once considered the possibility of her conceiving his child. It was an overwhelming thought even now, and Eden's eyes filled with tears as she realized Alex would never know he had fathered a child. That would be heartbreaking, but at the same time, Eden knew she wanted Alex's child with a desperation she had never before known.

Believing she had had ample opportunity to become pregnant, Eden sat up more slowly this time. After a brief struggle, she gained control of her rebellious stomach and rose to her feet. Making her way to her luggage with cautious steps, she was not too dizzy to search through her belongings for her diary. Her own body's rhythm had always followed as predictable a sequence as the moon, until that very month. She counted the days twice to make certain she had not made an error in her calculations, and just as she had suspected, her monthly flow was overdue by a week.

Had the tragedy of Alex's death upset her body as greatly as it had her heart and mind? That seemed possible, but she did not want it to be the case. The door swung open then, and Raven strode in carrying a teapot and basket of hot biscuits. Eden quickly clutched the small leather bound volume to her breast as though it contained her deepest secrets rather than only a listing of social engagements and a personal calendar.

"I thought you might want some breakfast." He placed the items he had brought on the table before turning to face her. Then noting her bewildered expression, he pulled out a chair. "I think you'd better sit down if you're not feeling any better than you look."

Eden swept her hair out of her eyes with a nervous flip, slid into the chair he had offered, and hid her diary in her lap. She watched him bring cups, a sugar bowl, and spoons from one of the cabin's many ingeniously designed cupboards and debated whether or not she ought to confide her suspicions in him. He was very bright. How long would it take him to realize she felt ill only in the mornings? Regardless of when that was, she knew he would promptly accuse her of lying to him for keeping such an important matter a secret. Maybe every recent widow felt as awful as she did, and hoped she was pregnant, so she did not want to share her suspicions for another few weeks. How long did a woman usually wait before announcing such news to her husband, one month, two?

She could imagine no greater comfort than having Alex's child to raise, but she had no idea what Raven would say to that. He had loved Alex too—would he be happy for her, or merely grow increasingly more infuriated as his pretty bedmate's figure took on the proportions of incipient motherhood? That she did not know the man well enough to judge his reaction saddened her greatly.

Amazed by the wide variety of emotions passing in fleeting moments across Eden's delicate features, Raven wasted no time in meaningless pleasantries. "I expected you to be relieved I didn't disturb your sleep last night, but that consideration doesn't seem to have improved either your spirits or your health. You needn't play the invalid on my account, but if you're truly ill, I'll summon a physician as soon as we dock this afternoon."

It was too soon for a doctor to confirm her pregnancy, so Eden had no interest in seeing one. "This last week has been extremely difficult for us both. I'm sorry that I haven't your strength, but I'm sure I'll survive without a doctor's attentions."

Raven poured their tea and took the seat beside her. "All right, I trust you to know what's best. We'll spend only a couple of days in London, but if you'd like to move into the townhouse, I'll arrange it."

Eden frowned slightly, not truly understanding his question. "Are you asking if I want to go there alone rather than stay on board the *Jamaican Wind* with you?"

With her rumpled nightgown and unruly mop of curls, Eden looked as childlike as she sounded, inspiring Raven to make a valiant effort to hold his temper. "No, that's not the choice at all. The both of us will either stay on board, or go to the townhouse. I have no intention of sending you off by yourself."

Eden added a spoonful of sugar to her tea, and took a sip, but it was too hot to drink yet and she quickly set her cup back down. She seemed to constantly be apologizing to the man, and after the easy rapport she had had with Alex, that was deeply troubling. "I didn't mean to upset you again, Raven. It was completely unintentional. Please don't think that I do it on purpose."

That would be too fiendish a practice even for her, in Raven's view, and he reached out to pat her hand lightly. "I'm not upset. I just don't want you to be confused. I want us to live as husband and wife just as we did at Briarcliff, not like some estranged couple who can barely tolerate each other."

Eden sighed softly, thinking them far closer to being estranged than happily married. "Alex loved and trusted you, Raven, and I'm trying to do the same, but it's awfully difficult when you don't trust me."

"Trust isn't something that can be won overnight, Eden. Now you didn't answer me. Which is it to be, do you want to stay on board, or go to the townhouse tonight?"

Eden did not want the memory of the one night she had spent there with Alex, their wedding night, ruined as she feared an inevitable fight with Raven would surely do. "I'd rather just stay on board if you don't mind. It will save us the trouble of packing our things again for such a short stay."

Delighted to find she also had a practical side, Raven began to smile. "I agree. Speaking of your things, I'll send a note to your aunt in the morning, and if she's free in the afternoon we'll stop by for a brief visit and pick up your trunks."

"Oh Raven, do you really think that we dare?"

Raven had completely forgotten he had warned Eden her reception at her aunt's home would not be warm. A clever man, he caught the intent of her question immediately and provided an appropriate answer. "Even if you had not left so many of your clothes there, we would still owe her the courtesy of a call before we sail to Jamaica. She will undoubtedly have heard about Alex's death, and that ought to ensure that she'll at least be civil. I was worried you would not be made to feel welcome if you

172

asked to return to her home. Our visit will be another matter altogether and shouldn't be too taxing for any of us."

"And when she learns we have married?" Eden asked shyly.

"I think we'd better save that announcement for when we are walking out the door." Raven knew that news would easily create a scandal that would far outlast her mother's elopement with an American. The excruciatingly well-mannered Lady Lawton would probably faint dead away, but that could not be helped. He started to laugh then, even though he knew Eden would never understand why.

Eden stared at her husband, shocked he could find anything humorous in what she knew would be an uncomfortable situation at best. Then she realized she had never really seen him laugh in such a lighthearted fashion. On numerous occasions he had used sarcastic laughter to taunt her, but that was not his purpose now. He was simply enjoying himself, and to her own amazement, she found she enjoyed watching him.

As Raven's deep laughter echoed against the cabin's teak paneling, Eden continued to study him. She had been thrilled by his rare smiles, but she had never before noticed that his lips had an appealing rose tint as though he had just finished a glass of burgundy or port. That she had kissed those lips with all the passion that still filled her heart made her blush.

At last Raven noticed the confusion in Eden's glance and, as usual, misread the cause. "I wasn't laughing at your aunt," he hastened to explain. "It's just that her kind is always more concerned with appearance than the truth so they are quite easily shocked."

"That's true," Eden agreed, for she had soon learned appearances meant far more to Lydia and Stephanie than they ever had to her. Her attention had been focused so closely on him she had completely forgotten about her aunt, though. When she found him staring at her with an equal intensity, she was horribly embarrassed.

"Oh I must look awful!" she complained in a helpless squeal. She had not paused to wash her face or brush her hair before searching for her diary. She had then been so lost in the thoughts of a child when Raven had entered the cabin that she had forgotten all about her appearance. That was an oversight that appalled her now.

Eden's sudden dismay sent Raven into another burst of hearty laughter. "You still look beautiful, even if your grooming does leave a little to be desired. But what difference does that make? I'm your husband and you needn't worry about how you look when you're with me. Would you like to bathe before you dress? If the cook isn't simmering soup in our tub, I'll bring it right in for you."

"You and your men bathe in a tub the cook uses for soup?" Such an unhygienic practice made Eden shudder. "Please remind me never to taste his soup."

Despite the elegance of her manners, Eden displayed a remarkable innocence at times. Her lashes had nearly swept her brows as she had apparently imagined him and his crew dining on vegetables cooked in dirty bath water. "I'm teasing you," he readily admitted. "The tub is only used for bathing, never for cooking. It was just a joke. I wanted to make you laugh too."

"Am I supposed to be flattered by that?" Eden asked, still disconcerted by his peculiar sense of humor.

Eden looked insulted rather than amused, and Raven grabbed a biscuit as he rose to attend to the promised errand. He leaned down to kiss her cheek, then left before he was tempted to push his luck any further.

"Strange man," Eden whispered to herself. He could be

direct to the point of cruelty. He had a terrible temper, but he certainly didn't brood over their disagreements. He would just go off by himself and the next time she saw him, more often than not, he would tease her as though no angry words had ever passed between them.

"It must be a trick of some kind," she mused with a perplexed frown, "some sort of bizarre strategy." She picked up her diary, and took care when she left the table. She still did not feel truly well, though, and nibbled a biscuit as she made up the bunk, hoping that having something more than tea in her stomach would be a help, and it was. She would just have to remember to move more slowly in the mornings, and pray she did not feel so ill she could not hide it until a babe was a certainty rather than merely a fond desire. She had absolutely no idea how she would reveal such monumentous news to Raven, but hoped by the time she had to do so, she would know him well enough to be able to do it in a manner that would make him as proud as she was sure to be.

Eleven

August 1863

As the day progressed, Eden was pleased to find Raven retained his good humor. She soon discovered it was the prospect of returning to Jamaica that had him in such an expansive mood. While his conversation at supper was again limited, he did not make another of his absurd accusations and she was too grateful for that to feel slighted that he made no effort to keep her constantly amused as Alex had.

They had reached London in late afternoon and she could hear the noisy traffic along the docks as she prepared for bed. Raven had again excused himself and gone up on deck, and when he had not returned in what Eden considered a reasonable length of time, she began to become concerned about him. Her worry soon turned to anger when it appeared he did not plan to return to his cabin at all that night. Disgusted to think he had abandoned her in favor of more amusing pursuits available along the waterfront, she climbed into his bunk and yanked the covers up to her chin.

She had suggested he seek out other women, and despite his emphatic refusal to do so at the time, where else could he have gone? If everything went well on the morrow, this might be their last night in London for some time. Had Raven chosen to make good use of it? She had been hurt and angry when she had accused him of being interested in her for only one reason. She had never made such a petty, vengeful remark in her entire life, but she had never before been so sorely provoked either.

Raven was not the only one with a temper, it seemed, but they continually brought out the worst in each other. Hot tears of frustration welled up in her eyes and she tried to blink them away. It was pointless to complain she did not understand her husband well enough to get along with him. The fact was Raven was her husband and she did not want him involved with other women, be it prostitutes who plied their trade along the docks or a pampered mistress in Jamaica.

Fuming over Raven's prolonged absence, Eden gave free rein to her imagination. She knew him to have not only a young man's natural appetite for making love, but the necessary stamina to sate that desire as often as he wished. For all she knew, he might have two or three women in bed that very minute rather than only one!

Thinking he had again given Eden sufficient time to fall asleep, Raven opened the door to his cabin slowly. He stepped in, pulled the door shut, then walked quietly to the cupboard that held the blackberry brandy. It wasn't until he had poured himself some and taken a sip that he glanced toward his bunk and saw Eden observing him with a darkly threatening glance.

"I'm sorry I woke you. I tried to be quiet."

Despite the tardiness of his return, Raven did not look in the least bit guilty to Eden. His clothes were not wrinkled as though they had recently lain on the floor of some loose woman's room. He did not reek of cheap perfume.

His hair was slightly windblown, but that was to be expected if he had spent the last couple of hours up on deck.

"I wasn't asleep," she informed him coolly, trying to hide the anxiety he had caused her and failing rather badly.

Raven noted her preoccupied frown and cautiously remained where he stood. "I hope you've not been worrying about how your aunt and cousin will respond to our visit tomorrow. There's just no way we can leave for home without telling them goodbye. Your wardrobe can be replaced easily enough, but I don't want anyone to get the mistaken impression that we're too ashamed of ourselves to show our faces in public."

He was providing the perfect excuse for her wakefulness, but Eden was in no mood to take it. "I'd planned to worry about Lydia and Stephanie tomorrow. It's you I've been worrying about tonight."

Confused by that remark since he had gone out of his way to be pleasant all day, Raven responded with a helpless shrug. "I can take care of myself. Why would you be worried about me?"

Thinking this conversation was going to be a long one, Eden sat up and made herself comfortable. "Did you mean what you said about being faithful to me?"

Raven downed the remainder of his brandy in a single gulp as he attempted to figure out why she had asked him such a ridiculous question, and why now of all times? It had been his experience that women were never direct. Even when they asked what appeared to be a direct question, the answer they truly wanted was never the most obvious one. What was Eden after then, some heartfelt vow of devotion? If so, he knew he would have to disappoint her.

"If I hadn't meant that, I wouldn't have said it in the

178

first place. I think you must have noticed by now that I'm not given to idle chatter."

"Do you think that I am?" Eden asked, fearing he had meant to insult her again.

"No, thank God, that's why I married you."

"No it isn't," Eden promptly pointed out, but she was too proud to cite the passion each aroused in the other as the reason.

"Is that what you've been brooding over tonight? That I've been forced into a marriage I'm bound to regret?"

"Not exactly," Eden admitted. Unconsciously she had tied the corner of the blanket in a knot and embarrassed to have displayed her inner turmoil so clearly, she smoothed out the covers and folded her hands in her lap.

"It's rather late for guessing games," Raven warned as he approached his bunk. He sat down on the end and pulled off his boots. "Since you asked if I were sincere about being faithful to you, is that what you've been worrying about?"

It was a question that had never crossed her mind with Alex, but Alex had seldom let five minutes pass without telling her that he loved her. Oh how she missed that! A single tear slid down her cheek and she hurriedly brushed it away. "I miss Alex terribly," she confessed softly. "It's very different being married to you. I fear that we'll never be as close as Alex and I were, and I don't want to settle for anything less."

Neither do I, Raven thought to himself. The first couple of times they had made love, he had thought that their passion for each other would bind her to him, but she had changed somehow and he had become determined to make her want him. If she was worried that he might be unfaithful, did that mean that she already did? Jealousy had to mean she felt something for him, but he rebelled at the thought she wanted him to be faithful to her while she spent her time weeping over Alex.

Raven rose to his feet and began to unbutton his shirt. "I think you expect too much from me too soon. I know I rushed you into marrying me, but don't you make the mistake of trying to rush me into being as adoring as Alex was. I might not ever be capable of it." Raven knew that was a long way from the truth when just looking at Eden made his blood race. It did not matter if she was wearing the finest satin or a sleep-rumpled nightgown or, best of all, nothing. He'd be damned if he'd make a fool of himself by admitting that to her though.

Eden did not know how to reply to a man who had just said he might never love her. She lay back down and moved over as far as she could to give him plenty of room, but when he joined her, he turned on his side with his back toward her. Knowing him to be a hot-blooded man rather than a cold one, Eden did not know what to make of his aloof pose. He had refused to allow her to sleep in Alex's cabin, but sharing a narrow bunk with a man who wanted to avoid her seemed ridiculous in the extreme. It made her feel even more lost and alone than she had when she had imagined him being with another woman.

"Raven," she called as she moved close and slipped her arm around his waist. "Couldn't you at least hold me?"

Rather than turn to face her, Raven merely laced his fingers in hers so that she could not move away. "I wouldn't stop there," he confided, thinking that if she wanted him, she would tell him that he needn't stop, but she did not speak again. She lay curled against his back and did not pull her hand from his, but she did not utter so much as a tiny moan that he could have construed as being a word of encouragement or acceptance.

Bitterly disappointed, he began to wonder if he had not made an incredibly stupid blunder by giving her a choice.

When he had not given her one, she had returned his affection eagerly, but as soon as he had backed off, she had lost interest in him. Had Alex been able to make sense out of the actions of such a contrary female? Probably, he surmised, but of the many skills Alex had taught him, he had never mastered any of his uncle's lessons in charm.

Instead, he had been perfectly content being a brash, headstrong rake, at least until that summer he had. Now he wished he had watched Alex more closely so he could have learned his far more gentlemanly techniques. The trouble was, the only woman Alex had attempted to charm had been Eden, and whenever the four of them had been together, Raven had not heard a single word that his uncle had said he had been so fascinated by his attractive blond companion.

Eden could feel the tension drain from Raven when he finally fell asleep, but she lay awake far longer. She wished she could ask her mother for advice, and overwhelmed with homesickness for her parents, it was all she could do not to sob out loud. That was the problem, she realized—all her thoughts led inevitably to sorrow. Alex's death, Raven's perplexingly perverse personality, the war that kept her from returning to those she loved, everything she cared about caused her pain.

Now she was sorry she had not pretended to be asleep when Raven had entered his cabin, for she was certain he would have embraced her as he fell asleep. What did that mean? Did he like her better when she was asleep than awake? Fearing she was making herself more sick with worry than she would already feel in the morning, Eden forced herself to breathe deeply and contemplate nothing but dreamless sleep, but a long while passed before she was successful.

* * *

Raven placed his hand over Eden's in a comforting clasp as they climbed the steps of the Lawton townhouse the following afternoon. She was clinging to his arm with a fierce grasp that revealed the true feelings her sweet smile failed to disguise. He knew he was partly to blame for her fright, but her imagination had clearly supplied a more vivid picture of a horrid confrontation than even he had predicted.

"Wait a minute." Raven paused as they reached the door. "If your aunt does not have the courtesy to treat us well, we'll leave immediately. I'll not subject you to a moment's unpleasantness. You have my word on that."

Raven wore such a determined frown Eden did not doubt him for an instant. "I'm not in the least bit ashamed for eloping with Alex, or marrying you, so nothing my aunt can possibly say is going to bother me. Nothing will never hurt me as much as Alex's death has, and a person can only feel so much pain. All I feel now is numb. I just want to get this over with as quickly as possible."

She looked tired as well as sad, and taking her at her word, Raven gave the large brass doorknocker several loud raps. "This is the first time we've appeared in London as Lord and Lady Clairbourne. Let's hope it does not prove to be a ill omen."

When the butler swung open the heavy oak door, there was not the slightest sign of trepidation in Eden's expression as she stepped over the threshold. Admiring her courage, Raven followed her inside. As they were shown into the drawing room, he saw Lydia glance at Eden's gray gown and stylish bonnet and wince, as though the sight of her recently widowed niece in anything but jet black was actually painful. Stephanie rushed to his side then, and he had to brace himself in order to hide his disgust at her touch.

Stephanie gave Eden only a hasty kiss in passing before

she threw herself into Raven's arms. "We are so dreadfully sorry about Alex. By the time we learned of his death, we knew we could not possibly arrive at Briarcliff in time to attend his funeral, so there was no point in our making the trip."

"We would have appreciated your expressions of sympathy, regardless of when you arrived," Raven instructed her coldly. It had not even occurred to him until then, but as Eden's close relatives, he really should have invited them to make the trip to Devon with him. Doubting their presence would have been any help to anyone, he decided that oversight had definitely worked in his favor.

"My darling," Lydia cooed as she gave Eden a brief hug. "I sent a letter to Briarcliff only yesterday beseeching you to come back to us. You'll not be expected to accept any invitations, of course, but we'll need to have some suitable mourning attire made for you immediately. Once Alex's friends learn you're here, they'll want to pay sympathy calls. I already had your trunks packed, but surely you don't want to move them to Alex's townhouse. I know your mother would want you to remain here with us."

Raven managed to elude Stephanie's possessive grasp and moved to Eden's side. He exchanged a brief greeting with Lydia and then waited until the ladies had all been seated before he took the chair next to Eden's. Stephanie had taken a place on a small settee and patted the cushion beside hers invitingly, but he pretended not to have noticed. He and Alex had been at the Lawtons' for tea on several occasions, but he had never been at ease. Now he felt a surprising sense of calm that bordered on elation and he could barely keep from grinning from ear to ear although he knew Lydia would consider it highly inappropriate.

"Thank you so much, Aunt Lydia, but I really can't

come back here to live." Eden accepted a cup of tea, but quickly set it upon the rosewood table at her side.

Lydia leaned forward as her tone became more insistent. "Listen to me carefully, child. Alex's untimely death has shocked and saddened everyone. In a few years the, shall we say, unusual circumstances of your marriage will be overshadowed by that tragedy. You might even have the opportunity to remarry one day. Why, in time, the War Between the States will surely end and you can return home. Your whole tragic stay in London can be forgotten then."

Uncertain where to begin her response when all of her aunt's remarks were unwelcome, Eden glanced first at Raven. He nodded, giving her all the encouragement she required to speak her mind. "Raven told me you'd been embarrassed by our elopement, and I'm very sorry for that but it couldn't be helped. Alex knew he didn't have long to live, and it would have taken months to plan a formal wedding. Time was very precious to us, and we didn't want to squander a second of it even if our behavior was viewed as highly unconventional. It didn't matter to us, but I am truly sorry for any embarrassment you might have suffered."

While Lydia was clearly shocked by that news, she quickly recovered. "Alex knew he was dying?"

"Yes, but it was the time he had to live that mattered most to us."

Lydia's eyes brightened, and she again moved slightly forward on her chair as she glanced toward her daughter. "That's a wonderfully romantic story, Eden. I'll see that it's soon common knowledge as it makes your elopement appear noble rather than reckless."

"It's not merely a romantic story, Aunt Lydia, it's the truth."

Lydia waved that comment aside as though it were unimportant. "Yes, yes, of course it is. The fact that it's so compelling a truth just makes it all the better. If we manage things properly now, I do believe we shall be able to salvage your reputation."

"Aunt Lydia, really—"

"You are so innocent at times, Eden. Don't you know that whenever a couple marries as hurriedly as you and Alex did, the rumors immediately begin to fly that the man was forced to make an honest woman of her?"

Eden felt her cheeks redden with a bright blush, but if her child was even one day premature she feared those rumors would begin circulating anew, and with a tiny babe in her arms, there would be no way to refute them. She would not care what anyone said about her, but the prospect of Alex's good name being dragged through the mud when he would be unable to defend himself was deeply troubling.

"We were well aware there might be malicious gossip about us, but we refused to allow it to taint the joy of our love. I hope that if anyone were so rude as to mention such scandalous suspicions to you, you did not dignify them with a response."

"No one dared say it to our faces, Eden, but it was what everyone was thinking, and I mean absolutely everyone," Stephanie promptly revealed, her mouth set in an unbecoming pout.

"Hush," Lydia scolded her daughter. "What's done is done, but now that we know Alex was in poor health, we can use that excuse to squelch any rumors that weren't quelled by his death. Thank God most people still have the manners not to speak ill of the dead but we can't give them anything new to talk about. That's why it's imperative that you return here to live. You can't possibly reside in Alex's townhouse. Raven is far too attractive a man not

185

to start the worst sort of gossip circulating about the two of you if you shared the same house."

It had been clear to Raven from the moment Lydia had begun to speak that she cared not at all about their grief at Alex's death. All that concerned her was maintaining her own spotless reputation and that of her spoiled daughter. Lydia was not about to allow Eden the independence her marriage to Alex should have won her. Instead, she obviously planned to take her niece in hand and manipulate her actions as a puppeteer did those of his marionettes. Thoroughly disgusted with her, he had heard more than enough.

"I think not," Raven informed Lydia with a confident smirk he could not contain. "Eden is now my wife."

"Your wife!" Stephanie sputtered through a mouthful of tea, then still attempting to catch her breath she rose awkwardly to her feet. "Eden, tell us that isn't true! Surely you would not have married him when you knew that I, well, you simply can't have married Raven!"

"Sit down!" Lydia commanded firmly, but it took several such orders to silence her daughter's hysterical outbursts and even then Stephanie sat whimpering unhappily.

Lydia fixed her niece with a fiercely hostile stare. "When I lost my dear Harold five years ago, I knew I'd never want to remarry. You are a far younger woman, however, but I can't believe you would remarry with such shocking haste. A year of mourning is considered the absolute minimum, a fact of which I'm sure you are well aware. Although you've already demonstrated little regard for our feelings, you must know your parents would never approve. Now what is this nonsense about marriage?"

Seeing no reason to involve her parents in the discussion, Eden wanted only to convey the truth and leave. "It's not nonsense, Aunt Lydia. Raven and I were married before we left Briarcliff," she announced with a pride she had not expected to feel.

With an anguished wail, Stephanie again lunged from her chair, and screaming and clawing, she went for Eden. Raven, however, had anticipated the hostility of her reaction and deftly moved to block her way. He grabbed her around the waist and simply swung her aside, then remained standing to prevent any further attempts to do physical harm to his bride. "I may have escorted you to several parties, Stephanie, but I never gave you any indication my feelings for you were as warm as those Alex held for Eden. You had no claim on me, and you have no cause to insult your cousin. I expect you to apologize to her immediately."

"Stephanie is not the one who ought to apologize!" Lydia declared harshly. "But first, who knows of this wedding?"

"Everyone at Briarcliff, my crew," Raven replied without taking his eyes off Stephanie, who was struggling to regain the dignity she had lost when she had again humiliated herself by speaking her feelings for him aloud.

Greatly relieved to hear that, Lydia rushed on with her plans. "No one of any consequence knows of it then. That's a stroke of luck we shan't waste. Your crew and the staff at Briarcliff will have to be paid immediately for their silence. Should any of them ever mention a wedding, we can simply deny that it took place. Our word will be believed over that of servants, peasants, or merchant seamen.

"You'll come here to live this very day, Eden, and live the quiet, contemplative life of a devoted widow until this time next year. You'll return to Jamaica, Raven, and no one need ever learn of this disgrace. My attorney will have the marriage discreetly annulled. It's the only way. Now when can you be ready to sail, Raven? The sooner

187

you leave London, the better." Without waiting for him to reply, Lydia turned to her niece. "I'll send for my dress-maker in the morning, and . . ."

Raven shot Eden a frantic glance for he knew she was not pleased to be his wife, but he had not thought there would be any way for her to get out of their marriage. Now that her aunt had provided one, he held his breath, dreading what her answer would be.

The look of absolute horror that had flashed across Raven's face mirrored the burst of pain that filled Eden's heart. She had told him she was too numb to feel another hurt, but she had been wrong. The prospect of losing him was a surprisingly painful one. "We married because it was what Alex wanted," she explained, as though that were the only reason. "That Raven has sacrificed whatever dreams he had of finding a wife to care for me is a noble gesture, not a disgraceful one. You'll not separate us, Aunt."

As Lydia's face filled with rage at that bit of defiance, Eden continued as though her comments had been calmly accepted. "Now I'd like to summon our driver and foot-man to carry my trunks out to our carriage. We'll be returning to Jamaica in a day or two, and I doubt we'll ever see each other again. While I appreciate all that you did for me while I was here, I can't allow you to do anything more."

Raven grabbed Eden's hand, and they hurried from the room before Lydia could draw the breath to scream the vile names each was certain had already come to the woman's mind. They could hear Stephanie sobbing that she had been betrayed, but neither was moved by the spoiled young woman's complaints.

"I still think I should make her apologize to you," Raven said. He opened the front door without waiting for the butler to do so, and gestured for the men from the carriage.

"It's not worth the effort," Eden assured him, but she was grateful when her aunt slammed shut the sliding doors of the drawing room so that they did not have to listen to Stephanie wail about how her American cousin had stolen the only man she had ever loved.

Her trunks were soon loaded on the carriage, and Eden breathed a sigh of relief as they rode away from her aunt's townhouse for what would definitely be the last time. "I've always thought my parents made a terrible mistake in sending me here, and now I'm sure my aunt and cousin agree."

"You'd never have met Alex had you stayed in Richmond." Or me, Raven thought, but he knew better than to include his own name.

"No," Eden assured him. "Somehow I would have met Alex. It was our destiny to be together." She just wished it could have been for far longer.

Raven greeted that remark with a puzzled frown, and Eden decided not to pursue it. "You thought I might choose to stay with Lydia, didn't you?" Her voice was filled with wonder, as though such a belief had been preposterous.

Embarrassed that his thoughts had been so transparent, Raven was again disgusted with himself for not having foreseen just how dangerous a visit to Lydia might have been. "I expected her to either be reserved and withdrawn, or loud and abusive, and not want to have anything further to do with us, but it never occurred to me the bitch would try and annul our marriage. I'd not have allowed that regardless of what your decision had been."

Eden had thought her refusal of her aunt's plan would have assured him she meant to remain his wife, but apparently he did not require any such consideration. She felt

189

rather foolish that his feelings meant so much to her, when hers meant nothing to him. She realized then how truly angry he was, and she did not want him to lose his temper completely now that they had left her outraged kin behind.

"When you told me you'd be faithful to me, you were thinking of only one aspect of a good marriage. There's loyalty too."

"And honesty," Raven added with an accusing glance.

"And sense enough to recognize it!" Eden shot right back at him. His dark eyes flashed when he reached out for her and for an instant she did not know if he meant to hug her, or choke the life out of her. Then his mouth covered hers, and it was like coming home.

Raven's kiss was slow and deep, seeking the passionate response Eden needed little such encouragement to give. She then wrapped her arms around his neck and pulled him down with her on the seat. Raven had tossed his hat on the opposite seat when they had entered the carriage. When Eden's elegant bonnet was knocked askew, she wished she had shown as much foresight.

Sensing her discomfort, Raven rose up slightly and, with a quick yank, untied the satin bow beneath her chin and removed the pretty bonnet before it became crushed. He leaned over to set it with his hat, then again pulled her into his arms. He covered her flushed cheeks with gentle kisses before returning to her mouth with renewed fervor.

Enveloped in his enthusiastic affection, Eden made no protest as he unbuttoned her bodice to her waist. He slipped his hand inside, but caressed her breast sweetly for only a few seconds before pushing her silk chemise aside so he could fondle her bare skin. When he bent his head to tickle her nipples with his tongue, she responded with a throaty giggle that encouraged him to become even more passionate.

A sudden shout from the street brought Eden back to her senses. They had not pulled down the shades, and anyone passing by who chanced to glance their way would certainly see more than they dared allow. Unaware of her concern, Raven was still nibbling playfully at her breasts, but she grabbed two handfuls of his glossy curls and pushed him away.

"Isn't your townhouse nearby?" she asked in a breathless rush.

Thinking she wanted him to stop, Raven answered in a defiant snarl, "So what if it is?"

Eden rose up to kiss his lips lightly then replied in a seductive whisper, "I would much rather make love to you there, than here. If we're seen being as indiscreet as this, I fear both our reputations will suffer irreparable damage."

Raven broke into a wide grin, and wasted no time in giving their driver their change of destination. When they reached the townhouse, their attire was as impeccable as when they had left the ship to pay their call at the Lawtons'. They walked to the door with the same sedate pace they had used earlier, but once inside, Raven handed the startled maid his hat and gloves along with a firm order.

"Lady Clairbourne and I are not to be disturbed. We'll be here for dinner, but not the night."

"Yes, my lord." The maid stood with mouth agape as the striking couple ascended the stairs with rapid steps. Raven had informed them of Alex's death, and she could not understand why his widow was not dressed in black and heavily veiled, or what she and Raven planned to do until time for dinner. Realizing there would be no fine meal unless she informed the cook, she rushed to the kitchen to do so.

Not wanting to use Alex's bedroom, Eden hesitated at the top of the stairs, but Raven quickly took her hand and led her down the hall to the room that had been his. He locked the door, then again removed Eden's bonnet and unbuttoned her bodice. Her kisses inspired him to even greater haste than he had shown in the carriage, and he hurriedly peeled away all her garments and carried her to his bed. A massive four-poster, it supplied ample room for an amorous couple and he swiftly joined her in it.

With Raven, Eden had never had to worry that the strain of making love would be too much for him. Her only thoughts now were of the pleasure they shared whenever their emotions overruled their equally stubborn natures, and after the clash with her aunt, she needed the devotion he was eager to provide with his muscular body if not in prettily spoken promises.

Raven was far too hungry to possess Eden to continue their loving play for long once he had drawn her lightly perfumed body into his arms. Eagerly sharing his passion, she clung to him with a wanton grace, and the sweetness of her surrender again excited him as no other woman's ever had. She not only drove him to the heights of desire, she gave pleasure in abundance and savored it in full measure, as always leaving him feeling wonderfully content, his soul as well as his body sated.

It wasn't until a long while after the room was completely dark that they realized the sun had set, and having ordered dinner, they ought not to be too terribly late for it. Raven helped Eden dress, and artfully arrange her hair, and she thanked him with teasing kisses as she tied his tie. Once again as beautifully groomed as they had been upon their arrival, they walked into the dining room hand in hand but the table was not set, and there were no savory aromas wafting from the kitchen. Then they noted the house seemed unnaturally quiet, and when the butler greeted them, they jumped in alarm.

"Good evening, my lord, my lady," Stewart called from behind them.

Raven was the first to turn toward the man who had been in his uncle's employ for more than a dozen years. He was a humorless fellow, small, with sharp features, but he had always run Alex's London townhouse with the same precision Jonathan Abbot managed Briarcliff.

"Good evening, Stewart. I know we gave you scant notice of our arrival and you needn't apologize if you were unable to provide dinner. We're sailing for Jamaica in the morning, and Lady Clairbourne and I will simply dine on board my ship."

"I excused the rest of the staff for the evening, my lord, when it appeared you required privacy rather than their services."

Stewart had been cordial, if somewhat stiff, when Alex had introduced him to her, but the butler's expression was so clearly filled with disapproval Eden was insulted and felt certain Raven would be also. Then she realized why the man was eyeing them with such a contemptuous gaze. "We neglected to inform the staff of our marriage, Raven. I'd forgotten that they wouldn't know of it when we came here."

"Your marriage, my lady?" Stewart drew himself up to his full height, which was still less than Eden's, and his expression grew even more hostile. "Surely I have misunderstood."

"No," Raven assured him with a broad grin. "With Alex's blessing, I thought I could best provide for Lady Clairbourne's future as her husband and we have married."

After a lengthy and uncomfortable pause, Stewart finally chose to respond, "Alexander Sutton was one of the finest gentlemen it has ever been my privilege to serve," he announced without a trace of a smile. "He was a man

193

of honor, and even if he did suggest that you two marry, I can't believe he meant you to do so before a proper period of mourning had elapsed."

When Raven raised his hand, Eden quickly caught his arm before he could throw the punch she agreed Stewart had earned. "Please Raven, we've had more than enough such scenes for one day. Let's just leave."

Raven was not about to allow a butler to pass judgment on his actions and said so. "You served my uncle well, but if being in my employ disgusts you, then you are free to seek another position elsewhere. Don't ask me for a reference as I'll not give one to a man who shows me such a disgraceful lack of loyalty."

Like many men of small stature, Stewart possessed the belligerent spirit of a bantam rooster and stood his ground. "If there is any disgrace here, my lord, it is you and Lady Clairbourne who have committed it. I don't want a reference from you, as it would hold little value."

Eden could not hold Raven then, and he slammed his fist into Stewart's face. The blow knocked the butler to his knees. Satisfied he had taught the opinionated man a valuable lesson, Raven took Eden's hand and hurried her outside, where their carriage was still waiting. His expression, however, remained filled with fury.

Twelve

August 1863

As they rode away from the townhouse, Eden laid her head on Raven's shoulder. "I'm so sorry. That was my fault. I should have realized the people who served Alex would never understand our desire to be together."

Still seething, Raven opened his mouth to respond with the bitter retort that had instantly come to his mind. Eden's casual pose was so dear, however, that he did not want to upset her and softened his tone. "I realize you've been a countess only a few weeks, but even so you ought to understand we needn't tolerate such insolent remarks from our servants. Stewart would never have dared speak to Alex like that. I may be young, but damn it all, I'm now the Earl of Clairbourne, and I expect to be treated with the proper respect. Alex was only nineteen when he inherited the title, and he never disgraced it."

That Raven was still in his twenties had slipped Eden's mind. He had such a forceful personality, she never thought of him as being as young as he was in years. She sat up slowly and turned to face him. The lamps that lit the carriage provided only dim illumination but she knew his face so well she did not need to see his expression clearly to recognize the hostility etched on his features.

"Alex and I used his health as justification for making our own rules, but I think you and I are going to have to be far more circumspect in our behavior. Are the people in Jamaica going to be as unforgiving as my aunt, Stephanie, and Stewart? They know you, of course, but all they'll know of me is that I failed to mourn Alex's memory for the proper length of time. Will they condemn me for it?"

"No more than once they won't," Raven vowed through clenched teeth.

Eden did not doubt that he would defend her, but she thought it would be more as a matter of his own pride than out of respect for her honor. She did not want him constantly put on the defensive on her account, though. Unable to think of a way to explain their marriage that lessened the scandalous nature of it, she again sat back and rested her head on his shoulder until they reached the dock where the *Jamaican Wind* was moored.

Raven barely tasted the broiled chicken they were served for dinner, while Eden took only a few bites before pushing her plate away. He hated to see her again so miserable and he racked his brain for a way to introduce her to Jamaican society that would not immediately make her the object of the most tasteless kind of gossip. Finally an idea struck him that he considered not only workable, but bordering on brilliant.

"News travels rather slowly between London and the West Indies," he began with an encouraging smile. "If I were to introduce you as my bride, and fail to mention that you were also Alex's widow, by the time the truth reached Jamaica, everyone would have had the opportunity to get to know you. Surely they would not judge us harshly then."

Eden could not believe Raven would seriously suggest such a devious ploy. "Do you honestly expect me to deny I was Alex's wife? I thought you abhorred pretense."

Raven sighed as he conceded that point. "I do, but you'll have to admit the circumstances of our marriage were extraordinary. Besides, I don't want you to deny anything. We'll just postpone revealing the truth until people are better able to accept it."

Eden shook her head emphatically. "No, you're wrong. They'll not become more understanding if they learn the truth several months from now. They'll just be all the more outraged by our duplicity and never trust a word we speak ever again."

"That's a risk I'm willing to take."

"Well I'm not," Eden insisted. "I won't have you compromising your dearest principles to protect me. I know this may be difficult to understand, or believe, but even if I have to spend the rest of my life as the object of gossip, the time I shared with Alex will have been worth it."

"A month with him would be worth a lifetime of scorn?" Raven asked incredulously.

"Yes, I loved him that much, Raven. I really did."

Impressed by her spirit, or perhaps merely her stubbornness, Raven reached out to take her hand. "No one is going to insult you. I'll not allow it. I'll call out any man who dares to whisper a single word of criticism about us and I'll think of a way to silence the women too."

"If you kill a man in a duel, it will be called murder," Eden reminded him. "I won't have it, Raven. I buried one husband, and I wouldn't survive if you were hanged for killing a man in a misguided attempt to champion my honor."

Raven hoped that meant she cared for him, at least a

little bit, but the prospect of being hanged for murder was not nearly as important a concern as avenging his honor, or hers. "I'm flattered you think I'd win any duels I fought. Thank you for that vote of confidence," he remarked with a broad grin.

"Raven, please. This is too important a matter for you to make jokes of it."

Raven disagreed. "I consider my good name, and yours, as important as my life. Just think about my idea. Old gossip isn't nearly as titillating as new. That I've married will astound most people. That Alex died, well, everyone who knew him will grieve with us. Those two events ought to keep everyone occupied for a good long while."

Raven's tone was soft and conciliatory, but Eden could not be a party to the deception he suggested. "We can't lie about Alex and me . . ." She got that far, but her cheeks began to burn with an incriminating blush when she couldn't bring herself to explain why.

Eden looked so stricken with guilt at the mere suggestion of a ruse, Raven could not help but wonder if he had not seriously underestimated her integrity. Wouldn't a woman who was concerned only about wealth and position have welcomed the chance to protect her name? He had not offered the option of postponing the announcement of her marriage to Alex as a test, but if he had been using it as a clever means to assess her character, she had definitely passed with flying colors. Had all of his impressions of her been equally unfair? There was too much to sort through for him to come to a just decision at the moment, but he began to suspect his desire to protect Alex from a devious female's wiles might have led him to misjudge her all along.

"I think I owe you an apology," he offered graciously.

"For what?"

"For always questioning your word. I've not known that many women well, and while that's no excuse, I should have realized that anyone who cares as passionately about a hopeless cause like the Confederacy, or who would brave a lifetime of shame to marry a dying man, had her own vision of truth and that it's an honest one."

Eden bit her lip to force back her tears. Only Raven Blade could pay such an insult-laced compliment, but while he clearly thought he had gained some sudden insight into her character, she knew he still understood far too little.

"I'm not a deceitful person, Raven. I know that's the way some men see women, but I think it's seldom the case. Oh I know there are women who are forced to lie, who pretend to love men in order to survive, but I have too much respect for myself, as well as men, to want to fool them. I never lied to Alex, and I won't lie to you either."

When Eden again looked away, her expression still troubled, Raven gave her hand an encouraging squeeze. "Maybe something else will occur to me before we get home. I won't force you to keep your marriage to Alex a secret if it would upset you so badly."

"I can't keep it a secret, Raven." Thinking only of how proud Alex would have been to have a child, Eden finally found the courage to confess the reason why. "I'm not absolutely certain yet, but there's a possibility I'm carrying Alex's child."

Raven was completely dumbfounded by that totally unexpected announcement, and needed a long moment to collect his wits in order to respond. Even then, his expression still mirrored his astonishment. "But you were only married to him for a month!"

That was not the sympathetic response for which Eden had hoped, but now that she had made such a difficult admission, she had no trouble discussing it openly. "A woman need sleep with a man only once to create a babe. You must know that. Alex was a very loving husband, and we had many such opportunities."

Raven slumped back in his chair, still too shocked to comprehend how this latest development was going to affect them. "Alex and Eleanora were married for three years and she was never able to conceive. It didn't even occur to me that you could have."

"Maybe I didn't," Eden mused. "It could just be wishful thinking and in a week or two I might know it's not true."

In the meantime, Raven knew he ought to be happy for Alex that there was even the possibility he had fathered a child, but he was too distraught to feel anything but dismay. He was as badly depressed as he had been when he had seen Eden's handwriting on the envelope containing the note summoning him to Briarcliff and had known instantly that Alex was dead.

The last two months had been the most trying of his life. First he had lost Eden to Alex without even being able to enter the contest for her affection. Then he had lost Alex, but Alex had always been generous to a fault, and had made it possible for him to make Eden his wife. Raven knew she had no idea how badly he had wanted her, but he had been unwilling to wait for her to grow fond of him and had seized his first opportunity to marry her. He had been positive that even if she had captured Alex's heart with a string of enchanting lies, he would not fall victim to any clever romantic illusions.

Now it appeared Eden's love for his uncle had been real, and even if she was not yet certain, he did not doubt that she was pregnant. Of course she was. She and Alex had been everything to each other and it was only natural that they would become parents as well. Where did that leave him? he wondered sadly. Alex had raised him, and he would never refuse to do as much for Alex's child, but the fact that he had again lost out to Alex, and that Eden's first babe would not be his, was almost more than Raven could bear.

"I know how desperately you must want Alex's child," he finally forced himself to promise, hiding his anguish as best he could. "I want you to know I'll be as fine a stepfather as any man can be."

Raven was concentrating on their hands rather than looking up at her, and Eden realized he was struggling with the same powerful emotions that continually tore at her. She left her chair then, moved to his lap, and hugged him with all her strength. "Thank you," she whispered, and when he responded with a kiss of nearly heartrending sweetness, she knew they were again taking comfort in the fiery desire that was so easily ignited between them but she craved the peace that followed in passion's wake too desperately to care.

Early the next morning, the *Jamaican Wind* began the voyage home. Exhilarated by the prospect of leaving behind the heartache she had encountered in England, Eden joined her young husband on deck. She had sailed frequently with her father, and had learned at an early age that she was not to distract a captain from his duties. She remained close to Raven, but kept to the rail and out of his way.

He turned often to smile at her, and she could not help but note the pride in his expression as he gave the orders Randy MacDermott promptly relayed to the crew. A well-disciplined group, they negotiated the crowded River Thames with care, but upon reaching the North Sea, all sails were unfurled and the majestic ship leapt forward as though she, too, were anxious to return home.

"Home," Eden whispered softly to herself, for while Alex had viewed Briarcliff with justifiable pride, it was on Jamaica that he had said he felt most at home. She was certain the plantation would be as beautiful a place as he had described, but without him, how could it ever truly be home to her?

Raven did not keep count as the morning progressed, but he knew that more often than not when he glanced toward Eden she was lost in thought rather than engrossed in the view of the sea he found so fascinating. Her golden gaze was focused inward, and he knew without having to ask that she was recalling the days she had spent with Alex. His expression became a defiant mask as he wondered if her marriage to him would ever hold the happiness she had found with Alex. He told himself repeatedly that it was far too soon for the beauty of her memories to have begun to fade, but that rationalization failed to assuage the aching need he felt inside.

Fearing she might be cold, he went to her side and slipped his arm around her waist to draw her close. "You mustn't become chilled," he cautioned.

"What? Oh, no, I'm fine. The day is far too pleasant to spend it in your cabin. I hope I'm not bothering anyone by standing here."

Raven would not admit how greatly she bothered him when it was the fact she was so remote rather than in his way that had proved to be so distracting. "No, you're welcome to stay on deck as long as you don't become overtired."

Eden blushed slightly, "I'm not in the least bit delicate, Raven. I've always love to ride and—"

"Good Lord," Raven interrupted. "You never should

202

have gone riding with me the last day I visited the tenants."

He appeared to be so troubled by that realization, Eden did not take his remark as a criticism. "Probably not, but I hadn't stopped to think about, well, about what might have happened. It really is too soon to consider a child a certainty. I hope you haven't told anyone yet."

News of Eden's possible pregnancy was the last thing Raven wished to confide in anyone but he caught himself before he declared that fact out loud. "I'd never discuss such intimate details of our lives with my crew, Eden. You needn't worry that I'll share our secrets with them, or anyone else."

"Aren't you and Randy close?"

"We were once," Raven readily admitted. "I'm now a happily married man, however, and we won't be spending as much of our time together as we once did."

Eden saw the beginnings of a smile tugging at the corner of Raven's mouth and understood just how they must have spent that time. "Even if you won't be spending your leisure hours together, aren't you still friends?"

"I think the fact that I'm now the earl will make it difficult for us to remain on such informal terms as we once were. My life has changed completely. If I no longer share the same interests as my former friends, I'll probably find myself making new ones."

While that was a reasonable assumption, Eden sensed more to Raven's response than what was immediately apparent, but she chose not to pursue it. With him by her side, she tried to take note of the crew's activities and ask questions about the voyage, but she soon noticed the men went out of their way to avoid coming anywhere near her. She knew they were not accustomed to having a woman on board, but she was not unattractive and wondered why none made any attempt to be friendly. The men who sailed with her father could always be counted upon to show off in every way they could when she and her mother were on board. She had expected Raven's crew to behave in a similar fashion. Thinking they were attempting to be respectful, she hoped they would soon become more relaxed and friendly.

As they ate dinner that night, Raven was again all too aware of how difficult it was to begin any sort of intelligent conversation with Eden. It seemed every subject that came to mind led swiftly to Alex, and not wanting to remind her of the husband she had lost, he kept still. There was the voyage, of course, but they had discussed it at length that morning on deck. The journey would take approximately a month, and he knew he would have to find a way to be a better companion, and soon.

Believing Raven to be a quiet man, Eden was content to dine in what she naïvely regarded as a companionable silence. She smiled whenever their eyes met, and not noticing his nervousness, she was grateful they were getting along so well.

"Do you like to play games?" Raven asked when the table had been cleared.

"What sort of games?" Eden replied, afraid his taste in amusements might be far different than hers.

Raven went to his desk, opened the bottom drawer, and removed a burl walnut box that measured a foot square. "This is a game Captain Cook supposedly liked so much his crew began calling it the Captain's Mistress."

Curious as to what the well-crafted box contained, when he returned to the table Eden leaned forward slightly to get a better look. "Perhaps my father's heard of it, but he never mentioned it to me."

Relieved he had succeeded in piquing her interest, Raven took the chair beside hers. He turned the box toward her and pulled up the lid. Designed to remain upright, the lid contained seven deep slots. The bottom of the box held forty-two wooden balls, each an inch in diameter. They were equally divided between light and dark.

"It looks interesting." Eden picked up one of the smooth wooden balls and rolled it between her palms. "How's the game played?"

"First you must decide if you want to take light or dark."

"Light," Eden responded, certain the dark should belong to him.

Raven made no effort to suppress a chuckle at her choice. "Then I'll take dark," he offered graciously. "Light always begins. The wooden balls are called rounds. The seven slots in the lid are chutes. The object of the game is to place four rounds of your own color in the chutes, either in a row vertically, horizontally, or diagonally. The rounds have to be in consecutive order, too."

"That sounds easy enough."

"It would be if I weren't also trying to do the same thing and block your moves in the bargain."

"Ah, now I understand. This is a game of strategy. Is that all there is to it?"

"That's all. Shall we begin?"

Eden responded by dropping the light-colored round she held into the first chute.

Raven appeared to consider his move thoughtfully before dropping a dark round into the second chute.

"All right," Eden mused aloud, "I can either place a second round on my first, or choose to block you."

"Whichever you like."

Eden dropped one of her rounds into the second chute to keep him from attempting a vertical series.

Raven chose to again ignore her and dropped a dark round into the third slot. Eden then put a light round into the fourth.

"Fiendish," Raven complained with another sly chuckle as he placed a second dark round in the third slot.

Keeping up her attack, Eden topped it with a light round and smiled prettily. She now had three light rounds on the diagonal across chutes one, two and three.

Undaunted, Raven dropped a round into the fifth slot.

"What good did that do?"

"Maybe none," he admitted. "We'll have to wait and see."

Thinking the man inattentive at best, Eden placed a light round on top of his in chute five.

Raven scooped up a dark round and, going back to the first chute, dropped it in on top of Eden's.

Eden countered by placing a second round in the fourth slot. Raven quickly topped it with one of his.

With a gleeful shout of triumph, Eden dropped another light round on top of it to complete a diagonal pattern across slots one to four. "There, I won!" she exclaimed excitedly. "This certainly is a simple game. Are you positive Captain Cook was exceptionally fond of it?"

"The story is he and the scientists who traveled with him played it every night."

"Really?"

"For hours and hours," Raven insisted with a wicked grin.

Eden's glance moved from the cleverly designed box to Raven's broad smile and she quickly arrived at a discouraging conclusion. "You let me win, didn't you?"

"Are you accusing me of cheating?" Raven asked in mock horror.

"No, of course not," Eden assured him. "I don't think what you did can be called cheating. I just think you let me win."

"Shall we settle the question with another game?"

"Only if you'll promise to play fair," Eden replied.

"You have my word on it." Raven gestured toward the game. "This slat that fits across the bottom of the chutes is called the gangplank. You just give it a tug, and it comes out. The rounds then drop back into the box, or locker, and we're ready to play another game."

This time Eden was concentrating so hard on blocking Raven's moves so that he would not be able to align four rounds on the diagonal that he managed to place four in a row horizontally before she realized what he was doing. "You won that game," she said with obvious admiration. "I didn't even see it coming."

"I was lucky."

"I think *clever* is a better word. I'll bet your strategy is always that good." When Raven broke into a charming grin and actually blushed at her praise, Eden was touched. "You have such a marvelous smile, Raven. If only you'd used it in London, all the women would have fallen in love with you."

Badly embarrassed by that observation, Raven concentrated on yanking out the gangplank to return the rounds to the locker. "It's a good thing I didn't smile all that often then. That much affection would have been lethal. Do you want to play again?" When he looked up and found Eden regarding him with a shocked stare, he realized he had just said the stupidest thing imaginable. "I'm so sorry. I didn't mean that."

Eden bit her lip to keep from bursting into tears. "Of course you didn't. I'm sure it just slipped out. Thank you for teaching me the game. I'd like to play it again another time, but if you don't mind, I'd rather just get ready for bed now."

"I didn't mean it, Eden, truly I didn't. Won't you please forgive me?"

While Raven appeared to be as horrified by his careless remark as she was, Eden could not help but wonder if it

207

had not been exactly what was on his mind. Tears welled up in her eyes as she decided it was. "I know people are bound to say unkind things like that behind my back, but it really hurts coming from you."

That only moments before Eden had been laughing with him made Raven feel like an inept fool. He had been well aware of the fact he lacked Alex's easy charm, but he had not meant to prove that point with such needless cruelty. "I don't like women fawning over me. I hate it, in fact. That's all I meant. I wasn't referring to you and Alex. I was talking about myself." When Eden looked away, too upset to respond, Raven knew his situation was hopeless. He closed the walnut box, and returned it to his desk. He knew Eden had enjoyed the game, but he doubted she would ever want to play it again. Unable to think of any way to make things up to her, he left the cabin and hoped he would not have to circle the deck until dawn before he felt like returning.

Attempting to analyze this latest misunderstanding, Eden remained seated at the table for a long while. Raven was such an intense young man, but his actions were totally unpredictable. He had abundant pride but little regard for hers, it seemed. Each time she thought they were becoming close, he would insult her with some vile question or opinion that drove them miles apart. Was he so terrified of her that he had to constantly keep shoving her away? Perhaps *terrified* is the wrong word, she thought dejectedly. Maybe he simply dislikes me.

As Raven paced the deck, his brow was furrowed with the deep concentration of a palace guard. The sea was calm, and the spray that shot up against the bow a light mist. The stars were bright but he was too depressed to notice anything other than the damp chill of night air and jammed his hands into his pockets.

He simply could not believe he had made such a tactless remark to Eden. On his best days, he possessed only a slight trace of charm, but he had never gone out of his way to impress anyone so that lack had never mattered. Now that failing took on the proportions of a fatal flaw.

"Good Lord," he muttered under his breath, quickly vowing never to use the word *fatal* in front of Eden for fear of making another unfortunate reference to death that she would surely take personally.

He was tempted to sleep in Alex's cabin that night, but after he had forbidden Eden to use it, he could scarcely seek refuge there himself. No, he would have to return to the cabin they shared and find a way to pass a comfortable night. No coward, he strode aft with a resolute step, but when he reached his cabin, he had never been less sure of himself.

Eden had been as lost in thought as Raven, but she had succeeded in reaching an important conclusion even if he had not. Clad in her nightgown, she was stretched out across the bunk. As Raven came through the door, her golden glance swept over him with the languid ease of a lover's caress before coming to rest at his mouth. As always, that his lips were far more inviting than his words ever were was disconcerting.

"The only time there's harmony between us is when we make love," she informed him boldly. "I don't want you in this bed if you're going to pretend you're alone again."

Raven slammed the door shut and locked it. "Is that a challenge of some sort?" It had certainly sounded like one to him and that had been the last thing he had expected. That was their main problem, he realized—not only was Eden's behavior impossible to successfully predict, but the way she interpreted his actions made no sense either.

"No, I believe you to be a man of great courage. I'm not daring you to prove it. I'm saying that if all we have is passion, then we ought not to waste it or we'll have nothing."

Raven crossed to the bunk and stood staring down at her, his expression filled with awe. "I swear that's the most brilliant piece of logic I've ever heard. Do you ever lose an argument?"

"Obviously those I have with you."

Raven did not turn away as he began to peel off his clothes. He had never met a woman who excited him more. In fact, none had even come close. "No, you've never lost anything to me."

Eden knew precisely what she was doing: she was attempting to create a bond between Raven and herself in the only way she knew how. She would have only a few months before her pregnancy became obvious, and not knowing if he would want her then, she had chosen not to waste any time now. If her methods were crude, he seemed not to notice, or perhaps he simply did not care. She rose from the bed, took his coat and hung it over the back of his chair, then returned to the bunk and slipped under the covers.

While he appreciated that wifely gesture, rather than fling his clothing aside as he had done in the past, Raven took the time to undress with care. If Eden wanted him, he saw no reason to keep her waiting, but he did not want to react with ungentlemanly haste either. He knew this had to be a trick of some kind, but when she was right about the pleasure they shared, why should he deny it while he pondered her true goal? When he was ready to join her, she had already removed her nightgown and laid it aside.

Making himself comfortable in the narrow bunk, Raven moved close, brushed Eden's sun-streaked curls away from her temples, then kissed her cheeks lightly. Eden responded by entwining her legs in his and he abandoned

210

his leisurely approach in favor of a far more aggressive one. There was no shyness in her response, only a joyous acceptance that made his passions soar.

"I think if a couple shares only one thing, it ought to be this," he whispered as he hugged her close. Not waiting for a response, he kissed her deeply, drinking in her taste and flower-scented fragrance until the velvet smoothness of her supple body stole his breath away and he was aware of nothing but the rapture they had always shared.

It was not until Raven lay sleeping, still cradled in her arms, that Eden began to recall the nights she had spent with Alex. Raven said little or nothing when they made love, while Alex had always given her as many adoring compliments as kisses. Unlike Raven, who always fell into a passion-drugged sleep, Alex had liked to talk after they had made love. She treasured each of those sweet conversations now, for they had also served to strengthen their marriage, just as surely as making love had.

Eden closed her eyes, expecting the memory of Alex's smile to come to mind instantly, but it did not. Instead, it was Raven's taunting grin that flashed before her eyes. She gasped sharply, and while Raven stirred, he did not awaken. In a moment, she could again relax, but Alex's image still refused to lead her into the world of dreams. The memory of his love would never fade from her heart, but her imagination played nothing but cruel tricks that night and kept his face veiled in shadows.

"No," she whispered softly, the anguish in her voice muffled by Raven's thick curls. She knew it was much too soon to let Alex go, but her usually vivid imagination refused to agree.

Thirteen

September 1863

Eden did not object to passing their evenings playing Captain's Mistress when Raven enjoyed the game so much. She doubted she would ever become as proficient as he, but their competition was lively enough to be entertaining. No matter how many times Raven beat her, she would simply smile and insist his run of luck could not possibly last much longer. She doubted his advantage would wane anytime soon, however.

"Do you like to play chess?" she asked one night as he put away the game. As usual he had won five games and she only two, but she wasn't discouraged by it. It pleased her to think that not only did Raven love the game, but Alex had as well.

Raven returned to the table and replenished their brandy as he replied. "Yes, I do. I beat Alex so often he quit playing with me when I was fourteen. I've never found anyone among my crew who could play, so I don't carry a set on board. Is chess one of your favorites?"

"No," Eden admitted with an embarrassed smile. "My father tried to teach me, but I never could concentrate deeply enough to give him much of a game. Maybe you two will be able to have a match someday. I think you'll like him. Like you, he's very bright."

"Then what's he doing fighting for the Confederacy?"

"There are plenty of intelligent men fighting for the South," Eden insisted as she straightened her shoulders proudly. She was badly disappointed he had not responded to her compliment in kind. She tried her best to be as charming a companion as possible for him, but as usual Raven appeared to be taking great delight in shattering the playfulness of their mood with an insulting question.

"Robert E. Lee is definitely a genius, I'll concede that. The Union doesn't have a general who can even come close to his brilliance. It's a tragedy he doesn't have a cause worthy of his talents."

Incensed by that comment, Eden's tone grew hostile. "Our cause is just. The North and South had become too different to remain together."

"Wasn't diversity the Union's strength?"

"Well, yes, I suppose it was until the Federal government began serving only the interests of the people in the Northern states." When Raven's response was no more than a skeptically arched brow, Eden became more specific, "In my father's case, his ships carried cotton to the mills in New England, but they took only one quarter of all the cotton the Southern plantations produced. The rest was shipped to European mills. That's how my parents met. My father was in London on business."

"I'll bet it was love at first sight," Raven guessed with more than a trace of sarcasm.

"Yes, as a matter of fact it was, but you're just trying to distract me from making my point," Eden scolded. "The problem was that while the European mills paid excellent prices for cotton, the planters couldn't get goods in return without paying tariffs of ten to thirty percent when they returned home. That expense made it difficult, if not impossible, to make a fair profit. The tariffs were designed to protect the commerce in the North from European competition, while it was the Southerners who were forced to pay them. That just wasn't fair."

Enjoying the bright sparkle their argument had brought to Eden's eyes, Raven decided to pursue it. He took a sip of brandy before he replied. "Weren't tariffs a minor issue?"

"Not to the Southerners who made their living in cotton it wasn't! Besides, my father agreed with those who believed the Southern states had the constitutional right to secede if they chose to do so."

"Yes, I heard that argument fairly often." Raven frowned slightly, obviously not convinced by it.

"There was the matter of land in the West too," Eden suddenly thought to add. "We wanted to see more land made available. Cotton depletes the soil, and plantations needed new land to remain in business. The Northern states opposed western expansion. They wanted the population concentrated on the East Coast so there would always be plenty of buyers for their goods. You see, the interests of the North and South were no longer compatible. The break between them was inevitable."

"What you're citing were minor issues, Eden, and you know it. It was the dispute over slavery that ripped America in two and I can't believe any sane person can see any morality in one man owning another."

"Only a small minority of Southerners owned slaves." Eden swirled the blackberry brandy in her snifter with a nervous twist, but did not sample any. "Many of those owned only one or two. My family has never owned a single slave, by the way. Despite the fact the majority of men were not slave holders, they answered the call to serve the Confederacy in great numbers."

"They've been dying in great numbers too." Raven finished the last of his brandy and set the snifter aside. "The South had neither the manpower nor the heavy industry to sustain a war effort. It was unconscionable to risk so much when there was no hope the Confederacy could win."

"That's simply not true!" Eden protested. "We've won many a battle."

"Yes, because Lee is a military genius, but eventually even he will run out of troops and supplies. When we were in London, there were many who said the South's loss at Gettysburg in July will prove to be the turning point of the war. Losing Vicksburg at the same time was a terrible blow. Not only weapons were being sent from Mexico through the port at Vicksburg, but food from the West as well. The War is as good as lost, Eden, you might as well face that fact now."

How Raven could be so coolly logical when they were discussing something of such great importance Eden failed to understand, but she was not about to agree with him. "Have you ever cared enough about anything to fight for it?" she asked instead, too committed to the South's cause to care that he would surely be insulted by her insinuation that he cared for nothing but himself.

Caught off guard by the vicious intent of her question, Raven's expression gave away his initial shock. He had certainly waged an aggressive campaign to win her consent for their marriage, but wisely did not remind her of that. That there had once been a time when he had had to fight simply to survive was not a story he cared to relate either. He would have argued with her all night about the War, but he had no interest in talking about himself. Rising to his feet, he started for the door.

"Excuse me please, I need to speak with Randy one last time before we retire."

Eden was amazed by how quickly Raven had lost interest in their conversation when she had put him on the defensive. He was very good when he was on the attack, but he used the same defense time and again: retreat. If only she could think of a way to use that insight against him when they played Captain's Mistress. Hoping she would find a means to do that, she got up and began to get ready for bed, but she was not at all satisfied with the way her latest encounter with her maddeningly aloof husband had ended. Losing a battle or two did not mean the South had lost the War and she remained infuriated for a good long while that Raven held such a repugnant opinion.

With constant efforts to be polite, Raven and Eden managed to pass the remainder of the first two weeks of the voyage without another confrontation or bout of tears over the War, or any of their other differences. Neither took any pride in the placid nature of their relationship, however. It seemed to each like an uneasy truce that would inevitably end in a renewed round of hostilities. While neither wished that to happen, the fear that it soon would filled them both with an unshakable sense of dread.

Raven could not allay the uncomfortable premonition that the next words to pass his lips would insult Eden so badly she would never speak to him again. As a result, he had become even more close-mouthed than was his custom. It was only when they made love that he felt free to express himself, and even then he dared not put his feelings in words.

As for Eden, she had expected the pleasure their lovemaking brought to make them close. She had sought to dissolve whatever remained of Raven's distrust with the passion he was always so quick to display, but she had no

216

evidence that her efforts were having any success. From their initial meeting she and Alex had been comfortable in each other's company, but with Raven not even the briefest conversation ran smoothly.

Now he seemed so reluctant to speak she made little effort to draw him out. While he was pleasant, if quiet, his smiles were too quick, as though forced. Whenever they were up on deck, he would keep her close, but his touch was possessive rather than affectionate. When darkness fell and they shared his bunk, Raven lulled her to sleep with loving so intense it left her too weak to crave more. But she would awake the next morning still feeling lost and alone and again be engulfed in a sense of hopelessness. She had begun to consider the possibility that Raven was simply incapable of sharing anything of himself with a woman, but she also thought that perhaps she was just not the right one. Because she was still in love with Alex, she knew she had no right to question Raven's feelings, and kept her painful doubts to herself.

As for the crew, the chill in their glances had grown no less icy. In fact, there were several men whose expressions could be described as contemptuous whenever she came into view. Eden had never done anything to deserve such blatant disrespect, and grew increasingly unnerved by it. At the same time, she did not want to trouble Raven by complaining that his men lacked the proper warmth. Instead, she concentrated on the sea's sparkle, or Raven's infrequent comments, and did not let the crew guess that she had even noticed their disdain, much less been deeply hurt by it.

Randy MacDermott stood with his back braced against the port rail. Eden and Raven were at the opposite rail, but although he had a few minutes of free time that morning, he was not tempted to join them. As he saw it, Raven was unlikely to ever forgive him for speaking his mind about his bride, and Randy had seen nothing in Eden's behavior that had inspired him to change his opinion of her. The lovely Lady Clairbourne seemed perfectly content to be Raven's wife, but he could not forget Alex so easily. A year of mourning had not been an intolerable burden for any widow he had ever met. That Eden had been unable to survive more than a week without a man in her bed disgusted him each time he looked her way. She was undeniably a beauty, and carried herself with the grace of a lady, but as he saw it, she was without a shred of virtue.

Out of the corner of his eye, the pensive mate caught sight of Max and Samuel swabbing the deck. They were casting sly glances at Eden, and whispering between bursts of hushed laughter that left little doubt as to the object of their humor. That the men shared his low opinion of Raven's wife did not surprise him, but Randy would not tolerate such an impudent display. He had just taken a step toward the mischievous pair when Raven suddenly turned toward him and waved. In response, Randy had to change his direction, and Raven moved across the deck to meet him half way.

The rowdy sailors were behind Raven now, but Randy still had a clear view of them. He saw Max kick over his bucket, deliberately sending several gallons of dirty water sloshing over the hem of Eden's full-skirted gown and thoroughly soaking her shoes.

Gazing out at the sea, Eden was unaware of Max's deed until she found the deck suddenly awash. She gasped in surprise and hurriedly clutched the rail, but only avoided falling by the narrowest of margins. When she turned, seeking the cause of the mishap, Max and Samuel appeared to be as horrified as she. They rushed forward with their mops, and made a great show of drying the deck where she stood.

Alerted by Eden's cry of alarm, Raven turned in time to see her grab the rail. Infuriated that Max and Samuel would be so clumsy around her as to have endangered her safety, he turned back and began to berate them severely. They begged his forgiveness with contrite expressions, but the other men on deck who had observed their actions turned away to hide their smiles.

Randy hesitated for a moment, but his loyalty to Raven would not allow him to remain silent. Although infuriated to find himself in such a difficult position, he walked to Raven's side. "I must speak with you privately, Captain."

"What?" Annoyed by that interruption, Raven scowled as he turned to face the mate. "What could possibly be more important than making certain the deck is safe to walk on?"

"It'll take only a moment," Randy assured him.

Randy was so angry his face was nearly as red as his hair, and after assuring himself that Eden was all right, Raven joined him a few steps away. "Yes, what is it?"

After making certain Eden could not overhear them, Randy explained what he had seen, concluding with, "It was no accident. Max will deny it, of course, but I saw him do it. He was deliberately being mean to your wife."

Raven glanced over his shoulder at the sailors in question. They were still mopping the deck while Eden shook out her dripping skirts and tried to stay out of their way. When he turned back toward Randy, his disgust was plain. "You told me the entire crew shares your misguided view of Eden. How many others would dare to do her physical harm?"

"None I hope. I was just on my way to tell those two to be more respectful when you called to me. If I'd been just a few seconds faster, this would never have happened."

Raven clasped his hands behind his back and lowered his voice slightly. "I told you to warn the men that I'd flog any who even dared frown at my wife. Did you convey that message?"

"Yes, sir, that I did," Randy answered, and he had the sinking suspicion Raven meant to carry out that threat now.

"I'm going to take Eden below to change her clothes. It's almost time for the noon meal, so she'll probably not want to come up on deck again. I'll be back in a few minutes, though, and I want the men assembled and waiting for me. It's only because Eden is such a graceful woman that she didn't suffer a serious fall. That might have been far more costly than any of the men imagines. I'll not have any others stooping to such malicious pranks. I'm going to order you to whip both Max and Samuel for being not only incredibly stupid, but unforgivably mean to a woman who deserves their respect. If you can't carry out that order, say so now and I'll whip them myself, but I don't want any arguments between us in front of the men."

Randy looked over at Eden, who appeared to have been completely fooled by the two sailors' excuse of clumsiness. As always, her expression was delightfully sweet, but he was unmoved. "I can't stop the talk about her. I should have been quick enough to stop Max, but there's nothing I can do about the talk."

"Not unless you try," Raven pointed out. "Now are you going to flog them or will I have to do it myself?"

"It was a thoughtless trick, and she could have been badly hurt. None of us wants that. I'll do it."

"Good." Raven turned away and, as promised, escorted Eden to his cabin, where he insisted she change out of her damp clothes.

Pleased by his concern, Eden brushed Raven's cheek

with a light kiss before he returned to the deck. She had seen the anger still smoldering in his eyes and was relieved it had not been directed at her. An overturned bucket was an insignificant matter to her, but she knew he expected the best from his crew and would not tolerate such sloppiness.

She had been amazed to learn Alex had given Raven command of the *Jamaican Wind* when he was no more than nineteen, but after seven years as captain, he had impressed her as knowing his business better than some men she had met twice his age. She had seen him settle disputes between sailors with the wisdom of Solomon, and his navigation was as precise as her father's. That he took such great pride in his ship and the performance of the crew that served him was justifiable in her view.

Eden had just begun to remove her soggy stockings when she heard a peculiar shout from up on deck. When it came again, she realized it had been more of a cry of anguish than a shout and grew alarmed. What could have happened now? she wondered. She hoped no one had fallen from the rigging or suffered some serious accident. She sat still, straining to hear the sounds from up on deck and heard the cry a third time. Too curious to remain below and wait for Raven to explain what had happened when he returned, Eden stuck her bare feet in her damp shoes, and hurried up the companionway to the deck to see for herself.

The crew were gathered around the mainmast, and Eden had to come forward to peer over the shoulders of the men in back to discover what held their attention. When she saw Max and Samuel had been stripped to the waist and that their hands were tied to the mast her heart leapt to her throat. It had been Max's cries of pain that she had heard, but the fact he had passed out before Randy had delivered ten lashes had not stopped the mate from completing the task with slow, deliberate strokes.

As Eden watched in horrified disbelief, Randy's whip sliced through the air with a threatening hiss, then ripped the skin from Max's back with a dull slapping sound that belied the sharpness of the cuts it inflicted. Eden felt each blow send a jarring wave through the crowd but the men remained silent. Only Samuel, who stood cringing helplessly as he awaited his turn, uttered a terrified whimper at what was to come.

Thoroughly sickened the sailors were being punished so brutally, Eden turned away without looking for her husband. She knew it would only infuriate him all the more if she questioned his orders in front of his crew, and not daring to embarrass him in such a fashion, she went below. Even in their cabin she had to hold her hands over her ears to shut out the sound of Samuel's piercing shrieks. She could not believe that either man deserved to be whipped. When Raven came to join her at noon, she told him she did not feel like eating.

Although she had not seen him, Raven had noted Eden's brief appearance on deck and he could read volumes in her averted glance. He was then faced with an extremely difficult decision. He could either refuse to explain his actions and allow her to think the worst of him, or he could tell her the truth. While he did not want to hurt her by revealing the crew's insensitive opinion of her, they had agreed to be honest with one another, and recalling that vow, his choice was made for him.

Kneeling by her side, he placed his hand under her chin to force her gaze to meet his. "I didn't want you to know I'd ordered Max and Sam whipped, but since you do, you ought to know why it happened. I'm not a cruel man, Eden, I swear I'm not, but when Randy told me that Max had drenched you on purpose, I—"

"What?" Eden studied Raven's pained expression, and was instantly convinced he spoke the truth. "Your men have never been friendly, but do they hate me that much?"

Raven shook his head sadly. "I'm sure they don't hate you. It's just that, well, they have little experience with cultured ladies and—"

Fearing he would never get to the point, Eden finished his sentence for him. "They think I've been disloyal to Alex, is that it?"

"You mustn't concern yourself with their ridiculous beliefs, Eden. You know Alex hoped we'd be together, and surely his opinion ought to be the only one that matters to us."

Eden believed that too, and leaned forward to wrap her arms around Raven's neck. "No one else is ever going to understand, though," she whispered as she hugged him tightly.

Caught off balance, Raven had to grab for the edge of the table. Once steady, he rose and pulled Eden up with him. "My men may be as ignorant as goats when it comes to being polite to a lady, but Max and Samuel will not risk playing another trick on you and neither will any of the others. Getting your clothes wet could be seen as no more than a schoolboy's prank, but if you'd fallen, and you know you almost did, you might have been so badly hurt you could have lost the baby."

That he had been so concerned about her child when she had not even considered the consequences of a fall left Eden all the more shaken. She still felt wretched in the morning, and with each passing day she was more certain she was pregnant. To have Alex's child was her fondest wish, but she had not until that very instant realized what a baby could mean to Raven. She took a step back to make it easier to converse.

"You know I'm unfamiliar with many British customs even though my mother is English."

"Treating women well is not only a British custom."

"No, of course not, but that's not what I meant. Forgive me if this question seems silly, or stupid to ask, but I know you're the earl because Alex had no sons. What if I succeed in bearing one?"

Her question was so obvious Raven could not understand why they had not discussed it when she had first told him of such a possibility. "You're my wife, Eden, and any child you have while we're married will be considered mine. If your child is a son, he'll be my heir, and become the earl upon my death. Our marriage will not have cheated him out of his rightful title. He'll still be the Earl of Clairbourne one day. Although I hope it will not be anytime soon," he added with a teasing grin.

When they were on deck in the bright sunlight, it was possible to tell that Raven's eyes were a deep brown. In his cabin, they appeared as black as the thick fringe of lashes that framed them. It was only when he was angry that Eden could read his mood in his glance; at other times, like now, it was impossible. While he frequently made jokes of serious matters, she never did. "And if we had not married?" she asked very softly.

"But we are married."

"But if we were not?" Eden asked again.

Raven frowned slightly, uncertain what she expected him to say. "Alex named me as his heir in his will. When we reach Jamaica, we'll have to go to Kingston and inform Alex's attorney of his death. You can read the will then. Alex had no other male kin. His title is rightfully mine."

The pride that filled Raven's voice as he announced that fact was warning enough that she ought not to pursue the matter with him. Eden was deeply disturbed, however, for even if her child had not lost the chance to inherit his father's title and wealth, Raven had certainly seized an opportunity that he might not truly deserve. She still did not understand enough about how titles were inherited to know if what he had done was illegal, or perhaps simply dishonest, but she intended to ask the attorney for his opinion on the matter.

A knock at the door signaled the arrival of their noon meal, but as Eden took her place at the table Raven knew she had not been satisfied with his answers to her questions. The very last thing they needed was another issue to create mistrust between them, but try as he might, he could not think of any way to erase the pensive frown from her brow.

When Eden lay down for a nap after Raven left her, she had far too much on her mind to sleep. As she had so often, she wished she could go to her mother for advice. Unfortunately, not only was her mother out of reach, but every other responsible person in the world as well. She was stranded on board a ship with at least a hundred men, none of whom was fond of her. The fact that grim group included her husband only made matters worse.

She did not want to believe Raven had taken advantage of her grief to rush her into marriage to preclude the possibility of her providing Alex with an heir. That was almost diabolical, and knowing Alex had had great faith in him, she hated to jump to what she feared was becoming the most obvious conclusion. She certainly could not confront Raven about their marriage when she was sure he would simply remind her that had she not been in "his" bed on the night of Alex's funeral, there would have been no need for them to marry. He would undoubtedly remind her of that night as often as it took to silence her questions concerning his motives. She had no doubt of that, for unlike Alex, Raven was no gentleman.

When he returned to his cabin that evening, Raven hoped to find Eden in a better mood. When she did not accuse him of plotting against her as they ate dinner, he considered the evening a success.

"As soon as we get home, I'll do what I can to send any message you'd like to your parents," he offered graciously. "It won't be easy, but I'm sure a way can be found to do it. They ought to know that you've married and left England."

Surprised he would be so thoughtful, Eden was at a loss for what to say. "That would be wonderful, but I've no idea how I could possibly convey any sort of a coherent message that would adequately describe what these last few months have been."

Raven drummed his fingertips on the table in an impatient cadence. "Why not simply say you've married the Earl of Clairbourne and have taken up residence on his plantation in Jamaica?"

Eden opened her mouth to argue that scarcely did justice to the truth when she suddenly had a better idea. "Raven, instead of failing to mention I was married to Alex when we reach Jamaica, why don't we keep our marriage a secret? After Alex's child is born, if we still want to be married, we can have another ceremony. There would be no scandal then, everything would be quite proper. My aunt will be far too embarrassed to tell anyone in London about us, and who at Briarcliff would have the opportunity? As for your crew, they seem to be so offended by our marriage that I'm certain you could convince them to keep it a secret."

Eden's topaz eyes were radiant with delight, as though

her sudden inspiration was the best of all possible solutions to their problems. Raven could neither understand nor believe how she could suggest such a stupid thing, however, and looked for something to throw to illustrate his opposition. His pewter plate was still handy and he flung it against the door with a force that dented the wood.

"Have you lost your mind? I did not force you to marry me; it was your choice. You've told me over and over again that the month you spent with Alex was worth whatever scandal your elopement caused. Are you completely unwilling to put up with any gossip to stay with me?"

Eden had explained her idea the instant it had come to her mind. Now she realized how truly desperate, and how insulting, it sounded. She had not dreamed she would hurt Raven's feelings as she so obviously had. "It would also work to your advantage to delay the announcement of our marriage."

Raven rose to his feet, placed his hands on the table, and leaned forward as he refused to consider her absurd suggestion. "You chose to be my wife, Eden, and I'll not allow you to deny it!"

Feeling at a disadvantage in her chair, Eden stood to confront him. "I married you because I refused to become your mistress. Don't try and make it sound as though I truly had a choice because I didn't!"

"You don't have one now either!" Raven shot right back at her.

"Oh yes I do," Eden boasted, overwhelmed by the frustration he continually caused her. She had tried her best to be a good wife to him, but she didn't need to waste the rest of her life on a marriage that was so one-sided. "When we visit Alex's attorney, I can ask him about an annulment. I was far too overcome with grief to have been thinking clearly and that's reason enough to void a marriage. If it's impossible to get an annulment, there's always divorce. I've had plenty of time to think since we left England and I'm much stronger now. I can manage on my own, I'm certain I can."

Raven circled the table. "That's a damn lie and you know it."

"It is not."

Rather than reply in words, Raven sought to prove his point by drawing her into a crushing embrace. When she turned her head to avoid his kiss, he grabbed her chin and held her still as he pressed his mouth against hers with a demanding pressure that swiftly parted her lips. When he tasted blood, he did not know if it was his or hers, but he did not care.

As Eden struggled to break free, she realized what a terrible mistake she had made in seeking to reach him with the passion it was so easy to arouse. That she had encouraged him to be an ardent lover, but had won neither his friendship nor respect, was shockingly evident now.

She was wearing a pale green gown of lightweight wool. She didn't bother wearing several layers of starched crinolines on board ship and there was so little between them she could easily discern Raven was fully aroused. As if that fact could have escaped her notice, he slipped his arm around her waist and ground his hips against hers. Disgusted by that blatant gesture, she tried to back away only to find the sturdy oak table at her back. Anchored securely to the floor, it was as unyielding as a brick wall.

Trapped in Raven's arms, Eden gave up her attempts to escape and relaxed against him. She hoped for a softening of his aggressive stance, but none occurred. Instead Raven leaned forward, bending her backward over the table until she was forced to grab his shoulders to retain her balance. His mouth had yet to leave hers, and gasping for

228

breath, she was outraged to find herself completely at his mercy when she knew that was a quality he sorely lacked.

Raven was past the point at which he could analyze his actions. All he could do was react with the violent emotions she had aroused. He wanted Eden for his own with a desperation he could no longer disguise, and yet at the same time he understood why there was no room in her heart for him. That was a torture that continually plagued him until he could no longer contain his inner rage. He wanted her to love him rather than mourn Alex and he had not another minute of patience to wait for that miracle to occur.

Eden felt the muscles in Raven's shoulders flex as he tightened his grasp. His linen shirt had been softened by a dozen washings but its smoothness provided no comfort as she dug her fingers into his well-muscled flesh. His skin was as hot as his fevered kisses and she felt seared by the heat. Convinced he intended to force her across the table and rape her, she grew faint, and it wasn't until Raven began plucking the pins from her hair that she realized he had at last slackened his hold on her. In the next instant he had pulled her upright and his kiss took on the magical sweetness of the very first kiss he had ever given her.

Not about to allow him to turn his abusive assault into a seduction, Eden finally succeeded in breaking free and turned her head. What had possessed her to threaten divorce she didn't know now, but in the heat of their argument it had seemed like her only choice. Had she expected him simply to walk out on her as he had so often? Now she wished that he had for his penchant for leaving in the midst of their arguments was certainly preferable to the violence he had just shown her.

She felt his chest heave as he drew in a deep breath and hoped he was again rational enough to think with his usual clarity. "What in God's name is wrong with you?" she whispered.

Raven slid his fingers through her curls and began to rub her back gently. "There's nothing wrong with me," he denied with the same stubborn defiance he displayed whenever she challenged him. "Did you expect me to be pleased that you no longer wish to be married to me? No man would be happy to hear that."

"He would be if he also thought the marriage was a mistake."

Raven took a step back, but kept his arms draped around her waist. "Is that what you think, that we don't get along well because I'm sorry I took you for my wife?"

"How would I know what you think?" Eden replied with a renewed flare of temper. "I know what you think of the War, the stuffiness of English society, the island of Jamaica, and the proper discipline with which a ship must be run, but I don't know what you think about me."

Raven stared down at her, his dark eyes aglow with a compelling light. Clearly she wanted him to swear his undying devotion, to which she would undoubtedly respond with wistful longings for Alex. That was a trap he intended to avoid for as long as it took for her to feel something for him. What was the point of mentioning love when she would react with pity? He had far too much pride for that. He kissed her gently as he knew Alex must have.

"Have you changed your mind?" he asked before kissing her deeply once again. "Is passion no longer enough?"

Eden lost count of his kisses before she realized he had still not revealed his thoughts about her. Her conscience scolded her crossly for being distracted so easily, but as her whole body began to ache with the need for him, she knew there would be many other days in which to discuss their marriage, but that night had been meant for love.

Fourteen

September 1863

When Raven returned to his cabin the next morning with Eden's breakfast, he found her still asleep. He shook her shoulder gently, but when she sat up and brushed her hair out of her eyes, he winced.

"I'm sorry about your mouth. I didn't realize I was that rough last night."

Eden licked her lips and immediately understood why he had been inspired to apologize. Her lower lip was not only swollen where his teeth had sliced the tender flesh, but also hurt rather badly, providing a painful reminder that their most heated argument yet had gone unresolved.

When his sleepy bride did no more than regard him with an anguished glance, Raven bent down to kiss her forehead lightly. "The weather turned foul during the night. I've changed our course to take us farther north in hopes we'll miss the worst of it."

Now fully awake, Eden could readily discern the rocking motion of the ship had grown more pronounced. As a result, the timbers creaked and groaned loudly in protest. Raven was having difficulty compensating for the changing angle of the ship and had to constantly shift his weight to remain upright.

"Confederate ships often put into Caribbean ports for supplies. If we're on a more northerly course, then it's possible we might sight some," Eden mused aloud.

"Not in this gale we won't, but when the weather clears, I'll tell the lookout to keep watch for the *Southern Knight*. That's the only ship you're really interested in seeing, isn't it?"

"I'd appreciate knowing of any Confederate ship, but yes, I'd especially like to see my father's."

"He could be sailing off the coast of France for all we know. Don't make yourself sick worrying about whether or not the *Southern Knight* will survive this storm."

"I won't. My father is an excellent captain."

"So am I," Raven assured her.

Eden had not meant to give him the impression she was comparing him to her father and hurriedly refocused his attention on the storm.

"Hurricanes hit the coast often enough for me to know we're in serious trouble if that's what this is. What do you want me to do?"

"Did I mention the word *hurricane?*" Raven asked.

"Well, no, but—"

"Not all storms at sea are hurricanes," Raven informed her with an easy grin. "Let's hope this one is no more than a passing squall. Please don't be frightened. The *Jamaican Wind* has sailed through far worse storms than this with no damage. My men know what to do. All you need do is stay here in my cabin where you'll be safe. Why don't you go back to sleep for a while and then just spend the rest of the day in bed reading? That way you won't risk a fall. I'll see you're sent something to eat during the day, but the cook's put out his fires to avoid any accidents, so other than this pot of tea it won't be anything hot."

232

"I understand." As usual, Eden didn't [...]
waking. She doubted she would get hungry, [...]
pect of spending the day in bed was enorm[...]
ing. "Don't worry, I'll behave. What abou[...]
Samuel? Will you be able to spare anyone to [...]
them?"

Raven could scarcely believe his ears. "After [...]
did to you, how can you be concerned about tho[...]

The answer obvious in her view, Eden shrugge[...]
she replied. "Just because they treated me badly [...]
mean I'll not show them compassion. Won't they be [...]
miserable for several days?"

"I certainly hope so. That was the whole point of flogging them. Look, even if the sea were as calm as glass, I'd not allow you to tend them. Caring for wounded in a military hospital is one thing; looking after disobedient seamen is quite another. Now I've got to get back up on deck. Be careful—do it for Alex's babe if not for me."

He had reached the door before Eden had the presence of mind to call out to him. She didn't want to let him go thinking she would have disregarded his wishes had he not invoked Alex's name. "Raven, don't worry, I'll stay put. You be careful too."

Raven winked at her before going out the door, and Eden again marveled at how short his memory was when it came to their fights. While not holding a grudge was an admirable trait, there was also the possibility he did not consider their conflicts important enough to merit remembering. That thought was so unnerving Eden lost all interest in going back to sleep.

She got up briefly, poured herself a cup of tea, then got back into the bunk to drink it while she munched a biscuit. As she ate slowly, she decided the greatest point Raven had in his favor was that he had enjoyed Alex's unequivocal trust and love. Alex would not have always

233

so highly of Raven if the young man were not
of such elaborate praise.

nething was definitely wrong between them, how-
Raven constantly showed her his worst side and he
ght out the same in her. They could make love and
Captain's Mistress without arousing either's anger,
there was little else that they could share without
sing each other at least verbally. Eden raised her hand
er swollen mouth. Raven hadn't hit her, but he might
well have since the resulting damage to her face was
same.

If all they could do was make love and play games, she
had made the wrong choice, Eden mused darkly. She
ought to have become Raven's mistress rather than his
wife. She had never heard of a man beating his mistress,
but she knew there were many men like Paul Jessup at
Briarcliff who thought nothing of hitting their wife.

Determined to avoid another wretched scene with Raven, Eden spent the day trying to decide how best to
approach him on the subject of their marriage. She knew
nothing about his parents. Perhaps they had had such a
stormy relationship he thought all husbands and wives
spent the better portion of their time together fighting.

"That's the problem," Eden surmised with the faint
smile she could still manage. "I don't know Raven well
enough to understand why he behaves as though he were
possessed by demons at times." They needed the opportunity to talk about topics which couldn't possibly create
any friction between them, and she decided their childhood was the best place to begin. Unfortunately the storm
continued to buffet the ship with such force that Raven
could not spare any time to spend with her.

The dark-eyed earl had intentionally underestimated
the storm's severity, for Eden's benefit. He had seen
worse, but not in recent years, and wasn't looking forward

to the backbreaking toil required to keep the ship afloat in heavy seas. There had been no point in complaining to his bride even though she was a captain's daughter, however. Knowing Eden, he believed she would probably have offered to take a turn at the bilge pump and he would not allow that.

Eighteen hours passed before Raven returned to his cabin. Drenched to the skin and chilled clear through, he wanted only to peel off his wet clothes and sleep for a couple of hours. His teeth were chattering so loudly as he lurched through the door he feared he would disturb Eden, but he found her wide awake.

Eden sprang from the bunk, then had to grab the side to keep from going sprawling. There were extra blankets stored in the drawers beneath the bunk and she hurriedly pulled out one. "I've been so worried about you! Come here and let me help you out of those clothes."

Raven started to protest that he could undress himself. Then he discovered his hands were so numb from the cold he couldn't unbutton his heavy wool jacket. He was wearing gloves, but removing them also proved to be a bigger chore than he could manage. "Would you please?" he mumbled as he made his way toward her, attempting to balance his steps against the ship's sway.

Eden reached out for him, and also timing her motions to those of the ship, she helped him drop into one of the chairs at the table. As soon as she had removed his coat, sweater, and shirt, she draped the dry blanket around his bare shoulders. "It's way past midnight. Are all the men working such long hours as you?"

Snugly wrapped in the blanket, Raven began to rock back and forth slowly in an attempt to get warm. "They have no choice. If the ship sinks, we'll all drown. That grisly thought inspires more work than even the threat of a whip would."

"I'll be damned if I'll drown!" Eden exclaimed as she yanked off his right boot. It was so saturated with water the leather squished like a wet sponge when she tossed it aside and reached for his left. "I've no intention of being widowed again either," she added as an afterthought.

Raven reached out to ruffle her curls. "None of us is going to drown. The *Jamaican Wind* is so well built she floats like a cork even in the worst of storms. A little rain will never sink her."

"What about the wind? It's been howling like a banshee for hours."

"It sounds much worse down here than it really is," Raven lied again. He recalled telling her how much he hated having women fawn over him, but Eden was pulling off his wet clothes with an abandon that was quite endearing. She was treating him as though he were a small boy who had fallen in a pond and gotten his best suit wet rather than as a sea captain who was no stranger to damp clothing. He had never been pampered as a child, and savored her attentions with a delight he found nearly impossible to hide. Only the fact his face was nearly frozen kept him from grinning from ear to ear. When she had stripped him down to his bare skin, he was sorry he had not been wearing another couple of layers of clothing to keep her busy longer.

Eden hung Raven's wet garments from the backs of the chairs and then dried his thick curls with a towel. His teeth were still chattering, which was most definitely not an erotic sound, but they so seldom touched unless they were making love that she believed the direction in which her thoughts were straying was understandable. She blushed at the indecency of them, however. She had forgotten that Raven's handsome appearance ought to be considered a point in his favor too.

Knowing she could scarcely expect him to take her

criticisms of their problems seriously if she allowed his attractiveness to distract her, she forced herself to think of him only as a very tired and cold man, nothing more. She helped him into his bunk still wrapped tightly in the blanket, climbed in after him, and snuggled close. She had added extra blankets to the bunk earlier in the day, and the bedclothes still held her warmth.

"You'll be warm in just a little while," she assured him. "I really have been terribly worried about you. I know you're too tired to talk now, but when the storm's passed, we've got to find a way to get along better than we have been. We've got to stop being so hateful to each other, Raven. We've just got to."

Eden waited for him to make some sort of reassuring comment, then she realized by the slow, even rhythm of his breathing that he had already fallen asleep. She had known he had to be exhausted, but she had not expected him to go to sleep without thanking her for helping him. Perhaps he had expected it because she was his wife, but she did not think it would have cost him anything to offer a word of gratitude in response. Again hurt that her feelings meant so little to him, she lay awake listening to the constant eerie wail of the wind and thinking Raven was a damn liar for telling her the storm was no threat to their safety. She then whispered a prayer for all those aboard the *Jamaican Wind* and the *Southern Knight* as well.

Raven awakened after only four hours' sleep. His circulation now fully restored, he managed the agility required to climb over Eden without waking her. Fortunately he had plenty of dry clothes and again dressed warmly before leaving the cabin for what he fully expected would be another exceedingly long day. Despite the brevity of his rest, the inherent danger of their situation was so exhilarating he felt a renewed strength that made him immune to the effects of fatigue. He relished a challenge, whether

it was one presented by man or nature, and relieved Randy with an eagerness that left the weary mate shaking his head in wonder.

Even though the hatches were securely sealed, the ship was still taking on water, but diligent manning of the bilge pump kept the level of the encroaching sea at a minimum. Raven assigned the men to brief periods of time at the pump so none grew exhausted and slow. It was hard work, and that it had to be done in the dank bowels of the ship made it no less tiresome. The consequences of slacking off at the job were so dire, however, that none of the men were prone to laziness when it came their turn.

Unable to light a fire to heat food, the cook asked for a barrel of salt fish, one of crackers, and another of beer to wash down the unappetizing fare. The sailors sent to the hold on that errand soon returned crying for help for one of their number who had suffered an accident.

Raven held his lantern aloft as he hurried down the ladder into the aft section of the hold where the ship's provisions were stored. That he didn't hear screaming struck him as a good sign until he reached the injured man and found he had suffered a crushing blow to the chest and couldn't utter more than an anguished whisper. Hanging the lantern on a peg, Raven bent down beside the young merchant seaman.

"I don't want to risk moving you, John, but we'll make you as comfortable as we can here." Raven looked toward the men who had been with him. "How did this happen?"

A burly man named Owen stepped from the shadows. "We'd untied the ropes to free one of the barrels of beers but before we could get a hold of it, it tipped and went rolling right over John. It's the storm, captain. We couldn't hold the barrel with the ship bouncing up and down like a fat woman's breasts. It weren't our fault."

Raven's expression mirrored his concern. He and Alex

had argued over having a surgeon on board, but Alex had always protested that Julian fussed over him so much when he was at home, he was not about to have another physician around to spoil his enjoyment of their voyages. That seemed a trivial complaint now that one of the men had been so badly hurt. Most mishaps on board ship were due to carelessness of one kind or another, and Raven thought that a cause in this case as well but there was no sense in berating Owen for not being more careful when John was gasping for breath like a fish out of water. Someone had brought a couple of blankets, and Raven used one to cover John, then doubled up the other to prop him up slightly. He seemed to be able to breathe easier for a short while, then he weakened and began to call a woman's name.

"Who's Molly?" Raven asked Owen.

"She's the redhead that works at the Fife and Drum in Kingston. John fancies he loves her, but you know the type of lass she is." Owen shrugged slightly, conveying the impression John's affection was misplaced.

When John closed his eyes and continued to moan Molly's name, Raven expected each breath to be the man's last. He hated to see anyone die in so senseless an accident. Suddenly realizing he could at least ease the man's mind, he rose and told the men gathered around he would return shortly. He hoped it would be in time to do some good.

Eden was dressed only in her nightgown, but Raven gave her no time to don more than her slippers and heavy black wool cloak. "I need you to do a favor for one of the men. He's been so badly hurt I doubt he'll live more than another minute or two, but I want you to pretend you're his girl. Can you do it?"

Readily grasping his sense of urgency, Eden could only promise to try. "I did that many times in the hospital in

239

ichmond. Near the end of a man's life, any feminine pice seems to sound like that of the woman he loves."

"Let's hope it works again then." Raven took her hand nd, exercising all possible caution, guided her down the uccession of ladders that led to the hold. Without further rompting, Eden started to make her way through the men athered around John.

"What's her name?" she turned to call over her shoulder.

"Molly, and he's John Rawlings," Raven whispered.

The men parted to allow Eden to approach John, but ieir expressions ranged from amazement to disgust as one could imagine why the captain had summoned her. ven if she possessed a talent for healing, their fallen ompanion was beyond her help.

Thinking Molly might not be fair-haired, Eden took the recaution of pulling her hood up over her curls before ie knelt at John's side and took his hand. She was sorry find him such a young man, no more than twenty at the iost. Leaning down, she kissed his brow and whispered, It's Molly, John."

John tried to smile, and a large tear rolled down his heek. "Molly, is it really you?"

"Yes, my darling, it's me." Eden reached out to brush a ray curl off his forehead as she imagined the woman he ived would do. He had thick brown curls, and eyes that ere more gray than blue. While his features were conprted with pain, she was certain he was usually considred good looking.

John savored that announcement for nearly a minute efore speaking again. "I always wanted to ask you to be iy wife."

"I'd be proud to be your wife, John. Didn't you know iat?"

Raven was as touched as the other men crowded into

the hold as they listened to Eden respond to John's halting remarks with such sweet replies it brought tears to their eyes. Her voice was soft, yet filled with affection and they found it difficult to remember she was not really the woman John loved, but instead a wonderfully considerate stranger. The injured man was nearly incoherent now, but he clung to Eden's hand as his lungs, pierced by his shattered ribs, slowly filled with the blood that would drown him. It was a pitiful sight, and yet none wanted to leave and miss a word of the poignant dialogue taking place.

When John lapsed into unconsciousness, Raven came forward and laid his hand on his bride's shoulder. "Come with me. It's far too cold for you to remain down here any longer."

"No, I want to stay with him until the end. Molly wouldn't leave him alone."

When she looked up at Raven, her golden gaze was filled with a haunted light. He could not help but wonder if she wasn't thinking of Alex and if it wasn't really Alex she couldn't bear to leave rather than John. Until that instant he had not realized just how great a favor he had asked but truly she was the last person on board he should have asked to sit with a dying man. He didn't have the heart to argue with her, and so knelt by her side and waited until John's heart ceased to beat. Less than an hour had passed since Owen had sent up the cry of alarm, and Raven noted the time so he could make an accurate entry of John's death in his log.

The weather began to clear by noon of the following day. Owen had insisted upon being the one to fashion John's canvas shroud. When it was time for the burial service to begin, he had the fallen mariner's body ready to be consigned to the depths.

"Are you certain you feel up to this?" Raven asked Eden considerately. He had again worked until after midnight. The weather had steadily improved during the night, but he had purposely stayed away from his cabin to give Eden time to be alone with her thoughts and memories. She had been sleeping soundly when he had been ready for bed, and while he was disappointed she had not helped him to again undress, he had not awakened her to assist him.

"Your crew thinks little enough of me as it is, Raven. Surely they'd consider me completely heartless were I to miss John's funeral."

Raven did not want to comment on the crew's opinions until he had had the opportunity to again observe the men when Eden was on deck. From the comments he had overheard during the night, he had gotten the distinct impression that, after her moving portrayal of Molly, most of the men had reassessed their thinking where she was concerned. If so, he hoped it would be apparent at the service as Eden's mood had been subdued ever since John's death and he would welcome any help to cheer her.

"A burial at sea usually doesn't consist of much more than a psalm or two and the Lord's Prayer. It won't take long."

"I hope you've not had to do this often."

"No, thank God, I haven't, but I've never had a man die of natural causes. All our casualties have been as a result of accidents as stupid as the one that killed John."

"What may seem like an accident to you might also be called fate. How else can you explain why one man dies of old age, and another loses his life in his teens?"

"You've given this subject considerable thought?" While Raven wasn't surprised, he did not think it healthy for her to dwell on such a morbid topic.

"Well of course, doesn't everyone? None of us escapes death. Why shouldn't the subject fascinate us?"

"You have a point there."

Eden smiled, pleased he saw the logic in her comments. She had chosen to wear her gray gown for John's service, and turned for Raven to help her on with her cloak. While the sky was now clear, the day was still a chilly one and she pulled on a pair of kid gloves before again covering her curls with her hood. Raven was dressed in black, but then he usually was.

"When we get to Jamaica, could we visit Molly?" Eden asked as she moved toward the door. "I know she'll be heartbroken to learn of John's death, but perhaps it will ease her grief to know his last thoughts were of her."

Raven swung open the door, but hesitated before moving out of her way. "I hate to disillusion you, but Molly works in a tavern in Kingston, and it's more than likely that she won't even remember who John Rawlings was."

Disturbed by that news, Eden frowned slightly. "I'd still like to see her. If there's even the slightest chance that she loved him, we owe it to John to make the effort to contact her."

Raven hated to lose a member of his crew and, like his bride, also thought he owed a man who had died on board his ship every courtesy. "If it would please you, we'll do it," he promised, but he thought she would change her mind about speaking with Molly once she saw how rowdy a place the Fife and Drum was. The matter settled for the moment, he took her arm as they made their way up on deck.

Eden stood at Raven's side as he conducted the burial service. She thought he had a marvelous voice, one perfect for intoning the Scriptures and yet there was nothing theatrical about his delivery. She wished he had taken part in Alex's funeral now that she knew how beautifully he read Bible verses. Alex had meant far more to him than John, however, and she understood why he had not been able to read for his uncle.

She didn't watch as John Rawlings' body slid from the plank held at the rail and sank beneath the waves. Her mind was too full of another burial to take note of this one. When Max came forward and spoke to her, she jumped in surprise.

"Lady Clairbourne, we heard what you did for John. You're a very kind and generous woman. Can you find it in your heart to forgive me and Samuel for what we did?"

Thinking Raven must have demanded that apology, Eden looked up at her husband, but he appeared to be as surprised as she by Max's request. Max had seemed sincere in his apology the day he had spilled his bucket; now she knew that had merely been an act. "I will forgive you, but only if you promise not to judge people you do not even know so harshly in the future."

Now believing her to be the most gracious of women, Max eagerly made that promise. Embarrassed that he had needed to do so, he hurriedly excused himself and rejoined the crowd of men on deck.

Not wanting to speak to any of the others, Eden turned toward the rail. She heard several men approach, and Raven's insistent response that she was not be to disturbed. She didn't understand the crew's sudden interest in her, and was not in a mood to be friendly. When Raven put his arm around her shoulder, she needed a moment to find a smile for him.

"I think you better go below before you become chilled."

"I've spent too many hours in your cabin the last few days. Please let me stay here awhile longer."

"If you wish," Raven reluctantly agreed, but what he truly wanted to do was take her below and make love to her until the sorrow in her eyes vanished for good. There had been plenty of times when he had gone for more than two days without having a woman, but not making love to Eden for that long was a far more horrible deprivation. A slow smile graced his lips as he began to look forward to nightfall.

When Raven seemed content to remain with her, Eden soon recalled the questions she had wanted to ask him. She had to move close to be heard above the wind that billowed out the sails, but she hoped Raven would give her the answers she felt she needed so badly. "What do you remember of your parents, Raven?"

Shocked by such an unexpected query, Raven had to swallow hard before he attempted to provide a believable reply. He had known sooner or later she would begin to wonder about his family, and he had promised himself that while he could not possibly reveal the truth and keep her respect, he would not tell her lies either. He leaned against the rail, and tightened his hold on her. "I can't remember anything about them. It was Alex who raised me, you know that."

"You don't remember your parents at all?"

Clearly she was disappointed to hear that, but Raven had always considered himself lucky that he didn't know anything about them since they could not possibly have been an admirable pair. "No, I don't."

Eden had been so certain the secret to his volatile personality had to lie in the way he had seen his parents behave, but she was not easily discouraged and just changed the focus of her questions. "What can you tell me about Alex and Eleanora then? Were they happy? Did they get along well?"

Raven was far too bright not to understand what had prompted Eden's curiosity, but he could not think of anything particularly interesting to tell. "Yes, I think they were happy, but they were nothing like you and me. Eleanora was so sweet I don't think I ever heard her raise her voice with anyone, and I never heard her argue about anything with Alex. Whatever he wanted to do, they did. I was only thirteen when they married, though, so I didn't pay much attention to them." That had been the same year he had discovered what made women such a fascinating diversion, but that was another secret he knew better than to reveal.

Eden was frustrated that her efforts to understand Raven were meeting with no success. Alex had mentioned that Raven had lacked a woman's influence while young. Raven had told her himself that he had known very few women well, and now she understood why. She was still left with her initial problem, however, that they got along so poorly she did not think their marriage would survive.

"There's a lovely painting of Eleanora at the plantation. When you see it, I think you'll understand what type of woman she was."

"I don't care about Eleanora!" Eden snapped angrily. "She was Alex's wife, not yours."

Not about to get into another argument with her in front of his crew, and especially since he had not the slightest idea why she'd just lost her temper, Raven took Eden's arm. "Let's go below."

Eden was not angry with him, merely exasperated that her plans to get to know her husband well had not worked. Her lip was no longer swollen, and when she tried to smile, she succeeded. "Yes, maybe we could have tea together."

"Tea?" Raven doubted either of them was in the mood to share a soothing cup of tea, but he thought it best not to comment on her suggestion. They had just started across the deck, when Randy approached carrying a spyglass.

"The lookout's just spotted smoke on the horizon." He

led them across the deck to the starboard rail, and then handed Raven the small telescope so he could see for himself.

Other than a cloud of black smoke, Raven could make out nothing. Knowing Eden would expect to have a look, he handed the spyglass to her. "What do you make of it, my dear?"

Eden knew that endearment was more for Randy's benefit than hers, but she was too curious about the smoke's origin to be offended by it. Like Raven, she could see only the smoke, but not its source. "There's nothing worse than a fire at sea. Hadn't we better investigate?"

Raven looked first at Randy, who wore an apprehensive frown, and then explained the situation to her. "The storm blew us way off course, Eden. We're much farther north than I intended us to be. That doesn't present much of a problem, but rather than a shipboard fire, it's far more likely we've sighted smoke from cannons."

Immediately she thought of the *Southern Knight* and in an instant Eden's expression went from one of concern to absolute horror. "All the more reason to get close enough to judge!" she insisted.

Knowing he would never be able to talk her out of that, Raven shook his head sadly. "We'll sail only close enough to learn whether it's a ship in distress due to a fire, or a battle. If it's the latter, then we'll not remain to see who wins. Is that clear? This is a British merchant ship, and I'll not involve her in your country's Civil War."

"Yes, I know, I know. You think the War's stupid, but while we're debating the issue, it could be a British ship that's sinking, and since we're close enough to render assistance, I think we should ascertain whether or not it's needed."

"My recommendation exactly, Captain," Randy agreed with an encouraging smile for Eden. Upon learning of how tenderly she had cared for John Rawlings, he had been as deeply impressed as those who had actually witnessed the deed. While he doubted he would ever be able to make up for his previous standoffishness, he was willing to make the attempt.

"Then set our course accordingly," Raven ordered. As the mate turned away to do just that, he reached for Eden's hand and pulled her close. "I meant what I said. I want no part of your War."

Eden nodded. "I understand." She took turns with him using the spyglass, but before anything was clear to the eye, they could hear the boom of what sounded like cannon fire in the distance. "It certainly sounds like a battle, but couldn't that just be gunpowder exploding?"

"If that's the case, we'll not be likely to find any survivors."

Eden held her breath, expecting at any second that Raven would change the ship's course again and that she would never know what had happened. She was far more concerned they would soon find a Confederate ship sinking, and dreaded that it would be the *Southern Knight,* than she was a British ship might be on fire, but she dared not speak her fears aloud knowing that Raven would only repeat his opposition to the War in response.

A sudden shift in the wind allowed Raven a clear view of what had been hidden by the smoke. He recognized the stars and bars of the Confederate flag immediately, and that it flew from the mast of one of the Commerce-Destroyers that had plagued the Union's merchant fleet to the point of ruin. He handed the spyglass to Eden.

"I've seen enough. It appears that one of your Commerce Destroyers is actually battling a ship that can defend itself. That must be a novel experience for the captain."

Eden ignored her husband's sarcasm as she strained to

make out the ship's name. Few people had the privilege of viewing a naval battle without having to dodge bullets and she was fascinated by the spectacle. Knowing Raven intended to change course immediately, she reached out to grab his sleeve. "We've got to get close enough to read the ship's name."

"That's completely out of the question," Raven replied sternly.

"Oh please, I've got to know if it's my father's ship. We can't just sail away not knowing whether or not it's his."

"I intend to do just that."

"Raven!"

Raven began to smile as he realized how much power the chance sighting of the naval battle had given him. Eden was devoted not only to the Confederate cause but to her parents as well, and he was not above using that devotion to further his own aims. "Is that all you want, just to be able to read the ship's name?"

"Yes!" Eden insisted, for indeed she was too excited to think past that point.

"Then we'll satisfy your curiosity, but I'll expect you to show your gratitude in a manner I can truly appreciate."

Eden considered the sly smirk that graced Raven's features utterly reprehensible. That she could have become aroused while undressing him now appalled her. "How Alex could have described you as the finest of men I will never understand."

"He was prejudiced," Raven replied with an even wider grin. "If you'll find it impossible to reward me for my consideration, then I'll risk going no closer."

As he raised his hand to wave to Randy, Eden gave in. "All right, I'll give you what you want! You needn't make threats." She then turned her attention back to the ships that were firing on each other with what could now be heard as thunderous volleys. With the beauty of a ballet, they fired their cannon as they sailed past each other, and then came about to begin another potential deadly pass. While neither ship had yet inflicted heavy damage on its opponent, when each seemed equally determined to sink the other, it appeared to be only a matter of time before one was successful. As the battle progressed, she was disheartened to see the Confederate ship appeared to be getting the worst of it.

Eden heard Randy's voice as he came up to seek new orders, and Raven's response that he wished to identify the ships. She paid no further attention to the men's conversation until the *Jamaican Wind* had drawn close enough to enable her to read the lettering on the Confederate ship's bow. There was no mistaking the words as they had been deliberately painted large enough to provide not only recognition, but a bold warning. She was the *Southern Knight*. Eden handed the spyglass to Raven, but as her eyes filled with tears, she could not bear to look up at him.

Raven had already read the ship's name in Eden's crestfallen expression, but the decision he now faced was not nearly as difficult a one as he had anticipated. He knew what he was about to suggest was at least wicked, if not evil, but he wanted Eden too badly to care. Excusing himself to Randy, he took Eden's arm and moved her a few feet down the rail so they could discuss the situation privately.

"Neither side in your War can afford to fire on a British ship. We'll observe awhile longer, and if your father can't score a victory, or escape harm on his own, I'll provide him with the opportunity to get away. But I'll expect something more from you than affection in return."

They could smell the smoke now, but Eden's initial excitement at coming upon a battle had become nearly suffocating dread. "You swore to me not ten minutes ago that you wouldn't become involved in the War. Are you saying now that you've changed your mind?"

"Yes, if it would please you."

She had understood his blatant demand for affection, but could not imagine what he wanted now. "That can't possibly be the truth. What is it you really want?"

Raven knew he deserved that insult, so ignored it and came to the point quickly. "I want your promise that you'll never seek either an annulment or a divorce. I also want your word that you'll do as I ask when we reach Jamaica and not reveal that you're Alex's widow until after his child is born."

Astounded by the enormity of his demands, Eden tried to find a way to avoid agreeing to them. "What if I say yes, and then the *Southern Knight* doesn't need your help? Will you then release me from that wretched bargain?"

That she was so clever a woman always amazed him. "No, each of us must be willing to take a risk, Eden. I'll not go back on my offer of help, and you must keep your promise regardless of the outcome of the battle, or our efforts to change it."

"I think the term *bastard* is too mild to describe you, Raven Blade."

Raven did not allow the pain of that insult to show in his expression either. "Was that a yes?" he taunted.

"It's the only choice I have!"

"No, it's not."

"Oh shut up!" Eden hissed. She grabbed the spyglass from his hand and leaned against the rail to steady herself. She didn't want to miss a second of the drama unfolding nearby, not when her father's future might depend on it, and hers as well.

Fifteen

Nathan Sinclair's situation was dire enough without having to worry about a British clipper ship lurking in the distance, so he simply ignored it. Like the other Commerce-Destroyers, the *Southern Knight* was a wooden ship of approximately 1,000 tons. It had eight guns, and two steam engines that were capable of producing a speed of twelve knots. By adding sails, they could make fifteen. The Confederate raiders had been built for speed, and while they were more than a match for any merchantman afloat, they had never been intended for the task of battling Federal warships.

The corvette that had attacked the *Southern Knight* carried eighteen guns mounted on the upper deck. The class of warship under the frigate, corvettes were used for scouting, convoys, and privateering. Nathan had at first attempted to elude the more heavily armed ship and, having failed, was determined they would defend themselves until dusk when they would make good an escape under the cover of darkness. The success of that plan was dependent upon their ability to inflict damage without suf-

fering an equal amount in return, and being so badly out-
gunned made that task a considerable challenge.

Despite being under heavy fire, they had suffered few
casualties, but with their supply of gunpowder running
low, Nathan began to fear their store of munitions would
be depleted before dusk arrived to shield them. Fighting
against time as well as the corvette's relentless assault, he
was doggedly determined not to lose either battle and
ordered his men to make every shot count.

Standing on the quarter-deck, Nathan turned in response to a distress-filled cry and found the British clipper bearing down on them at an alarming speed. Knowing
the corvette's captain was bound to be equally distracted,
he ordered a momentary cease-fire until they could discover the clipper's purpose. When he saw the British vessel meant to traverse the channel between them and the
Federal warship, he could not believe his eyes.

Thinking no sane captain would set such a suicidal
course, he nonetheless chose to use the ship's passing to
every advantage, and ordered the starboard cannon to fire
the instant each had a clear shot at the corvette. As that
command was relayed to the gun crews, Nathan continued
to stare in wonder at the audacity of the British maneuver.
At one time there had been many Englishmen who were
in sympathy with the Southern cause. That such an individual had appeared on that of all days was a stroke of
luck he would not waste.

The *Jamaican Wind* passed within thirty feet of the
Southern Knight, and Nathan's mouth dropped agape as
he recognized his only daughter standing at the rail. She
was waving and blowing kisses, and while her tawny curls
were being whipped wildly by the wind, her expression
and gestures were unmistakably ecstatic. She was standing between a tall man dressed in black and a signalman
waving semaphore flags to transmit an urgent request for

the *Southern Knight* to follow the British vessel. It was easily the most remarkable spectacle any on board the Confederate raider had ever seen.

The first of their cannon fired then, followed in rapid succession by the other three on the starboard side. Not nearly so alert to the possibilities of using the British clipper as a shield, the corvette was repeatedly struck amidships before firing a single round. Seeing the enemy's wooden hull splinter at the waterline, a loud cheer went up from his men and Nathan was satisfied the Federal ship had suffered sufficient damage to prevent it from giving pursuit. He therefore broke off the engagement and, setting the engines at full speed, followed the helpful British vessel without further delay.

Pleased the *Southern Knight* was following in their wake, while the Federal corvette appeared to be in distress, Raven dismissed the signalman, folded his arms across his chest, and leaned back against the rail. Eden was using the spyglass, and he waited for her to hand it back to him before he spoke.

"It looks as though our ploy worked, undoubtedly because it was so damned unexpected. That should make the terms upon which we agreed easier to follow than if the venture had ended in failure."

While the sarcasm had not left Raven's voice, Eden was too amused by her father's startled expression to react negatively to her husband's mood. At least her parent had not been so befuddled by their bizarre attempt to help him that he had allowed the opportunity they had provided to slip by unused. She had always considered him the best of captains, and it was readily apparent that Raven was of equally high caliber. She was too thrilled by their success to be goaded to anger by his reminder of their bargain.

"I know I sounded very ungrateful before, and I'm sorry. I don't want you to think that I put a higher value on the lives of my father and his crew than you and your men."

That she could speak such an outrageous lie with a straight face didn't amaze Raven, only that she had bothered. "We agreed on honesty, remember? Just how little you think of us is far more plain in your actions than your words." When she opened her mouth to protest that opinion, he promptly cut her off. "You got what you wanted and so did I, so there's no point in arguing about how we went about it."

"You're being very unfair," Eden insisted stubbornly. "In the first place, you offered your help, I didn't demand it. But I'm sure you'd have done the same thing had you had the opportunity to save . . ." She paused as she tried to think of someone he cared enough about to rescue, and had to give up the effort when she realized she didn't know any such person now that Alex was dead. "A friend," she finally added. "You'd not allow someone you cared about to come to harm if you could prevent it."

Raven continued to regard Eden with a skeptical glance. They had hurriedly draped canvas over the *Jamaican Wind*'s bow and stern so her name could not be read and he doubted he would ever be called upon to explain his actions that day. "Your opinion of me seems to change with the hour. As soon as we're certain there are no other Union vessels nearby, I'll invite your father to come aboard. I'm sure he's as anxious to speak with you as you are to see him. You may tell him the truth about Alex, of course, but not about our bargain. I'd rather my father-in-law didn't consider me the bastard you do."

Raven had gotten his way, and Eden did not understand why he was being so obnoxious. Maybe he had not expected her to accept his terms and was angry she had forced him to keep his side of their bargain. Whatever his reasons, she had no time to pursue them now when she would need all her wits to devise a means to describe the recent events in her life to her father that would not prompt him to instantly disown her.

When Nathan Sinclair and several of his officers came on board, Eden rushed into her father's arms, and he responded to her affectionate greeting with equal enthusiasm, lifting her off her feet in a boisterous hug. He had taken the time to clean up and change into a uniform that wasn't blackened by smudges of gunpowder. He had had no hope of seeing any of his family anytime soon, and could not truly believe Eden was standing in his arms until he had hugged her repeatedly.

Hoping that Eden would soon introduce him, Raven stood back and attempted to wait patiently, but she continued to embrace her father with what he began to regard as nearly hysterical fervor. While he was sorely tempted to reach out and restrain her, he forced himself to observe Nathan instead. He was surprised to find Nathan was his equal in height, but not that he was quite handsome since Eden was so pretty. The man's hair was a deep auburn, touched lightly at the temples with gray. When he at last glanced toward him, Raven was startled to see Eden had inherited her striking golden brown eyes from her father. In a young woman the unusual shade was stunning; in a man, the very same hue was shockingly dangerous in its effect. Thinking the devil himself would also have eyes of molten gold, Raven knew instinctively he wanted his father-in-law as a friend rather than an enemy.

Equally intrigued, Nathan's gaze swept over Raven's muscular frame and well-tailored attire before focusing on his face. He had not really expected to recognize the captain of the ship that had enabled him to get the better of the corvette, but he was still disappointed that he did not. "You are either the bravest man I've ever met, or a damn fool. Which is it?"

Eden was still clinging to her father, and Raven decided he would have to introduce himself. "That's a matter of opinion," he replied with the most charming grin he could manage while his wife was ignoring him so completely he was certain she had forgotten his existence. "I'm Raven Blade, your daughter's husband."

"Oh, I'm so sorry," Eden apologized as she realized she should have made such an introduction herself the instant her father had come on board. "Raven is much too modest, Daddy. He's also the Earl of Clairbourne."

Nathan responded with a mock bow. "My lord. When we sent Eden to England, we hadn't dared hope she would return home a countess. I hope neither of you will be offended if her mother and I fail to show the proper respect."

Raven was uncertain if Nathan were joking and he found that fact as unsettling as the man's amber eyes. From his firm grasp on Eden's waist, and sarcastic tone, Nathan scarcely appeared pleased to welcome him into the Sinclair family. What disturbed Raven most, however, was that he recognized the undercurrent of hostility that flowed through his own personality in Nathan's every word and gesture.

"Why don't you take your father to our cabin where you can talk in private. I'm sure you both must have many questions." Raven moved aside, but the look in Eden's eyes was one of panic rather than gratitude at his suggestion and he didn't understand why. He leaned down to kiss her cheek lightly. "I realize ours is a most unusual love story, but you needn't be ashamed to tell it."

Consumed with curiosity without Raven's remarks,

Nathan took his daughter's hand in a firm grasp. "I can't stay long. Let's not waste what little time we do have."

Eden had wished so many times that she could talk over her problems with her mother, but a conversation with her father was an entirely different matter. Fortunately he knew the location of the captain's cabin, and she had only to follow rather than lead the way.

As Raven watched them walk away, he realized Eden had not responded to his demand that she keep the terms of their bargain a secret. For all he knew, she might beg her father to take her off the *Jamaican Wind,* and when he refused to allow her to leave, there would be hell to pay. He started after her then, but had taken only a few steps before he realized he did not want to listen to her conversation with her father. He simply could not bear to hear her tell him how dearly she had loved Alex, and still did. He turned around then, and seeing the half-dozen officers who had come aboard with Nathan, he made certain they were given whatever they wanted to drink while they waited for their captain.

Eden took her usual place at the table, while Nathan regarded the neatly kept cabin with a cursory glance. "Does your earl keep anything stronger than tea on board?"

Eden gestured toward the appropriate cupboard. "He has all manner of spirits. The blackberry brandy from Briarcliff is his favorite, though."

"Briarcliff? Is that the ancestral estate?" Nathan browsed through Raven's store of liquor until he found a bottle of whiskey. He then reached for a pewter mug, poured himself a shot, and downed it quickly.

"Yes, there's Briarcliff in Devon, a townhouse in London, and a plantation on Jamaica. That's where we're bound. Had a storm not blown us off course, we'd not have been anywhere near here."

"Well, it's damn lucky you ran into foul weather then." Considering the weather of no further interest, Nathan poured himself more whiskey and, bringing the mug, took the seat across from his daughter. "I've met an earl or two, but your Lord Clairbourne certainly doesn't look English to me. What's his background, Greek perhaps, or is he a descendant of the Spanish Conquistadors with Indian blood?"

Eden shrugged helplessly. "I've no idea, but I do know he considers himself British. The European aristocracy intermarries so frequently I doubt any of them knows what nationality they truly are anymore." It disturbed Eden to think her only thoughts of Raven's looks were how handsome a man he was. She had never bothered to question the reason for his dark coloring, and it struck her as being totally irrelevant now. "You know what I mean, don't you? Not only was Queen Victoria's mother German but her darling Prince Albert was one of her German cousins. The French general Bernadotte was adopted as the heir to the Swedish crown, and—"

Nathan interrupted impatiently. "I'd rather skip the lecture on European history and hear how you became a countess. Your husband said the story was unusual. In what way?"

Eden would have much preferred to continue tracing the genealogy of as many royal families as came to mind rather than discuss her own situation. It was not that her father was an unsympathetic man, but only that her story was such a painful one to tell. He had every right to hear it, however, and taking a deep breath, she forced herself to begin. "I want you to know the truth, but it's difficult to know where to start. Raven is my second husband, you see, not my first."

Rather than respond with one of his favorite oaths, which certainly seemed appropriate, Nathan left the table to pour himself another drink and this time he brought the bottle of whiskey back to the table. "I wish your mother were here to hear this. Just tell me the whole story slowly so I can repeat every word the next time I see her."

Encouraged that he appeared to be more curious than outraged to learn she had been wed twice since he had sent her to England, Eden tried to honor his request, but soon found herself speaking in an excited rush. She was too anxious to make him understand how difficult their time apart had truly been to concentrate on the manner of her delivery.

Eden experienced no difficulty describing the idyllic days she and Alex had spent at Briarcliff, but when she came to the night of his funeral, she knew the truth was a secret she dared not reveal. That her love for her late husband had overwhelmed her reason and allowed her to succumb to Raven's passionate advance was far too shameful an event to relate to her father, or anyone else.

Her father loved her dearly, but she feared he would lose all respect for her if he learned she had behaved in such a wanton fashion. She was satisfied in her own mind that her grief had betrayed her rather than a previously undiscovered weakness of character, but still, the story was too sordid to admit. After all, her silence would protect not only her own reputation, but Raven's as well. She and Raven had married, she disclosed tearfully, because it had been what Alex had wished.

When Eden began to weep dejectedly, Nathan first handed her his handkerchief, but when the square of linen offered little comfort, he rose, scooped her up into his arms, and sat down again with her cradled on his lap. He could not recall the last time she had sat on his knee, but she had been an affectionate child and had done it often

260

so he felt comfortable holding her now. He had been amazed to learn she had wed a man of thirty-eight, since he was forty-two, but she had spoken of Alex in such adoring terms that he did not doubt she had loved him. He had readily felt his daughter's anguish as she had described her husband's sudden death, but his understanding had ended abruptly when she had announced she had wed Raven Blade within a week of Alex's demise.

"Forgive me for interrupting, sweetheart, but I know the members of the British peerage marry more often for reasons of amassing property, and creating ties between families than for love. Is what you're describing merely a marriage of convenience to prevent Alex's fortune from being divided between you and Raven?"

That was a lie Eden had not even considered telling, and she swiftly rejected it now. "No. Alex's wealth would not have been divided if we'd not married. It was all to go to Raven, although I would have received a generous allowance." The second part of his question was far more difficult to answer, and she could not manage to do so with more than a whisper. "Our marriage is not a pretense. Raven truly is my husband."

Nathan was at a loss for words for a long moment, and when he finally spoke, his anger was plain in his abrasive tone. "I see. Raven not only inherited his uncle's title and fortune, but his beautiful bride as well. That was damn clever of him, and for him to sail through the midst of a battle as he did today makes me think he thrives on danger as well. A rogue with a title is a rare combination. Do you love him?"

Eden did not know how to describe her second marriage, but she considered it sadly lacking in the love that had filled her first. She did not want to give her father a worse impression of Raven than he had already gathered, however. "Raven could not be more different from Alex, but I might be able to love him someday."

That wistful remark was as depressing to Nathan as the rest of his daughter's story. "Do you realize nothing you're telling me makes any sense? I'm sorry you lost Alex, but if you loved him as you swear you did, how could you have replaced him so quickly?"

"I didn't 'replace' him," Eden protested immediately. "No one could ever take Alex's place in my heart, not Raven, nor anyone else."

Nathan was frustrated by her lack of understanding. "I'm sorry to say this, sweetheart, but if you feel that way, I'm afraid you'll soon regret marrying Raven. Your mother could offer far better advice than I can, but other than to love you, there's nothing I can do for you until the War's over. None of us expected it to last more than a few weeks, or months at the most, and now it looks as though it will continue until the last Southerner is dead. That my own situation is too desperate to permit me to help you is no excuse, I know, but do you think you can stay with Raven until I'm able to do something for you?"

Grateful for that offer, Eden hugged him tightly. "Your love is all I'll ever need. I intend to stay married to Raven, forever."

"Because Alex wanted it?" Nathan asked incredulously.

"No, not just because of Alex." Eden stopped there, unwilling to describe the bargain she had made with Raven when revealing it would only infuriate her father. As perverse as Raven was, she did not want Nathan to hate him. "Raven is most definitely a rogue, you're right about that, but he's also very bright. He's a fine captain, firm with his crew, but not abusive. He has many admirable qualities," Eden paused as she tried to think of some, but when none came to mind, she gave up the effort. "I hope once we reach Jamaica, we'll be able to lead normal lives. I know we'll never love each other the way Alex and I did, but I don't expect that either."

Eden was more slender than when Nathan had last seen her, and if anything, more beautiful. She had the same maturity about her now that he had seen in all too many young widows of late. "Your mother and I had hoped you'd be happier in England, sweetheart. We really did."

"I was happy, Daddy. Once I met Alex, I was happier than I've ever been. I'll never forget him, nor be sorry that I was his wife." She tried to smile so he would not think her situation bleak, but she could not keep her lips from trembling.

Raven had expected Eden and her father to talk for an hour at most. Nearly two had now elapsed and he was becoming worried. He rapped lightly at his cabin's door before peeking inside. "I'm sorry to disturb you. I neglected to offer refreshments, and it's growing late." He was astonished to find Eden perched on her father's knee, her arms draped around his neck, in what he considered far too familiar a pose.

Unmindful of the critical nature of Raven's thoughts, Eden slipped off her father's lap and went to the door. She stood on her tiptoes and whispered in his ear. "I didn't have time to mention the arms, but if we gave them to my father, it would save us the trouble of disposing of them elsewhere."

Raven had already learned from the Confederate officers they were entertaining that the *Southern Knight* was dangerously low on munitions. Those young men had had no idea that was exactly what the *Jamaican Wind*'s hold contained, however. Considering her comment an invitation to join her, he moved through the door and closed it behind him. "You've told him about Alex?"

Eden nodded as she wiped away the last of her tears on her father's handkerchief. "Yes, I did."

"Good." Raven took note of the half-empty bottle of whiskey on the table, and decided no further offer of refreshments was needed. He helped Eden return to her chair, then sat down beside her. "My uncle wished to aid the Confederacy. We've not only got a great deal of gunpowder on board, but also Enfield rifles and Kerr revolvers and ammunition for them. I'll be willing to transfer it all to your ship if you'll give me your personal guarantee that I'll be paid what the munitions are worth in gold. I'll not accept Confederate currency."

Nathan was astonished not only by the mention of arms, but also that Raven would launch into such a discussion without making the slightest attempt to get to know him first. He had had no love for the British before that day, and his son-in-law's cool arrogance did nothing to change his opinion. In the back of his mind, he began listing the Southerners his daughter might take for a third husband and he found it easy to smile.

"You'll take my personal note for the cost, is that what you're saying? If I give you my word that you'll receive gold for the arms, you'll give them to us?"

"Well, I'd prefer a straight exchange, but I'm assuming you don't carry gold in sufficient quantity on board the *Southern Knight*. If I'm wrong and you can pay me now, then there'll be no need for a note."

"Is this why you were so damned reckless? Did you come to our aid simply to make a profit on arms?"

"Daddy, I'm sure the thought never crossed Raven's mind. We were concerned only about you. I don't think his actions can be described as reckless either. *Daring* is a far better word, and since our intervention worked to your advantage, it's rude of you to question Raven's motives."

Nathan was not about to argue that he could have gotten along without help when he doubted he could have. He was startled that Eden would defend her husband so staunchly, however, when she had given him the impression she was indifferent to him. "Forgive me, my lord," he began with exaggerated care. "I'm more than a little drunk, but I did not mean to insult you. Draw up the note, and I'll sign it. Perhaps we can decide upon some deserted isle where we can safely load the munitions on the *Southern Knight*. We've so many repairs to make we have great need of a safe harbor."

"Raven?"

Raven read Eden's question in her anxious expression. "Our plantation is located on the Rio Bueno and has docks up the river that aren't visible from the sea. They'd make the perfect place for you to conduct your repairs. If you're low on munitions, you must need other supplies as well, don't you?"

"Well yes, of course, but . . ." Nathan did not want to be indebted to a son-in-law he found so difficult to like.

"Jamaica can't be that much out of your way, Daddy, especially not if you'll be safe from attack while you're there."

Nathan rose to his feet, but kept his hand on the back of his chair to keep his balance. "You said your uncle wished to help the Confederacy. What are your feelings on the matter, Lord Clairbourne?"

Raven also stood, and when he drew himself up to his full height, he was pleased to find he was perhaps a fraction of an inch taller than his father-in-law. "I'd rather you called me by my name," he requested first. "I think your misguided cause was doomed from the start. I'm helping you only because you're Eden's father. I'd not have intervened if we'd sighted another Confederate ship in the danger you faced. Don't make the mistake of thinking I believe in your cause, because I don't."

"But you're not averse to making a profit on it?" Nathan pointed out shrewdly.

"I'm merely trying to complete a venture Alex undertook. I've no desire to build our wealth on your country's pain. If I didn't have to protect Alex's investment, I'd have dumped the whole lot overboard long before this."

Nathan saw no difference between protecting an investment, and turning a profit, but even after one drink too many he could see the futility of arguing with Raven Blade. The handsome young man was not only bright, but determined as well. He was most certainly not the type of man he would have chosen for Eden, but because that choice had already been made, Nathan would not waste his breath decrying it when he could do nothing about it.

"Give me the course settings for your plantation, then should we have to separate, we can rendezvous there later. You have my word that I'll not sail into your harbor with a Federal ship anywhere in the vicinity. I'm sure your actions today will be seen as those of a lunatic, but protecting the *Southern Knight* in a private harbor would be another matter altogether."

"I've gotten myself out of worse situations," Raven replied flippantly, but he went to his desk, sketched a quick map, and made the course notations Nathan had requested.

"Yes, I just bet you have." Nathan leaned down to kiss his daughter goodbye. "Stay where you are. I'm sure it's too cold for you to be out on deck again. Oh, by the way, Michael Devane's one of my officers. I couldn't bring him with me today, but I know he'll be looking forward to seeing you."

"Tell him I'll be looking forward to seeing him too," Eden responded sweetly, but when Raven returned from making certain her father got back to his own ship safely, she soon realized she had said the wrong thing.

266

"Who is Michael Devane?" Raven asked before he had gotten through the door.

"He's a boy from home, is all."

"A boy, or a man?"

"Well, I suppose he should be called a man. He's about your age."

"And what is he to you?"

"Nothing really. He's just one of the boys, or young men rather, that I used to dance with at parties. I've not thought of him once since I left home so there's no need for you to be jealous of him."

"I am not jealous," Raven denied through tightly clenched teeth.

Unwilling to argue with her volatile husband, Eden turned away. She was still seated in her chair, but that allowed for some freedom of motion. "I won't fight with you. I'm sorry my father wasn't more gracious. He's usually a very charming man. I think he was just too surprised to see me today to be as friendly as he should have been."

Raven noted the stubborn tilt of her chin, and knew he ought to follow her example and change the subject before her mood deteriorated to the foul level of his. "I'm sorry he wasn't able to stay for dinner. I'll tell the cook we're ready to eat."

Eden let out a sigh of relief as she heard the door close. Alex had never made her feel the way Raven did, as though she had to watch every word she spoke or constantly be on the defensive. She had always liked Michael Devane, and she truly was looking forward to seeing him again, but not if it was going to send Raven into a fit of jealous rage.

Raven returned a short while later with Kipp, the cook's helper, who served all their meals, and Eden realized she felt hungry for the first time since the voyage had begun. Her mouth watered as she watched the young man set the table and serve thick slices of ham and boiled potatoes. As soon as Raven had finished the brief blessing he repeated every evening, she took a bite of ham.

"This is absolutely delicious. When was the last time we had a hot meal?"

"It was too long ago to remember," Raven replied between bites. Knowing they would both feel better with full stomachs, he refrained from asking questions until they had finished eating.

"Your father took the news of our marriage more calmly than I'd expected. How did you manage that?"

Eden wiped her mouth on her napkin before admitting she had mentioned only Alex's desire that they wed. "That is the truth, if only part of it, so please don't accuse me of lying."

Raven could not help but laugh at her request. "I didn't expect you to tell him we'd slept together before the wedding, Eden. No one admits that to their parents, although I'll bet not every bride is a virgin and, with a widow, who can say?" When his wife blushed with embarrassment at the indecency of that opinion, he tried to find something she would find easier to discuss. "Was he excited about becoming a grandfather?"

"I'm afraid I didn't get that far. I was still talking about you when you came in, and then, well, I guess I just forgot."

"How could you forget something so important as that?"

Pressed for an explanation, Eden gave the only one she could. "I was just so thrilled to see him, that it was difficult to remember everything."

"You certainly forgot me quickly enough." Raven had meant to control his temper, but that remark slipped out before he could stop it.

"I did not!"

"I was gone in the blink of an eye."

"Raven, don't do this. Just because I was excited to see my father doesn't mean that I'd forgotten you! I should have introduced you earlier. I know that and I'm sorry. It won't happen again."

"Aren't you a little old to be sitting on his lap?"

"Nothing I ever do pleases you, does it?" Eden answered with the same caustic tone he had just used. She was getting as good at doing an imitation of him as he was at mimicking Alex, but she had heard that critical tone of voice too often not to be able to duplicate it. Tears stung her eyes and she knew they were only seconds away from another of the beastly arguments that had made her second marriage far closer to hell than the paradise her first had been.

Raven took a deep breath, then finished the rest of his wine. It pained him to think his jealousy was so plain Eden could see it the minute he had asked about Michael Devane, but he was grateful she didn't seem to realize he was jealous of her father as well. Apparently she thought him overly critical, but didn't understand why. That he craved the attention and affection his wife had no interest in giving him was too painful a circumstance to bear in silence, but his pride wouldn't allow him to beg for her love. He was angry with himself for wanting something he couldn't have so badly it hurt. It was the agony of that longing that made him lash out at her and he knew all that did was give her a damn good reason to hate him.

She had agreed not to divorce him, however, and although he had not worded his request as precisely as he wished he had now, she had also promised to reward him for going to her father's aid. He wanted her so badly his whole body ached, but he was not going to ever be as rough with her as he had been before the storm. She never took more than a sip or two of wine, and she didn't care for brandy, so he had no hope of getting her drunk. He did want her in a far better mood than her present one, so he suggested the only thing that occurred to him.

"There's plenty of fresh water thanks to the rain. If you'll excuse me, I'll go and heat some so we can bathe."

He was making another strategic retreat, but Eden wasn't about to criticize him for it. "A bath would be wonderful," she said instead. When Raven leaned down to kiss her, she raised her hand to caress his cheek. "That's really very considerate of you."

"Believe me, it's not gratitude I'm after," Raven informed her, and as he strode out the door, he was glad she couldn't see the width of his grin.

Sixteen

September 1863

Raven brought the tub and several pails of hot water, then left the cabin while Eden bathed. She washed her hair, then remained in the tub to soak while the water cooled. It had distressed her that she had been unable to enumerate at least a few favorable characteristics when she had described Raven to her father. Now she was sorry she had failed to mention he had always been a gentleman when it came to assuring her comfort and privacy.

A review of the days they had spent together at Briarcliff quickly brought to mind the admirable fact her husband had assured his tenant farmers he would not raise their rents. He had also insisted quite forcefully that Paul Jessup take better care of his family. How could she have forgotten those actions when they so clearly illustrated the goodness of his character?

Asking her to pretend she was John Rawlings's sweetheart had shown Raven had a regard for the members of his crew she knew many captains lacked. Surely if she had had time to tell her father about the baby, she would have remembered Raven's promise to be the best of stepfathers too.

Ashamed of her negligence, she quickly left the tub, wrapped herself in a towel, and using the pen and ink in Raven's desk, began to make notes in the back of her diary. She would keep a running list of every worthwhile activity her husband undertook so she would not be at a loss for reasons to praise him in the future.

When Raven could not stand to be away from Eden for another minute longer, he was dismayed to find her taking such poor care of herself. "This cabin is far too cool for you to wear no more than a towel," he scolded crossly.

Eden closed her diary and replaced his pen and ink in the desk. "I wanted to write myself a note. I'm finished," she remarked with a smile, hoping she did not look as guilty as she felt at having him catch her at it.

Raven had already reached for another towel and stepped behind her to dry her dripping curls. "I mean it, Eden. You've got to be more concerned about your health."

Eden had not even noticed the chill in the air until Raven had complained of it. She leaned back against him now and enjoyed his warmth while he continued to blot the last of the moisture from her hair. He could be very gentle and sweet at times, and she knew she ought to have remembered that too.

"Now hurry and put on a nightgown," he ordered just as sternly. "I'm going to fetch more hot water for my bath." Raven tossed the damp towel on a handy peg on his way out the door. He then had to stop and catch his breath before going up the companionway. When Eden was such an alluring woman, why had he not realized drying her hair would only fuel his desire? This was just another example of his usual lack of foresight where she was concerned, and angered by his own stupidity, he stomped off to get the water.

As soon as Raven had poured the fresh water into the

tub, Eden came forward to help him remove his coat. "I'll help you undress if you like," she offered graciously.

"No, you needn't bother. Just get into bed." Raven brushed her hands aside and turned his back on her. He had the evening planned down to the last second, and he didn't want her upsetting those plans with the enticing ways that would swiftly make him lose all control of his senses. He'd vowed not to behave like the love-crazed idiot he had been the last time they had made love, but he would not be able to be otherwise if she touched him now.

Eden took one look at the rigid set of Raven's shoulders and backed away. She had thought he wanted to make love, but that icy rebuff chilled her ardor more thoroughly than the cool temperature of the cabin. Her feelings hurt again, she turned away and got into the bunk as she had been told. She pulled the covers up to her chin and hoped she would be sound asleep before Raven came to bed.

Raven hung his coat over the back of his chair, yanked his shirt off over his head, then sat down to pull off his boots and socks. His pants soon joined the heap of discarded clothes, and in less than a minute he was seated in the tub. He washed his hair, scrubbed himself clean, and was out of the water and dry in less time than it took Eden to make herself comfortable. He then joined her in the narrow bunk, swept her curls aside, and began to playfully nuzzle her nape with a flurry of eager kisses.

Eden had expected to be ignored, not ravished, and completed confused, she sat up abruptly. Raven had left the lamp burning low, and she could see his smile plainly, but was determined for once not to be influenced by it. "I'm trying my best to understand you so we can live in something approaching harmony, but when you shove me aside one minute then grab me the next, I don't know what to make of you."

While Raven had to agree his actions did seem contradictory, he knew in truth they were not. Rather than protest her accusation, he reached for her wrist, and with a gentle tug pulled her back down into his arms. There was no way he would admit his need for her was becoming an obsession he could neither explain nor control.

"I want you," he whispered against her mouth, which was set in a fetching pout. His lips brushed hers lightly as he shifted his position to trap her beneath him where she could not escape him again.

Making a list was going to prove pointless, Eden decided. It would be of no use to keep track of Raven's good deeds when his erratic behavior would erase them faster than she could write. She had promised herself to never again allow thoughts of Alex to fill her mind when she lay in Raven's arms, but she had never missed the dear man more.

Raven propped himself up on his elbows so he could study Eden's expression since she was not usually so quiet. Her golden eyes appeared a soft brown in the dim light. She was looking directly up at him, but he doubted she saw him when her gaze seemed focused many miles away. Unable to hide his disappointment, he reminded her harshly, "You promised me a reward."

His deep voice jarred Eden from her reverie, but she was only dimly aware of his words. "You must want me all the time, Raven, not merely when the whim strikes you," she complained wistfully.

Raven groaned in despair. "There's not a second of the day that I don't want you," he admitted before he could stifle the impulse. "But I had to risk getting us all killed to win your promise you'd want me."

That was the first time Raven had even hinted that he cared for her. Responding with the unabashed delight that had made her the belle of Richmond, Eden could not

274

resist teasing him. "And what about the nights?" she asked in a seductive purr.

A bright sparkle now lit her eyes with a mischievous gleam, and that she so clearly wanted him too kept Raven from feeling she was making fun of him. No other woman had ever dared tease him, and he was amazed to find that he liked it coming from Eden. "The nights," he confided in a husky whisper that was flavored with his own sense of humor, "would be worse torture than the torments of hell without you."

Eden favored him with a bewitching smile before she laced her fingers in his damp curls to draw his mouth to hers. Her tongue swept his mouth slowly, and this time when he groaned softly, she knew it was not prompted by frustration but by desire. She pulled him closer still, anxious to savor more of his delicious taste and slow, sweet affection.

The amorous couple kissed until they were both so breathless they had to stop for a moment. "My gown," Eden murmured softly, and Raven, no longer fearing she might elude him, moved aside momentarily to help her discard it. She then returned to his arms before he could reach for her. She had forgotten their bargain. She wanted him for the pleasure they had always shared, not because of a promise she had been forced to give.

The cabin was too cool, and the bunk far too narrow, for the way Raven truly wished to make love, but he knew those constraints would no longer hinder him once they reached Jamaica. They would again have wide, comfortable beds, and the gloriously warm nights that would allow them to give their passions free rein. With the exotic memories of his island home in mind, he made love to Eden with a newfound tenderness that thrilled her as deeply as it did him.

Her touch was even more tantalizing than the first time

he had felt her caress. Her kiss was far more flavorful than his favorite brandy, and the warmth of her inner heat as he brought their bodies together radiated clear through him. He could not even imagine another man ever finding the blissful happiness his reluctant bride provided in such abundance, and he was overjoyed that she had given him her word never to leave him. Basking in the afterglow of her loving, he knew whatever risks he had to take to keep her would be well worth it.

They had gone to bed earlier than was their usual custom, and when Eden realized Raven had not fallen asleep in her arms, she seized the opportunity to make the closeness they shared last far longer than it ever had. She slid her fingers through the crisp curls that covered his chest, and snuggled against him.

"Talk to me, Raven. I know so little about you. Won't you please tell me something about yourself?"

Raven drew in a deep breath rather than react angrily to that request but he didn't want to talk. All he wanted to do was hold her and pretend that she loved him. "Is that what Alex did? Did he keep you constantly entertained with amusing stories?"

That was exactly what Alex had done, but Eden did not want to compare the two men in her life. "I want to talk about you, not Alex. You're my husband, but I don't know you well. Can't you think of something to tell me?"

With a perverse sense of pleasure, Raven rose up slightly and propped his head on his hand, but he kept Eden pulled close to his side. "All right, I'll tell you a story if you insist I must."

"Thank you." Eden reached up to kiss him, for truly she was thrilled that he had agreed to confide in her.

"I told you I outgrew Alex's clothes in my teens. I must have been six feet tall by the time I was thirteen. There are a great many advantages to having a man's height at an early age, and I used them all."

"To do what?" He'd made her too curious to keep still.

"Just hush and listen. When I was almost sixteen, Alex decided I ought to know about women so he took me to the most expensive brothel in Kingston."

Now Eden was really intrigued. "That was when he was married to Eleanora, wasn't it?"

"Yes, but he didn't intend to avail himself of the services, he was just taking me there. Now are you going to be still and let me finish or not?"

"Yes, m'lord," Eden replied through a burst of giggles.

Raven began to laugh too then. "The whole point of the story was, that when Alex took me to the brothel to introduce me to the pleasures of the flesh, every last woman in the place already knew me."

Eden knew that was surely the most shockingly inappropriate story any man could ever tell his wife, but she was so amused by it she laughed right along with him. She was certain he had told her far more than he had intended to, for now she knew exactly what type of women, the few he had admitted to knowing truly were.

"If you were that good a customer, you obviously resembled a grown man in more than height," she remarked with her usual ready wit.

"I'll not deny it," Raven admitted through another burst of deep chuckles.

They had never shared such a relaxed mood, and Eden pressed for every advantage. "You promised to be faithful to me. I know the women in Kingston are going to miss you terribly. Will you miss them?"

Eager to make love to her again, Raven moved over her. "That's entirely up to you," he replied with a wide grin but his real answer flavored his kiss with a devotion Eden could never mistake. No other woman would ever take her place in either his bed or his heart, but he could not bring himself to put that promise into words until he was confident his love was returned in full measure.

While Nathan Sinclair did not board Raven's ship again, the sight of the *Southern Knight* off the stern kept Eden's spirits so high the remainder of the voyage passed swiftly for her. The crew, while still somewhat shy around her, had become friendly. She found it difficult to believe the kindness she had shown John Rawlings had changed their manner toward her so drastically, but she accepted their pleasant smiles without questioning what had prompted them.

The weather continued to be mild and the winds brisk, allowing them to make up the time they had lost during the storm. Unlike the gray-green Atlantic Ocean, the waters of the Caribbean were a dazzling sapphire blue that promised with every sparkling drop that Jamaica would indeed prove to be the paradise Alex had described.

That Eden had not once complained of their bargain left Raven slightly perplexed, but he enjoyed her ample affection too greatly to bring up the topic himself just to test her resolve. Once he had discovered how much he liked making her laugh, he had continued to tell her stories he had once thought unfit for her ears. After making love, she would lie in his arms listening to his hushed confessions until they had each laughed so hard tears came to their eyes. They would make love again, and when Raven fell asleep, he always knew Eden's dreams would be as sweet as his own.

Alex had had a gift for telling the most trivial incident in an enormously entertaining fashion. Raven made no attempt to duplicate his late uncle's style. Instead, he would merely relate one of the many ridiculous and sometimes dangerous incidents he had managed to survive unscathed. He had never regarded his life as being particularly amusing until Eden had asked to hear about it and then had reacted in such an appreciative fashion. That he could entertain her so easily continually amazed him, but best of all, he found the laughter they shared late at night brought a closeness that lasted all the following day.

That he would surely run out of stories eventually worried him, but he hoped by the time that happened they would be home and have enough to talk about without him having to describe his past. He was careful never to mention the days before he had come to live with Alex, for the stories he could tell about his childhood were all tragic rather than amusing ones.

"The entrance to the Rio Bueno is just ahead." Raven handed Eden the spyglass so she could see it. "Kingston is on the opposite side of the island, but apparently the first Earl of Clairbourne to come here valued privacy more highly than companionship and chose the site of his plantation accordingly."

Eden scanned the palm tree-lined coast for the mouth of the river. The beach was littered with palm fronds but the contrast of the rich green of the foliage, the sparkling white of the sand, and the startling blue of the sea was magnificent still.

"From the looks of the beach, they have had stormy weather here too."

Raven took the spyglass when she offered it, then had to agree her observations were correct. "I've not seen a gale severe enough to uproot the palms, but you're right about the amount of debris lying about."

Raven was obviously concerned, and Eden stepped

close and took his arm. "A few palm fronds doesn't mean your home was damaged."

"Let's hope not." He had frequently gone over how he would tell Alex's staff and friends about his passing, but the possibility that the storm that had driven them off course might have struck the northern coast of Jamaica had not occurred to him. He had been looking forward to coming home with a nearly painful anticipation, and he did not want to find the plantation any less perfect than when he and Alex had left it, for Eden's sake as well as his own.

Enchanted by Jamaica's verdant natural beauty, Eden remained by Raven's side as the ship entered the Rio Bueno. The river bottom had been dredged in the early years of sugar production, and frequently since, to allow ships to be loaded at the plantation docks which stood approximately one hundred yards upriver. As the wooden structures came into view, Eden turned back to watch for the *Southern Knight,* which had been closing the distance between them rapidly, while Raven was interested only in assessing possible damage from the storm.

As soon as the gangplank was lowered, Raven excused himself. "I want to go up to the house first and tell everyone about Alex. I don't want them all weeping and wailing when they should be at their best to welcome you. I hope you won't mind staying on board for a while."

Eden considered it very thoughtful of him to ask. "Of course not. I'll wait here for you."

Raven kissed her cheek lightly, then hurried away. Remaining at the rail, Eden watched him start up the dirt road toward the plantation that still lay out of sight. Apparently the staff had sighted the *Jamaican Wind's* masts above the tree tops, however, for half a dozen women were already running toward the river. Raven waited where he stood, then held out his arms to keep the enthusiastic group from going past him.

Eden had expected him to have Negro servants, and was surprised when one appeared to be a most attractive Spanish woman. She was tall and slender, with ebony hair worn in a chignon. Unlike the others, she was not wearing an apron, although she was dressed in a simple gray gown that a servant might wear.

While Eden could not overhear Raven's words, she saw the shock and grief register in the women's faces and knew they had loved Alex too. Only the Spanish beauty appeared unmoved, but in the next instant she swayed slightly, and had Raven not caught her when she fainted, she would have fallen in the dirt of the road. Thinking her husband would surely need her now, Eden started toward the gangplank, but Randy MacDermott swiftly blocked her way.

"Yadira Morales is the dramatic sort. You needn't concern yourself about her. She'll have recovered by the time she reaches the house."

Eden sighed impatiently, then decided to accept Randy's word rather than argue since Raven had asked her to remain on the ship for a while. "She's very attractive. Is she one of the maids?"

Randy shook his head. "She's the housekeeper, came here right after Eleanora died."

That neither Alex nor Raven had ever mentioned they employed such a lovely housekeeper puzzled Eden for a moment, until she realized each had described only the beauty of the island, and never the residents. Actually, she was pleased to find the housekeeper was a young woman and hoped they would get along well and become good friends.

"Here's your father's ship now," Randy pointed out. "I'll bet he's anxious to see you again."

"Oh yes, I'm certain he is and I can't wait to see him either." Eden did not think she would upset Raven if she remained at the docks, and with Randy by her side, she left the *Jamaican Wind* as soon as the *Southern Knight* had tied up at the dock behind them. She returned her father's wave, and nearly danced with excitement as she waited for him to reach her. When she saw Michael Devane following him, she hurriedly glanced over her shoulder to look for Raven and was relieved to see he had not yet returned.

Nathan again wrapped Eden in a boisterous hug, but he had encouraged Michael's interest in her, despite the fact she was now a countess, and he swiftly stepped aside to allow the young man to speak with her. Not about to waste an opportunity to kiss the pretty blonde, Michael did just that.

Startled by what she considered an overly affectionate greeting, Eden took her father's arm. "Will you please excuse us for a moment, Michael? I need to speak with my father."

While he was disappointed Eden did not seem particularly happy to see him, Michael responded with another broad smile. Blond and blue-eyed, he knew he was handsome and was confident that she had always liked him since all the other girls in Richmond most certainly had. "Of course, talk as long as you please. We'll be here for a week at least and there will be plenty of time for the two of us to talk."

Although she was uncertain just what she and the overly attentive officer had to discuss, Eden replied that she would look forward to it. Once she had drawn her father aside, she forgot Michael completely. "Have you told everyone that I was widowed before I married Raven?" she asked in a breathless rush.

Because that was not the type of news he wished to

circulate, Nathan glanced toward the heavens in a silent plea for the strength to handle the tangle his lively daughter had made of her life. "No, I said only that you'd wed the Earl of Clairbourne. I didn't reveal how many times you'd done it."

"Good. Raven wishes to keep the fact I was married to Alex a secret until after the baby comes."

"Good Lord, Eden. Whose baby are you having?"

Eden had forgotten her father didn't know she was pregnant, and he wore too horrified an expression for her to think he was pleased about it. "I'm sorry. I should have told you when last I saw you. Please forgive me for not doing so."

Nathan dismissed that request with an impatient wave. "Whose child is it?" he asked again in a hoarse whisper that readily conveyed his annoyance.

"The babe is Alex's, but I didn't realize there would be a child when I married Raven."

"Well of course not, he didn't give you time to consider anything at all!"

"Daddy, please don't be angry with Raven. We did the only thing we could under the circumstances."

Nathan turned away to shield her from the string of oaths he could not suppress, but when he faced her again, his expression was no less dark. "The man is up to no good, sweetheart. I can't believe that you don't see that. He rushed you into marriage, and now he expects you to keep your marriage to Alex a secret so no one will know what a scoundrel he is. I don't like the sound of any of this and I'll tell him so, too!"

"Daddy, please! After Raven was kind enough to invite you here where you can make your repairs without fear of attack it would be most ungrateful of you to insult him. Don't forget the arms either. I know you need them too badly to refuse them out of pride just because you suspect Raven's motives."

He was thoroughly disgusted, but Nathan had to admit she was right and nodded. His scowl didn't lessen, however. "All right, I'll hold my tongue for the time being, but the minute the War's over—"

Eden interrupted her father's threat with a hasty kiss. "Thank you. There's so much about Raven that you don't know, but please believe me, his character truly is an admirable one." She caught sight of her husband out of the corner of her eye then, and hoped her father would act like a gentleman as he had promised.

Raven was not surprised to find Eden with her father and, after greeting him briefly, introduced the young black man at his side. "This is Azariah Dunn, my overseer. If you'll give him a list of what you need, he'll see you receive it promptly."

"Thank you, I'll do it first thing in the morning."

Raven glanced over at the blond officer who was watching them with more curiosity than he considered polite. Making a determined effort to ignore him, he simply turned his back on him. "The slaves were freed here nearly thirty years ago. As you might expect, the sight of a Confederate ship at our docks makes those who can remember slavery more than a little nervous. I know there's nothing you can do about your gray uniforms, but will you at least strike your colors?"

Eden saw the fire fill her father's eyes and used her elbow to provide a sharp jab to his ribs to remind him of his promise. He looked down at her with a warning glance, then surprised her by agreeing to Raven's request to lower their flag without argument. "Of course, I consider it only prudent to do so when it's highly probable not all your neighbors are so willing to disregard Britain's neutrality as you are, my lord."

Raven was certain he had asked his father-in-law to call him by his name, and did so again. Nathan smiled as he said that he would, then motioned for the young officer who was obviously eager to join them to come forward.

"Lord Clairbourne, this is Michael Devane, my first officer. He'll be the one supervising the repairs."

"Raven Blade," Raven repeated as he extended his hand. "I would prefer that you called me by my name, Lieutenant Devane." He had taken an instant dislike to Michael when Nathan had first told Eden the young man was on board the *Southern Knight*. He saw no reason to change that view now. Michael had struck him at first glance as an arrogant dandy and he knew they would never become friends. He again introduced his overseer, and explained one of his many talents.

"Azariah is a master carpenter, so if you need help with your repairs, just ask him to assist you."

Michael Devane dismissed the handsome Negro with no more than a disdainful glance. "I'm sure we'll not require his help. We do need fresh water, though."

"Help yourself to the river, Lieutenant." Azariah inclined his head in a mock bow, turned away, and walked over to the men who had begun unloading the arms that were to be transferred to the Confederate ship.

"You ought not to allow such insolence from your servants," Michael pointed out sharply.

Amused by his overseer's obvious contempt for the arrogant lieutenant, Raven broke into a wide grin. "He's an employee, not a servant, and I don't consider him insolent at all."

Raven was a couple of inches taller than Michael, and a good deal more muscular. While Nathan would have liked nothing better than to see a fight break out between the two young men, he saw no point in encouraging such a contest when Michael could not possibly win. "Will you excuse us?" he asked his daughter instead. "I imagine you're anxious to see your new home, and we've more than enough to do ourselves."

"You'll come for dinner tonight, won't you?" Eden asked.

"We'll have to make that tomorrow night, Captain," Raven corrected. "We'll be unable to entertain tonight."

"Oh, I'm sorry." Eden was badly embarrassed she had not considered that the household staff had just learned of Alex's death and should not be asked to entertain. "Is everyone upset?"

"Devastated is a better word." Raven found it difficult to believe Eden would have expected Alex's servants to feel otherwise.

"We'll have to let you know about tomorrow night then." Eden reached up to kiss her father goodbye, but offered Michael no more than a smile.

When Raven took her arm, she apologized again as they started up the road toward the house. "I don't know how I could have been so thoughtless. It's just that we speak of Alex so often, it doesn't seem as though he's really gone."

"I understand."

Eden studied Raven's pensive frown and doubted that he did. "Should we have some sort of memorial service here for him? He must have had many friends who'd like to attend."

"Let's discuss it after your father leaves."

"Was he right about your neighbors? Will people be upset that we have a Confederate ship here?"

Raven shrugged. "It's possible, but they'll surely understand my reasons for wanting to aid my wife's countrymen."

"I certainly hope so." Eden clung to her husband's arm

more tightly, but thought it prudent to change the subject. "Tell me about Yadira. Is she all right?"

Raven came to a halt in midstride. "How did you hear about her?"

Eden explained her conversation with Randy. "She's very pretty for a housekeeper. Is she efficient as well?"

"Yes. She runs the house as though it were her own."

"That's good."

Raven was relieved Eden had been curious only about Yadira's housekeeping skills. He had had too much on his mind on the voyage home to worry about Yadira, but now that they had arrived, he hoped the hot-tempered woman would not prove troublesome for Eden. Hoping to avoid any such conflict, he vowed to tell Yadira to keep her memories of Alex to herself. He patted Eden's hand lightly, and continued to escort her on up the wide road.

"A violent storm did cut through here a couple of weeks ago," he told her as they walked around a heap of wilted palm fronds. "But fortunately they caught only the edge of it here, just as we did. Other than some damage to the foliage, which they've nearly cleared away, there was no serious harm done."

They rounded a slight bend then and Eden got her first glimpse of the house Alex had regarded as home. It was an imposing structure with the ground floor built of stone and the upper story of shingled wood. It had multiple roofs, and was surrounded by a shady veranda overgrown with native orchids and brightly blooming hibiscus. The windows were covered with louvers, which assured privacy at the same time as they allowed the breeze easy access to the large home.

The well-designed house was every bit as beautiful as the rest of the island, and suddenly Eden was overcome with longing for the man who had described it with such pride and had wanted to bring her there to live. Raven was standing quietly by her side, but she could not bear to look up at him her heart was so full of love for Alex. He had insisted she was as lovely as the orchids that grew in such abundance on the plantation and she knew she would never be able to look at the exquisite flower without remembering his whispered words of praise as they had made love.

Raven felt Eden hesitate, and when he looked down and saw her golden eyes filling with tears, he knew without asking where her thoughts had strayed. He had already carried Yadira over the threshold that day, but he scooped up his tearful bride and carried her into the house as though they were like any other happy couple who were beginning their marriage in a new home. That neither of them could manage a smile did not faze him.

Seventeen

September 1863

The portraits of Alex and Eleanora were on display in the drawing room. Eden immediately agreed with Raven's opinion that this painting of her late husband was superior to the one at Briarcliff. Completed in the last year of his first marriage, Alex's hair shone with the silver light Eden had thought a wonderfully attractive complement to his deeply tanned skin. The blue of his eyes held precisely the right amount of sparkle to reveal his lively wit, and his slight smile, while suitably serious for a formal portrait, readily conveyed his engaging personality. Had she never met the charming man, she would have fallen in love with him with a single glance of the remarkably flattering portrait.

Grateful she would be able to appreciate it daily, Eden turned to study the one of Eleanora and found Alex's first wife had been a brunette, with large hazel eyes. She appeared to have been petite, for her features were delicate and the hands which lay folded in her lap were as small as a child's. Her expression was one of such innocent sweetness, it was easy to believe Raven's comment that she had never raised her voice to anyone.

Raven had not stopped to contemplate Eleanora's portrait since the day it had been hung. Now he wondered what Alex had seen in the shy young woman. She had been undeniably pretty, but completely devoid of either the keen intellect or passionate temperament that made Eden such a fascinating woman.

"We'll have to have our portraits painted next summer when we visit Briarcliff," he mused aloud. "England has several excellent artists who can make us look as attractive as we truly are."

"Why Raven, I've never heard you say anything in the least bit conceited before today."

"I've no need to be conceited," the dark-eyed young man responded confidently. "Besides, you must know you're a beauty without having to hear it from every man you meet."

Eden regarded Raven with a skeptical glance, certain he was teasing her for a purpose and unwilling to walk into some clever verbal trap. She looked up at Eleanora's portrait rather than respond. "Was she truly as childlike as she seems?"

"Even more so, but Alex was happy with her, although I doubt he knew what happiness was before he met you."

"Are you trying to make me as conceited as you?"

Raven knew from her smile that his comment had pleased her too much to argue the point. He took her hand to draw her away. "Come on, there's lots more to see. This house isn't a quarter of the size of Briarcliff, but it's always been my favorite of the two."

"I think it will soon become my favorite too." Eden was uncertain if Raven's teasing had been a deliberate attempt to raise her spirits, but regardless of his intent, it had had that effect. "I'd like to see the whole plantation tomorrow."

"Wouldn't you rather spend the day with your father?"

"Yes, but I doubt he'll have much time to devote to me. He may have put Michael in charge of the repairs, but I know he'll want to oversee the work himself. He's as particular about the running of his ship as you are."

Pleased that she thought he and her father shared such an important attribute, Raven was happy to grant her request. "We'll ask him first then, and if he'll be occupied all day, I'll be happy to take you on a tour."

"Thank you." They had reached the stairs without seeing any of the servants, and Eden wondered aloud where they were.

"I sent them all home for the remainder of the day. Yadira is the only one who lives in the house. Her room is on the ground floor, next to the back stairs. She's very high-strung." Raven found it difficult to return Eden's inquisitive gaze when he had no intention of revealing more than a small portion of the truth about the attractive housekeeper. "She's been here for nearly a decade, and takes a great deal of pride in maintaining our home well. Because the house has been without a mistress for so long, she may be reluctant to take orders from you at first. I'll speak to her about that tomorrow. After learning of Alex's death, she was in no condition to discuss anything."

Eden could readily understand how Yadira might regard her as an interloper. "No, please don't talk to her about me. I didn't expect to come here and immediately begin giving everyone orders. If Yadira has managed this long without a mistress to provide direction, she'll undoubtedly regard any suggestions I make as interference. Please give her a chance to become comfortable around me. Then if there's something I want done differently, she won't feel insulted when I approach her about it."

"You're right, of course."

"Alex's death will make things difficult too. I want to

be sensitive to whatever grief the servants here may feel but my father won't be here but a few days, so I hope your staff will understand why I'm anxious to entertain him. I don't want any of them as outraged as Stewart was, or to think we aren't mourning Alex as respectfully as we should."

It never failed to amaze Raven that Eden was not only beautiful, but practical as well. "That we've had longer to deal with his loss than everyone here has might make things difficult for us for a while, but we don't have anyone here with such a strict sense of propriety as Stewart had."

"Not even Yadira?"

"No, she keeps very much to herself so I don't think she'll be concerned about appearances if we invite your father and his officers to dine with us. I'll tell her only that I want her to offer you every possible assistance. Do you want everyone to know about the baby yet?"

Eden frowned thoughtfully. "Are you going to say we were married in July rather than August?"

The timing of her child's birth was not something Raven had considered. "Yes, we'll have to, won't we? I don't want everyone counting on their fingers."

"They'll be doing it regardless of what we want, but I'd rather keep them from beginning that for as long as possible. Besides, I doubt the fact we'll have a child next spring will be obvious until after the holidays. Let's just keep it a secret for as long as we possibly can."

Eden looked so distressed by their discussion, Raven reached out and placed his hands on her shoulders. "I know you think the ruse I've demanded you play is ill advised, but I want you to trust me to know what's best for us."

That Raven had asked for her cooperation now puzzled Eden. "I gave you my word. I'll not go back on it. What

292

about your crew? Did you tell them to keep my marriage to Alex a secret?"

"Yes, I most certainly did and they'll do it too." Raven raised his index finger to her lips. "Now hush. Alex always treated the staff here like family, and if one of them ever overhears such a tantalizing conversation as this, I can guarantee they'll all be buzzing with curiosity within five minutes."

Eden nodded. She did not share her father's view that Raven was a scoundrel intent upon covering up his own foul deeds, but she would never agree that convenient lies were better than the truth, no matter how damning that truth might be. "You helped my father as you'd promised, and I'll keep my part of the bargain. Now why don't we go on upstairs and see the rest of the house?"

Raven knew she would keep her word, but the cynical light in her eyes didn't please him. Clearly she was going to do as he had asked as a point of honor rather than because she believed he was right. He was equally certain he had chosen the proper course, however. Taking her hand, he started up the stairs. "I think I'll remain in my own room for the time being. You may choose the bedroom on either side. The one on the north was Eleanora's, the one on the south was used only by guests."

As they reached the top of the stairs, Eden began to smile. "Don't tell me, let me guess. Was Eleanora's room decorated in shades of lavender?"

"How did you know?"

"I think the color would have suited her. I'd prefer the other room, please. Will someone bring my trunks from the ship?"

"Of course." Raven hesitated at the first door to the left. "Do you want to see Alex's room?"

Eden shrank back slightly. "No, I'd rather not. I suppose we'll have to dispose of his things someday, but I'd rather not begin today."

Raven readily understood her reluctance to enter Alex's room and continued on down the wide hall to the adjoining one. "This room was Eleanora's."

Eden took in the decor from the doorway. Not only was lavender the predominant color, but the furnishings were of such a delicate design the room could have belonged to a young girl, or an elderly woman, just as easily as to the mistress of the house. The louvers at the windows were open to admit the afternoon breeze and there was a graceful stem of green orchids in a bud vase on the dresser. As immaculately kept a house as Briarcliff, the room appeared to still be in use, rather than long vacant.

"Does Yadira place fresh flowers in all the rooms regardless of whether or not they're occupied?"

"That's scarcely wasteful, Eden. The plantation is overgrown with flowers and bringing a few into the house will never deplete the supply."

Eden was surprised by the sharpness of his tone. "I wasn't being critical," she quickly denied. "All I meant was that it was a very gracious gesture for an empty room."

"I'm sorry. I didn't mean to snap at you." Again taking her hand, Raven opened his door as they walked by, but went on past it to the bedroom she had requested. He threw open the door, and stepped aside to allow her to enter first. "If the pink wallcovering and upholstery does not suit you, the room can be redecorated. We can shop for whatever you'd like when we go to Kingston next week."

"This room isn't really pink, Raven, it's more of a dusty rose and I like it just the way it is." Again the louvers were open, and a vase of orchids sat on the dresser. While the bedroom had mahogany wainscoting, as did all the other rooms she had seen, the pale rose of the walls above the dark paneling kept the room from being masculine in appearance. She walked over to the connecting door between their rooms and tried the knob.

"It's locked. Where's the key?"

Raven could not help but laugh at that question. "I had no idea you were so eager for my company. I'll see you're given a key immediately."

Eden had not realized how her question must have sounded until she heard his deep chuckles. "On the contrary," she countered. "I knew you'd be eager for mine for a few more months at least and I didn't want you to have to break down the door to get to me."

When she turned away rather than toward him, Raven knew that, despite her feisty response, she was badly embarrassed. He waited until he could control the impulse to laugh again, and then followed her to the windows. "I have always regarded pregnant women as especially attractive rather than repulsive. Don't think my interest in you will wane when your condition begins to show. It won't."

"Will that be safe?"

A shadow of apprehension filled her golden gaze now, and Raven hastened to reassure her. "I'll ask Julian Ryan about it. He was Alex's physician. He's sure to know."

"Don't you think he would be shocked by such a question?"

"No, I'm certain I won't be the first husband to ask it." Raven thought Eden's concern charming and pulled her into his arms. When she hesitated only a moment before relaxing against him, he tilted her chin and provided what he hoped would be a reassuring kiss. "I'd not risk either the babe's health, or yours, for my own pleasure. Don't you know that?"

Eden nodded, then rose up on her tiptoes to return his

kiss. The idea of a child was still too new for her to want to plan how long they would be able to make love. That they could do so now was all that mattered to her. When his affectionate hug became a far more fervent embrace, she tightened her hold on his waist. Raven had always been able to sweep all reasonable thought from her mind, and she was aware only of the sweetness of his taste until she heard a light rap at the door. Badly startled, she backed away from his arms as though she had no right to be there.

Yadira Morales stood at the door. Apparently completely recovered from the shock of Alex's death, her expression was one of cool detachment rather than the deep distress Eden had seen earlier that afternoon.

"Forgive me, my lord, I did not mean to intrude. Is this where you wish your men to bring Lady Clairbourne's trunks?" the housekeeper asked, when Raven glanced her way.

"Yes, please." Raven quickly introduced the two women. He then explained the *Southern Knight* moored at their docks was captained by his wife's father. Yadira nodded slightly as if that information were of interest, but she did not come forward to bid Eden welcome.

"I thought Alex meant for you to have an English bride," she remarked coolly.

Yadira's voice was husky, and so soft it barely carried across the room. While her tone was not critical, her comment certainly was and Raven took exception to it. "Let me assure you that Eden was Alex's choice, as well as mine. Now if my men are here, please send them up with my wife's belongings."

"As you wish, my lord." Yadira turned away without saying more than her initial greeting to Eden, and left them as silently as she had come.

Eden sighed unhappily. "I think winning that woman's

friendship is going to be far more difficult than I had thought."

"She was devoted to Alex, and I expected her to take the news of his death badly. I'm sure she didn't realize how hostile she sounded."

"I just don't want her to think us unfeeling."

Raven kissed his worried bride again before he replied. "She's here to make our home comfortable, not to add to our worries. You needn't be so concerned about her."

Again distracted by his affection, Eden decided to give Yadira the benefit of the doubt and tend to her unpacking rather than worry that the housekeeper might continue to be aloof.

After an early supper Yadira had managed to produce even without the assistance of the rest of the staff, Raven and Eden walked down to the docks to visit Nathan. As eager for exercise as they, the captain joined them in a stroll along the riverbank. The evening was warm, and still light enough to make a walk enjoyable.

"I've not had the time to sit down and write up that agreement we talked about," Raven admitted as the three started toward the beach. He had ordered the munitions unloaded, but he would not allow them to be transferred to the *Southern Knight* until he had his father-in-law's promise of payment in writing.

"We were able to repair most of the rigging on the way here. I doubt we'll need to stay the week Michael mentioned. I think we can be ready to sail again in about four days. I'd appreciate it if we weren't delayed waiting for you to draw up that document."

Eden was walking between the two men, and pressed her father's hand in hopes he would become less argumentative. "That's a simple matter. I'm sure you can do it tomorrow, can't you, Raven?" she asked pointedly.

"I'll attend to it first thing," he promised.

"You realize, of course," Nathan cautioned, "that if I'm killed before I can provide your gold from the Confederate treasury, you'll have to recover the amount due you from my estate. Or to put it more bluntly, you may find you have to ask Eden for the money. I hope that won't prove bothersome."

"Daddy, please!" Eden yanked on his hand hard enough to stop him this time.

"Well it's the truth, sweetheart. Your husband is very clever and I'm sure he knows he can't collect debts from a dead man."

"Stop it!" Eden demanded tearfully. "I'll not listen to you talk like that."

Raven put his arm around Eden's shoulders and drew her near. "Your father's merely trying to be realistic, Eden. But I'm sure that I'll be paid for the arms so there's no need to agonize over how that might come about."

"I want to go back to the house," Eden replied without glancing up at either man. She knew Alex and her father would have gotten along beautifully, but it was apparent that, other than their interest in sailing, Nathan and Raven had no grounds for mutual respect. The antagonism that flowed between them made her too uncomfortable to want to remain with them. "I expected too much from you both," she announced suddenly, and pulling away from her husband, she started back up the path on her own.

Raven turned to follow her, but Nathan reached out to stop him. "Let her go. She can't possibly get lost and we may never have another chance to talk privately."

While Raven didn't like the idea of leaving Eden alone when clearly she was badly upset, he decided his father-in-law deserved at least a few minutes of his time. "That you obviously don't like me is unfortunate, but I think you ought to make an effort to at least be civil for Eden's sake."

"To hell with being civil!" Nathan replied with a disgusted sneer. "I think you're a lying opportunist, and I'm sorry Eden ever met you, let alone married you. For some reason she's determined to defend your actions so I have no choice but to leave the matter in her hands for the time being. At the War's end, however, you'll have to answer to me for her happiness."

Raven was not the type of man who would calmly listen to threats. "The last man who made the mistake of calling me a liar didn't live five minutes. What makes you think you can do any better?"

Nathan eagerly accepted that challenge. "If you'd rather settle this now, that's fine with me." Although born into a wealthy family, he had gone to sea at sixteen and considered himself as tough as Raven any day. He ripped off his jacket and tossed it aside, then waited while his son-in-law shrugged off his. The path by the river was wide enough for a fistfight, but just barely. Nathan took the precaution of placing his back toward the palms and then swung at Raven with a blow that would have torn off his head had it connected.

Raven dodged that blow, but wasn't as fortunate on the next. For a man in his forties, Nathan was surprisingly agile and strong, but Raven doubted he would have much endurance and responded to the Southerner's savage blows with sharp jabs that kept the older man constantly moving. The strategy was a good one, and while Raven took as much punishment as he meted out, he was counting on gaining the upper hand when Nathan began to tire. Unfortunately, Nathan was too angry to feel fatigued for a good, long while.

The men slipped in the mud of the riverbank, and ca-

reened into the trees as they recovered. Soon both were so
battered and muddy it was impossible to tell which man
wore gray pants and which black while neither's shirt
would ever be worn again. When finally the furious pace
of Nathan's attack began to slow, Raven went for him with
a renewed burst of determination. He struck him a brutal
blow to the chin, then seeing he had Nathan dazed, he
shoved him into the river.

The water's chill quickly revived Nathan, and he
crawled up the muddy bank still intent upon giving his
daughter's husband a well-deserved beating. Slyly, he
staggered as though beaten as he rose to his feet, but in
the next instant he tackled Raven with a flying leap and,
hanging on to him tightly, rolled back into the water,
where he hoped the arrogant English lord would quickly
drown.

While Raven had been in numerous fights as vigorous
as this one, he had to admire his father-in-law's spirit as
well as his unexpected stamina. He still thought he would
eventually get the best of Nathan, but now it looked like
that might not happen before midnight. A strong swim-
mer, he broke free of Nathan's grasp before the man could
hold his head under for more than a few seconds. As they
scrambled out of the river, both men slipped so often their
fight swiftly deteriorated into a wrestling match in which
neither could get a secure enough hold on the other to
gain an advantage.

When he had to spit out a mouthful of mud for the third
time, continuing the fight suddenly struck Raven as being
so totally senseless he began to laugh. He cuffed his father-in-law playfully. "I'm willing to call this fight a draw
if you are."

Suspecting a trick, Nathan hesitated to agree, but when
Raven made no further move to hurt him, he struggled to
his feet and leaned back against the palm tree he had

slammed into several times that night. He ached all over, but he wasn't ready to concede defeat. "It may have been a draw this time. It won't be the next."

Raven was on his feet too now. "Are you always so stubborn?" he asked before scooping up a handful of water to rinse out his mouth.

"Oh hell yes," Nathan swore.

"Well, so am I." Raven regarded his father-in-law with renewed respect as they both caught their breath. "You would have liked Alex. He would have challenged you to a game of chess rather than settle an argument with his fists."

"I would have had no quarrel with your uncle," Nathan reminded him. "Eden loved him."

That was something Raven didn't need to be told, but hearing her father say it in his soft Southern drawl hurt worse than any of the man's smartly landed punches. "Come on," he said. "You can't go back to your ship looking like that. You can bathe at my house."

The young man's attitude had changed so abruptly, Nathan knew he had scored some sort of victory, but he failed to understand just how. "Wait a minute. Eden explained Alex's heart condition was hereditary. Is there any chance at all that she'll have a healthy child?"

"What do you mean?"

That he had befuddled Raven completely was too obvious to merit comment so Nathan rephrased his question. "If the Suttons have had weak hearts for several generations, isn't it likely Eden's babe will be sickly? Perhaps too weak to survive infancy?"

It was Raven who reached out for a conveniently placed palm tree now. "Please don't voice those questions to Eden. I've never stopped to consider them myself and I certainly don't want her to. I doubt she and Alex ever

301

discussed this, but he was the eldest of five children. None of the others lived longer than a few months."

"If he had no brothers or sisters who reached adulthood, then how could Alex have been your uncle?"

Instantly Raven recalled his conversation with Alex before he had agreed to go to England to look for a wife. He had been certain someone would surely ask him that question, but Nathan was the first. "The Sutton family tree is too complex for me to trace it here." That was the truth, and so was Raven's next statement. "Everyone knew I was his heir, without having to do it either. Now come on, it's getting late and I'm worried about Eden."

Nathan reached down for his coat, and tossed Raven's to him. "You're a lot tougher than I thought," he offered grudgingly. There was still something suspicious about Raven Blade but he decided perhaps he ought to give the young man more time to prove himself because Eden spoke so highly of him. "I'm worried about Eden too. She seems to have survived Alex's death well, but I wouldn't want her to lose his child. Have you a good physician to attend her?"

"Yes, Julian Ryan is very conscientious. He looked after Alex for several years so I'm sure he'll know what to do for his child. I'll ask him to join us for dinner tomorrow night if you'd like to meet him."

"I'd appreciate that, thank you. I promise I'll be on better behavior then too."

"Well, I'd certainly appreciate that," Raven replied in a drawl that mimicked his father-in-law's so perfectly the older man began to laugh.

Eden was seated on the veranda, and when she saw two mud-covered men approaching the house, she did not at first recognize the pair. When she did, she was horrified to see they had obviously been fighting, and confused that they seemed to be talking quite amicably now.

"Hasn't either of you a lick of sense?" she called out, but they just laughed and waved as they went on by her and headed for the rear of the house. Certain they were on their way to the separate structure that contained the privy and bathing facilities, Eden ran after them.

"If you want to be helpful," Raven teased, "go and get us some clean clothes. We're close enough to the same size to both wear mine."

Astonished the two men could have gotten themselves so dirty, and yet now smile as though they were the best of friends, Eden left them to run that errand. She entered the house through the rear door, and nearly ran into Yadira before she saw her standing in the dimly lit hall.

"Is there something you require?" the soft-spoken housekeeper asked.

"No, just a couple of changes of clothes and I can get those."

Yadira turned away, and seemed to vanish into the shadows before Eden remembered her room was nearby. "Thank you all the same," she called after her, but there was no reply. Still thinking the housekeeper a bit odd, Eden hurried up the back stairs to her husband's room. He had not bothered to unpack his clothing, but she found all he and her father would need without too great a delay. When she climbed the stairs of the stone structure to reach the room containing the large copper tub, she found Raven waiting at the door.

"I let your father bathe first. I'll take him the clothes. While I'd appreciate your helping me with my bath, I doubt he would enjoy your company."

Eden regarded her husband with a murderous stare. "I know he was being obnoxious, but couldn't you have at least tried to get along with him?"

Knowing that remark was uncalled for, Raven

shrugged impatiently. "He was the one who wanted to prove something, not me."

"From the looks of him, the fight was scarcely one-sided."

"Would you have preferred I not defend myself? I would have sworn you told me you didn't want to be widowed twice."

"My father tried to kill you?" Eden scoffed in disbelief.

Raven reached for the doorknob, "Do you want to ask him about it?"

Certain he had been correct that her father would prefer privacy to her company, Eden turned away and started back down the stairs. "There's no point in bothering him," she replied flippantly. "Had he wanted you dead, you would be."

Raven thought she was probably right. Nathan had not wanted him dead, though, merely aware of the fact he would defend his daughter aggressively should she ever need it, which Raven was certain she would not. That he had asked Eden to help him bathe had apparently escaped her notice, and that annoyed him. First she had been concerned about Alex, and now her father. Wasn't she ever going to have time for him?

By the time Raven was ready for bed, Eden was sound asleep. She had lowered the mosquito netting to form a cozy cocoon around the bed and her expression was one of sweet contentment rather than the anger he had expected. That she had chosen to sleep in her own room rather than his only added to the blackness of his mood, however.

Where his mind had been he didn't know, but he had not once considered the possibility that his beautiful bride might not have a healthy child. He had expected her to

304

have a fine son, a bright-eyed boy who would follow him around as he had once tagged along after Alex.

What if the little fellow were pale and weak instead? Eden would be devoted to the child. He knew that without question. She would pamper the baby, and blame herself if he did not survive. She would feel that she had failed Alex too. That was something else Raven knew for certain and he did not know how he could spare her the anguish of that unwarranted guilt.

God help him, he had wanted Eden for his wife and had taken her, but he had never imagined she would already be pregnant. Nor had he dreamed that her expected babe would be other than the picture of health. If only Eden loved him. He was certain that while it would be terrible indeed, they could overcome the sorrow of losing their first child and have others if Eden loved him. The problem was, she did not.

Eden awakened to find Raven looking down at her. Even through the fine mesh of the mosquito netting she could make out his expression. That he appeared to be on the verge of tears alarmed her badly. Sitting up, she parted the netting and reached out to take his hand.

"Oh Raven, I never stopped to think you might be hurt. If Daddy hurt you, I'll—"

When she paused to think of a suitably horrible punishment, Raven began to smile. "I'm not hurt, just disgusted you're in the wrong bed."

It had not been disgust Eden had seen, but an emotion far more poignant. Saddened that he would not confide in her, she let the matter drop rather than challenge him on it. "You had no time this afternoon, and there were no servants to put away your things. My room is in good order, though, so I thought you'd prefer to use it tonight."

"Really?"

"You gave me a key, Raven. Was my door locked?"

305

Raven turned to glance back over his shoulder. Not only had the connecting door between their rooms not been locked, it had been standing wide open, and he had had to step over several valises to reach it.

"I'm sorry," he mumbled softly as he began to remove the clean clothes she had brought him.

"After I left you, I got to thinking," Eden revealed as she studied the muscular contours of his body with an appreciative glance. "I've seen boys get into awful fights, and then become the best of friends. While I think that's an exceedingly stupid way to make friends, if that's what it took for you and my father to reach an understanding, I'll not say another word about it."

Raven was soon undressed, and joined her in bed. "I'll agree, not only is fighting a stupid way to make friends, it's also quite painful."

"Then you are hurt?"

Eden looked so alarmed by that possibility, Raven's smile grew wide. Maybe she didn't love him as deeply as he would like, but she did care at least a little for him. "Come here," he whispered as he pulled her into his arms. "I think I know how to make the pain go away."

With the first brush of his lips against hers, Eden realized he could not possibly be in much pain and she was glad she was no longer angry with him. It would have been impossible to stay mad at him anyway, her conscience reminded her, for she had never been able to concentrate on anything but pleasure when she was in his arms.

Downstairs, Yadira walked slowly through the darkened rooms, the candle she carried providing an eerie light. She paused here and there, remembering the times the house and been filled with Alex's laughter. She had known he

306

did not have long to live, but she had expected him to die there, in her arms, not in far-off England. She felt doubly cheated that not only had she lost him, she had also lost the chance to share his last hours. How precious those would have been to her.

When she reached his portrait, she placed the candle on the mantel beneath it. She would leave one burning there each night, as a reminder he would never be forgotten. She was certain Raven and his bride were too lost in each other to remember Alex, but he was the only man she had ever loved, and she would keep his memory alive forever.

Eighteen

September 1863

Eden awakened first the next morning. While she was accustomed to falling asleep in Raven's arms, she could not recall ever awaking there and it was a most enjoyable surprise. The whole length of his sleek body was cuddled snugly against her. After delighting in his comforting warmth for a long moment, she moved over slightly, propped her head on her hand, and took advantage of a rare opportunity to study the handsome young man while he slept.

In repose, his thick curls and long lashes lent his face a boyish quality that was quite endearing. Eden could not resist the temptation to touch his jet black hair, but afraid she might wake him, she drew her hand back quickly. She had not noticed the bruise on his right cheek, nor the cut that sliced through his brow, when he had come to bed. The perfect symmetry of his features was scarcely marred, but she felt a sharp stab of sorrow nonetheless. Fearing he had suffered other injuries as well, she peeled the sheet away to scan his shoulder and arm. Not only did she find numerous bruises, which she was certain were precisely the size of her father's fist, but cuts and scrapes as well.

Ashamed she had not realized how badly battered Raven was, Eden leaned over and placed a light kiss on a deep purple bruise on his shoulder. When she moved back, she was startled to find him observing her with an amused smile.

"That you're covered with bruises isn't a bit funny," she scolded softly. "I'd never have left you two alone last night had I known you'd behave so badly."

Raven scoffed at her sympathetic gesture and words of regret. "Don't pretend you were concerned with my health just now. If you want to look at me, you needn't be shy." With one easy gesture, he flung aside the sheet that covered them, completely exposing not only his well-muscled frame but her delectable figure as well.

Eden's long curls covered her breasts with a modest drape, and after bending her knee slightly, she did not feel as though she were on display nude merely to satisfy his curiosity. As for him, she already knew how attractive he was without needing another look. Her kiss had been a spontaneous show of affection she had been unable to contain, and she was truly sorry he bore so many marks from a fistfight that should never have taken place. That he had responded not with equal sweetness, but with an arrogant challenge, was not only disappointing, but unnerving as well.

"I was worried about you, not admiring how handsome you are," she responded defensively.

"You mean that was pity I saw in your glance rather than wifely pride?"

Eden noted the scrapes on his knuckles as he reached out to trace a light path from the cleft between her breasts to her navel. They had made love only once in the morning. That had been at Briarcliff, the day after Alex's funeral. At that bittersweet memory, her eyes stung with hot tears of shame for she recalled how badly she had wanted Raven, and why.

"Eden?" Raven had awakened in such a good mood he had been unable to resist teasing her. That another of his attempts to make her laugh had failed miserably baffled him.

Eden could not meet his gaze. She knew only that all too often Raven's words hurt and confused her, or like now, filled her with nearly unbearable remorse. "I know our marriage is an unusual one, but a wife ought to be able to show concern for her husband without him laughing at her."

"I wasn't laughing at you," Raven denied as he pushed her down on her pillow. There was nothing he liked better than pinning her beneath him where their arguments could lead only one place. "If my efforts to amuse you make you cry rather than laugh, I'll give them up." He kissed away the drops of moisture that clung to her lashes, then nibbled her earlobes until she began to giggle.

"That's much better."

That Raven's dark eyes could hold a charming warmth rather than merely a menacing light was something it had taken Eden a long while to learn. That she still understood so little about him was troubling, but as he began to kiss her gently, obviously taking care to keep his beard from scraping her skin, she was content for the moment with what she did know.

While he waited for Eden to dress later that morning, Raven struggled to compose a note to Julian Ryan that not only imparted the sad news of Alex's death, but also invited him to attend a dinner party in honor of his bride's father. He had not realized until Nathan had questioned him that Julian would have to know who had fathered

Eden's chid, but he did not even attempt to reveal that secret in writing.

After entrusting the message to Azariah to deliver, Raven turned his attentions to the document Nathan seemed so anxious to sign. He had the invoices for the munitions, and asked for exactly what they had cost. When Eden joined him in the study, he showed her what he had written.

"You've included nothing for transporting the arms from England, or to allow for a profit?" the fair beauty asked in surprise.

"No, the cost is all I want. Greed has never been one of my vices."

Another point in Raven's favor, Eden noted silently. Still enjoying the loving mood he had created that morning, she reached up to kiss his cheek. "My father may not be as gracious about this as he should, but there are hundreds of others who will bless your name."

Rather than being pleased by that promise, Raven frowned darkly. "I don't want my name even whispered in connection with the arms. Is that clear? I'll make certain your father understands that too. That I was drawn into this is bad enough, I certainly don't want any credit for it."

Feeling as though she had been dashed with cold water for the second time that morning, Eden turned away as though distance would soften the bitterness of his tone. She was sorry she had forgotten how much he despised the cause she held dear. It made her feel not only lonely, but sad. "It's nearly noon, I'd rather we postponed the tour of the plantation for a few days. In fact, let's wait until next week. If my father can come for dinner tonight, we ought to stay here and make certain everything's ready."

"The kitchen is fully staffed today, Eden. You'll not have to don an apron and cook." Raven had often heard it was a woman's prerogative to change her mind, but he thought she had made a poor choice for the day's activities. "I can show you the plantation any day you like, but next week we'll be in Kingston. I want you to meet Alistair Nash, our attorney, and—"

Eden raised her hand to still his protest before his list grew any more lengthy. "I want to go, Raven. You needn't try and convince me that I should."

"Good." Raven so frequently ran into a brick wall with Eden that he felt as though he were wandering through a maze. He had no doubt he was a totally rational person, but in his view, her moods were as changeable as the direction of a butterfly's flight. It certainly made their lovemaking exciting, but he longed to be able to complete a conversation without constantly having to worry he would inadvertently upset her. That was another question he wanted to ask Julian. Perhaps all well-bred young ladies had such delicate natures, or may be it was merely pregnant ones.

"Let's take this note to your father to sign. That will give us the chance to confirm the dinner invitation too."

Thinking that idea a good one, Eden walked back toward Raven, but she was worried still. "My father must have nearly two dozen officers. Do you want to invite them all to dine with us?"

"Why not?"

"I thought perhaps you'd prefer a smaller group since you don't share our views. I don't want you to be uncomfortable in your own home."

"Our home," Raven corrected her. "I think I can stand to listen to the glories of the Confederacy for one evening at least. I've also invited Dr. Ryan and his sister, Rebecca. Your father wanted to meet him. That will make three people for my side."

"That's just the point. I don't want anyone taking sides.

I'm certain my father must have a surgeon on board. Why did he want to meet this Dr. Ryan?"

Raven slipped his arm around Eden's waist as they started for the door. "He wants to be certain you'll receive the best of care."

"Oh, I see."

"You don't seem pleased." Raven held his breath, hoping she would not object to the doctor's presence that night.

"I feel fine. I don't need to be under a doctor's care."

"Humor us, Eden. I want you to stay well and so does your father."

Eden tried to smile, but she already felt as though she had to work much too hard to humor her husband as it was.

As Eden came down the stairs that evening, she was alarmed by the sound of angry male voices coming from the study. They had visited her father's ship without mishap, and she had been so looking forward to spending a pleasant evening with him. As she drew close, she was relieved it was not her father's voice that was raised in harsh tones, but nonetheless dismayed that someone was having a heated argument with her husband. She hesitated to enter the study, and yet did not want to stand at the door and eavesdrop. When she sensed, rather than heard, someone approach, she turned to find Yadira watching her from the hallway.

"Do you know who's with my husband?"

Yadira was dressed in black that night, and seemed almost to float her steps were so light as she drew near. "It is Julian, and his sister. You were not downstairs to greet them when they arrived."

Eden thought that point too obvious to merit comment,

and could not imagine why Yadira thought she had the right to mention it either. She had checked the time. The doctor and his sister were early; she wasn't late. Not about to make excuses to the housekeeper, though, she dismissed her with a nod and entered the study without further delay.

"You must be Dr. Ryan," she greeted him graciously, "and Miss Ryan, I'm so pleased to meet you, too."

Riven could not suppress a smile as he observed Julian's startled expression. The physician had obviously not expected Eden to be such a stunning young woman, but as always, Raven was filled with pride that she was. She was wearing the ice blue gown that night, and that also pleased him.

Eden judged Julian to be in his early forties. His light brown hair lacked even a hint of a curl and dipped low over his forehead. His eyes were gray, his nose quite prominent, and his square jaw jutted out at a belligerent angle. He was not quite six feet tall, with a build as solid as his features. He was the type who could be described as distinguished rather than handsome, and yet she could not help but think a smile would improve his appearance enormously. Unfortunately, the physician appeared to be in no mood to smile.

Rebecca shared her older brother's fair coloring, but her features were far more refined. While no one had ever remarked on her beauty, she was actually quite pretty. She seemed almost painfully shy as she greeted Eden. "I'm Mrs. Yardley, a widow," she explained after an anxious glance at her brother.

Eden wished Raven had told her something about this pair so she would have known what to expect. Rebecca was dressed in a black satin gown of modest design whose high neckline and long sleeves covered her petite figure completely. Her only jewelry was a gold wedding band. Eden could not help but wonder when Mr. Yardley had died, as there was a great deal of difference between a woman who had been recently widowed and one who simply chose to wear mourning garb forever.

Despite Eden's presence, Julian was unwilling to be distracted from his purpose, and swiftly resumed the argument. "It is Queen Victoria's own edict that ships engaged in war may not occupy her ports for more than twenty-four hours. Clearly the *Southern Knight* has already exceeded that limit."

"The ship isn't docked in one of her majesty's ports, but in mine," Raven pointed out.

"Alex would never have flaunted the queen's wishes," Julian replied in the same strident tone that Eden had overheard. "I can't believe you actually think you can do it and escape censure."

Raven flinched at the mention of his late uncle's name. His dark eyes narrowed, but before he could give what Eden was certain would surely be a scathing response, she moved to his side. "You're mistaken, Dr. Ryan. Alex and I spoke frequently about America's Civil War, and he graciously offered whatever assistance he could provide. Were he here tonight, I know he would ask you to keep your thoughts to yourself, and if you could not treat our guests politely, he would bid you good night without further delay."

Raven broke into a wide grin as he slipped his arm around Eden's waist and drew her near. "She's right, Julian. While I invited you here in hopes you'd have a pleasant evening, if you feel that's impossible, I won't insist that you stay."

Julian looked toward his sister, who shook her head in a silent plea for restraint. "You really should have told us in your note that your father-in-law was a Confederate officer and I would have sent our regrets. Since we're already here, we'll try and make the best of it."

"That's very kind of you, Dr. Ryan," Eden assured him with an enchanting smile even though he had been less than gracious about remaining. "Why don't we all go into the drawing room to wait for my father and his men. They should be here soon."

Julian's frown hadn't lifted, but he followed Eden from the room without further complaint. His sister, however, seemed greatly relieved the matter was settled for the time being.

Eden was able to exchange only a few words with Rebecca Yardley before Nathan arrived with eighteen of his officers. Clad in their dress uniforms, she thought they looked absolutely splendid, although in his evening clothes, Raven looked equally dashing. Besides Michael Devane, there were a couple of others she recognized from home but she greeted every man with equal warmth. She was pleased when, although Rebecca blushed constantly, the widow seemed interested in meeting everyone, even if her brother did no more than reply to introductions with a scowl and a nod.

Raven had vowed not to do or say anything to embarrass Eden that night, but it came as something of a surprise that the men gathered around his table were so charming a group he had no desire to challenge them on their political beliefs. Some were barely out of their teens. Only the ship's surgeon and Nathan were older than thirty. While they did want to discuss the War, it was only their own exploits they wished to recount.

"Captain, have you told Eden how we were nearly caught by blockaders because of a bird?" Michael Devane inquired once the meal was under way. He was disappointed he had not been seated beside the lovely blonde, where there would have been an opportunity for him to converse with her privately.

Nathan took a long swallow of wine before shaking his

head. "That's a story I'll not repeat but go ahead if you must. Just don't mention where it happened."

"Tell us all about it, Michael," Eden coaxed enthusiastically. "It sounds like an amusing story."

Michael hesitated a moment, then seized the opportunity to capture her undivided attention and began to spin the tale. "It was in the dead of night. We'd managed to slip through the blockade and come in close to shore. The fog was so thick we were all straining to make out the entrance of the, well, of the river, and expecting that at any second a half-dozen Union gunboats would appear. Gradually the fog began to lift, but before your father could give the order to start the engines, there came the most gawdawful shriek you can imagine. It was so loud it nearly rattled our teeth. The devil himself couldn't have produced a whistle that shrill. We all knew that unless a blockader had a stone-deaf crew, they would have heard, it, too and be steaming our way at full speed.

"Then it came again. Only this time we were all holding our breath waiting for it. The man closest to the chickencoop realized it was the rooster warming up to greet the dawn and made a dive for him." Michael paused a few seconds as everyone began to chuckle. "Problem was, he'd yanked the head off the wrong bird before he'd realized it. The hens were all flapping about making a terrible racket and the rooster kept right on crowing."

Nathan was too chagrined to listen to any more. "He finally killed the cock, we slipped into the river without getting caught, and we had chicken and dumplings for dinner, but I'll not sail with a rooster on board ever again."

Realizing a noisy rooster had seriously jeopardized the crew's safety, Eden could easily understand why that wasn't one of her father's favorite stories despite the obvious humor of it. It was difficult to read Raven's expression since he was seated at the opposite end of the long and crowded table, but she was pleased he appeared to be as amused as everyone else. In fact, everyone seemed to be enjoying themselves that evening, even Julian Ryan, whom Eden had cleverly seated next to the ship's surgeon, Clifton Endecott. Although several years younger, and a good deal better-looking, he seemed as serious a man as Julian. The two had become engrossed in a medical discussion from the moment they had been introduced.

Eden surveyed the table and found not only the men seated closest to Rebecca doing their best to charm her, but those seated across from her as well. They gave the shy young woman few opportunities to speak, but Eden could tell from her expression she was enjoying every word of their conversation. While Eden had feared the evening held all the elements of potential disaster, she was delighted to find things going so well.

The table was set with crisp white linens, the finest English bone china with a delicate floral pattern, gleaming crystal goblets, and ornate silver. Deep purple orchids were entwined around the bases of the four silver candelabras. Their brightly burning candles gave off a seductive spicy scent and filled the dining room with their tangy perfume. Yadira had merely nodded as Eden had described what she wanted, but obviously the housekeeper was as talented as Raven had promised.

Taking another bite of succulent pork baked in a flavorful orange sauce, Eden considered the cook's work excellent as well. She had never tasted breadfruit, but was certain the large green fruit had been roasted to perfection. The dinner was truly superb, the wines Raven had selected from Alex's cellar exquisite, and their guests all seemed to be enjoying themselves. That the first party she and Raven had hosted as Lord and Lady Clairbourne was an unqualified success kept Eden smiling all evening.

With only two ladies present, Raven insisted Eden and Rebecca remain with the men when they returned to the drawing room for brandy. The conversation grew more serious, but the Confederate cause was defended with such fervor he had to admire his guests' conviction even though nothing he heard changed his opinion on the ultimate futility of the War.

Time and again he heard that shortages of essentials such as food and clothing plagued not only the Confederate troops, but the civilian population as well. The shortages Raven had considered readily predictable had combined with inflation to wreck the South's economy. Yet the officers present clung to the belief that any hardship was worth enduring for the sake of preserving the South they loved.

The majority of soldiers in any conflict were always painfully young, but as Raven studied his guests' earnest expressions, he did not understand how any commander could send such fine young men to their deaths over something so trivial as a political dispute. There had to have been a better way to bridge the chasm between the customs and needs of the North and South than civil war and he thought it a great tragedy neither side had had men with sufficient brilliance to find it.

Raven had said little that evening, but Nathan did not need more than one glance at the young man's pensive frown to know they ought not to overstay their welcome in his home. He spread the word it was time to leave, then bid his daughter and her husband good night shortly before ten. "Your hospitality will not be forgotten, Lord Clairbourne."

Rather than again ask to be addressed by his given name, Raven took note of Nathan's grin and did not make an issue of it. The only evidence the Southerner wore of their fight was a gash in his chin, and Raven hoped they would not ever come to blows again. He was then ashamed to realize how quickly they had resorted to violence to settle a problem that really existed only in Nathan's mind. It was no wonder countries could not live in peace when individual men could not, he thought sadly.

"I'm looking forward to entertaining you and your wife someday soon," Raven assured him.

Nathan seemed pleased by that invitation. "You'll find Sarah is as charming as her daughter, and I know she'll be eager to meet you."

"Let's hope that will be very soon." Eden kissed her father good night, and remained by the door to say a final word to their other guests.

Michael Devane stepped out of the line and moved to the rear in hopes he would be able to have a few moments alone with Eden if he was the last to leave, but he was able to say no more than a brief thank-you before Raven slapped him on the back and ushered him out the door. Disgusted, but not defeated, he hurried to catch up with the others, and promised himself he would not leave Jamaica without spending some time alone with the lovely blonde.

Julian and Rebecca had been invited to spend the night so they would not have to return home after dark. Eden hoped she might now be able to become better acquainted, but before she could encourage them to return to the drawing room, the doctor took his sister's hand and started toward the stairs.

"It was a lovely party, but I'm afraid Rebecca has become overtired and I want her to go on up to bed."

Rebecca's cheeks were flushed, but Eden thought that was from excitement rather than fatigue. The young woman appeared reluctant to say good night but did so after a regretful sigh and, accompanied by her brother, retired for the night.

Eden took Raven's hand and led him back into the drawing room. "Thank you for being such a marvelous host tonight. I know it must have been difficult for you to hold your tongue, but I'm so pleased that you were able to do it."

"I can scarcely demand silence from you on certain matters, and not give the same in return," Raven replied as he took a clean snifter from the tray and poured himself more brandy.

"Well, whatever your reasons, you were the soul of tact tonight and I appreciate it. Now tell me about Rebecca. Is Julian always so overprotective of her?"

"Yes. He's quite a bit older than she is and after their parents' deaths felt responsible for her. She was married several years ago, but only briefly. Her husband was an accountant from Kingston. He died of yellow fever, as I recall. Rebecca came back home to live with her brother and there's nothing more to tell."

"Is he the one who insists she wear black, or is that her choice?"

"I have no idea. Why don't you ask her in the morning?"

"Really Raven, that's not the type of question that can be asked in casual conversation."

Raven observed Eden with an appreciative glance as she walked to the windows. Despite the warmth of the evening, she looked as pretty and fresh as when their guests had first arrived. The louvers were open and she raised her chin slightly to enjoy more of the fresh air they provided. "Be careful," he cautioned. "The evening breeze comes off the land. It's called the 'Undertaker Wind,' because it can cause quite a chill."

"How gruesome," Eden laughed as she turned back

321

toward him. "There's a breeze off the sea in the mornings. What's it called?"

"It's the 'Doctor Wind,' because it helps keep everyone cool while they work."

"I'll bet you know all kinds of stories about Jamaica, don't you?"

"I grew up here," Raven reminded her with a shrug. "Besides, it's not all that large an island, so there isn't a great deal to learn."

Eden quickly covered her mouth to hide a yawn. "I'm afraid I'll have to ask you to tell me more another night."

Raven set his snifter aside and came forward to meet her. "That's fine with me. I had other plans for tonight anyway."

Knowing by the devilish gleam in his eyes just exactly what those plans were, Eden lifted her arms to encircle his neck and eagerly returned his kiss. When at last she stepped back, Yadira was at the doorway. The woman came and went with the stealth of a ghost, but Eden was too pleased with the way the evening had gone to be annoyed with her.

"Everything was perfect, Yadira. Please tell everyone in the kitchen how delighted we were."

"I will do that, my lady." Without asking if she would be disturbing them, Yadira entered the drawing room and began gathering up the brandy snifters their guests had used.

"We were just leaving," Raven announced as he took Eden's hand, and he hurried her out of the room and up the stairs.

"In which rooms are Julian and Rebecca staying?" Eden whispered as they started down the hall.

"Those opposite Alex and Eleanora's so you needn't fear we'll disturb them."

Eden knew he was teasing her this time, and returned

322

his taunting grin with a smile. He went past his room to hers and, pulling her into his arms, waltzed her through the door. The lamp beside the bed was burning low, and the rose-colored room held a romantic glow.

"Raven," Eden mused as he continued to dance her toward the bed. "Most husbands visit their wife's bedroom, not the other way around. There was no reason for you to scold me for not being in your bed last night."

Raven released her and stepped back to give a courtly bow. "You're right, of course. It was only that finding you in my bed at Briarcliff set the pattern."

Rather than again attempt to explain what she had been doing in Alex's bed, Eden simply turned her back toward him and lifted her hair out of his way so he could undo the buttons that ran down the back of her gown. The touch of his fingertips against her bare skin made her shiver, but when she noticed the small lavender bottle sitting on the night stand, she felt the worst chill of her life.

The delicate bottle was shaped like a newly opened rose and its stopper was topped with a hummingbird. Even without opening it, Eden knew exactly what it contained. When Raven had said he had plans for that night, she had not dreamed he meant to use the oil she and Alex had shared. "How could you?" she gasped.

"How could I what?" Raven asked, having no idea what she meant.

Eden's gaze remained fixed on the exquisitely hand-crafted bottle, her memories of her wedding night as clear in her mind as those of the evening's party. She could not only see Alex spread a drop of the fragrant oil on the tip of her breast, she could feel the warmth of his hand. Her breath caught in her throat, suffocating her in a stifling wave of panic.

"I didn't kill him. I know that I didn't. But you can't make me use that with you."

Completely mystified, Raven looked up from the row of buttons to follow Eden's glance. When he saw the bottle beside her bed, his reaction was as intensely negative as hers. "I didn't bring that in here, and I'll get rid of it right now."

Raven strode across the room, and grabbed up the bottle. After opening the louvers at the window to their widest point, he tossed it outside, then turned back to face her. "Yadira brews that stuff. She undoubtedly just wanted to make you a present of it. There's no way she could have known you wouldn't want it."

Yadira, the dark-eyed beauty who moved through the house with the grace of a spirit, made that intoxicating oil? That the woman who created the love potion would surely have been the one to teach Alex how to use it shattered all that was left of Eden's hold on reality. With no more than a slight sway, she slid to the floor in a faint.

Nineteen

September 1863

A few whiffs from Julian's vial of smelling salts revived Eden. She was lying on her bed with Raven standing on one side and the physician and Rebecca on the other. All wore anxious frowns and Eden could not immediately recall why she should be the object of their concern. Then the painful memories returned and her eyes again filled with tears.

Raven was overcome with guilt as Eden turned her anguished gaze toward him. She had asked to keep the small lavender bottle she had had at Briarcliff, undoubtedly as a souvenir of the beautiful love she and Alex had shared. Now the sight of a similar flagon was more than she could bear and he knew it was because his bitter accusations would echo in her memory for as long as she lived. The pain of his own folly cut him as cruelly as her tears and he sat down on the side of the bed and drew her into his arms.

"Thank you, but Eden will be fine in a minute or two," Raven assured his companions. "You needn't stay."

Julian noted the tears pouring down Eden's cheeks and

shook his head. "Your wife's hysterical, and I'd like to know why."

That was something Raven would not explain. "It's really none of your concern."

"Women do not faint for no reason, Raven. Clearly Eden's suffered a dreadful shock and I'll not leave her in such a sorry state."

Raven hugged the distraught blonde all the more tightly. "You're wrong. It's just that she's very sensitive and easily moved to tears."

"Surely not like this."

Raven would not admit that he had seen Eden sob so wretchedly on only one other occasion, and that it had been entirely his fault. "Perhaps not, but she'll soon fall asleep and she'll be fine in the morning. You needn't worry about her."

As concerned as her brother, Rebecca circled the bed and reached out to take Eden's hand. "Do you want us to stay?" she asked.

Eden was horribly embarrassed that she could not control her tears, but when she tried to assure Rebecca that she would soon recover her composure, her words were no more than a string of unintelligible sobs.

Julian had carried his doctor's bag into the room when Raven had summoned him. After replacing the smelling salts in the black leather satchel, he withdrew another bottle. "I'm going to give her some laudanum to help her sleep. Don't argue with me about this, Raven, or I'll send Rebecca to fetch Eden's father."

Nathan was the last person Raven wanted involved and he had no choice but to give in to Julian's demand, but he tried to appear unconcerned. "Since I've no objection to your giving her laudanum, there's no need to threaten to summon Nathan."

"Good, I was hoping you'd see things my way." Julian

waited while Rebecca brought a glass from the wash-stand. He poured in several ounces of the alcohol-based opium solution, and then handed it to Raven. "Make her drink it all."

Raven took the glass of brownish-red liquid and gently coaxed Eden into swallowing it. He set the empty glass aside, then looked up at Julian. "Thank you, but I can take care of my wife now."

"Shall I summon one of the maids to help her get ready for bed?" Rebecca asked helpfully.

The innocence of that question brought a smile to Raven's lips. "No, thank you, I want to help her myself."

Julian hesitated for a moment, and then spoke his mind as he usually did. "As soon as she's asleep, come down to the study. I want to talk to you."

Eden had already grown calmer, and Raven thought she would be all right if he left her for a few minutes while she slept. "Fine, I've something to say to you too." He did not move from his bride's side until they were again alone in the room. Then he began to remove her satin gown with the same tenderness he showed when they made love.

"I don't want to ever see you this sad again, Eden. Not ever. I think it's more difficult for me than it is for you."

The laudanum had made her too drowsy to respond, but Eden watched with a sleepy gaze as Raven peeled away her clothes. He returned her gown and starched slips to the wardrobe, then folded her stockings and lingerie and draped them over the arm of a chair to be laundered in the morning. He brought her a nightgown, slipped it over her head, and then took her hands to pull her arms through the sleeves the way he would dress a child. He removed the pins from her hair, ran his fingers through the glossy curls, then leaned down to kiss her lips lightly.

"This isn't the way I wanted tonight to end," he whispered as he tucked her in but her eyes were already closed in sleep. Pleased that her expression was a relaxed one, he gave her another kiss then eased the mosquito netting down around the bed. Determined to keep his conversation brief so he could return to his bride, he hurriedly left her room.

Julian was alone in the study, and he stopped pacing as Raven came through the door. "The whole point of your trip to England was to find a suitable English wife whose bloodlines would complement the Clairbournes'. That you've returned instead with not only a Southern belle, but an unstable one, is as tragic as Alex's death. I'm certain he would never have risked making the trip had he known you'd disregard his wishes so completely."

Raven eyed the older man coldly, and clasped his hands behind his back to force away the impulse to throttle him. "I'm going to give you the same warning I gave the last man who made the mistake of insulting my wife. If you ever do it again, I'll call you out for it. Now I want your word before I continue that you'll not breathe a word of what I'm about to tell you to anyone, not even Rebecca."

Despite the fire in the young man's eyes, Julian considered Raven's threat of a duel absurd since he would never accept such a challenge, and simply ignored it. "Doctors are trained to be discreet, Raven."

"I'm not asking for discretion, but complete and absolute silence."

"If Eden is ill—"

"This has nothing to do with disease."

"All right then, you have my word that I'll keep your confidence," the physician offered grudgingly.

"Thank you." In no mood to sit down, Raven walked over to the fireplace, and leaned back against the mantel. In as terse a manner as possible, he explained that Eden was not only his wife, but Alex's widow, and pregnant with Alex's child. "Yadira put something in Eden's room that reminded her of Alex. There...

known Eden would be upset by...

tional. Eden's not in the least...

Alex dearly and at times her g...

"You've married your wid...

I'm supposed to keep?"

"Christ, Julian, we aren'...

incest."

Julian frowned as he mulled over...

revelation. "Were you that terrified she'd g...

son?"

Again Raven found his temper nearly impossible to control. "Our marriage had nothing whatsoever to do with the fact I'm Alex's heir."

"Well, that would certainly be difficult to prove in a court of law, wouldn't it?"

Raven had heard enough and went to the door. "I had thought that because you treated Alex for so many years that you would be the best man to deliver his child. Obviously I was mistaken. You've no respect for either my wife or me and I'll not burden you with another invitation to our home. Rebecca, however, will always be welcome."

Raven slammed the door on his way out, but Julian made no attempt to go after him. He sank down into the leather chair Alex had favored and mulled over what he had just learned. That Alex would have married when he was in such precarious health troubled the conscientious physician deeply. That Raven had married the same ravishing young woman with such shocking haste was equally disturbing.

From all he had heard, the Suttons were bright, responsible men who never behaved in such an unpredictable manner. Raven was not actually a Sutton, however, but from some other branch of Alex's family. Perhaps a fear of death had prompted Alex to seize whatever happiness

ing Eden, but what reason could Raven
ad for rushing to the altar other than to
n interests? Whatever their reasons, neither
aved as Julian thought a titled Englishman
ven had always been hot-tempered, though, and
expected him to apologize in the morning. As for
ing Alex's child, Julian doubted Eden could carry
abe to term if she possessed so little control of her
otions.

He remained in the study, his expression a troubled
one. He was going to miss Alex badly. It had never mattered to Alex whether or not a man held a title. As long as
he was honest, Alex would call him a friend. Apparently
Raven would extend his friendship only to those who
promised to keep the scandalous nature of his marriage a
secret. Julian could not help but think the young earl was
going to find himself with very few friends.

When he left the study, Raven walked to the back of the
house. A faint light shone beneath Yadira's door, and
thinking he had already delayed speaking with her too
long, he knocked lightly. She opened the door, then
leaned back against it in a provocative pose. She was
wearing a simple white cotton nightgown and her hair,
freed of its confining chignon, fell past her waist like a
stream of liquid ebony.

She smiled knowingly. "I did not expect you to come to
me so soon."

That she had had the audacity to imagine he would ever
seek her favors disgusted Raven completely. "We've
never been lovers, and we never will be either. All I
wanted was to ask you to be careful of what you say about
Alex around Eden. She was very fond of him, and deeply
saddened by his death. She's expecting our first child in
the spring, and I don't want her to suffer the slightest
distress about anything, not Alex, or problems with the

house, or staff. I want you to take care of everything as you always have so she'll not have any unnecessary worry."

Yadira's eyes were as dark as Raven's and she had no difficulty reading the emotion displayed in his glance. "I did not think you would ever fall in love."

Raven drew in a deep breath rather than respond to what he regarded as an uncalled-for remark. "All I want is your promise that you'll make our home tranquil for Eden."

"That will present no problem if she does not interfere."

"She has not the slightest interest in interfering with your work, Yadira. Don't create problems where none exist."

Yadira nodded slightly, then again regarded Raven with a seductive smile. "I can make your life very pleasant too," she offered in a husky whisper. "If not tonight, then in a few months when your wife's waist grows thick with your child."

Raven did not know which was worse, Julian's distasteful assumptions or Yadira's blatant attempt to seduce him. Now there was an unlikely pair, he thought slyly. "I'll have no need of you tonight, or ever, but Julian might be feeling lonely. I think he's still in the study." He turned away then, hoping she would consider the straitlaced doctor an exciting challenge.

Thinking Raven's suggestion absurd, Yadira closed her door, but by the time she heard his footsteps ascending the stairs, she had reconsidered. Julian Ryan's looks were too rugged to be called handsome, but she had never thought him unappealing. She had had no interest in him while Alex was alive, but now everything had changed. She took care to close her door quietly, and after leaving

331

a lighted candle beneath Alex's portrait, she made her way to the study.

Julian was seated in Alex's chair, and had to turn to see her. He looked startled then rose clumsily to his feet. "Has one of the servants fallen ill?" he asked nervously. In all the years he had been coming to Alex's home, the attractive housekeeper had always been so prim in her manner that he was flabbergasted by how different she looked in her nightgown with her hair loose.

Yadira moved across the room, and came so close Julian was prompted to take a step back. "Raven suggested you might need some company tonight. Surely you must need a woman as badly as other men do."

Again Julian was so badly shocked it took him several seconds to find his voice and then he stuttered badly. "Miss, Miss Morales, really, you, you ought to be in your room."

Yadira outlined her lips slowly with the tip of her tongue, then slipped her hands inside his jacket and laid her palms on his chest. His heart was already beating wildly and she considered that a compliment. "You do like women, don't you, doctor?"

"Well, of course, I do, but, but . . ."

Yadira moved her hands down his body in a sensuous massage but her eyes never left his. She did not stop when she reached his belt, but merely unbuckled it and unbuttoned his trousers. The man looked terrified but he was already hard, and she responded with a throaty laugh as she began to caress him more boldly. "You've not been with a woman for a long, long time, have you? Have you forgotten how good it feels?"

She took Julian's anguished moan for assurance her assumption was correct and abruptly stepped back. "If you want more, you'll have to come to my room." When she turned and left the study without a backward glance,

Julian had to grab the waistband of his trousers to keep them from falling down around his ankles. Then he followed her with the eagerness of a homeless puppy.

The next morning, Julian asked to see Eden again before he and his sister left for home. Raven did not object, but she was still sleeping so soundly the doctor did not attempt to wake her.

They went into the hallway outside Eden's door, and Julian took the precaution of making certain none of the servants were nearby before he spoke. The memory of how Yadira had insisted he remain stark naked when she had walked him back to his room shortly before dawn still made him feel as though he were being watched. She had stopped him just outside his sister's door, where he had nearly gone mad trying to remain silent as she had told him goodbye in a manner he would never forget. The woman had done things to him he had not dared ask the prostitutes in Kingston to do and had given him the most remarkable night of his entire life.

To have to concentrate on his medical duties after such an erotic interlude was nearly impossible. He had not forgotten her comment that Raven had sent her to him, but there was nothing in the young man's expression that led him to believe she had been telling the truth. Besides, it was far more flattering to think she had sought him out on her own.

"Have Eden remain in bed today, and tomorrow as well if she still seems a bit shaken when she wakes," Julian instructed in the most professional manner he could affect while so preoccupied. "I imagine she must want this baby rather badly, and that ought to inspire her to keep a better control of her emotions than she did last night."

"It was the Suttons' heart problems that worried me,

not my wife's nerves." Still feeling the sting of the doctor's insulting innuendos, Raven found it difficult even to look at Julian, let alone converse with him. He just wanted him gone.

"Let's pray the babe takes after his mother's side of the family rather than his father's. Other than that, there's nothing anyone can do until the child is born. If he's healthy, he'll need no special care, and if he's not, there will be precious little that anyone can do for him."

"What marvelous advice. Don't forget to send me a bill for your services." Without waiting for a reply, Raven turned toward his wife's door, but Julian reached out to stop him.

Realizing Raven was not going to apologize, Julian hurriedly did. "Wait, I said some very harsh things to you last night, and I want you to know I'm sorry I wasn't more sympathetic. I'd like very much to continue to treat your wife. Rebecca has very few friends, and I know she'd not come here to visit Eden without me."

Although surprised by Julian's apology, Raven remembered his devotion to Alex and accepted it graciously. "All right, I'll still consider you Eden's physician then."

"Good." Julian sighed in relief. "I'll stop by to see her as often as I can."

"You've always been welcome here," Raven reminded him before bidding him goodbye.

Julian took out his handkerchief and mopped his brow before joining Rebecca downstairs. He still thought Raven had extremely suspicious motives for marrying, but if he failed to attend Eden, he would have no excuse to see Yadira again. Fascinated by the exotic seductress, he planned to pay all his calls in the late afternoon so he would be invited to spend the night. Thrilled with the hope of again sampling the housekeeper's affections, Julian vowed to return within a week.

By nature a restless man, Raven paced Eden's bedroom waiting for her to wake until the sight of her wistful smile and graceful pose drove him so mad with desire he had to ask Amy, the youngest of the half-dozen maids, to take his place. He went down to the study to sort through the invoices for the portion of the *Jamaican Wind*'s cargo that he planned to sell in Kingston, but he found it impossible to keep his mind from wandering so badly he got little accomplished. It was his wife that mattered most to him, not how much he would earn from the voyage.

When Amy came to tell him Eden was awake, Raven dashed up the stairs two at a time. He paused outside her door to smooth the curls off his forehead and catch his breath, then strode into the room as though he had nothing more pressing on his mind than wishing Eden a good day.

Despite Amy's protestations that she was not to leave her bed, Eden had not allowed the girl to send for Raven until she had gotten up and made herself presentable. She had returned to bed, but planned to get up again as soon as she had assured her husband she felt fine. When he leaned down to kiss her, she raised her hand to caress his cheek fondly.

"I'm so sorry about last night. I feel very foolish now. What must Julian and Rebecca think of me?"

Raven sat down beside her, and took her hands in his. "It really doesn't matter what they think. You're the only one who matters. How do you feel?"

"I'm always a little queasy when I wake, but other than that, I'm fine."

"Good, but you mustn't rush things. Julian wants you to stay in bed for a day or two."

"But why? Did I make that great a fool of myself?"

"No, not at all. I told him about the baby, and whose it is. He just wants to see that you get plenty of rest and don't become so upset ever again. I'm sure you must know as well as I do that it isn't good for the baby."

Eden thought it exceedingly unlikely that the babe could discern her state of mind, but she wanted no repetition of the previous night's emotional turmoil for her own sake as well as her child's. "You told me Yadira made that oil," she reminded Raven self-consciously, concentrating on their clasped hands rather than risk meeting what she feared would be an impenetrable stare.

"That's only one of the many things she does, Eden. She makes the scented candles, the fragrant soap, our cologne."

At the mention of the cologne that had once caused her to mistake him for Alex, Eden's head shot up, but she was relieved to find Raven's expression sweet rather than hostile. She prayed that he would remain in such an understanding mood for a few more minutes. "She's obviously very clever so it shouldn't be too difficult to find her another position. Would you arrange that, please? Just find her a housekeeper's job elsewhere."

"You want me to dismiss her just because of that oil?"

"No," Eden responded. "I think you know why I want her to leave. Please don't make me say it."

Raven had hoped Eden would never question the intimacy of Alex and Yadira's relationship, but obviously she already had so he did not insult her by denying it. "Alex hired Yadira nearly ten years ago, and I can assure you it was because of her talents for running the household, not for any other reason. He was not yet thirty, a recent widower, and she took advantage of his loneliness. She was merely convenient, Eden, he never loved her. As far as I know, he hadn't slept with her in several years."

"He just used her. Is that what you're saying?"

"No! She used him. I think she hoped that eventually Alex would marry her, but he had no intention of remarrying, and most especially not to her. They had an affair, but it meant nothing to him. There's no reason to dismiss Yadira when Alex is dead and whatever existed between them was over a long time ago."

"Did he stop sleeping with her because of his heart?"

"I don't know what excuse he gave her, but believe me, it was over long before he met you."

Eden clung to Raven's hands more tightly as she tried to make him understand the reason for her request. "I don't want to have to share this house with Alex's former mistress. Don't ask that of me, Raven. It's positively obscene."

"You're pregnant and not feeling completely well. We ought to begin looking for a nanny to be certain we'll have one next spring. This is no time for you to take on the added burden of hiring a new housekeeper too."

Eden could not believe that Raven would be so obstinate, but she would not give in. "I want Yadira gone, Raven. We can find her a new position when we're in Kingston next week, and send her to it with a generous severance bonus when we return. I won't live in this house with Alex's mistress. I won't do it."

There was not a trace of moisture in Eden's glance now, but instead the menacing glow of fierce determination. Cut to the quick by her narrow view of the world that included no one but Alex, he released her hands and rose to his feet. "It hasn't even occurred to you that there might have been something between Yadira and me, has it? Probably because you wouldn't care one bit if there were. All you care about it your precious Alex. Well, the man is dead and I'll not send Yadira packing just because she once slept with him. Christ almighty, if every woman fired all the servants her husband had slept with, there wouldn't be a single English lord with a female on his staff!"

Raven stormed out of her room and slammed the door so loudly Amy came running to find out what was the matter. When she found Eden staring into space, she grabbed her shoulders and shook her. "Oh my lady, what's wrong with you now?" she began to wail.

The girl's pitiful cries jarred Eden from the shock of Raven's bitter farewell and Eden brushed her hands away. "There's nothing wrong with me. I want to bathe, Amy. Go heat the water and I'll be there as soon as I gather my clothes."

"But you're supposed to stay in bed."

"Do as I say," Eden scolded, in no mood to argue. She and Raven had far too much to straighten out for her to lie in bed all day waiting for him to cool down enough to return. He had been right, of course, she had not stopped to consider what his relationship might be with Yadira, but that he had failed to understand how that possibility hurt her now, was heartbreaking.

When Eden didn't find Raven downstairs, she walked down to the docks. While the decks of the *Southern Knight* were alive with activity, the crew of the *Jamaican Wind* were either fishing in the river or huddled in small groups playing cards. Randy MacDermott directed her to the captain's cabin, and thinking Raven would be alone, she did not bother to knock before she opened the door.

Both Nathan and Raven turned when she entered, but Nathan alone looked pleased to see her. "Can you give us a few more minutes, sweetheart? We're discussing something important."

Raven was eyeing her with so threatening a stare Eden had no desire to remain. "I'll go for a walk, and see you later, Daddy." Embarrassed she had disturbed them, she left the ship as swiftly as she had come. She paid no attention to those she passed as she started down the path beside the river, but when Michael Devane saw her, he quickly gave the men he had been supervising a break and ran to catch up with her.

"Good afternoon, Eden."

"Oh, hello, Michael. Is it afternoon already?"

"Of course, it's after two."

Eden laughed, as though keeping track of the time was beyond her. "The day is so lovely, I thought it was morning still."

"It's not nearly so pretty here as it is back home."

Eden smiled again and, with only an occasional nod, allowed Michael to monopolize the conversation. If he wanted to talk about home, she had no objection, but she did not bother to listen too closely to his comments either. When they reached the shore, she was surprised to find her father had stationed sentries there.

"Is such a precaution really necessary?" she asked apprehensively.

"Of course. If Union vessels are in the area, we want to know about it. When we return to sea, we'll sail before dawn so no one will see us leave the Rio Bueno. We're always that cautious. We're fighting a war, remember, not merely involved in the merchant trade like your husband."

Eden preferred looking out at the endless motion of sea rather than at her companion's adoring expression. "The War's not going well for us now, is it?"

"Let's not talk about the War," Michael begged. "When I found out you'd gone to England last fall, I knew I'd been a fool not to propose long before then. It broke my heart to learn you'd married someone else. Are you happy with Lord Clairbourne, or do you want to leave him and come home to me?"

Raven had made her promise she would never divorce him, but Eden knew she had not been thinking clearly when she had mentioned ending their marriage or she would have known she could not really do it. Raven was a complex and continually perplexing man, but Eden knew she would never leave him. While she could not describe their marriage as one of blissful contentment, there was definitely something precious in her relationship with her husband and she did not want to lose it.

"This is my home now, Michael," she assured him. "There was never anything special between us. Don't try and pretend that there was. I'm certain there are still plenty of young women in Richmond who are praying for your safe return. Give your love to one of them."

While Michael was deeply disappointed she had not thrown herself into his arms, he could not help but break into a grin at the mention of other women. "Well, if I can't have you, let's hope the prayers of the Richmond girls are answered."

"Yes, let's do," Eden agreed. She reached up to kiss his cheek, then took his hand as they started upriver. They had not gone far before they encountered Raven standing in the middle of the path.

"Go on back to your ship, Lieutenant," he ordered brusquely. "I want to talk to my wife in private."

When Michael hesitated, Eden encouraged him to go, and although reluctant, he did. She waited until their conversation could not be overheard to speak. "I was so anxious to see you, I didn't stop to consider the fact you might be busy. I'm sorry I disturbed you."

Eden was wearing the pale apricot gown Raven had always liked, but now it reminded him of the dreadful argument they had had on the cliff when he had stupidly thought she was about to leap to her death. "I thought you understood Julian's orders and planned to remain in bed

340

for a couple of days. It was bad enough that you went down to the docks, but to walk all the way out here is totally irresponsible."

Raven was standing with his feet wide apart and his hands on his hips as though he were shouting orders to his crew. It took all of Eden's willpower not to react angrily to his criticism. Instead, she took a step closer, as though he had spoken to her sweetly. "How could you have expected me to allow you to go on believing I didn't care about you?"

"What are you saying?"

If anything, Raven's frown had deepened, but Eden did not back down. "You were right. It was very thoughtless of me to think only of Alex and not of you. While I don't for a minute believe that all English lords amuse themselves with their servants, I know things might be different here in Jamaica. I know you mean to be faithful to me, but if there are women in our employ who once, well, who once provided services of a personal nature, I want you to find them work elsewhere immediately. It's not an unreasonable demand. It's what any gentleman would do to ensure his wife's peace of mind. You must know you'll not need other women. I'll never turn you away."

Raven stared down at Eden, amazed that she was able to discuss such an intimate matter so calmly. He was embarrassed he had allowed her to see how badly she had hurt him. He had not meant to beg for her affection but now it seemed as though that was exactly what he had done. He looked away for a moment as he tried with only partial success to gather his thoughts.

"The slaves were freed here in 1834, three years before I was born. Before then, just as in America, there were plenty of white men who slept with their slaves, but here children who were part white were free. Many were recognized as members of the family and some were even

341

sent to England for schooling. Alex's father was not one of those men, however, and I like to think it was because he was a man of high principles rather then merely one in poor health. Alex followed his example. He did not abuse the women in his employ and I haven't either.

"I should never have made that stupid remark about sleeping with servants. I have no idea what most English lords do. All I know is that in all the time Yadira has been here, she's never given anyone cause for complaint. Alex didn't let her go when he ended their affair so it seems ridiculous to fire her now for it." Raven glanced back at Eden, and finding her expression one of interest rather than dismay or scorn, he continued. "There's never been anything between Yadira and me. Alex and I didn't share the same women."

He had not realized what he had said, but shocked by his words, Eden certainly did. "Except for me, you mean."

Raven winced. "No! You mustn't think that. I never have."

Raven's pose had relaxed, but Eden felt far more tense than when their conversation had begun. "I believe you about Yadira and the others. We need never discuss this matter again, but I beg you to at least give some more thought to finding Yadira work elsewhere."

Raven felt as though he had already revealed too much of his feelings that day. If he agreed to send Yadira away, wouldn't Eden think him no better than her slave to command? Squaring his shoulders proudly, he refused to give in. "This is only the third day you've been here, Eden, and you barely know the woman. If after the baby is born you still want to hire another housekeeper, we'll discuss it again then. I don't want to hear any more about it until then. Is that understood?"

Eden nodded unhappily. There was something about

Yadira that had made her uneasy from the instant she had laid eyes on her and she doubted she would ever change her mind. "I suppose there's always the hope that Yadira won't like me, and that she'll leave of her own accord."

"The subject is closed, Eden. Now what were you doing out here with Devane?"

"Why nothing. I'd just gone for a walk while waiting to speak with you and he followed me."

Raven had never seen a more innocent expression than the one Eden wore, and not wanting to sound like a jealous husband if there was no reason, he let the matter drop. With a slow smile, he scooped his bride up into his arms and started back toward the docks. "I will tie you to your bed if I must, but you are going to stay there until sundown tomorrow."

"No, I can't stay in bed while my father's here. Please believe me when I tell you I'm well. If I get in the least bit tired, I'll go to bed early, but I don't want to miss seeing my father."

Raven frowned slightly, but since he had not granted her request about Yadira, he decided to allow this one. "All right, I understand why you don't want to worry your father, but you must be certain not to worry me again either."

Eden had already slipped her arms around his neck and gave him an enthusiastic hug. "Thank you."

"You're welcome," Raven replied. The day was warm, Eden's perfume as enticing as her slender figure, and he would have liked nothing better than to carry her off the path into some secluded arbor to make love. Thinking he would have to control that impulse until a better time presented itself, he continued on up the path but his body ached as badly as his heart that he had to keep such a tight rein on his emotions.

Twenty

Nathan Sinclair came to dinner again that night, this time bringing the six officers who had been on duty the previous evening. The smaller party was no less elegant, however, and the conversation was just as spontaneous and enthusiastic. Raven could not help but compare the recent gatherings in his home to the stilted dinner parties he had abhorred in London. He had not thought he would enjoy the company of Confederate officers so much, but these men were so honest and open a group he found it impossible to dislike them. That they had dedicated their lives to a cause that would never prevail saddened him more than he had thought possible.

"Raphael Semmes, who captains the *Alabama,* had a head start on us, but the *Southern Knight* has sunk her share of merchant ships," Nathan boasted proudly. "We don't loot them. All we confiscate are the nautical instruments. We take the crews on board, and then scuttle the ships. We've never had a captain put up much of a fight. Usually all we have to do is identify ourselves, and the ship surrenders."

"I assume you'd fire on any vessel that refused to do so?" Raven asked.

"Of course. Our mission is to cripple the North's maritime fleet. The *Alabama, Florida,* and the other raiders, we've done all we can to make the North suffer the same shortages of goods that we've had to endure."

"And your prisoners?" Eden inquired hesitantly. "What becomes of them?"

"We've had days when we could hardly move around the deck for the captured crews underfoot. When that happens, we demand a ten-thousand-dollar bond from the next ship we take, and send the prisoners ashore with them. We've not harmed civilians, sweetheart, nor turned over any to our prisons."

"From what I've read, most of the owners of ships you've not sunk, or intimidated into keeping their vessels in port, are transferring their registries to foreign countries. Haven't you found it increasingly difficult to find a merchantman flying the United States flag?" Raven asked pointedly.

"Yes, but those we do find still go straight to the bottom," Nathan replied with a satisfied grin.

"And when the War's over, you'll make a fortune replacing those ships, won't you?"

Nathan was not certain whether or not Raven was deliberately trying to insult him, but he had succeeded. All trace of humor left his expression as he responded. "I'm going to assume you didn't realize the implications of your question, Lord Clairbourne, but I am most definitely not fighting for the Confederacy in hopes of personal gain. You'd be wise not to make such slanderous accusations when your own conduct is so far from exemplary."

Eden was appalled by how swiftly the mood of the party had gone from lighthearted to venomous, but all conversation at the table had come to an abrupt halt. Fearing Raven would end the uncomfortable silence with a demand her father again back up his opinions with his fists, or worse, the weapon of his choice, Eden rose from her chair. "Gentlemen, our brandy is excellent. Shall we return to the drawing room?"

Raven remained in his chair as the men wearing gray uniforms filed out of the room. When his bride came to his side, his glance was filled with cold fury. "My question was so damn obvious, I can't believe no one else has ever asked it."

"Yes, it was obvious, and you should have known the answer without asking it too. If the South loses the War, I doubt my family will be left with the resources to build a dinghy, let alone a merchant vessel. That you'd accuse my father of sinking ships to create business for his shipyard is every bit as despicable as he claimed. I imagine you'd prefer your own company to ours for the rest of the evening."

Eden's full satin skirt swirled about her ankles with a dramatic flourish as she turned away with all the dignity a countess should possess, but even without her rebuff Raven had no desire to follow. Alex had often cautioned him that he was too honest for his own good, and he had certainly proven it that night. While he and Nathan had not developed the warmest of friendships, they had at least been able to get along together with some accord until now. Perhaps no man ever truly admired his son-in-law, but Raven feared he had just made it impossible for Nathan ever to like him.

Even without Raven's company, the conversation in the drawing room was strained and Nathan soon suggested he and his officers return to their ship. After the others had said good night, he took his daughter aside. "We'll sail before dawn, sweetheart, so this will be goodbye."

"But Michael said you'd be here for a week," Eden

protested anxiously. She reached out to clutch at her father's sleeve, unwilling to let him go so soon.

"Well, obviously Michael isn't all that good at estimating the time required to get things done. Now don't waste what time we do have, just listen. I asked Cliff Endecott to question Dr. Ryan and he's satisfied the man is a competent physician. He went to visit him at his home this morning, but I think that was mainly to have a chance to speak with Rebecca again rather than to see Julian's medical facilities."

Having no interest in whether or not Dr. Endecott thought Rebecca Yardley appealing, Eden frowned unhappily. "I've no doubts about Julian's competence. You're the one I care about and I don't want you to leave when you and Raven have nearly come to blows again."

Nathan laughed at her fears. "I'd say this is precisely the time to leave because your husband came dangerously close to getting his nose broken tonight."

"I realize he was being difficult, but—"

"Sweetheart," Nathan scolded gently. "What I'm trying to say is that, with Julian's care, you'll be fine. I doubt I'll be able to return before the War's end, and until then you'll have to get along with Raven as best you can. I certainly don't trust him, despite the fact he's been more than accommodating while we've been here, and it's plain he doesn't trust me."

Eden blinked back her tears. "Raven has never learned to keep his thoughts to himself, no matter how vile they are. But I can't bear to have you at each other's throats. Let me go and get him so he can at least tell you goodbye."

"He knows I'm leaving. I told him so this afternoon. That's what we were talking about when you came into his cabin."

That neither man had confided that information in her

347

made Eden feel all the more wretched. "Raven is fond of saying that this is now my home as well as his. If you ever need a safe port again, I'll demand he make you welcome."

Nathan gathered his daughter into a loving hug. "I love you too much to put you in the middle, sweetheart. There are many ports in the Caribbean where we're able to buy coal and provisions, so I can't imagine returning here unless our situation becomes truly dire. Now smile for me, so I can remember how pretty you are."

When he took a step back, Eden did her best to grant his request, but she wasn't all that successful. "I love you too, Daddy. Please be careful." Her father gave her a quick kiss, then let himself out the front door. Eden hoped with all her heart it would not be the last time she saw him. She turned and went back into the drawing room and, still distraught, was quite naturally drawn to Alex's portrait. His engaging smile reminded her all too painfully of the love she had lost, and she could not bear to think she might lose her father too.

As she rested her hands on the mantel, a drop of wax caught her eye, and Eden wondered which of the servants had carelessly left a candle burning so near Alex's portrait. She made a mental note to tell Yadira to caution the staff to be more careful, then thought better of it. One droplet of wax was scarcely cause for alarm, and since she did not want to discuss Alex with the housekeeper, she decided to keep the matter to herself.

Having absolutely no idea what to say to Raven, Eden did not look for him before going upstairs to bed. Perhaps he had actually tried to keep his opinions to himself, but he had certainly failed. To make matters worse, her father was every bit as proud and stubborn a man as Raven was. Neither had a forgiving nature and there was probably no hope they would ever develop a mutual respect now. She was positive insults less bitter than the ones they had exchanged had caused permanent rifts in other families, and would be no less damaging to hers.

When she reached the second floor, Eden saw the housekeeper about to enter her room. She called out to her and Yadira remained by the door. "Thank you for providing another wonderful evening, Yadira. Did you need to speak with me?"

The soft-spoken housekeeper held out a small silver tray on which she had placed half a dozen crackers. "I thought you might feel ill in the mornings, my lady. A cracker or two will settle your stomach."

Although she was puzzled by Yadira's suggestion, Eden accepted the tray. "My health is excellent, but I appreciate your concern."

Yadira's dark eyes remained devoid of warmth despite her smile. "You need not pretend with me. Raven told me you will have his child in the spring. You must be very proud."

Proud did not begin to describe how Eden felt at that moment. "Yes, of course," she managed to lie smoothly, and she slipped into her room before Yadira noticed she was gripping the small tray so tightly her knuckles had turned white. Not caring whether or not the housekeeper's remedy for morning sickness was effective, she set the tray on her dresser and went into Raven's room. When she found it empty, she sat down to wait for him.

Nearly thirty minutes passed before Raven appeared and by then Eden's anger had become a full-blown rage. By the time he had closed the door, she was out of her chair and half the way across the room. Her voice was low so it would not carry past the door, but her tone was vicious. "That you would insult my father is bad enough, but that you would tell Yadira about the baby when we agreed not to tell anyone until after the holidays is unforgivable. I can understand why you felt you had to confide in Julian, but not Yadira. I don't even want her in this house! How could you possibly have imagined I'd want her to know something so personal?"

After the way they had parted downstairs, Raven had not expected their next conversation to go well. He had already steeled himself for what he considered an unavoidable confrontation, and his mood was one of icy calm. He peeled off his jacket, tossed it aside, then removed his tie. He could not recall Eden ever losing her temper with him twice in one day, but the way she told it, he certainly deserved it. Knowing the best defense is always a vigorous offense, he ignored her hostile accusations.

"I've just been down at the docks talking with your father. I told him that I'll supply whatever capital he requires when the War's over. The shipyard is still in operation, but the Confederate government owes him more money for keeping their ships afloat than they've paid and you know as well as I do that he'll never see it. Like most loyal Southerners, he's funding the War with his personal fortune and he'll not be able to recover his losses. While he didn't leap at the chance to have me as a partner, he didn't turn me down either. He told me the Sinclairs have been building ships since Colonial times, and I find becoming part of that tradition appeals to me.

"As for Yadira, I spoke to her before you asked me to send her away. She has a maddeningly superior attitude at times and I had hoped telling her about the baby would make her more sympathetic. Believe me, she's not prone to gossip and our secret will go no further."

Eden preferred Raven's anger to the arrogance he was displaying now and she felt no less abused. Letting his offer to her father slide for the moment, she concentrated on the baby. "How many others have you told?"

"I've not told anyone else, nor do I intend to."

"This whole farce is a mistake, Raven. Neither of us is comfortable with lies, and—"

"You gave me your word, Eden, and I intend to see that you keep it."

Recognizing his mood as an intractable one, Eden simply channeled her anger in another direction. "There are some people who thrive on danger. Most are gamblers and adventurers who don't feel alive unless something's at risk. I'm beginning to suspect you're that kind of man."

"That's possible," Raven agreed with a slow smile. "The placid life we could lead at Briarcliff has never appealed to me."

Briarcliff was associated with too many poignant memories of Alex for Eden to want to talk about it. "No, a quiet country life definitely does not suit you," she said instead.

"Going to sea as young as I did spoils a man. There's only one thing that compares with the constant challenge of sailing."

"And what is that?" Eden asked flippantly.

Raven did not respond with words. Instead he slipped his arms around her waist to draw her near for a kiss he did not end until she had not only relaxed in his embrace, but had begun to cling to him, silently begging for more. At that precise instant he released her. "You were the one I wished to protect when I insisted we marry. Regardless of what your father mistakenly believes, I had no other dark, devious motive. If I have a flaw, it's that I'm too honest, not that I'm deceitful."

"If you have a flaw?" Eden asked sarcastically.

"You think I have a great many?"

Eden found it impossible to meet his gaze, and hoping he would not realize how difficult it was for her to respond to that question, she began to unbutton his shirt.

"You're not only bright, Raven, but rich as well, and that gives you a clear advantage over most people. If things don't go your way, I think you're capable of taking whatever action necessary to see that they do."

As Eden's fingertips brushed his chest, Raven began to pluck the pins from her hair. While her words were insulting, her actions were so seductive he did not know what to make of her mood now. "Give me an example."

His shirt was now unbuttoned, and Eden laid her palms on his chest rather than attempt to move back when she knew he would surely follow. "My father knows he'll face financial ruin if the South loses the War. So when he questioned your motives, you responded by offering him the money he'll need to remain in business. That would certainly silence his objections, and it would also make it impossible for me ever to leave you."

Scattering her hairpins in a dozen different directions, Raven reached out to grab Eden's upper arms with enough pressure to lift her clear off her feet. "Is that what you really think, that I want your father in debt to me merely to prevent you from divorcing me? Is that what you and Michael Devane were talking about? Did he beg you leave me and marry him? Well, did he? If I loan your father money, will it put an end to those plans?"

Raven had again unleashed the violence of his temper, and Eden was more than merely frightened. "Put me down," she requested with a calm born of stark terror. To her utter amazement, Raven set her down gently, but he did not release his hold on her, nor did his hostile expression soften.

"I'm not in love with Michael."

That was not the answer Raven longed to hear. "He did ask you to leave me, didn't he?"

"What are you going to do? Go down to the *Southern Knight* and beat him senseless for having such childish dreams? Don't bother, Raven. He understands that I plan to stay with you."

"Is it impossible for you to believe that I'd want to help your father simply because he's your father? Or that any man would be as offended as I am if another man tried to seduce his wife?"

Eden found it difficult to accept Raven's assertion of innocence when he continually forced choices upon her she would never make on her own. "You've nothing to worry about, Raven. Michael's talents at seduction do not even begin to compare with yours."

That was a challenge Raven could not ignore. While his dark eyes still smoldered with anger, after a moment's pause his grasp became gentle rather than confining and he began to trail light kisses from her temple to the throbbing pulse in her throat. He retraced that tempting path, straying this time to her earlobe before reaching behind her to unfasten her gown. Eden stood quietly in his arms, fighting him with neither words nor actions, and he continued to lavish tender kisses on her cheeks and throat as he slid her gown off her shoulders. She pulled away for a moment then, but it was only to cast aside the elegant dress, not to escape him.

There were buttons, hooks, ribbons, and he undid them all to strip her nude and the whole time his lips caressed each tantalizing inch of newly exposed flesh. Finally he dropped to his knees and rubbed his cheek against her stomach, whose smooth flatness still gave no hint of the child growing deep within. Her flawless skin held the delicate fragrance of her perfume, and her body's own far more enticing scent. When Eden leaned against him and drew him close, he rose and carried her to the bed but this time rather than laying her on it, he sat her on the edge.

As he again dropped to his knees in front of her, he turned his attentions first to the elegant line of her right leg and then her left. Slender and shapely, her legs were perfect from toe to hip and he spread adoring kisses along them, all the while listening to her breath quicken until it echoed the rapid rhythm of his. He slowed his pace then, savoring the tender flesh of her inner thighs with slow, deep kisses until she could stand no more of his erotic teasing.

He felt Eden's hands move over him then, her nails raking his shoulders, her fingers tangling his curls. She wrapped her legs around his neck and pulled him down into the depths of her sweetness, but in driving her mad with desire, Raven had also sent his own passions reeling. The kisses he gave her now were as fevered as his blood, and seared the delicate recesses of her body with a tongue of flame.

As Eden writhed beneath him, Raven felt her whole body tremble first with the need for release from the unbearably sweet agony of desire, and then with endless waves of ecstatic deliverance. He moved over her then, pulling her up on the bed where he barely had time to free himself from his clothing before he sought his own release embedded deep within her. Her velvet soft center was wet and hot, and enfolded him in convulsive tremors that cost him the last of his sanity. He had never made love to another woman with such untamed abandon but the thrill they had shared was too exquisite to claim as a defeat for either of them.

Still flooded with her warmth, when at long last Raven could again think rationally, he rolled over on his back and brought Eden atop him where he could hold her in his arms without crushing her with his weight. She was completely relaxed now, languidly draped over his chest, her fair curls spilling over his shoulder, her hands resting lightly on his arms. He did not want to talk, and was grateful when she fell asleep without murmuring a word of protest at the way he had chosen to make love to her.

Then with a sudden chill of recognition, Raven recalled there had been no hesitancy in Eden's gestures. She had not been in the least bit demure or shy, but instead demanding and eager for the intimate kisses that had given them both such intense rapture. A wicked grin graced his lips then, for he had not even suspected Alex would have been that bold with his delicate bride, but obviously the man had taught Eden more than Raven had guessed, and he had taught her well.

Raven stroked Eden's curls as he tried to force the image of her lying in Alex's arms from his mind. To him, his actions had never been devious, but all too painfully obvious. He had fallen in love with his wife, and there was nothing he would not do to keep her. He was not the conniving bastard Eden and her father seemed to see, but merely a lovesick fool who would die for a woman who did not love him, and probably never would.

When Eden awakened the next morning, the sky was overcast and gray. Raven was seated near the window, his chair tipped back, his foot resting on the sill. While she felt wonderfully rested, he looked as though he had been up all night. He was clad only in a pair of tight-fitting black pants, and the long red trails her nails had cut in his shoulders were clearly visible. She winced when she noticed them.

Raven glanced toward her then. "There's another storm brewing. Your father's gone, but we'll wait this out before going to Kingston. If the storm's another bad one, the *Jamaican Wind* will be better off on the river than in a crowded harbor."

He had thoughtfully placed her silk wrapper across the

foot of the bed, and Eden donned it before going to him. "I understand. I'm sorry, I didn't realize I'd scratched you so badly last night. Do you have anything to put on those cuts?"

Raven looked up at her, his stare curiously blank. "Look on the washstand. Yadira makes an herb cream that's good. It ought to be in a green jar."

"Is there anything Yadira doesn't do well?" Eden asked in an exasperated sigh. Finding the cream exactly where Raven had said it would be, she removed the lid and sampled the aroma. Surprisingly, the thick herbal remedy had a fragrance as light as spring rain. "Well, it smells good at least."

Raven was wise enough not to comment on Yadira's talents and he kept still as Eden began to smooth the cool salve on the deep scratches. Her touch was light now, without the urgency that had caused her to use her nails on him. When she apologized again, he refused to accept it. "Look, it was my own fault, so stop blaming yourself. A scrape or two won't kill me."

"It was most certainly not your fault, Raven." Eden coated each of the cuts with the salve, then leaned down to kiss his right shoulder, which was still bruised from one of her father's many blows. When he reached out to catch her wrist and pulled her down on his lap, she did not fight him. It was easier to concentrate on replacing the lid on the jar than on her husband's face and Eden took her time with the task.

"Look at me, Eden."

He had not combed his hair, nor bothered to shave as yet, but Eden thought him incredibly handsome. She wanted to snuggle against him, to make love slowly, and this time on her terms rather than his. She let neither of those thoughts show in her expression though. "Yes?" she asked sweetly.

Raven rested his forehead against hers and was silent for a long moment before he finally spoke what was on his mind. "To hear you and your father talk, I'm some hideous spider who's trying to ensnare everyone in my web. I know you don't love me, but the very least I expect from you is more loyalty than that."

That so astonishingly attractive a man would describe himself as a spider appalled Eden. That he would demand loyalty when in her opinion she had shown him an enormous amount was even more upsetting. But most troubling of all was when they made love, all trace of Alex's touch was gone from her memory. She responded solely to Raven now, and in ways she had never thought possible. Was that being disloyal to Alex? she wondered fretfully.

"I have given you my loyalty, and if it doesn't seem so to you, then I am truly sorry," she explained hesitantly. "I never gave any thought to why a widow waits a year to remarry, but now I think that custom is a wise one. Had we not gotten married, we'd not have half the problems we do."

Raven moaned way back in his throat for her words cut him far more deeply than her nails had. "No," he denied forcefully. "Marrying you was the most honorable thing I've ever done, and even if our lives never run smoothly because of it, I'll never be sorry."

Eden did not want to debate the issue when he seemed so anguished over it. Taking care not to hurt him, she rested her hands lightly on his shoulders and leaned forward to kiss him. Her gesture was both sympathetic and enticing, but Raven did not respond as she had hoped.

Instead, he tightened his hold on her waist and set her on her feet. "I don't want to lose myself in you again this morning. Get dressed, and we'll go downstairs and have breakfast together. Since we can't leave or tour the plantation, we might as well clean out Alex's room. That will take us the whole day."

While Eden didn't look forward to that chore, she didn't argue, and carried Yadira's salve back to the wash-stand before going to her room. Once there, she decided to bathe before getting dressed and went outside to the room above the privy to do so. Water was heating on the stove, and not bothering to summon a maid, she poured it into the copper tub herself. She hung her wrapper from one of the hooks on the back of the door, and turned to step into the tub.

It was not until then that she noticed the small lavender shadows Raven's impassioned kisses had left on her inner thighs. It seemed each of them had marked the other, but she bore only the pale imprint of his mouth, while he wore bloody cuts from her nails.

As she sank down into the tub, Eden knew there was a message in that contrast, and while its meaning taunted her, it existed only on the edge of her mind and refused to come clear. She stayed in the tub until the water was too chilly to remain. Than recalling Raven was waiting for her, she got out, dried herself off, tied the silk wrapper tightly around her waist, and hurried back to the house to prepare for the day.

Twenty-one

October 1863

The storm brought high winds that again left the shore littered with palm fronds and heavy rains that soaked the fields. Although not of hurricane force, it delayed Raven and Eden's trip to Kingston for a week. They did not count the time lost, however, for Raven's confident assumption that they could sort through Alex's effects in a day proved to be woefully inaccurate.

At first Eden feared they would come across a reminder of Alex's affair with Yadira, or possibly love letters or tokens of affection from other women he had known, but the room was devoid of any evidence of romantic liaisons. Other than a miniature of Eleanora, there were no mementos of her either. What his bedroom did contain were countless things that called forth a flood of memories for Raven.

Eden had not been surprised to find he had as perfect recall of incidents that had taken place in his childhood as those that had occurred since she had met him. It took little to catch his interest: a favorite waistcoat Alex had worn until threadbare and then never discarded, a dog-eared volume of poetry, or an unusual piece of jewelry.

He would stop working then, take it to her, and with what usually evolved into a colorful tale, explain why Alex had treasured it. She was the perfect audience for him, and deeply grateful, he was willing to share so many of his precious memories. With such distractions frequent, they would often spend more time at the windowseat reminiscing than working to clear the room.

Occasionally they would look up to find Yadira standing at the door. She would shake her head and wander off, but she made no comment on their project, or the slowness of their pace while completing it. She had soon realized from the reverence with which they handled Alex's belongings that she need not fear anything he had loved would be thrown away. She had already known that Raven had idolized his uncle, and assumed Eden listened with such rapt interest as he spoke of him because she adored her handsome husband and would have been content to listen to him talk all day no matter what the subject. Having lost her only love, it saddened Yadira to be around the affectionate couple, and she devoted herself to her other duties as soon as she realized they did not need her help.

With their days spent in such a loving pastime, no new arguments had sprung up between the newlyweds, nor did they resort to recalling their old ones. At the close of each day, they made love with a touching sweetness rather than a reckless passion, but it was no less pleasurable. When fair weather returned, and Raven announced they would leave the next day for Kingston, Eden hated to see the tranquil week come to an end. Being with Raven was never dull, but she doubted they would have many other opportunities to complete a project with such perfect accord.

After the blissful calm of the plantation, the boisterous port of Kingston provided Eden with a noisy return to the real world. Bordered on the east by the rugged Blue Mountains, the town had a spectacular natural setting but it was as vulgar and corrupt a place as any in the civilized world. While Raven was eager to show Eden something of the town, he intended to choose those sights with care.

Eden, however, wanted to go straight to the Fife and Drum to meet Molly McCay. "You haven't forgotten that I wanted to speak with her, have you? I'm sure if John Rawlings frequented the place, there are others among your crew who do as well. She ought not to learn of John's death from some careless comment one of them might make."

"No, I'd not forgotten," Raven said, but he was still reluctant to escort Eden to the dockside tavern. "It's just that you'll surely be the first countess who ever set foot in the place."

Eden was dressed in her gray gown and bonnet, and held out the skirt as she turned slowly in front of him. "Oh come now, surely I look more like an industrious captain's wife than a countess, don't I?"

How she looked was exquisitely beautiful, but that compliment stuck in Raven's throat. "Well, I suppose we could go over there now. The place might not be too crowded in midafternoon."

"Will we have to rent a carriage?"

"I wish that we did, for the Fife and Drum would undoubtedly be far more respectable if it weren't so close to the docks. It's only a short walk, however, so none of the sailors who enter the port can get lost on their way there."

"My goodness, it certainly sounds popular."

"That it is," Raven assured her, and offering his arm, he left Randy to supervise the unloading of the cargo and guided his bride to the Fife and Drum. A drunken sailor had just been forcefully ejected and, after picking himself up off the walk, would have reeled into them had both Raven and Eden not been so light on their feet.

"You see what I mean?" Raven asked with a rueful shake of his head. "This is no place for a lady."

"We won't have to stay long," Eden assured him as she peeked through the open doorway into the tavern's dimly lit interior.

On a sudden impulse, Raven moved ahead of her. "Wait here a minute. I'll go and ask for Molly. If she's not working this afternoon, we needn't stay."

Before Eden could argue with that idea, Raven had disappeared into the smoke-filled tavern. She had no choice but to stand back from the doorway then, and try to ignore the curious glances she was drawing from the sailors strolling by. Only a few seconds had passed before three amorous young men mistook her nervous smile for an invitation to stop and chat.

"Well, aren't you a pretty one," the most gregarious of the trio greeted her enthusiastically. "My name is Robert, but I always ask women to call me Rob. This is Paul and Jack but you needn't bother to remember their names."

Eden clutched her reticule more tightly, but did not respond, a fact Rob and his companions failed to notice. Rob stepped closer still and again flashed a wide grin. "We got into port too late yesterday to have any fun, but we intend to make up for that today. Do you want to go into the Fife and Drum for a pint or two of ale first, or would you rather take us straight to your place?"

Eden did not appreciate the men standing so close. They were at least clean, and sober, but she knew she had done nothing to encourage their company and just wanted them to go away. The boys she had known at home were certainly a lot better at sensing a woman's lack of interest but she hoped these men would get that message soon. Not wanting to be drawn into a conversation with strangers, she turned to look into the tavern, praying she would see Raven on his way out. Unfortunately, Rob again misinterpreted her actions. He slipped his arm around her narrow waist, simply picked her up, and carried her inside with Paul and Jack following close behind.

"I'd hoped you'd go for the ale. It always helps to make things friendlier."

Raven had located Molly and had just begun to explain his wife wanted a word with her when he saw the three young sailors whisk Eden through the door. Not understanding why she had not been able to stay out of trouble for the short while they had been apart, he quickly excused himself.

Rob paused to allow his eyes to adjust to the tavern's dim lighting before showing Eden to a table, but the first thing he saw was Raven striding toward him wearing so murderous an expression he quickly looked behind him hoping it was being directed at Paul or Jack rather than him. When his friends squared their shoulders and stepped closer rather than turning tail and running away, he knew they would back him up if there was going to be a fight over the pretty blonde. He braced himself and prepared to stand his ground.

Raven did not bother to introduce himself. He simply reached for Eden's hand, plucked her from Rob's arms, and swung her out of his way. He then belted Rob in the chin with a crushing blow that lifted the astonished sailor clear off his feet. Rob came down on legs that wobbled so badly he staggered back into his friends and would have slid to the floor had they not caught him. Raven took another step forward, clearly prepared to deal with Paul and Jack just as harshly, but they had seen enough, and keeping a firm grip on Rob's arms, they dragged him out the door.

Grateful to have settled the matter with one punch, Raven straightened his jacket, and then turned around in time to see Eden and Molly McCay hurrying through a door at the back of the room. While he was pleased his wife had had sense enough to get out of his way, he was still mad she had not stayed outside where he had left her. His expression grim, he ignored the whistles and cheers of those he passed as he hurried to catch up with her.

When Molly had rushed up and taken her hand, Eden had been glad to flee what she feared would surely become a brutal brawl. Once they had reached the safety of the storeroom, she sat down on a barrel of ale and struggled to catch her breath. Molly was used to scuffles between the tavern's patrons, however, and hoped the fight would be a fierce one so she would have an excuse for a long break. When Raven entered the storeroom almost on their heels, she was badly disappointed.

"You ought to have known better than to bring your sweet little wife down here, Captain." Molly laughed as she viewed Eden's ashen face and trembling hands. "I always consider it a compliment when men fight over me, and you should too, darlin'."

"I didn't ask them to bring me inside," Eden hastened to assure Raven. "I was just minding my own business and—"

"Well, clearly they mistook what business you're in," Molly interrupted with another throaty laugh.

That Eden appeared to be terrified that he would blame her for causing the fight stopped Raven cold. He had been annoyed with her, that was certainly true, but he did not want his wife to be frightened of him. He bent down on one knee by her side and took her hands in his. "I should never have left you alone, not even for the minute I intended to. I thought the fact you're a lady would be obvious to anyone, but apparently those three wouldn't recognize a lady even if they saw Queen Victoria wearing her crown. The mistake was mine, Eden, not yours. Now smile for me."

That Raven had not accused her of inviting Rob and his pals into the Fife and Drum simply amazed Eden. She studied his smile for a long moment, and then delighted to find it sincere, she threw her arms around his neck and hugged him tightly. "No, I'm sure I should have been able to send those men on their way so you wouldn't have had to deal with them."

"Oh please," Molly sighed. "You two lovebirds can apologize to each other later. I'm supposed to be serving ale, not just wasting my time chatting."

That Molly would describe them as lovebirds embarrassed both Raven and Eden, and they quickly drew apart. Raven rose to his feet, and dusted off his pants. Certain the two women had not introduced themselves, he attended to that chore but gave only Eden's first name, without referring to her as Lady Clairbourne. He then asked if Molly remembered John Rawlings.

"Is that why you've come looking for me, to ask if I remember one sailor from another?"

Clearly Molly thought that feat impossible, but Eden did not. Molly had the curly red hair many Irish women possess, blue eyes, and a flawless complexion. Her figure was lovely too, but the girl had so brash a manner Eden found it difficult to believe John Rawlings had wanted to marry her. "Perhaps you would recall him if we'd brought some of his friends from the *Jamaican Wind* with us."

"The *Jamaican Wind?*" Molly frowned slightly. "That has a familiar ring to it. Is that your ship, Captain?"

Raven nodded. "John was in his early twenties, good-looking fellow with curly brown hair and gray eyes. I imagine he would have tipped you generously."

Molly favored him with a seductive smile. "They all do, Captain, every last one."

Convinced their errand had been stupid in the first place, Raven helped Eden to her feet. "I'm sorry we've wasted your time."

"Wait a minute," Molly demanded crossly. "Is that all there is to this?"

When Raven looked down at her, Eden answered. "John was injured on the voyage from England. He talked about you just before he died. We thought if you two had been close, you would want to know."

Molly flung open the door. "Sorry, the name John Rawlings means nothing to me. I hope he asked you to give me his pay, though."

While Eden gasped at the coldness of that comment, Raven had expected it. "No, as a matter of fact he didn't and I'll send it to his mother." He tipped Molly for her time, but did not return her delighted smile. With a tight grip on Eden's elbow, he escorted her out of the tavern. Once outside, he looked up and down the walk to make certain Rob and his buddies were not waiting to jump him from behind. Pleased to find them nowhere in sight, he started back toward the *Jamaican Wind.*

The couple had gone only a few yards when a petite barmaid came running out of the Fife and Drum and called out to them. Raven and Eden turned and waited for the girl to catch up with them. She wore the same white blouse and blue skirt Molly had, but there was no other similarity between the two. This girl had straight brown hair, hazel eyes, and more freckles than most red-haired children. Plain rather than pretty like Molly, she needed a moment to catch her breath.

"I knew John Rawlings," she assured them. "I knew him real well. Molly just told me he's dead. Is that true?"

Eden noted the girl's tear-filled gaze and reached out to take her hand. "I'm afraid it is."

The girl began to cry then, her pitiful sobs in stark

contrast to Molly's flippant dismissal of the news of John's death. Raven pulled a handkerchief from his pocket and handed it to her. "What's your name?" he asked considerately.

"Mary, sir," she managed to mumble through her tears.

"Mary," Raven repeated the name slowly as an idea began to take shape in his mind. "I think my wife and I may have made a terrible mistake, Mary. John was in a lot of pain, and we thought he was asking for Molly. But now that we've met her, I'm certain we must have misunderstood. I think he was calling for you."

Eden listened incredulously as Raven told what she knew to be an outright lie. She had heard John say Molly just as clearly as she could hear Raven's words now, but when Mary responded with a radiant smile, Eden was not even tempted to tell her the truth. It was as obvious to her as it was to Raven that John Rawlings had fallen in love with the wrong woman, and if they could set the matter straight now, she was all for it.

Before bidding her goodbye, Raven placed several gold coins in Mary's hand. "I'm sure John would want you to buy yourself something to remember him by, a gold locket perhaps?"

"Oh yes," Mary agreed as she clutched the money tightly. "I'll buy one, but I'll never forget John, not for as long as I live I won't. Here, you'll be needing your handkerchief."

"Keep it. Tie the coins in a corner so you don't lose them," Raven suggested. "I think it would be a good idea if you didn't mention any of this to Molly. It would hurt her feelings to know John wasn't thinking of her after all."

"I understand. It will be our secret." Mary placed the coins in the soggy handkerchief, then gave both Raven

367

and Eden a kiss on the cheek before hurrying back to the Fife and Drum.

As she took his arm, Eden paid her husband a sincere compliment. "I think that was the kindest thing I have ever seen anyone do."

While Raven had been grateful Eden had not disputed his word in front of Mary, he was nevertheless surprised she would condone a lie. "John was a nice fellow. I didn't think he'd mind my telling Mary he loved her since Molly didn't even recall who he was."

"Regardless of your reasons, that was a wonderfully sweet thing to do."

When Eden gave his arm a loving squeeze, Raven covered her hand with his. No one had ever accused him of being sweet, but if he had pleased her, he considered the trip to the Fife and Drum an afternoon well spent. That he had again scraped all the skin off his knuckles was a small price to pay.

The next afternoon, Raven took Eden to meet Alex's attorney, Alistair Nash. This time he had hired a carriage, and told the driver to make his way to Nash's office by the most scenic route possible. That took them up King Street, where the most elegant shops were located, and around Victoria Park. After the previous afternoon's tour of the docks, Raven was glad for the opportunity to show Eden some of Kingston's better neighborhoods.

"The original settlement, Port Royal, was east of here, but it was destroyed by an earthquake in 1692. Everything you see today dates from after that time."

While Eden found Raven to be an entertaining tour guide, she was so worried about visiting the attorney she simply smiled and nodded rather than ask questions as she might have on a less stressful day. He had not cautioned her to be silent, but he had not encouraged her to speak freely with the attorney either. Rather than bring up the subject herself when she feared it would spoil his congenial mood, she was left to fret about it unhappily.

Raven was too perceptive a man not to notice Eden's distress, and wanting to avoid a scene in the attorney's office if at all possible, he encouraged her to speak. "Is it merely having to listen to the reading of Alex's will that has upset you, or is it something else? If it's a legal question, I'd appreciate hearing it before you consult Alistair."

It had been after Raven had flogged Max and Samuel that Eden had decided to ask Alex's attorney to explain the inheritance laws to her. That now seemed like years, rather than merely a few weeks, ago. With Raven's prompting, she realized how badly he would misconstrue her intentions if she failed to explain them first. "We discussed this once before, but I still don't really understand," she began hesitantly.

As always, Eden's expression looked deceptively innocent, but Raven was positive her question wouldn't be. "Tell me what it is, and if I can't provide you with a satisfactory answer this time either, then maybe Alistair can."

"It's merely a point of curiosity, Raven."

That Eden was looking down at her tightly clenched hands rather than at him gave Raven a clear warning, and expecting the worst, he braced himself. "We're almost there. Tell me what's bothering you."

Eden did look toward him then, her golden eyes lit with a compelling light rather than scorn. "I gave you my promise I'd stay married to you. You know that I mean to keep it."

"Yes," Raven replied impatiently, already confident that she would.

"Well, if we hadn't married, who would be the one to inherit Alex's title? Would it be my babe, or you?"

"But we are married, Eden," Raven reminded her firmly, now recalling their earlier conversation. "There's absolutely no point in confusing the issue with hypothetical questions."

"Perhaps not, but the answer's important to me."

"Why?"

"It just is!"

Raven exhaled slowly. "Alex had no other male kin. He named me his heir in his will and he spent nearly twenty years grooming me to take his place. The possibility he might remarry never entered his mind. Did he ever tell you he hoped you would give him a son?" Raven held his breath, knowing Eden could say whatever she pleased, but praying she would tell the truth.

"No, we never discussed having children. We were far too busy enjoying the moment to consider what the future might bring."

"Then it ought to be obvious to you that Alex was confident that I wouldn't disgrace the Clairbourne name."

"Raven, please. That isn't really the issue here. I just want to know who is legally entitled to be Alex's heir. I'd rather not ask Mr. Nash that question because it will look as though I'm accusing you of doing something underhanded and that's not my intention. I just want to know which of you is the rightful heir."

"Did your father put you up to this?"

Sorry that possibility had even occurred to him, Eden glanced away for a moment. "He questioned the speed with which we married and indeed it does look suspicious, but that's only because I dared not explain our reasons."

"So you allowed him to think I'd rushed you into marriage for some devious purpose of my own rather than describe how willingly you'd shared my bed?"

Eden recoiled as though he had struck her. "No! I lied to protect you, not to make you look like a scoundrel."

"But he thinks I'm one anyway, doesn't he? You were protecting only yourself, Eden, not me."

"It wasn't that way at all," Eden contradicted sharply. "It's only that he wants the best for me. When he has the opportunity to get to know you better, he'll see what a fine man you are."

Raven shook his head in disbelief. "If you truly think I'm such a fine man, then why are you asking if I'm really entitled to be Alex's heir? Why can't you just accept that I am?"

"I can accept it, Raven, but I'd still like to know what would have happened had we not married."

Raven lowered his voice to a threatening whisper. "Had we not married, I would still be Alex's heir. Do you honestly believe he would have preferred to pass his title on to a brat he did not live to see rather than to me?"

Shocked that he would refer to her unborn child in so hostile a manner, Eden again pulled away from him. "You promised to raise my child as your own. I'll not have you calling him a brat."

"There's only one way out of this mess," Raven pointed out caustically. "You realize that, don't you?"

"And what is that?" Eden asked apprehensively.

"You'll have to have a daughter!"

Eden's eyes opened wide, for indeed she had not once considered the possibility her child might not be male. She was in no mood to think about baby girls now either. "No, it isn't," she argued, now dreadfully sorry she had brought up the subject of Alex's title in the first place. She could not take back that question, but she could at least attempt to repair the damage it had done between them.

"You're right," she stressed as she reached out to take Raven's hand. "Alex meant for you to succeed him as earl. It's Alex's wishes that ought to be respected regardless of what the technicalities of the law might be. I'll not ask Mr. Nash, or anyone else about it. You are now the earl and that's all there is to it. I didn't mean to insult you, Raven. Please forgive me that I did."

Although he was relieved beyond measure that Eden had made such a sensible decision, that she had again cited Alex's wishes as her reason disgusted him completely. Was she never going to appreciate him herself, but instead always rely on Alex's judgment of him? He gave her hand a perfunctory squeeze, but he was so discouraged his expression was still an obstinate one when they arrived at Alistair Nash's office.

Raven had been coming there for nearly twenty years, and in all that time the elderly gentleman had not changed one bit. He was barely five feet tall, and had to hook the heels of his shoes on the rung of his chair to prevent his spindly legs from dangling a foot from the floor like a small child's. His sparse white hair stuck out from his pale head in wispy clumps like a bizarre halo, giving him a comic appearance no matter what his mood, but his bright blue eyes shone with intelligence, and his greeting was sincerely warm.

"I am pleased to see you looking so fit, my lord, and to meet you, my lady. I was badly distressed to learn of Alex's passing. He was like a son to me, you know, as was his father."

Eden would not have been surprised had Alistair sworn a similar affection for Alex's grandfather as well. She was certain he had to be ninety at the very least, and wondered why Raven had not remarked on the man's advanced age. He had Alex's will ready to read, and donned a pair of gold-rimmed spectacles for the task. While he and Raven were familiar with the wording, she had to sit on the edge of her chair and strain to understand Alistair's high-pitched, mumbling recitation. When he reached the end and set the document aside, she nodded thoughtfully.

Still in the foulest of moods, Raven took a perverse pleasure in goading his bride into breaking her word. "Is there anything that's unclear to you?" he asked. "I'm sure Alistair would be happy to answer any questions you have."

Eden could readily discern from the taunting light in Raven's eyes that he was presenting her with a test. That he still did not trust her was unfortunate, but she had absolutely no desire to leap to her feet and challenge his right to be earl. Wars had been fought over which man had the right to a title or throne and she certainly didn't want any such derisive contest going on in her own family.

"Why no, I'm certain everything is in order."

Raven still did not smile. Like everyone else, Alistair believed him to be Alex's nephew. That he had inherited Alex's title and all his worldly goods was as it should be in the attorney's view, but as he had on so many occasions, Raven felt like an impostor. He sat up abruptly then, and forced himself into the uncomfortable role of a fine gentleman.

"I'd like for you to draw up a new will for me," he began. "The previous one left everything to Alex should I predecease him. The new one should leave everything to my beloved wife, Eden, and whatever dear little children we might have."

"I shall begin immediately," Alistair promised. "Please allow me to congratulate you on your marriage and offer my hopes that the children you mentioned will soon become a reality."

When Eden began to blush, Raven's anger dissolved in

an unaccountable rush of fatherly pride. "Do you mind?" he asked her.

"No, go ahead," Eden encouraged.

"Our first child will be born next spring."

"Well, that is good news!" Alistair's smile grew broader still. "You must bring the little fellow to see me as soon as you can. Do you remember coming here with Alex? You were such a solemn child, all eyes it seemed then."

Raven could recall being that child all too easily. He rose to his feet and reached for Eden's hand. "We appreciate your good wishes. We'll be returning to the plantation in a few days. I'll stop by to sign the new will before we leave."

"I'll have it ready, my lord."

Raven breathed a sigh of relief as they left Alistair's office. The visit had gone remarkably well, but he could not shake the horrible feeling that if Eden ever discovered he was not really Alex's nephew, there would be hell to pay.

Twenty-two

October 1863

Eden wanted to focus her attention on the sights of Kingston as they returned to the *Jamaican Wind,* but Raven made no attempt to provide either information or entertainment. Instead, he kept his thoughts to himself as though he were traveling alone rather than with a lovely young woman who was all too aware of him.

When she could bear no more of his stony silence, Eden moved closer and looped her arm through his. "Raven, there's a vast difference between a question and an accusation so I wish you'd stop acting like I've committed some heinous crime. You and Alex were closer than most fathers and sons and I'm certain that even if he had lived long enough for us to have half a dozen sons he would still have wanted you to inherit his title. That you were his choice was spelled out quite clearly in his will. We needn't discuss this issue ever again and I'd appreciate your ceasing to condemn me for bringing it up."

Raven found it difficult to return Eden's level gaze. He knew he was behaving badly, but it was far easier to cling to a stubborn silence than to speak and embellish the fanciful lie that Alex had begun the first time he had introduced him as his nephew. Despite his passion for the truth, Raven did not even consider admitting it about himself when he knew how disgusted Eden would be to discover she was married to a man Alex had rescued from the Kingston streets. That he could pass as a gentleman was no more than a trick of fate that had given him a handsome appearance, and Alex's diligent tutoring.

"Alex often complained that I lack proper manners," Raven reminded her. "But you mustn't allow my faults to prevent you from speaking your mind. I would rather that we had ten bitter arguments each day than have us get along by skirting every issue of any importance."

Raven's features were still set in a sullen frown, but Eden considered his words encouraging even if his expression was not. "We didn't have a single fight last week at the plantation. In fact, we got along better than I ever thought we could. I want that kind of happiness for us always."

"So do I," Raven was quick to agree, for he recalled the previous week as fondly as she did. The possibility of living a lie for the rest of his life made him horribly uncomfortable, but the prospect of losing Eden's respect, and whatever small chance he had of winning her love, made telling the truth an impossible alternative.

When they arrived at his ship, Raven had work to do, and taking care to stay out of his way, Eden also remained on deck. The day was warm and the activity on the docks was lively enough to hold her interest but her thoughts strayed frequently to her husband. Raven could be so charming at times, and at others so withdrawn she feared he might be hiding some terrible secret. When he suddenly appeared at her side, she was relieved to find him wearing a smile. He was easily the most puzzling individual she had ever met, and yet when he was pleasant, she found him wonderfully appealing.

Her mood now far more relaxed, Eden made what she hoped Raven would find a considerate suggestion. "As soon as we get home, let's begin making plans for your birthday. It was so easy to entertain my father and his men with your staff's help, I'd like to plan a nice evening for your friends."

Surprised that she wished to give a party, Raven rested his forearms on the rail as he explained why it was impractical. "Most of my friends are on board this ship and they don't expect to be entertained in my home. Alex didn't really mix with the owners of the neighboring plantations, so I'd not invite any of them. Besides, I think a birthday celebration might be considered highly inappropriate when we should still be in mourning."

Eden had wanted to please Raven, to do something especially for him that had nothing to do with Alex, but she understood his concerns. Grateful he had not sounded critical, she revised her idea aloud. "If we must, we'll have a party all by ourselves then, but I want the day to be a special one for you. A man only turns twenty-seven once."

"Don't you think that ought to be enough?" Raven joked easily.

"Yes," Eden agreed, enormously pleased his mood had turned good.

"You usually rest in the afternoon when we're at home. I think that's a habit you ought to continue here."

Eden shook her head. "I'm not in the least bit tired."

"Neither am I," Raven confided as he took her arm. "But let's go to my cabin anyway."

Raven was again displaying the quicksilver nature that kept Eden constantly in a quandary in her attempts to understand him, but she hesitated no more than an instant before placing her hand over his in a silent gesture of consent. Earlier that afternoon his anger had unnerved her completely, but the affection he offered now was far too sweet to refuse.

The goods Raven had brought from England were swiftly sold, and although he had kept several bolts of silk and brocade for Eden to have made into new gowns, she surprised him by complaining she had too many clothes already. She kept the fabric at his insistence, but said she would save it until after the baby was born.

"I suppose Yadira is a wonderfully talented seamstress," Eden remarked with the sarcasm that always crept into her voice when she mentioned the housekeeper.

"No, she considers sewing beneath her. There are several women on the plantation who are very talented, though. I'll give you that tour I promised the day after we return home. You'll meet them then. Perhaps you'd like to ask them to make some baby clothes."

"Not until after the new year."

Seemingly preoccupied, Eden turned away, leaving Raven to wonder if she might not also be worried about her babe's health. If she had not realized the child she was carrying might share Alex's heart defect, it would be cruel to point it out and frighten her. Then again, if she was agonizing over such a terrible possibility, it seemed equally cruel to allow her to do so alone. Unable to decide what was the wisest course, he stepped up behind her and kissed her nape tenderly. When she relaxed against him, he kept his fears for Alex's babe to himself. It was merely one more secret of the many he dared not share.

After a week-long stay in Kingston, the *Jamaican Wind* carried Eden and Raven back to the plantation on the Rio Bueno, along with one hundred barrels of coal Raven had decided might prove useful should the *Southern Knight* again need their help. As soon as the coal was unloaded,

Randy MacDermott took the helm, and the ship returned to Kingston, where it would remain for the winter. As promised, the next day Raven had Arabella, their cook, pack a picnic lunch, and once Eden was comfortably seated in the buggy, they began the long delayed tour.

The first of the sugar cane fields was not far from the house, and with Raven providing a running commentary, they proceeded along the road to the mill, where the cane was ground to extract the juice. Next they visited one of the boiling houses, where the juice was boiled with lime to reduce it to a thick syrup. Raven showed Eden how the brown sugar was crystallized out, leaving molasses.

"We ferment most of the molasses and distill it to make rum. It's a highly profitable business, but it takes a great deal of labor."

After leaving the curing house, where the hogshead barrels of rum were stored, they returned to the buggy. Raven clucked to the horses and the matched pair of bays got them under way again. While he had shown Eden how sugar cane was processed, there was something far more important he wanted her to understand.

"When the slaves were freed, they were forced to put in a three-year apprenticeship and had to work for their former owners for pay. After that, most fled the plantations, but William, Alex's father, had always treated his slaves well and made a bargain with them. He divided the plantation to give each some land of his own to farm in exchange for a promise that they would spend part of their time working for him, but he paid them honest wages for that work. He set up a school so that all the children, plus anyone else who wanted to learn, could get an education. Most of his neighbors thought him a fool, or just plain despised him for supporting emancipation, but he was able to keep the plantation running without resorting to using indentured laborers."

Raven paused for a moment, choosing his words with care. "The Africans had lost everything when they were brought here, their language, customs, and family ties as well. William felt responsible for their welfare and didn't want them to lose everything again. He thought by keeping them here, he could make certain they had better lives than the poor souls who ran off to live in the hills. He helped them build houses, and provided medical care. None of his people disappointed him either. While most of the freed slaves had nothing but their freedom, the people here had that and their dignity as well."

"Raven, please," Eden interrupted. "I told you my family has never owned slaves. You needn't feel you must justify William's actions to me."

"That's not what I'm trying to do," Raven countered impatiently. "I think William was right. Slavery was wrong, but to turn slaves free with no education, no place to go, and no means to support themselves was even more evil. He repaid his people several times over for the free labor they had given him as slaves. I never knew him, but Alex used to speak of him often and always with deep affection and admiration."

They had now reached the fields where ginger was grown for its aromatic roots and others planted with Jamaican pepper whose berries were dried and ground to make allspice. Raven then left the main road for a far-less-traveled lane that wound its way toward the river through uncultivated land still covered with lush, tropical vegetation.

Continuing to be an informative guide, he pointed out several of the Jamaican hardwoods: mahogany, ebony, mahoe, and juniper. There were stands of dogwood, and cedar logwood from whose yellow flowers a vivid dye was made. Among the ferns and bamboo, a profusion of orchids bloomed in a myriad of hues. Overhead brightly colored parakeets, hummingbirds, and butterflies darted in and out of the trees.

Eden found Jamaica's beauty absolutely magnificent and told Raven so repeatedly. "This is like a trip through paradise. Where are we having our picnic?"

Relieved she had not found any of his comments offensive, Raven regarded his bride with a sly smile. "Are you hungry? It's not much farther, and it's such a pretty spot it's worth the trouble to get there."

"It can't be any more beautiful than this."

"You'll see."

Raven left the horses tethered within sight of the river and then, taking Eden's hand, carried their basket down a seldom-used trail that curved upward away from the river before ending in a sylvan glade. At the center, a creek running toward the river spilled over an outcropping of moss-covered rocks to form a small, but utterly charming waterfall. A rainbow glistened in the air above it like a sparkling crown.

"Oh Raven, this must surely be the prettiest place on earth."

While Eden's rapt expression mirrored her delight, Raven forced back the desire to kiss her and busied himself laying out their tablecloth and lunch. He was happy that he had pleased her, and yet still apprehensive that her opinion of him might change once her child was born. Such conflicting emotions troubled him constantly, but he did not know what to do about them.

"I've always thought so. Now come sit down, I'm hungry even if you aren't."

Arabella had packed roast chicken, sweet rolls, banana slices sprinkled with coconut, and crisp ginger cookies. Raven opened the bottle of wine and poured Eden the two sips he knew she would drink while he filled his own mug to the rim.

"How did you happen to find this place?" Eden asked between bites of chicken.

"It's near the spot where Azariah and I used to cut bamboo and build rafts. When I was a child, rafting on the river was what I loved to do best."

"Azariah grew up here too?"

"Yes. Like most of our workers, he's a descendant of one of William's slaves. He liked rafting on the river, but I could never convince him to come to sea with me."

Eden had been impressed by the friendliness of all the people she had met that day. She could not help but note the admiring glances the young women had sent Raven's way. That he appeared completely unaware of the special attention he received had amused her, but she knew better than to tease him about it and commented on Azariah instead. "He appears to be an excellent overseer; apparently the sea simply was not his calling."

Raven shrugged. "I guess not, but Alex was harshly criticized for giving him the overseer's job rather than hiring a white man. From the time Englishmen started plantations here, the owners generally lived in England and relied upon white overseers to run things. Alex didn't care any more about tradition than his father had when he believed it was wrong. I think you can understand why the Suttons have never been particularly popular here. They regarded Jamaica rather than England as home and visited only for the social season each summer."

"But Alex was very popular in London. I never saw anyone snub him."

"That's true, but you've got to remember that, by the time slavery was abolished, sugar was no longer so vital to England's economy as it had once been. Without free labor, owning a plantation was no longer as appealing an investment, so the lands of many were divided up and sold. What we did here no longer mattered in London. We do have neighbors upriver, but most are either in awe of an earl, or so incensed by the way we run things they want nothing to do with us either. You asked about a memorial service once, but I'd rather not hold one when our neighbors would probably attend out of curiosity rather than respect."

"I understand." As always, the mention of Alex filled Eden with longing for the dear man. She did not want to think about Alex that day, however; she just wanted to enjoy the beauty of Jamaica with Raven and talk about happy things. When she glanced toward him, she found him regarding her with the tender expression she had glimpsed only a time or two while they were making love. When she smiled, he seemed embarrassed that she had caught him staring at her and hurriedly grabbed another piece of chicken.

Eden looked away then, focusing her attention on the shimmering waterfall while the truth of what she had seen rocked her clear to the marrow. In an unguarded moment, Raven's expression had been filled with the love he had never expressed in words. She remembered telling her father that she might one day come to love her second husband, but she had never dreamed Raven already loved her. When he knew that she still loved Alex, how could his love for her bring him anything but pain? Overwhelmed by the sorrow of that thought, she sighed sadly.

"I'm sorry," Raven said. "I didn't mean to remind you of Alex."

"It's all right. I enjoy hearing about your life here. I was just wishing that *we* could go rafting."

"You want to go rafting?"

Eden laughed. "Of course. It sounds like a lot of fun. I'm sure Julian would forbid it now, but would you take me after the baby's born?"

"Can you swim?"

"Probably better than you," Eden announced proudly.

It was Raven who laughed this time, "All right, we'll do it as soon as you feel up to it."

Eden continued to wear a mischievous smile as they finished eating. When Raven offered her a cookie, she took one bite then set it aside. "It's really too pretty a day not to enjoy it fully, don't you think?"

Confused, Raven frowned slightly. "I'd say that we're already doing that."

Eden had been seated across from him, but now moved to his side and reached for the top button on his shirt. "You have more imagination than that, Raven Blade."

Despite his doubts about her, Raven responded with his first impulse and pulled the blond beauty down across his lap, where he covered her face with kisses before savoring her ginger-flavored lips. He gloried in the affection Eden gave so freely and for the moment ceased to care what the future might bring.

They made love several times that afternoon, their passion as natural as the verdant beauty that surrounded them. It was not until the sun began to set that they regretfully forced themselves to leave, and even then, neither truly wished to depart. On the journey home, Eden wore a lingering smile. She knew it would be too dark to search for the lavender bottle in the shrubbery beneath her bedroom windows when they reached the house, but she intended to look for it first thing in the morning. Raven's birthday was not that far away, and she could think of only one present she wanted to give him: a night of love he would always remember.

When they returned to the house, Eden was surprised to find Julian waiting to see her. She again assured him that she felt well, but after the way she and Raven had spent the afternoon she found it almost impossible to keep a straight face while she answered the reserved man's questions. Because of the lateness of the hour, Raven invited him to remain for supper and to spend the night. The physician said little during the evening meal then, pleading appointments the next morning, retired early. That they would not have to entertain Julian when they much preferred to amuse themselves did not trouble his amorous hosts in the least.

When she had greeted Julian at the door, Yadira had behaved with the same aloof professionalism she had always shown. She had given him no opportunity to speak with her privately, nor had she provided even a hint that she recalled the last night he had spent in the house. When he retired to his room, the anxious physician paced for one hour and then two, hoping with each minute that passed that Yadira would come to his door. When finally he was too excited by the prospect of seeing her again to wait a moment longer, he stole down the back stairs and rapped lightly on her door.

Yadira's long glossy hair covered her breasts, but otherwise she was nude when she opened her door. She found Julian's obvious consternation at her lack of apparel highly amusing and reached out to draw him into her room. Her quarters were dimly lit, and filled with the heady fragrance of the incense she burned each evening.

When he reached out to clutch her breasts, she backed away. "No, you must undress first."

"Oh please," Julian moaned. His fevered gaze swept over her exquisite figure with a hunger he could not disguise. "I don't think I can wait that long."

As Yadira turned away, she called over her shoulder. "I can teach you many things, doctor, but if you have no better control than a schoolboy, it will be very difficult for you to learn." With her usual grace, she lay back on her bed, and propped herself on her elbows. After a shake of her head, her inky tresses fell back to reveal the lush fullness of her breasts. When Julian nearly drooled at that sight, she laughed at him.

"Undress," she insisted.

Julian had trouble removing his tie, and then his hands shook so badly he could not get the buttons on his shirt undone. All the while he struggled with his clothes, Yadira continued to tease him. Her suggestive comments were humiliating, and yet he wanted her so badly he would have listened to any abuse. When he had finally thrown off the last of his clothing, he rushed toward the bed, but again the dark-eyed beauty stopped him.

"You must please me first, doctor," Yadira ordered in a husky whisper. "I want to feel your mouth on me, the hot wetness of your tongue. Not until you have pleasured me will I let you have what you want."

Julian thought Yadira a wanton whore, but he would have satisfied any conditions she put on their affair. As before, she demanded more of him than any woman ever had, but it did not even occur to him to say no. He satisfied her every whim rather than risk losing the exotic rapture of her favors. When she again made him return to his room carrying his clothes, he was too busy planning when next he could visit to worry that they might be seen.

On November tenth, Eden asked Arabella to prepare all of Raven's special favorites for dinner, but this time the lively blonde gathered the orchids to decorate the table herself. She donned her ice blue gown that evening, but rather than wearing the diamond and ruby ring Alex had given her on her right hand as she usually did, she wore only Raven's diamond wedding ring. She was always beautifully groomed, but that night she took extra time with her hair and was very pleased with the result.

She was now in her fourth month of pregnancy. Her breasts had a new fullness but her stomach had only a slight swell, and she thought her figure as alluring as ever. As she and Raven talked easily during dinner, she could tell from his admiring glances and charming comments that the evening was going to be a wonderful success.

Raven had not expected a present from Eden. In the month they had been home from Kingston, there had been scarcely a moment when she had been out of his sight so he knew she could not possibly have bought or made one. But when she told him she had something special to give him later that night, he could not help but become not only curious, but excited as well. He had been unable to banish his fears that they might have horrible conflicts in the future, but Eden had not once mentioned Alex's will, and he had no desire to bring up the subject again himself. Especially not on his birthday, when Eden made him feel more like a king than an earl.

Eden had found the delicate lavender bottle unbroken. It had fallen among the orchids that grew beside the house and, cradled by their softness, would have been there indefinitely had she not come looking for it. She had given a great deal of thought to how she wanted to use the magical oil, and the possibility Raven might react angrily to the first taste of the heavenly liquid had not escaped her. That what she intended to do contained an element of risk served only to make her more determined to carry it off well, however.

When they went upstairs to Raven's room, Eden kissed him lightly and then drew away. "There's something I want to do tonight simply for the joy of it. There's no other reason, so you mustn't accuse me of having any other purpose."

Greatly intrigued, Raven readily agreed. "What's my part in this?"

"Slip off your clothes, get into your bed, and I'll join you in a few minutes." Eden blew him a kiss as she started for her room. She was too enchanted with her idea to reconsider it now, especially when Raven was in an equally playful mood.

She undressed, donned her most exquisitely beautiful nightgown, and brushed out her elaborate hairstyle. She then sat down on the edge of her bed and counted to one hundred slowly to make certain Raven would already be in bed before she returned to his room. When she was satisfied she had allowed sufficient time for his anticipation to build, Eden opened the bottle of exotic oil and applied a liberal amount to her lips. It would take only one kiss to know if the evening would go as she had planned. Concealing the bottle in the folds of her gown, she made no effort to hide her smile as she returned to her husband's room.

Raven broke into a wide grin as Eden sat down on the edge of his bed. He could not imagine what she was up to, but she looked so pleased with herself, he knew he would surely enjoy it too. When she leaned over to kiss him, he slipped his arm around her waist and hugged her tight. He had always loved the way she kissed, and enjoying it to the fullest, he did not at first recognize the source of her delicious taste. When he finally did, he was so badly jarred he shoved her away.

Eden had expected Raven to be shocked, and hastened to reassure him. "Yes, I know. I'm the very last woman that you would ever expect to bring this delicious oil to your bed." She set the lavender bottle on his nightstand to give him a few seconds to absorb the fact that she had. "That each of us has used it with another doesn't matter.

I want us to create some beautiful memories of our own tonight. Will you help me?"

Had she asked him to set himself on fire in so tempting a fashion, Raven would have readily agreed. "What did Yadira say when you asked her for more?"

Eden removed the bottle's elegant stopper and shook out a few drops to rub on Raven's lips. "I didn't. This is the same bottle you threw out the window."

That the lovely Lady Clairbourne must have had to crawl through the bushes on her hands and knees to find it amused Raven no end. "Come here," he ordered with a wicked grin. "If it's memories you want, I'll give you a night you'll never forget."

"Is that a promise?" Eden whispered just before her lips met his. Raven had no time to respond in words, but she felt his answer all the same. His lips were soft, his caress gentle, and his imaginative use of the sweet-tasting oil endlessly exciting but she did not allow him to distract her from her goal. Alex had provided her first lessons in loving, but she had also learned a great deal from Raven. With each touch of her hands and lips, she sought to give her dashing young husband the most exquisite of pleasures and she could tell by his satisfied moans that she was succeeding.

By midnight, their bodies glistened with a light film of oil and neither could have spoken a coherent sentence. Their thoughts were a blur of loving dreams, and their senses awash with the passion that flowed so easily between them. It was too soon for Eden to speak of love, but the affection she had long felt for Raven deepened immeasurably that night.

As for Raven, the evening was too perfect to risk spoiling it with declarations of love he feared Eden would only be embarrassed to hear. There would be time enough later, he told himself. If not in the spring, then in the summer, or again next fall when they celebrated his birthday. When Eden had given him such a marvelous night, he hoped the next year would pass quickly so he could ask her for the same present when he turned twenty-eight and every year thereafter.

Twenty-three

December 1863

Eden had to cover her mouth with both hands to stifle her giggles until their three visitors had left the house. Equally amused, Raven drew her into his arms and muffled his own deep chuckles in her tawny curls. Despite his assumption that his neighbors would continue to be standoffish, the news of Alex's death coupled with that of his marriage had inspired so much curiosity they had had frequent callers.

"I don't mean to laugh at them," Eden began, "but when the Sidneys learned I was from Virginia rather than England they did not even try to hide their disappointment. They made it almost painfully obvious that they thought you should have wed their daughter instead of me. The poor girl was so embarrassed she flinched every time her mother spoke."

"And with good reason," Raven added. "I had almost forgotten what the London season was like, but a wealthy bachelor is even more highly prized here than there. Thank God I'm no longer in that category."

Because he had left the bachelor ranks for reasons she did not care to discuss, Eden chose not to pursue that comment. "I think we're simply far more sophisticated than any of your neighbors and that's what makes carrying on a conversation so difficult. I am sorry we've not found anyone who shares our interests, though, as I'd like for us to have some good friends."

"I'm certain we'll have plenty of friends in time," Raven assured her, but he was relieved beyond measure that, for the present, he would continue to have Eden all to himself.

It was not until the middle of December that details of the Confederate defeat at the Battle of Chattanooga reached them. Raven debated the wisdom of revealing the devastating loss to his bride, then realized he would be foolish not to and allow her to harbor false hopes for the Confederacy.

Eden read the report of the War's progress in the Kingston paper and then looked up at Raven with tear-filled eyes. She knew the railroad center at Chattanooga had been vital to the Confederacy. With its loss, Tennessee was now firmly under Union control and the South no longer had any strength west of the Alleghenies. The Union needed only to subdue the four seaboard states: Virginia, North Carolina, South Carolina, and Georgia, to win the War.

"I don't want to hear that this loss was inevitable. Please spare me one of your lectures," the distraught blonde pleaded sadly.

There had been a time when Raven had striven to make Eden see the futility of the War, but now that she did, he found absolutely no pleasure in seeing her distress. He sat down beside her, pulled her into his arms, and cradled her head on his shoulder.

"Now that I've met your father and his men, it's difficult to analyze the War as though it were only a military exercise. You must have thought me insufferably rude."

That a man with Raven's pride would make such a statement astonished Eden, and she moved back slightly so she could study his expression. "You were entitled to your opinions, and you were never rude in the way you expressed them."

Raven could see Eden was struggling to be diplomatic. "What about *arrogant* then? Is that a better term?"

"Well, if you want me to be completely honest, yes, there have been times when you've been arrogant."

"Wouldn't you like to include *overbearing* and *tyrannical* too?"

Eden licked her lips thoughtfully. "You can be overbearing, but you're never tyrannical, Raven. That's an exaggeration."

While she had scarcely paid him a string of compliments, Raven began to laugh. The newspaper slid from her lap as she slipped her arms around his waist, and as their lips met, he was glad that he had at least temporarily distracted her from the sorrow of the War.

As Yadira passed the drawing room, she glanced in and wondered how long it would take before the newlyweds' enchantment with each other wavered. She was certainly sick of them always holding hands, or hugging and kissing the moment they thought they were alone. Disgusted with them both, she decided to make the choices for dinner without consulting Eden and left to give Arabella her selections.

For Eden's Christmas present, Raven wrapped the diamond earrings and necklace that had been in Alex's family for several generations. He was pleased that he could give her the exquisite jewelry until he awoke in the middle of the night two days before Christmas and could not recall whether or not Eleanora was wearing the elegant jewels in the portrait that hung in the drawing room. Unable to wait until morning to look, he took care not to disturb Eden as he left his bed. He donned his robe, and hurried downstairs to make certain he was not about to give Eden the same gift Alex had once given Eleanora.

To his immense relief, he found that, rather than the diamonds, Alex's first wife was wearing a dainty emerald pendant and matching earrings in her painting. He did not recall ever seeing Eleanora wearing the jewels he wished to give Eden, but the possibility she might have worn them for her portrait had given him a bad start. What disturbed him now was not Eleanora's selection of jewelry, but the candle that had been left burning beneath Alex's portrait.

As always, he and Eden had gone upstairs together that evening, so he knew she had not been the one to light it. No, it had to have been Yadira. Alex had been a fine man, but Raven did not think it proper to place lighted candles beneath his portrait as though he had achieved sainthood. He not only blew out the candle, but carried the brass holder to Yadira's room and left it on the small table beside her door. He knew her to be a clever woman, and trusted that she would discontinue its use without him having to give her a direct order to cease the practice.

Raven had just turned toward the back stairs when he heard Julian's voice coming from the housekeeper's room. The physician stopped by at least once a week to see Eden, but Raven had not suspected the frequency of Julian's visits was due to anything more than solicitous concern for his wife. He had not been serious when he had mentioned Julian to Yadira, but at that hour of the night he did not need to overhear the details of their conversation to know the man was not providing medical attention.

Thinking how the unusual couple wished to spend their time was their own business, Raven started on up the back stairs. Eden and Yadira still treated each other with a stilted reserve, but his wife had abided by his decision not to discuss replacing Yadira until after the baby was born. If Yadira and Julian had fallen in love, though, perhaps the housekeeper would soon be leaving of her own accord. That prospect would certainly please Eden, but Raven did not want to raise her hopes and therefore chose not to tell her he had discovered Yadira and Julian were lovers.

The next morning when the haughty housekeeper found the candle had been extinguished and moved during the night, she was not merely disappointed to find the owners of the house did not share her devotion to Alex, she was incensed by their callousness. They were young, of course, but true gentlemen like Alexander Sutton were rare, and she was certain he deserved to be remembered with far more devotion than Raven and his bride ever showed. She carried the white taper into her room, where she vowed to continue to light it each evening. She loved Alex still even if Raven and Eden had forgotten him.

Having heard of his talents with wood, Eden asked Azariah to make a jewelry box for Raven, and when he unwrapped it on Christmas morning, the young man was both surprised and touched by her thoughtfulness. Made of highly polished mahogany, the elegant box was slightly more than a foot square. When unlocked with a brass key, the two panels at the front folded back to reveal four drawers, each divided into velvet-lined compartments. Perfect in every detail, it was as splendid a piece as any Raven had ever seen.

"I don't think I've ever received anything made especially for me," Raven explained with obvious pleasure as he ran his hand over the reddish brown wood. "That you had Azariah make it means it's all the more precious."

"It's difficult to find something you don't already own. I'm glad that you like it." Eden was thrilled she had been able to arrange for a unique and beautifully made gift and responded to Raven with a delighted smile. She had insisted he open his present first, and now began to open hers. When the diamond necklace and earrings spilled out into her lap, she was so stunned it took her a long moment to find her voice to thank him.

"Oh Raven, these must be worth a fortune."

"Every countess ought to have diamonds, and those are rightfully yours. They'll look especially nice with that light blue gown I like so much. I hope you'll wear them when we have our portraits painted."

Christmas had quite naturally brought longings for home and that she had received such expensive jewelry when she doubted her mother and the rest of the residents of the South would be celebrating the holiday filled Eden with a sudden sense of shame. "I'll be happy to wear them for the portrait, and any other time you choose."

His bride looked so far from pleased, however, Raven reached over to lift her chin. "Would you rather have emeralds, or rubies? I can get whatever you want."

Eden had never seen any jewels more beautiful than the ones she now held in a reverent clasp. The round, marquee and emerald cut stones were set in graceful golden swirls to create a design resembling entwined flowers and ribbons. The matching earrings duplicated the same exquisite pattern.

"These are far too lovely to exchange, Raven. I was just thinking about my mother and what a miserable Christmas she must be having. No one in the South has enough to eat, and with me and my father gone, she'll be all alone."

Raven reached out to give Eden's hand a loving squeeze. "There's nothing I can do today, but we'll make it up to her next year, or whenever we can. Now there's another present for you. It's from your parents."

"But how could they have sent me something?"

"You'll see. If you'll excuse me, I'll go and get it." Raven left her for a few minutes, then returned with a cumbersome object wrapped in a sheet and tied with a lopsided bow. He set it on the floor beside her, then leaned down to give her a kiss. "Azariah must have really been busy. Your father asked him to make this for you when he was here. I think you'll like it."

Eden had been on the verge of tears, but she was so excited by the surprise gift she began to laugh as she untied the bow and pulled the sheet out of the way. "Oh Raven, this is the prettiest cradle I've ever seen!"

"I didn't know about it until Azariah brought it to the house yesterday or I would have had some little sheets and quilts made for you. Babies need lots of those, don't they?"

Perfectly proportioned and balanced, Eden found the finely crafted mahogany cradle rocked easily with just a slight push. "They must. I'm sure Azariah will be busy with his own family today, but I want to thank him for this tomorrow. My mother still has my cradle. Where's yours—is it at Briarcliff?"

That question caught Raven completely off guard. He sat down beside his wife, picked up the diamond necklace, draped it around her neck, and secured the clasp while he tried to come up with an answer. "No, Alex was born there but I wasn't. There's all kinds of old furniture stored in the attic. We'll have to look next summer. Maybe we can find his cradle."

Eden put on the sparkling earrings, then turned to show off their beauty. "It would be nice to know where it is, but I'm sure I'll still like this one best."

Raven took Eden's hands and drew her to her feet. He slipped his arm around her waist and led her over to the mirror so she could appreciate the magnificence of the diamonds too. He was delighted when she smiled at him, and extraordinarily relieved that she had not asked him where he had been born since he had absolutely no idea.

As Eden studied her reflection, she could not help but notice Raven was watching her rather than looking into the mirror too. She thought it only natural that anyone standing in front of a mirror would glance at his own image, but unless Raven was shaving, she had never seen him give a mirror a second look. For so handsome a man he was not in the least bit vain. Another of his many admirable qualities, she thought with a knowing smile. The baby gave a sudden kick then, and laughing she took Raven's hand and pressed it to her abdomen.

"The babe seems equally impressed with your gift," she teased.

It was impossible to tell through the folds of her gown if that had been a tiny foot, elbow, or knee, but Raven was thrilled all the same. Often when Eden lay sleeping in his arms he would feel the baby move and it never failed to fill him with awe. Surely such a lively child had to be a healthy one. He knew there was no point in praying the child favor Eden's side of the family, as Julian had once suggested, for surely the infant's fate was already decided. But every time to he looked at Eden, he said a silent prayer to beseech God to give her a healthy child.

Drawing his lovely bride into his arms, he again wished her a Merry Christmas with affection as well as words.

After the holidays, Raven astonished Eden by announcing the first ship he wished to build when he went into partnership with her father was one of his own design.

398

"Do you actually have the plans drawn?" the startled blonde replied, not nearly as certain her father would welcome him as a partner as he seemed to be.

"No, but I will by the time we're ready to go into business together," Raven assured her confidently. "I want to build a fleet of merchant ships. I think the days of combining steam and sail will soon be over and that we ought to concentrate our energies on building steam-powered vessels that will be so fast and reliable no one will ever miss the sails."

Eden arched her brows slightly. "I doubt you'll ever convince my father of that. I'm sure the only ship he thinks can do without sails is a canoe."

"A canoe is a boat, not a ship."

"You know what I mean, Raven."

"It's been a long while since we had an argument, hasn't it?"

Eden did not have to reflect for more than a few seconds to realize their life had been remarkably placid of late. She then responded to Raven's rakish grin with an equally warm smile. "Yes, it certainly has, and I don't think we ought to be arguing about the merits of sail versus steam either."

"Just wait until I draw up the plans, and then you'll agree with me."

Amused by that boast, Eden shook her head, "We'll have to wait and see." She knew her husband was bright, and supposed if he wished to design a steamship he could certainly do so, but she had been unprepared for the enthusiasm he displayed for the project. He did not turn out the rough sketches she had expected, but meticulously detailed drawings that took him days to produce. None seemed to satisfy him, but rather than grow discouraged, he would simply begin another to incorporate the refinements that continued to occur to him almost daily.

When February arrived, Eden entered her seventh month of pregnancy and found it increasingly difficult to be as active as she had once been. She spent most of her time reading or sewing tiny garments and was grateful Raven had found something to occupy his days. He rode about the plantation every morning, and for the first time knew as much as Azariah did about the status of the crops, but he spent each afternoon working on his designs as that was where his real interest lay. Yet even with their separate activities, each would have said they spent all their time together.

During the last week of the month, Raven and Eden had just sat down to dinner when they were interrupted by a fierce pounding at the front door. "I think I better see who that is myself, but I want you to stay here," Raven ordered firmly.

Eden did not argue as Raven left the table, but she had no intention of waiting meekly in the dining room until he returned to explain who their heavy-fisted caller had been. While she moved far more slowly than he, she left the table too, and crossed to the door where she could overhear what was transpiring in the entryway. When she recognized Michael Devane's voice, she joined the two men as quickly as her condition allowed.

While Raven was annoyed his wife had not obeyed him, he did not scold her in front of her old friend. "The *Southern Knight* has just tied up at our docks."

While her husband's words had been spoken calmly, Michael looked so distraught Eden knew she had every right to be alarmed. "Why didn't my father come with you? Is something wrong?"

The lieutenant was exhausted, and while he thought she had a right to know, he could barely provide a coherent response. He gestured toward the leather satchel he had set down beside the door. "We've little time so he sent me to deliver Raven's gold for the arms and to ask if we might leave our more severely wounded men here. The Union has so many ships out looking for us we don't dare risk staying past dawn and leading them here."

"You said we'd take the wounded, didn't you, Raven?"

The uncertainty in Eden's voice broke Raven's heart, for he could not even imagine how she could think he would refuse. "Of course, but I'll not ask you to carry a stretcher. I think it would be best if you waited here while Michael and I go back to the ship and work everything out."

"No, I want to go with you and talk to my father. If he'll be here only a few hours, there's no time to waste."

Eden started for the door, but Raven reached out to catch her elbow. "Wait a minute. I'll go and tell Azariah to hitch a team to the wagon and we'll ride with him. Go on back to your ship, Lieutenant, and tell Dr. Endecott we'll take as many wounded as he wants to give us. Let him know we'll bring the wagon."

"We didn't know where else to turn," Michael mumbled as he started out the door.

"You needn't beg, Lieutenant. I've already said we'll care for your wounded and I would have done it even if you hadn't brought the gold."

Seeing that he had unintentionally angered Raven, Michael nodded and hurried away.

"I don't understand why my father didn't come to see us himself. He can't possibly have planned to drop off the gold and his wounded without at least saying hello."

"You must remember a captain's first responsibility is to his crew. It's not surprising he hasn't the time to pay social calls."

Not understanding that her question about accepting the wounded had brought the caustic edge to Raven's voice, Eden regarded him with an angry glare as he left the house to summon the wagon. If the crew of the *Southern Knight* had suffered so many casualties they could not be tended on board, she feared they must have come up against another warship. At least they had gotten away without being taken prisoner, but the mere thought of how narrow their escape must have been left her badly shaken. Fortunately, she did not have long to fret over that possibility before Raven and Azariah returned with the wagon.

Raven helped Eden down from the wagon as soon as they reached the docks, but when she did not see her father among the men standing on the deck of the *Southern Knight,* she continued to cling to his arms. "Just exactly what did Michael tell you?"

"Nothing you don't know." But Raven also thought it odd that Nathan was not there to meet them.

Instead, it was the ship's surgeon, Clifton Endecott, who came down the gangplank to greet them. He was in his shirtsleeves and looked every bit as distressed as Michael Devane had. "I can't tell you how grateful we are for your help, Lord Clairbourne. I've listed the men's names, and the treatment they've received so far in this letter. Will you please give it to Dr. Ryan?"

Raven recalled the lengthy conversation between Julian and the Confederate physician when they had dined in his home and hoped Clifton's assumption that Julian would care for the *Southern Knight*'s wounded was correct. "I'll see that he gets it. How many men do you need to leave with us?" he asked as he slipped the letter into his pocket.

Clifton massaged his forehead as though the number had slipped his mind. "Did Michael tell you what happened?" When Eden and Raven shook their heads, the doctor did his best to relate the news. "We docked in Havana earlier this week to take on coal. Before it could be loaded, we were attacked by a Union ship."

"In a neutral harbor?" Raven asked incredulously.

"Yes. They didn't even make a pretense of allowing us to leave first. It was clear they wanted to take the ship undamaged because they did no more than rake the deck with rifle fire in an attempt to kill the crew."

Raven was stunned by Clifton's tale. Wars were fought with rules to which all civilized countries agreed. Both Union and Confederate ships purchased supplies in neutral ports, where they were supposed to be equally safe from attack. That the Union had violated so basic a rule disgusted Raven as thoroughly as it did his wife.

"Now do you see what unprincipled bullies the Yankees are?" Eden questioned harshly. "They will go to any lengths to beat us into submission. Can you understand why we're fighting them now?"

Raven had no interest in reopening that debate and merely nodded. "How did you manage to get away?"

Clifton shrugged. "The Union captain made the mistake of thinking we'd surrender without firing a shot. Our cannon were not only loaded but fired before the fool realized his mistake and at that range we couldn't miss. Then there was such confusion we were able to steam out of the port before they could respond. We took a great many casualties, though."

"I don't care how many there are. We'll find a way to care for them," Eden promised.

Clifton's lips trembled slightly as he tried to smile. "We all hate to impose on your kindness. I'll not leave any of the men who can walk, but there are seven whose injuries are too severe for me to tend them properly. If you could just take them for a few weeks, I'm sure they will all be more than willing to work to pay for their keep just as soon as they are able."

"I've never asked a guest in my home to earn his keep, Dr. Endecott, and I'll not begin now," Raven assured him.

"I didn't mean to insult you, my lord, but you are a

British citizen, and as such are under no obligation to assist us."

"Rendering medical attention to wounded will not violate Great Britain's neutrality, nor will supplying coal. If you were unable to load any in Havana, I think I have all you'll need."

Michael Devane had joined them in time to hear the offer of coal, and certain he could not have understood, he asked Raven to repeat it. When he did, the lieutenant was still amazed. "It did not occur to any of us that you would have coal here."

"I've become interested in steamships of late," Raven informed him, rather than admit he had stocked the fuel anticipating just such an emergency. "There are one hundred barrels of coal in the first storehouse. Tell your men to load all they need. Of course, I'll require Captain Sinclair's written promise of payment, but I'm sure that will be no problem."

The anxious glance that passed between Michael and Dr. Endecott alarmed Eden so badly she reached out to touch the lieutenant's arm. "Was my father one of those injured? Is that why we haven't seen him yet?"

Unable to allay Eden's fears, Michael found it easier to direct his reply to Raven than her. "Dr. Endecott has advised Captain Sinclair to leave the ship here with the others, but he won't even consider it. Perhaps if the two of you would speak with him, you could convince him to stay."

Raven felt Eden sway slightly, and quickly slid his arm around her waist to make certain she did not fall. He was furious with Michael Devane for so thoughtlessly subjecting her to such needless worry and angrily lashed out at him. "I wish you had had the presence of mind to tell me about this when we spoke earlier, Lieutenant. Just how badly was Nathan hurt?"

Aghast they had again provoked Raven, Clifton Endecott hurriedly explained, "He was shot in the thigh, but fortunately the bullet passed through his leg without hitting either the bone or an artery. His prospects for recovery would be excellent if he would stay in his bunk but he refuses to do so. Every time he gets up he reopens the wound and a man can stand to lose only so much blood. There's also the danger of infection. I've told him he could lose the leg if he doesn't rest, but he won't heed my advice."

Raven pursed his lips thoughtfully as he wondered just how far the doctor and Michael had gone in their efforts to convince Nathan to recuperate on Jamaica. "Other than serving in the Confederate navy, I've no idea how much experience either of you has at sea, but you must realize that forcing a captain to leave his ship against his will is an act of mutiny."

Michael's eyes widened and he had to swallow hard before he could reply but clearly he spoke with conviction. "When the choice appears to be forcing him off today, or burying him at sea next week, isn't demanding he leave the better alternative?"

Eden was leaning against Raven now, but her weight was a slight burden. He knew without asking what her choice would be. "What do you have here, two dozen officers and about a hundred in the crew?"

"Minus those that will be left here, we'll have twenty officers, and ninety-one in the crew."

"How many of those men are willing to leave Nathan here?" Raven asked bluntly.

Michael glanced away for a moment, then again summoned his courage to respond. "All would vote to leave the captain here if you will agree to take his place."

That remark was greeted by a stunned silence.

"You can not possibly be serious," Eden gasped when

405

she finally realized what Michael had said, but seeing by the solemnity of his expression that he most certainly was, she insisted he consider the obvious. "My husband is a British citizen. How can you possibly ask him to fight in a War that does not concern him?"

While Raven was as startled as Eden by the absurdity of Michael's request, he found it strangely exhilarating. "If you don't mind, I'd like to ask the questions," he whispered as he gave her a loving hug. "What's the real reason you came here tonight, Lieutenant, to request aid for your wounded, or to involve me in the most bizarre proposal of mutiny I've ever heard?"

Michael could not back down now and straightened his shoulders proudly. "The *Southern Knight* has the finest crew afloat, but without Captain Sinclair, well, I think we would have been better off to surrender in Havana than try to continue our mission. At least there none of the men were in danger of drowning as they would be if we're attacked at sea."

Raven started to laugh. "If you're trying to make me feel responsible for the lives of the men on board the *Southern Knight,* it won't work. My father-in-law is the only one who concerns me. Now is he up to seeing us?"

Dr. Endecott gestured toward the captain's quarters. "I'll take you to his cabin. Talk with him, and then give us your decision."

Eden looked up at her husband. He did not seem particularly concerned, but she was certain his decision was already made. He was opposed to the War. How could he take her father's place and fight in it? She had felt sick to her stomach ever since she had learned of her father's injury, and she hoped she would not become ill in front of him. When they reached his cabin, he was stretched out on his bunk, but there were navigational charts lying on the table and she wondered if he hadn't lain down at the precise instant they had knocked on his door.

Nathan not only felt weak, but was also badly embarrassed to have his daughter and her husband see him in such a pitiful state. He tried to smile, but failed. "Michael told me you're taking the wounded. I'll find a way to repay you for their care."

Eden would have liked to sit down by his side, but fearing she would cause him pain, she leaned down to kiss his cheek, and then remained standing. "We don't expect to be paid," she assured him, but not before sending a questioning glance Raven's way.

Raven, however, had more important things to discuss. "For a Union ship to attack you in Havana's harbor is deplorable. For you to disregard your surgeon's advice and not take care of yourself is even worse. Are none of your lieutenants capable of performing your duties until you're well enough to resume command?"

"I've not relinquished my command," Nathan insisted stubbornly.

"A minor point. Just answer my question."

"Well, my lord, Lieutenant Devane is the executive officer and I fear he would have difficulty commanding a rowboat, let alone the *Southern Knight*. She'd be sunk or on display in Boston Harbor in less than a week if he attempted to take my place. I'll not do that to my men. Don't get me wrong, Devane is sincere and hardworking, but like the rest of my officers, he just doesn't have the experience to command."

"Would you be willing to recuperate at my home if someone could be found who did?"

Nathan was baffled by that question. "I've already told you, we don't have such a man on board."

Nathan's face was pinched and drawn. His golden eyes had a feverish sheen, and when Raven leaned down to touch his hand, his skin felt much too warm. Clearly he was already more seriously ill than Dr. Endecott realized. "I'd hate to see you lose your leg, or worse, your life. I don't believe in your cause, but I'm willing to sail the *Southern Knight* up and down the coast often enough to discourage shipping. Apparently your crew was so impressed with the way I sail they're willing to trust me. Are you?"

That was the last offer Eden had ever expected Raven to make, and she was now shaking so badly she had to sit down at the table. "Could we talk about this?" she asked weakly. "After all you have said about the absurdity of the War, I can't believe you want to enlist in our navy."

Ignoring Nathan momentarily, Raven sat down beside his bride and took her hands in his. He had wanted only to save her father's life, but he knew the first time he had made that offer he had coupled it with a demand that she remain married to him, and also keep her marriage to Alex a secret as well. Perhaps it was no wonder that she would question his motives now, but it hurt him all the same. Despite the rapport they had enjoyed since coming to the plantation, he knew neither of them trusted the other as completely as a husband and wife should. This was certainly no time to discuss the causes of their doubts, however.

"I'm not going to join the Confederate navy, Eden, I'm just offering to take your father's place until he's well."

"I can't believe you would even consider such a mad scheme, let alone agree to it." Eden's gaze swept his face, searching for a clue that would reveal his reason.

Raven had expected Nathan to object, and strenuously, but not Eden. "What is it you really want to know—what I expect in return?"

Eden tried to withdraw her hands from his, but he increased the pressure of his grasp to prevent her escape and she ceased to struggle. "You'll have to admit it isn't like you to do anything unless you'll receive some type of gain."

Raven glanced toward Nathan, who now appeared several shades paler than when they had entered his cabin. Eden was all the family Raven had, but he understood why she would question his efforts to save her father's life and thought he probably deserved it. If his character actually had a noble side, he knew she had seen damn little of it. Seeking to give her a reason he knew she would readily understand, he released her hands and rose to his feet.

"You're right. I do have an ulterior motive. For once I'd like to do something for you that Alex hasn't done first. Let me know what you decide."

Stung by the bitterness of that retort, Eden made no attempt to prevent Raven from leaving the cabin. As tears started to pour down her cheeks, she turned toward her father. "I'm sorry, Daddy, but what Raven really wants is to be a partner in the shipyard. I'm sure that's why he's willing to take your place."

Nathan's whole body ached, while his right leg burned with an agonizing pain that never let up. As he saw it, the only choice he had was whether he would be buried on Jamaica, or at sea. The least he could do was give his men a fighting chance to survive, and with Raven Blade, they would certainly have it.

"Ask him to come back, sweetheart. I don't care what the bastard wants. The *Southern Knight* is his."

Twenty-four

March 1864

Julian Ryan hurriedly read the instructions Clifton Endecott had left for him and then waved the neatly penned pages for emphasis. "I thought Raven had taken leave of his senses when he allowed your father's ship to use his docks for repairs. Now you tell me he's the acting captain of the *Southern Knight* and that I'm expected to run a Confederate hospital?"

As this was one of the few times he had paid a call at the Clairbourne plantation in the morning, Rebecca Yardley had accompanied her brother hoping for a chance to visit with Eden. While she thought Julian was being very rude, she was as astonished as he by the reason he had been summoned to the house. She had always admired Raven Blade's dashing good looks, but going off to fight in America's Civil War struck her as being reckless in the extreme. She stood at Julian's side, her eyes wide as she tried to think of some way to help him control his temper when she was every bit as dismayed as he.

Eden had been up all night and was in no mood to coddle Julian's outraged sense of propriety. "If your principles will not allow you to attend my father and his men, then there's no point in prolonging this discussion. Yadira is talented in the preparation of medicines and we'll simply rely on her until another physician can be found."

"You can't treat gunshot wounds with folk remedies!" Julian contradicted belligerently.

"It appears we have no choice," Eden responded coolly.

Julian glanced down at his sister's anguished expression. Clearly she was siding with Eden and thought he should treat the injured without regard to their nationality, but he was loath to agree. The deciding factor was not one of principle, however, but one based purely on self-interest. The care of seven severely injured men would require him to make more frequent visits to the plantation and the prospect of Yadira making every one memorable was irresistible.

He drew in a deep breath and exhaled slowly as though his decision had been a difficult one to reach. "I don't approve of Raven's involvement in the War, but as a responsible physician I can't in good conscience refuse to treat wounded men regardless of who they are or how they received their injuries. Where have your father and his men been quartered?"

While Eden thought Julian a pompous ass, she was relieved she would not have to send to Montego Bay or Kingston for another doctor. "My father is in Alex's room. We put cots in the room next door for the others."

"Eleanora's room?" Julian asked in surprise.

"I saw no reason to scatter them among the guest bedrooms. It will be far easier for us to care for them if we don't have to constantly traipse up and down the hall to do it."

"I'll not argue with that, my lady. I was merely surprised at your choice of room."

"From what I've heard, Eleanora was too sweet a woman to object to her room being used temporarily as a hospital ward. I'd like for you to see the men now, so if you have any suggestions for their care, we can implement them immediately."

Julian picked up his bag. "Of course, but I think I should give whatever directions I have to Yadira. It wouldn't be wise for you to tend the men yourself, my lady. There's too great a risk you'll become overtired and that could easily bring on premature labor. You mustn't take that risk."

Eden had been far too worried about her father and his men to consider her own well-being and refused to do so now. "You know our servants are either former slaves, or their descendants. I can scarcely ask them to tend Confederate soldiers. I worked in a hospital in Richmond before going to England, so I'm experienced in caring for wounded and I can do it again. I'll rest whenever I'm tired."

"I could stay and help," Rebecca volunteered, and when her brother started to object, she interrupted him. "I really want to do this. You've trained me as your nurse and we can't expect Lady Clairbourne and her housekeeper to care for seven men on their own."

Grateful for Rebecca's offer, Eden accepted before Julian had time to forbid it. "Thank you, but I must insist both of you call me Eden rather than Lady Clairbourne."

"If you wish," Rebecca responded shyly while Julian merely frowned at the young woman's disregard for tradition.

Nathan had been asleep, but awakened long enough to tell Julian he would appreciate being left alone. "Daddy, please," Eden scolded gently. "Dr. Ryan only wants to help you get well."

Unable to believe that was even a possibility, Nathan had to force himself to lie still as Julian examined his leg. Unlike most of the other wounded, he had been spared the

412

agony of having a bullet dug out of his flesh, but he was certain that was the only misery he had escaped. Noting Julian's sullen frown, he issued a stern warning.

"Don't even consider taking a saw to my leg or I'll take one first to your neck!"

Insulted, Julian fixed Nathan with a hostile stare. "If you follow the instructions here that you disregarded on board your ship and remain in bed, there will be no need for anyone to use a saw. You're just not drinking enough fluids, that's why you're feverish." He turned to his sister then. "Pour all the tea you can into him, and tie him to the bed to keep him in it if you must. Now let's look at the others."

Eden took her father's hand and squeezed it gently as Julian and Rebecca crossed to the door that led to the adjoining room. "I wish Mother were here, but since she isn't, will you at least try to treat us as kindly as you would her?"

The mention of his wife made Nathan feel thoroughly ashamed but he could make no promises. "If I live through this—"

"What do you mean 'if'? You know Mother could not bear to live without you and I do so want you to be able to see your first grandchild." Eden spoke in a light teasing tone, but she was badly frightened all the same. "I'll bring you some herb tea with plenty of lemon and you're going to drink the whole pot before you go back to sleep."

"You shouldn't be waiting on me, sweetheart."

"Nonsense. Fetching a pot of tea won't hurt me." And yet by the end of the morning, Eden had lost count of how many times she had traversed the stairs. Arabella and Yadira had gotten into a lengthy debate on which herbs made the best tea to quell a fever and had never run out of advice on how it was to be dispensed, but there always seemed to be something she had forgotten downstairs that

413

she had to search for herself. When she could no longer stay awake, she told Rebecca to call her should any man's condition worsen and went to her room for a well-deserved rest.

While she had managed to put on a brave front for the others, once alone, Eden was overwhelmed by the enormity of the task she had undertaken. She had wanted to care for her father and his men, truly she had, but the responsibility was proving to be a far greater strain than she had ever imagined. She had planned to rely on her experience in tending wounded, but she had not once stopped to consider she had not been seven months pregnant when she had last done it.

Adding to her worries about her ability to provide adequate care was her disappointment over the brief kiss with which she and Raven had parted. He had been the one to supervise the transfer of the wounded to the house and he had also taken it upon himself to make certain the *Southern Knight* had plenty of provisions as well as coal. While he had not seemed to be deliberately avoiding her during the night, it certainly seemed that way now.

In the last few months she had thought they were getting along well, but in retrospect perhaps their accord had been an illusion they had created by studiously avoiding conflict. While she feared the obvious state of her pregnancy made her far from desirable, Raven had been no less affectionate, but he had yet to put his feelings into words. Not even the danger involved in the voyage he was about to undertake had prompted him to reveal the depth of his emotions before he had bid her a hurried farewell.

Then again, Eden agonized, perhaps Raven didn't love her at all. Maybe it was vanity that made her see love in his glance when it might have been no more than desire, or need. He had certainly leapt at the chance to leave her and she knew Raven was not an impulsive man, but a coldly calculating one. She had had no opportunity to thank him for taking her father's place, regardless of his motive, and that bothered her too for she did not want him to think her ungrateful. That he would be gone for a month at least, perhaps even longer, left her with a curious sense of emptiness she had not expected and feared would linger indefinitely.

"There was so much I should have told him," she whispered as she wiped away a tear. Although Alex had died suddenly, there had been nothing left unsaid between them. She had buried him with a deep sense of loss, but she had not been burdened with the regret she now felt over the way she and Raven had parted. When he returned home, she was going to do a much better job of letting him know how much she appreciated all he had done for her. All she could do now, unfortunately, was pray that he returned safely so that she would have that opportunity.

Too weary to dwell on their problems any longer, Eden fell into a troubled sleep, in which she dreamed Raven felt as lost and confused as she did.

During the first week Julian treated the injured Southerners, he cautioned Eden repeatedly about becoming overtired, but as the men slowly began to improve, she grew increasing pale and drawn. Finally he took her by the arm and escorted her to her room.

"I can't allow you to endanger your health another minute, my lady. You are to get into your bed and stay there until I say you can get up."

"But there's too much to do," Eden protested unconvincingly.

"Do you remember the night we met? I'll never forget how desperate Raven looked when he came rushing into my room to ask me to do something to bring you out of hysterics. Perhaps the threat of giving birth prematurely doesn't scare you as greatly as it does me, but I don't want to have to face Raven with the news Alex's child was born early and didn't live.

"That there is a very good possibility that you're already too weak to survive the ordeal of childbirth terrifies me even more. I think Raven would probably kill me if I lost the both of you. So, my lady, if you've no concern for yourself, the very least you can do is spare me and your precious infant early deaths."

Considering Julian's melodramatic appeal absurd, Eden nevertheless chose to humor the man and obediently climbed up on her bed. She placed a pillow at her back, and crossed her ankles to get comfortable. "There, I'm in bed."

Julian read the defiant gleam in her golden eyes correctly. "You'll not get up when I leave either because I'm going to tell your father, as well as Yadira and Rebecca, that you're not to tend the men. Providing their care is simply too strenuous and you're not to do so much as read to them let alone change bandages or lift them to help them eat and drink. Is that understood?"

Eden continued to regard the surly physician with a level stare. "I'll not be treated as though I'm an invalid too."

"Has your back been bothering you?"

Eden shrugged. "Isn't that to be expected?"

"No it isn't. If the ache becomes a steady throb, and then cramplike pains, it means you're in labor. I should probably leave some chloroform here for you now just in case you deliver the child while I'm away. Yadira tells me she's served as a midwife, and Rebecca has assisted me."

Without realizing it, Julian had finally frightened Eden sufficiently to cause her to remain in bed because the prospect of having Yadira deliver her child was an extremely repugnant one. "I'm sure there will be time to call you."

"And if I'm away on an emergency? No, it's not too soon to begin preparing for the birth. I hope to be here, but if I'm not, Yadira and my sister will take good care of you."

"Maybe Raven will be back by then," Eden mused aloud.

"He expects the babe to be born around the first of May, not this week."

"It won't be born this week," Eden insisted stubbornly, but she had known before Julian began to scold her that she had not been getting nearly enough rest. And her back did ache, almost constantly, but she had thought that was because she had been doing too much, not because the baby was in danger of being born early.

Julian considered Eden's preoccupied frown a positive sign she had finally taken his warning seriously and reached out to pat her hand. "Amy and the other maids can take turns caring for the men. They were born free, and I'm certain none is worried they'll end up slaves by caring for Confederate wounded when, by all reports, your side is losing the War."

"You certainly have a way with words, Dr. Ryan."

Not understanding the subtlety of her sarcasm, Julian blushed slightly as though that had been a compliment and left her room to finish seeing his other patients.

A man of his word, before Julian left the house the next morning he gave Yadira a bottle of chloroform. "I fully expect to be the one to deliver Eden's babe, but as a precaution, I want you to have the means to ease her pain should that not be the case. You need give her only a few whiffs in the beginning. You don't want to render her unconscious until the birth is imminent."

"I understand." Her interest in Eden's comfort minimal, Yadira set the bottle aside. "She appears rather fragile. It is probably a good thing you put her to bed."

"Oh yes, it certainly is. I would hate for Alex's child to be lost."

"Alex's child?"

Julian realized his mistake instantly, but saw no harm in revealing the truth to Yadira. "Yes. Raven wants it kept a secret, but Alex was Eden's first husband, and the babe is Alex's, not Raven's."

The housekeeper accepted that chilling news with outward composure, but inwardly she felt as though her heart had just been ripped to jagged bits. "I had no idea," she said calmly. "Eden always seemed so devoted to Raven."

Julian regarded the dark-eyed beauty with a sly smile. "Well, I'm sure she is, but as you well know, things are not always what they seem."

Yadira's placid expression remained unchanged until Julian had departed, then she went to her room and gave vent to the furious rage his confidence had inspired. "The slut!" she snarled as she twisted her pillow until the fabric ripped and a flurry of goose down billowed around her. That in one summer Eden had gone from being Alex's wife to Raven's, apparently without a moment's pause to mourn her first husband's passing, was the most hideous crime she could imagine. Obviously the girl had married Alex for his money, undoubtedly hastened his death with her ardor, and then wed his heir to secure her position as Lady Clairbourne.

"The bitch should have been buried with Alex!" She remembered the chloroform then, and hurriedly went to fetch it. Julian feared a premature birth, and Yadira was certain if that occurred, and Eden failed to survive, no one would suspect her of murder. She began to scheme with a triumphant smile, thinking it could all be arranged so easily. On Julian's next visit, she would ask him for pow-

418

ders to help her rest, and she was certain he would give her enough to put his mousey sister and the ailing men to sleep.

There were several possibilities then, but wanting the joy of raising Alex's babe herself, she decided upon the one that would ensure the dear child's safety while at the same time allowing her to put a quick end to his mother. It was too risky a plan to implement as yet, however. The baby would be stronger at eight months than seven and she was doing this for him.

A wicked smile graced her lips as she climbed the back stairs and walked toward Eden's room. She had been too stunned by Alex's death to welcome the girl to his home properly, but now, she was determined they would become the best of friends. Yes, Eden was going to trust her with her life, and that would be the frail blonde's last mistake.

In his first days at sea, Raven poured all of his energy into familiarizing himself with the *Southern Knight* so he could command her with the same confidence he had shown on board the *Jamaican Wind*. He found that chief engineer Douglas Owen, a man in his late thirties, knew how to coax the maximum performance from the ship's two engines. Confident they had the speed to outrun the larger, heavier Union warships, and keeping out of the range of the swifter blockaders, Raven set a course for the east coast of America, where their presence would be most likely to discourage whatever shipping continued under the United States' flag. Nathan had told him that at the end of the month they were to rendezvous with another Confederate ship off the coast of Norfolk to receive new orders, and he wanted to make certain they had accomplished all they could by then.

Despite his preoccupation with his task, Raven never once forgot the forlorn expression Eden had worn when he had kissed her goodbye. While he had not walked out on her in the midst of a fight as he had so often in the past, he could not shake the uncomfortable sensation that somehow he was guilty of deserting her. He could not have refused to take her father's place and kept her respect, and indeed, he had not even considered that option when he had learned how serious Nathan's injury was. He had wanted to help, and he knew Eden must have wanted him to make exactly the choice he had, but he could not believe how stupid he had been to have mentioned Alex as the reason why. He had let his jealousy over the love he knew Eden still felt for her first husband erupt into a spiteful comment that had hurt her. That he had left without apologizing for his thoughtlessness had only compounded the error.

As Raven lay in his bunk each night, missing Eden terribly, he reminisced about each minute they had spent together. Gradually he began to understand how complex their problems truly were. Eden's devotion to Alex was only one aspect of them. There was also the sorry fact that he had never revealed the truth about himself. He had made the mistake of waiting, and not at all patiently, for Eden to fall in love with him, when everything she believed about his background was a lie.

He knew then that he could no longer wait indefinitely for her to fall in love with him and then confess the truth. She would only feel betrayed then. No, he would have to tell her the truth as soon as he returned home. All he could do was hope that someday she could love him in spite of the fact that he and Alex had not really been kin, rather than despise him for keeping that secret so long.

Michael Devane had had to swallow most of his pride to ask Raven to command the *Southern Knight,* but when he saw how hard the young earl worked at being the ship's captain, his resentment gradually became grudging respect. Within a week Raven could not only call each member of the crew by name, but knew which were the most dependable, and which the slackers, and he tempered his comments accordingly.

When Raven had come on board, the crew had been discouraged not only by their close call in Havana, but also by the relentlessly depressing news they had received of the South's losses. Raven made no reference to the conflict between the North and South, however. He stressed only the professionalism he expected his crew to display, and following his example, they all began to regain their badly damaged pride.

By late March of 1864, the morale of the crew of the *Southern Knight* was at an all-time high, and Raven was as eager as the rest of them to continue their destruction of United States shipping. President Lincoln had promoted Ulysses S. Grant to the rank of lieutenant general and given him command of all the Union armies, but the men on board the *Southern Knight* neither knew, nor cared.

When they sighted a schooner flying the Stars and Stripes off the New Jersey coast, Raven announced that he intended to be among the boarding party. "But how can you?" Michael argued. "Captain Sinclair's uniforms fit you well enough, but as soon as you open your mouth, they'll know you're British."

Raven regarded his executive officer with a slow smile. "On the contrary, they will believe me to be Captain Nathan Sinclair," he responded in a perfect imitation of the Virginian's gentlemanly drawl. "I meant what I said my first day as captain of the *Southern Knight*. I'm taking

Nathan's place, and even in the unlikely event that we're all taken prisoner, no one will ever learn I'm not he."

Michael shrugged helplessly. "You sound just like him."

Not needing the lieutenant's approval, Raven turned back to observe the schooner. He had announced to the crew that he would not sink any ships nor take prisoners, but that he had come up with an idea he thought would be equally effective in discouraging the merchant trade. Predictably, the schooner surrendered without putting up any resistance and Raven went on board as planned.

"This is a fine ship," he complimented the captain in the dulcet tones of a Southerner. "I'm going to give you a choice. We'll take you and your crew prisoner and scuttle her, or if you give me your solemn promise you'll not sail her again until the War's end, you may dump your cargo overboard and return to port."

Astonished the captain of a Confederate raider had offered him a way to save his ship, the captain of the schooner had the hold emptied within an hour. Raven stepped close and lowered his voice to a threatening whisper before bidding the grateful man farewell. "This is a favor I'll not repeat," he warned. "You understand that, don't you?"

"Yes, sir, that I do."

Raven stared at the now quivering man, certain his imagination was providing far worse punishments than he would ever inflict. He was confident that the fact the ship had lost what was undoubtedly a valuable cargo would be enough to discourage the owners from attempting another voyage to Europe anytime soon. With one last evil grin, he and his boarding party returned to the *Southern Knight*, where they were heartily cheered.

The next day they repeated their success by capturing a bark in the morning and a brig in the afternoon. By the time a dozen ships had been forced to dispose of their cargoes and return to port, Raven decided they had pushed their luck far enough. Certain the Union must already have warships out searching for them, he had no intention of allowing the *Southern Knight* to be found, and he set a course toward Virginia, where they were to receive their new orders.

Shortly before dawn on the appointed day, a sloop appeared out of the mist and Raven waited at the rail as a messenger came aboard the *Southern Knight*. He did not like bringing the ship so close to shore and had no intention of extending their stay beyond the few minutes it would require to read and acknowledge the receipt of whatever the new mission might be. When the cloaked messenger came toward him, then drew back, he greeted him impatiently.

"I'm Captain Sinclair. If you have papers to give me, then hurry up about it."

While Sarah could make out the silhouette of a man of Nathan's height, the timber of his voice wasn't right and she wasn't fooled. "You are most certainly not my husband, and I'll speak with no one else."

Raven stepped forward then, and dropped the Southern accent. "Sarah? Is that you?"

Sarah could see him clearly then, but that a total stranger knew her name frightened her, and thinking she had stumbled into a trap of some kind, she turned to flee. When she slammed into Michael Devane, who had stepped up behind her, she cried out and then, recognizing him, demanded an explanation.

Michael looked to Raven. "I didn't know it would be her. I swear I didn't."

"What's going on?" Sarah asked again. "Where's my husband?"

Raven took the precaution of searching the mists for signs of another ship and, seeing none, gave Michael a terse order. "I'll need no more than five minutes with Mrs. Sinclair. Tell Mr. Owen to be ready to give us all the speed he can when I give the order." Raven reached out for Sarah's arm then and hurried her back to his cabin.

Raven scarcely knew where to begin but decided he should attend to business first. "You do have the new orders, don't you? I think I should read them first."

"Well I don't, not until you tell me just who you are and where Nathan is."

Raven inclined his head in a mock bow. Sarah had thrown back the hood of her cloak and he found her resemblance to her daughter striking. Not only were their features nearly identical, but Sarah also had the same honey blond hair. Her eyes were different, though. They were a cool, bright green rather than golden-brown.

"If you insist. I'm Raven Blade, your son-in-law. Your husband is recuperating from an injury he sustained last month. Both he and Eden are at my plantation on Jamaica."

Sickened by that distressing news, Sarah sank into the closest chair. "How badly was he hurt?"

"He should be completely recovered in just a few weeks." Raven could readily understand Sarah's concern for her husband, but that she seemed not to care that he was Eden's husband both confused and hurt him. She was holding a leather pouch, and assuming it contained his orders, he reached for it. "May I?"

"Yes, of course."

Raven found an unmarked envelope inside. He tore it open and scanned the contents. The *Southern Knight* was to proceed at once to California and continue their mission of disrupting shipping on the Pacific Coast. That was most definitely not a voyage he would undertake in Nathan's place and he shoved the brief message in his pocket.

"We've got to be under way before sunrise. Come on. You'll have to leave."

Sarah looked up at the dark-eyed young man. Other than her own dear Nathan, he was easily the handsomest man she had ever met. "You'll be returning to Jamaica soon, won't you? I want to go with you."

Before Raven could reply, Michael came to the door. "There's a ship approaching and I have little hope it's one of ours. You'll have to leave now," he urged Sarah.

"Oh no, I'm going to stay," the determined woman replied.

"That's not a good idea," Raven declared, and again taking his mother-in-law's arm, he escorted her up on deck. The mist now only partially hid their identity. They could make out a steamship approaching and knew they had been seen. Before he could stop her, Sarah waved to the men in the sloop and they pulled away, heading for shore without her.

The steamer hailed them then. "What steamer is that?"

"I want full speed now," Raven ordered, and as Michael conveyed that message to the engineer, he responded to the call to identify the ship himself.

"This is Her Majesty's ship *Princess Royal*. What steamer is that?"

"The *Princess Royal?*" Sarah asked in a hushed whisper.

"A *ruse de guerre*," Raven responded with a sly wink.

"This is the United States steamer . . ." The name was lost when the engines of the *Southern Knight* came to life and the whole ship shuddered as the twin propellers began to turn. Raven then sent men into the rigging to unfurl the sails to give them additional speed. The Union ship overtook them, however, before the *Southern Knight* could gain sufficient speed to draw away.

Raven had been hoping to avoid firing on a Union vessel, but now he had absolutely no choice and they managed to get off the first round of cannon fire. The volley hit the steamer broadside and echoed with a hollow ring that loudly proclaimed the ship was built of iron. He had no time to argue with Sarah as a hail of rifle fire came their way, but she did not need to be told to get below deck and ran back to his cabin of her own accord.

Raven knew none of the crew would accuse him of cowardice for attempting to outrun a heavily armed iron ship rather than coming about to fight. Luck was with them, and as they gathered speed, the mist thickened into a blanket of fog that veiled their retreat. The Union vessel doggedly pursued them but the Confederate raider had been built for speed and the Yankees had no opportunity to use their cannon. With Raven changing their course repeatedly, they soon escaped unscathed into the open sea.

After ascertaining there had been no wounded, Raven congratulated his crew for their fine work. He then wiped his brow on his sleeve and returned to his cabin. As he came through the door, Sarah looked up at him, her glance filled with the curiosity he had expected her to show earlier.

"As I said, I'm Eden's husband and I think it's a good thing we're bound for Jamaica as it may take me until we get there to tell you our story."

Sarah sighed with relief. "I really didn't plan this. I had hoped only to see Nathan for a few minutes. That was all."

Raven nodded, then began to search his mind for a way

to begin. Because he had already decided to tell Eden the truth, he thought for once he ought to use it. After all, he could certainly use the practice.

Twenty-five

April 1864

Rebecca admired Eden greatly and had eagerly accepted her invitation to talk with her each evening before she went to bed. Perched on the edge of the blonde's four-poster, she found it easy to converse about subjects she dared not broach with her brother.

"You and Raven seem to be very happy together," she began shyly.

"We have had our problems, as I'm sure all couples do." Eden had not had such an opportunity in their previous discussions, but seized it now. "Have you ever considered marrying again?"

Rebecca's cheeks filled with a bright blush. "Oh no, one marriage was more than enough for me."

"You weren't happy?"

"Raymond was a wonderful man, but, well, there were certain aspects of marriage to which I just didn't seem suited."

"You didn't enjoy keeping house?" Eden teased.

"No, it wasn't that," Rebecca admitted, but she knew Eden had not been serious. Certain her confidence would be respected, she asked the question that troubled her most. "Raven is such a handsome man, but despite that, don't you find marital relationships rather distasteful?"

Eden did not think she dared admit just how greatly she enjoyed making love. "In what way?" she asked instead.

"Well, I know all men enjoy it, but how can a woman feel anything but humiliated to be used in that way?"

"Raymond did not hold you, kiss you, make you feel as though you were being loved rather than used?"

Rebecca shook her head "I think he sensed I didn't like his attentions, and just got them over with as quickly as possible."

For a moment, Eden considered what that must have been like, then reached out to touch Rebecca's hand with a fond caress. "It's unfortunate that Raymond didn't know how to please you, but I think you ought to give another man the opportunity to try. All of our patients like you. Is there one of them you consider special?"

Rebecca tried to hide her smile, but failed. "They are all sweet boys, but Dr. Endecott is the only man I've met since Raymond's death who, well, who seems to share my interests."

"He's very nice, isn't he?" Eden paused to cover a wide yawn. "I'm sorry. Let's talk about him again tomorrow night, shall we?"

"I didn't mean to tire you." Rebecca rose to her feet, then turned as she heard the door open.

Yadira entered the room carrying a cup of warm milk for Eden. "You know Dr. Ryan wants you to be asleep long before this, my lady."

The housekeeper had been wonderfully considerate of late, but Eden still felt uncomfortable around her. Each night Yadira brought warm milk, and knowing it would be good for the baby, Eden always drank it without argument. "We had just said good night," she explained as she took the cup.

"Good. I left some warm milk in your room too, Mrs. Yardley," Yadira explained as she walked Rebecca to the door. "You'll feel far more rested in the morning if you drink it."

"Why thank you, Yadira. That's very sweet of you."

"It is my pleasure."

Eden bid them good night as they left her room, then began to drink her milk. After several sips, she noticed it had a peculiar taste, but thinking Yadira had added an herb or spice flavoring, she took several more mouthfuls before deciding she did not want any more. She set the half-empty cup aside and settled down among her pillows. It was not all that easy to get comfortable, but curled up on her side, she usually did not have too much difficulty falling asleep. When Yadira came into her room half an hour later, she stirred lazily before opening her eyes.

"You didn't drink all your milk," the housekeeper scolded gently. "You must finish it now."

"No thank you. Did you put something in it tonight? It didn't taste as good as it usually does."

"No one else mentioned it."

"You fix warm milk for everyone? That's really so thoughtful. I didn't realize you did that." Eden yawned sleepily. "I really don't need the milk to get to sleep. Good night."

For the last two weeks, Eden had drunk every last drop of the milk Yadira had brought her and the housekeeper had expected that night to be no exception. The injured men had been trained to expect warm milk too, and with the sleeping powders with which it had been laced that night, none would stir before morning. Rebecca's milk had been drugged as well and she would not awaken either.

After Yadira had taken care to see that she would be the

only one in the house to be awake and alert that night, she would not allow Eden to foil her plans. She had waited as long as she could for the babe's sake, but fearing it might soon choose to be born during the day when Julian was there, she dared delay no longer.

"As you wish," she agreed softly as she stepped away from the bed, but in a few minutes she returned with the bottle of chloroform, and a towel. She had a razor-sharp knife in her apron pocket, but she would not use it until Eden was unconscious. When Eden opened her eyes and regarded her with a sleepy stare, Yadira could not resist taunting her with what was to come.

"I know Alex fathered your babe. He refused to give me a child, but I intend to raise yours."

Frightened by Yadira's malicious tone, Eden tried to sit up but her body was slow to respond. Her limbs felt too weak to support her weight and her mind was not at all clear. "We'll talk about this tomorrow, Yadira. It's too late tonight."

Yadira's laugh was as husky as her speaking voice. "You'll not see tomorrow, but I trust you will die happy knowing that Alex's baby will."

While most of what Yadira said was blurred by the sleeping powder that had sapped Eden's strength, she heard the word *die* distinctly. Yadira had opened the bottle of chloroform, but with a strength born of terror, Eden knocked it out of her hands, spilling it all around them. The sickening scent of the anesthetic filled the room instantly and both Eden and Yadira began to gag.

Eden tried to get away from the housekeeper, to leave her bed by the opposite side, but Yadira reached out to grab her arm and yanked her back. Incensed that her plan had not gone smoothly, the housekeeper grabbed a pillow and forced it down over Eden's face. She had meant to render her unconscious with chloroform, slit open her belly to deliver the child, then let Eden bleed to death.

If she had to suffocate her instead, it would make no difference. Her story would still be the same: that Eden had gone into labor during the night, died of heart failure, and that she had had to act quickly to save the child.

Eden did not need to know the details of Yadira's grisly plan to realize she was in grave danger and that spurred her to fight as hard as she could. She clawed at Yadira's arms, but she was too weak to cause her any pain. On the edge of blacking out, she slid her hands down the housekeeper's apron, and she felt the knife in her pocket. Eden struggled with her last ounce of strength to get a hold of it and did, but deprived of oxygen, her grasp was too feeble to make good use of the weapon.

When Alex appeared in Eden's mind, she knew she was dying and that he had come for her. He was dressed as he was in his portrait downstairs and he looked young and strong. She reached out to him, still holding the knife. He whispered that he loved her as his hand closed around hers. His image faded away as she lost consciousness, but when the pillow slid from her face, she was still wearing a peaceful smile.

Raven had been even more anxious than Sarah to reach his plantation, and when darkness fell before they could enter the Rio Bueno, he dropped anchor off shore and took her and Dr. Endecott upriver with him in a life boat. While it was late, the trio was certain the occupants of the house would not mind being awakened, and they hurried up the steps.

Raven lit the lamp on the table just inside the front door, then carried it to light their way up the stairs. "Let me check to make certain Nathan is still using this room."

He peeked inside, and finding his father-in-law asleep in Alex's bed, he motioned for Sarah to enter. Certain Nathan would be thrilled to see his wife, Raven waited as she sat down on the bed and shook his shoulder. When the sleeping man did not immediately awaken, both Raven and Clifton Endecott followed her into the room.

Raven set the lamp aside and spoke to Nathan himself. When the man still did not respond, he turned to the doctor. "Could Julian have given him something to help him sleep?"

Cliff examined the cup on the nightstand and nodded. "That's what this smells like. I'm sorry, Sarah, Nathan probably won't be awake until morning."

While obviously disappointed, Sarah leaned down and kissed her husband's brow before turning away from the bed. "I'd like to see my daughter."

"Let's go through here." Raven took them into Eleanora's room, knowing the doctor wanted to see the men who had been convalescing there. A lamp was burning low in the corner, but even in the dim light he realized as soon as his companions that the men were all sleeping far too soundly. "What the hell is going on here?"

"Where's Eden?" Sarah asked with growing alarm.

"Come on." Raven dashed from Eleanora's room and sprinted down the hall. The instant he came through Eden's door the last traces of the spilled chloroform assailed him but it did not slow his step. Eden lay sprawled across her bed in an unnatural heap, but it was not until he rounded the end of the bed that he saw Yadira's lifeless body on the floor.

The doctor had been following close behind and turned back to block Sarah's way when he caught sight of the dead housekeeper. "Wait, you don't want to see this."

Unwilling to be shoved aside, Sarah lurched past him,

but then she, too, came to an abrupt halt. "Who is that?" she whispered hoarsely.

"Yadira Morales, the housekeeper," Raven answered. Yadira lay on her back. The knife that had slit her open from navel to chest was still embedded in her flesh and there was no need to feel for a pulse to know she was dead. Taking care not to step on her blood-splattered skirt, Raven sat down on the bed and pulled Eden into his arms.

"She's been drugged too," he announced when his first efforts to wake her proved fruitless.

Cliff Endecott took Eden's wrist to take her pulse, and once satisfied it was strong, he turned both her hands over and studied them carefully. "While it certainly looks as though Eden stabbed Yadira, there's no blood on her hands or nightgown. The men are all asleep in their beds, but Yadira certainly didn't commit suicide. Who could have killed her?"

"There must be someone else in the house," Sarah whispered as she cast an apprehensive glance toward the door.

Eden moaned softly then, and Raven shifted her position slightly and tried once again to wake her. In a moment, her lashes fluttered slightly, then she opened her eyes. When she recognized Raven, she broke into a delighted smile. "I never said that I love you, but I do. I love you very much."

"I love you too," Raven responded without hesitation. "But we can talk about that later. Can you tell us what happened here tonight?"

Eden looked puzzled, and when she saw her mother standing at the end of the bed with Cliff Endecott, she was all the more confused. "Mother? Is that really you?"

"Of course it is, sweetheart, but we have to know what's happened here."

Eden sighed softly, and frowned with concentration.

"Yadira tried to kill me. She said she wanted to raise Alex's baby."

"Who is Alex?" Cliff asked.

"Later," Raven ordered. "I should have sent Yadira away as you asked me to when we first got home. I'm sorry. This is all my fault, not yours. Julian must have told her the babe was Alex's without realizing the consequences."

"Did you catch her?" Eden asked fretfully. "I'm afraid she'll try to kill me again."

"She's dead, Eden. Don't you know how it happened?" Raven prompted gently.

Eden remembered how she had seen Alex then, but surely Alex could not have killed her. "It must have been me. She was trying to smother me, but I got a hold of her knife just before I blacked out."

Cliff Endecott did not need to take another look at Yadira's body to know whoever had stabbed her had done so with brutal force. He doubted Eden would have had the strength to do it. Taking care not to step on the body, he walked around to the nightstand and picked up the cup of milk. A single taste assured him it contained a strong sleeping potion. There was also the unmistakable odor of chloroform in the room. No, a pregnant woman who had been given a drug to sleep, splashed with chloroform, and then smothered with a pillow could not possibly have stabbed Yadira.

"Your father's been drugged, and so have the six other men I left here. Is there anyone else in the house?" Cliff asked.

"Rebecca's room is across from my father's," Eden replied.

"I'll go and check on her," Cliff volunteered immediately, but he soon returned with the news she was also sleeping too soundly to wake. "Is there another room where you can take Eden? I'll clean up in here."

"I'll take her next door." Raven got up and walked around to the other side of the bed, but as he started to lift Eden, she cried out. "Are you hurt?"

Eden bit her lip as the pain of a contraction increased. "I think it's the baby."

"Then I am definitely taking you into my room," Raven exclaimed. "You'll be needed, Cliff, just leave Yadira. She's not going anywhere."

"I've never delivered a baby," Cliff admitted with a helpless shrug.

"Then it's time you learned how to go about it." Sarah looped her arm through his and they followed Raven into his room. "After what my daughter has been through tonight, having a child should be easy."

And with three such devoted attendants, it was.

Nathan slept until nearly noon, and when he awakened to find his wife sharing his bed, he reached out to touch her to make certain she was really there. She opened her eyes as his caress brushed her cheek, and gave him such a pretty smile he knew she had to be real.

"Hello, Grandpa," she greeted him.

"Christ, Sarah, I'm not that old."

"Oh yes you are. Eden had a baby girl at two this morning. I love our son-in-law already, don't you?"

Nathan was silent a moment too long, then admitted grudgingly, "I think he's too much like me."

"Yes, he is. That's why I find him so easy to love. Now don't you think we ought to celebrate becoming grandparents?"

Nathan had had six weeks in which to recuperate, and while Julian still did not let him out of bed for more than a couple of hours at a time, he thought he would do all right as long as he stayed in it. "Do you have any idea how much I've missed you?"

"Yes, I certainly do." Their loving exchange was muffled by kisses, and more than an hour went by before Nathan had the presence of mind to inquire how Sarah had come to be in his bed.

By the time Julian arrived that day, the *Southern Knight* had tied up at Raven's dock. Rebecca was seated on the veranda with Cliff Endecott, and knowing all the wounded were now well enough to return to duty at least on a limited basis, Julian asked the Confederate officer what Captain Sinclair's plans were.

"We'll sail at dawn tomorrow. We all appreciate what you did for our men, and if you'll give me your bill, I'll pay it before we leave."

"Thank you. I'll make one out just as soon as I've seen how Lady Clairbourne is today."

"I can tell you that. She's in excellent health, as is her daughter."

Julian was disappointed that he had not been there to attend her, but grateful to hear things had gone well. He noticed the fond glance with which Rebecca regarded Cliff, and thought perhaps it was time she found love again.

"I'll want to tell the men goodbye. Are they still here?"

"Yes, they're staying for dinner."

Rebecca shaded her eyes with her hand as she looked up at her brother. "Eden's mother has come for an extended stay. I'm sure she'll be a big help since Yadira left yesterday."

"Yadira's gone?" Julian asked much too quickly.

"Yes. She said she couldn't abide babies and found another position."

Julian shrugged as though the matter didn't concern

him and went on in the house. He knew he would never meet another woman with such a hearty sexual appetite, but after a brief moment of sorrow that she left without saying goodbye, he was overwhelmed with relief that she was gone.

The birth had been an easy one, but that exertion combined with the lingering effects of the sleeping powder kept Eden asleep until early afternoon. She awakened to find Raven seated beside the bed, gently rocking the cradle in which her infant daughter lay sleeping.

"I meant what I said, I do love you," she told him. "I wish I'd said it before you went away, but I didn't realize it until you were gone."

" 'Absence makes the heart grow fonder'?"

"Something like that."

"Then I should have left sooner," Raven teased. "There's something I wish I'd told you too, and last summer."

He suddenly looked so serious, Eden grew worried. "Are you in some kind of trouble?"

Raven flashed a rakish grin. "Maybe. Just listen and then you can say." Wanting to get the ordeal over with quickly, he plunged ahead. "I told you that I'd lived with Alex since I was a child, and that's true, but there's one important point I never explained."

Eden plumped up her pillow to get more comfortable. "Well, why don't you do it now?"

"That's what I'm trying to do. Just hush. The first time I saw Alex, I was down at the docks in Kingston. There was a magnificent black horse tied up near the wagons being used to load provisions on his ship. I was standing there petting him when Alex walked up and asked me if I'd like to go for a ride. He was wearing the finest suit of clothes I'd ever seen, and I knew he had to be very rich. I told him I'd never ridden a horse but that I'd like to and he picked me up and put me into the saddle. Alex was twenty then, and I think I was eight.

"He led the horse up and down the docks and then offered to take me home so my mother could see me ride." Raven paused for a moment, but he had rehearsed the story so often while he had been away, he could have finished it in his sleep. He kept his glance focused on the baby, though, rather than Eden.

"I told him that I didn't have a mother and he asked with whom I lived. I said I swept out The Blue Parrot tavern and that the owner let me sleep in the back. Alex didn't say anything until I got to that part. Then he told me he needed a cabin boy, and if I'd rather go to sea than sweep out taverns, he would be happy to hire me for the job. Of course I said I'd do it. He helped me off the horse then and we shook hands on the deal.

"He asked my name, and I said I didn't have one and that he could call me whatever he liked the way everybody else did. He just laughed at that and told me he would give it some thought. The next day he bought me the first new clothes I'd ever owned and two days later we sailed for England. By the time we got there, Alex had decided to call me Raven Blade simply because he liked the sound of it.

"When he asked if I'd like to be his nephew, I thought it was a fine idea. So the first time I went to Briarcliff, that was the way I was introduced. When we returned home to Jamaica, everyone assumed I was a nephew who had been orphaned in England. Your father was the first person to ask me how a man with no brothers or sisters can have a nephew, but I didn't explain.

"Alex thought it was a harmless ruse, one that benefitted us both when Eleanora died without giving him a so-

When he died without telling you the truth, I didn't dare reveal it either. I was so proud of the fact everyone mistook me for Alex's kin that I didn't want you to know I was just someone he'd picked up off the street.

"I wish I'd had the sense to be honest with you from the start because it hurt to have you constantly questioning my motives, when all I ever wanted was to win your love."

Tears were now sliding down his face and Eden had to wipe away her own before she spoke. That he had once been a child without even a name to call his own explained so much about him. It was no wonder he grabbed for whatever he wanted the instant it came within his reach.

"Why did you marry me?" she asked softly.

Raven had not realized he was crying until his tears fell on the baby's blanket. Horribly embarrassed, he pulled out his handkerchief and hurriedly dried his face. "Alex took me to London so I could find a wife. You were the only woman I wanted, but he had seen you first. I didn't care what wild scheme had brought you to my bed. Once we'd slept together, I had a reason to force you to marry me and I did. It wasn't to cheat your child out of a title. I'd never dreamed you would have a baby with Alex. It was simply you that I wanted."

Eden was not even tempted to admit she had imagined him to be Alex the first few times they had been together and chose to talk about him instead. "Why do you think everyone has always believed that you're Alex's nephew?"

"You know what Alex was like. He was so charming he could have said day was night and everyone would have agreed with him."

"No, that's not it at all," Eden argued. "I know you don't like to look at yourself in the mirror but you really ought to study your reflection someday soon. I'm certain your parents loved you dearly, and I'd be willing to wager they had titles too."

"No, you're trying to be kind, but you're wrong. My mother must have been a whore and I doubt she could have told you my father's name. Either she died, or just found me in the way and left me, but I've always believed I was better off not knowing anything about her."

"No," Eden insisted stubbornly. "I think you're probably the son of some wealthy Spanish couple whose ship was lost on a voyage to the Caribbean. You might have been the sole survivor, and too young to explain who you were to the people who found you."

"That's a nice story, but it's not true, Eden."

"You can't prove that it isn't."

"And you can't prove that it is. I don't even know how old I am. Alex was the one who thought I looked about eight. He picked my birthday too. November tenth was just a convenient day to celebrate."

"What can you remember before the time you worked in The Blue Parrot?"

"Nothing. It's almost as if my life began when I went to work there."

"That's odd, don't you think? If your life was as awful as you imagine, I'd think you have plenty of memories, even if they were all bad."

"Well, I don't."

"Undoubtedly because you nearly died in the shipwreck too. It's no wonder you forgot your name and all the other details of your past."

Raven began to laugh now. "I don't blame you, Eden. I don't like to think of myself as a whore's son either."

"While I do not believe that for a minute, even if it were true, it would be the very least of the things you are, Raven. Besides, I fell in love with you, not your parents."

"It certainly helped that I was Lord Clairbourne, though, didn't it?"

A slow smile spread across Eden's face as she shook her head. "No, it wasn't that at all. You have your own brand of charm, Raven Blade, and I would have fallen in love with you even if you had not been an earl."

The baby began to cry then, but she stopped as soon as Raven handed her to her mother. "She has Alex's blue eyes and I'll never ask you to tell another lie about who her father is. What do you want to name her?" he asked.

"Alexandra. If that's all right with you."

"I think it's the perfect name."

"Good." Eden leaned down to kiss the baby's cheek. "Cliff says she's healthy. I've been so afraid the baby wouldn't be."

"Why didn't you say so?"

"There was nothing you could have done."

"Well, you could have at least given me the chance to try."

Eden nodded, "I'm sorry." Now that they were alone, there was something else she wanted to say. "Since we are being so honest with each other, there's something I didn't tell you about last night."

"No, we needn't talk about it ever again. We'll simply say Yadira left our employ. Her body will never be found, so that story won't be questioned. It was clearly self-defense anyway, but I would have sworn I killed her rather than allow you to take the blame."

"Raven . . . "

"Hm?"

Eden described the last few seconds before she had lost consciousness. "It was Alex who killed her when I couldn't. I felt his hand on mine. I really did."

While that was one of the most bizarre stories Raven had ever heard, he did not find it impossible to believe

"That explains a lot. Cliff told me he didn't understand how a woman your size could have caused Yadira's death, especially after what you had suffered. Whether it was his spirit, or merely your memories of his love, I'm certain Alex helped you."

"You believe me?"

"Yes, I believe you, but I think we better keep that story to ourselves, as not everyone believes in guardian angels the way we do."

"I do love you, Raven."

"I love you too, but doesn't it bother you that I'm not the man you thought I was?"

"Don't be silly. You're precisely the man I thought you were. You're proud, stubborn, and wonderfully bright. I'm sure you can convince my father to build the steamship you've designed."

"I intend to, but for now, I have all I want right here." Raven proved that with a lingering kiss, then sat down on the bed so he could hold Eden in his arms while she nursed their daughter. "She has your blond hair, and I think she'll be as beautiful as her mother. I wish Alex could have seen her."

"After last night, I think he can."

"I hope so." Raven gave his wife a fond hug, and for the first time in his life he was completely content with who he was. He was the man she loved and that was all that truly mattered.

Note to Readers

Writing love stories is a fascinating career because the dilemmas that can complicate a romantic relationship are endless. When the idea of having a dashing young hero marry the widow of the man who had raised him first occurred to me, I found it too intriguing to resist. Because wealthy men frequently wed women many years their junior, that the widow could be a ravishing young woman was not only possible, but highly probable. While Raven and Eden's love story could not help but be fraught with constant problems, they were such a passionate pair that writing their tale was simply a delight.

The significance of the Confederate Commerce-Destroyers during America's Civil War was another story I wished to tell. The most famous of the raiders, the *Alabama,* sank more than sixty merchant ships before it, too, was sunk by the *U.S.S. Kearsarge* off the coast of Cherbourg, France, in June 1864. The *Florida* was captured in October of that year in Bahia, Brazil. That the *U.S.S. Wachusett* had attacked the ship in a neutral harbor brought an outcry of world protest, and proved to be a great embarrassment to the United States.

When General Robert E. Lee surrendered at Appomattox on April 9, 1865, the *Shenandoah* was patrolling the Pacific coast and the crew did not learn of the War's end for several weeks. While the *Southern Knight* was [...] tional ship, that she could have seen service in the [...] was indeed a possibility. The attack she suffered [...] vana, Cuba, was inspired by the *Florida* incident.

At the end of the War, Americans made claims a[...] Great Britain for the damage done by the Commer[...] stroyers. Referred to as the Alabama Claims, the [...] was settled by a tribunal which met in Geneva, S[...] land, and consisted of representatives from the [...] States, Britain, Switzerland, Italy, and Brazil. Grea[...] ain was found guilty of a breach of neutrality la[...] building the ships, and the United States was aw[...] damages of $ 15,500,000.

Great Britain, however, received $2,000,000 fro[...] United States for injuries and property loss suffer[...] British subjects, and $5,500,000 for violation of f[...] rights off the North Atlantic coast. This agreement, [...] was the first use of arbitration in an international s[...] was seen as one of the great achievements of the [...] teenth century. Had Raven Blade been a real p[...] rather than a product of my imagination, I know he [...] have been proud to see the United States and Great[...] ain settle their differences in so rational and peac[...] manner.

I would love to hear from anyone who would l[...] comment on Raven and Eden's romance. Please w[...] me in care of Zebra Books, 475 Park Avenue South, [...] York, NY 10016.